"You're coming with us," I

"I'm not going anywhere with you," Jessie said.

Zeke moved to protect her, keeping his body between the intruders and Jessie. Sure, he knew a few self-defense moves from prison, but Forman had every discipline of martial arts in his programming. He could anticipate any fight move Zeke made. He was a helluva lot faster, too.

Top that off with the intruders' well-muscled bodies, and Zeke's chances of fighting his way out of this underground hell diminished to zero.

But he had to try. He got in one minor lick on the shorter guy, but the larger one flattened him with a solid punch. By the time Zeke had lunged to his feet, Forman had Jessie in his grip. Out of ideas, Zeke padded along with the entourage.

They traveled down two empty corridors, turning first right and then left before they entered a larger room, one with day-bright lighting, carpeting, a utilitarian desk, and several chairs.

A stocky brunette in a black shirt and trousers rose when they entered. "Excellent work, team. Release the girl. Robot, secure the male. Guards, step outside."

When the men left, Zeke felt better about the odds. Two of them, two of us. Jessie shied away from Forman and the brunette. Smart woman.

"You have the keystone," the brunette said to Zeke. "Surrender it now, or suffer the consequences."

"I don't have what you want." Zeke winced as Forman yanked his wrists together behind his back. "I never had it. I don't know where it is. I'd never heard of a keystone before today."

The woman's unusual amber eyes blazed. "Now I know you're lying. You have, what—three, four college degrees, and you expect me to believe you don't understand the term?"

"I understand what a keystone is. It's a specially shaped piece that unites the others around it, such as the wedge in the crown of an arch. It isn't the terminology that has me baffled, but the application. I don't know of any keystones in my work, my family, or my home."

"You lie."

"I speak the truth," Zeke said. "I have nothing to hide."

PRAISE FOR G-1 BY RIGEL CARSON

A fine read from start to finish, you will love this book if you are a science fiction buff. —the Great Reads, Amazon Top 500 Reviewer

This was a thoroughly engaging and fast moving novel. I read it the span of twenty-four hours, finding it hard to put down. Carson has a flair for plotting and is particularly skilled at mixing in elements of science and technology. There's a dire warning in her message, both political and environmental, and that's what makes this novel so relevant to our times. I highly recommend this book! –Joseph Souza, author of Unpaved Surfaces

In a race against time, Dr. Zeke Landry must discover his legacy and activate his powers to save the world. G-1 is a page-turning ecological thriller that could become chillingly real. —Nancy Cohen, author of Bad Hair Day Mysteries

I'm not usually a sci-fi reader, but I've read other books by Ms. Carson, AKA Maggie Toussaint, and love her writing style. There are quite a few interesting characters in this book, but my favorite was Forman, the brilliant robot. —Polly Iyer, author of Diana Racine Mystery Series

2065 Sci-fi landscape, roiling mystery, international intrigue, eco-terrorism, an embattled scientist who is ethical to his core, and the cherry on top is the re-programmed gigolo-robot turned hacking wiz, add a little rock and roll, and you have the formula for an excellent weekend read. —Fiona Quinn, author of Weakest Lynx

G1

The Guardian of Earth Series

RIGEL CARSON

To Isabella & Ethan,

Thanks for loving the Georgia coast!

Enjoy!

Maggie Toussaint

Contact information: maggietoussaint@darientel.net
Cover art by *Maggie Toussaint*

Muddle House Publishing
1146 Tolomato Drive SE
Darien, GA 31305
Visit us at www.muddlehousepublishing.com

Publishing History
First Digital Edition, Kindle Press, 2015
First Print Edition, Muddle House Publishing, 2015
Print ISBN: 978-0-9833614-8-0

Published in the United States of America

Dedication

This book is dedicated to all people out there who march to their own beat.

Acknowledgements

This book wasn't written in a vacuum. I had help, lots of it. Steve Covey, Virginia Baisden, and Craig Toussaint helped me figure out plausible ways to hide the missing water. Critique partner Polly Iyer and literary agent Holly McClure had input into the plot, while Caroline Carr and the Kindle Scout team added an extra polishing touch to this Kindle Scout winner for their digital version. Any mistakes in G-1 are mine and mine alone.

A feature of this series is the Georgia barrier island setting. I'm very thankful of the many opportunities I've had during my lifetime to visit Sapelo Island by boat. Thank you to all the boat captains who made this possible. The storied mysticism of the island and its heritage are indeed special and precious to me.

One
July 2065

Zechariah Landry checked the time again. His new assistant should've already exited the transpo tube onto the ferry platform by now. Supply Central had assured him the unit would arrive before the last boat, but so far the unit was a no-show. Supply needed to get their act together and fast. He couldn't afford any more delays.

At a flash of color near the gate, Zeke studied the new arrival's suave looks, and then turned away with a snort. Some lonely heart on the island had ordered the premier entertainment model robot. He wanted nothing to do with the gigolos. They were an aberration against nature as far as he was concerned.

An ill wind blew across the bustling ferry platform, rippling palmetto fronds, snapping the plastech nautical streamers along the waterfront. The familiar scents of seawater, marsh, and home rode the breeze, infusing Zeke with a desire to see his parents. Not possible. Though the summer sun shone brightly, the stark emptiness of loss still took his breath away.

Not now. Zeke squelched the six-month-old grief and tried to hold it together. He ripped off his sunglasses and rubbed his throbbing temples. All morning tied up in meetings on the mainland and now he'd been stood up by a robot. This day couldn't get any worse.

Footsteps stopped nearby. A shadow fell across Zeke's body. He turned to gawk at the gigolo robot.

It grinned at him. "Sir, I believe you're expecting me."

Zeke blinked, aware that every person on the platform was watching him converse with an oversized sex toy. "You've mistaken me for someone else. Move along."

"No mistake, unless you're not Dr. Zeke Landry, super brain and ultracool guy?"

Zeke ignored the flattery. "I ordered a Bob. Not a Gary. Never a Gary."

The A.I. unit cocked its head to the side like an inquisitive parrot. Genetically altered human skin and hair covered the artificial life form's inner machine, which was maintained at a precise ninety-eight point six degrees. "Sir, my programming—"

Zeke's hand shot up to silence the bronzed Adonis. He was not amused. Leaning in, he read the name inscribed in gold on the mandatory identification collar. "Forman. While I'm sure your programming is extensive, I'm not looking for a hookup. My request was for a laboratory unit to assist in my hydrology research. Catch the next tube back to Hollywood."

Forman's blue eyes widened and his head bobbed back, a perfect mimic of human disbelief. "Sir, I can explain—"

"Not interested. Excuse me." The hovercraft would dock any minute now, and Zeke's com link wouldn't work in transit to Tama Island. Turning his back on the robot, Zeke hailed Supply Central on his wrist com. After being routed through six automatic menus, he reached an interactive prompt. "This is Dr. Zeke Landry." He sucked in a breath, and fury flowed out on the exhale. "You have a big problem. You shipped me the wrong unit."

"Sorry for the error, sir," the androgynous voice soothed. "Do you have your authorization number?"

"No, I do not have my authorization number. I'm standing on a pier notifying you of your screw up. I need it corrected immediately."

"One moment while I query requisitions."

The silky voice returned. "Sir, we were unable to fill your request and, due to your Level Five priority, shipped you an alternate unit. You are dissatisfied with Forman?"

The leaden clouds offshore and the changing barometric pressure aggravated his headache. "You sent me a gigolo. I need a research assistant. Where's the Bob robot I requested?"

"We show a two-month backlog on the Bobs. Rest assured we will fulfill your request when possible. Our inventory will replenish once the Mechatronics Federation approves the Ginright circuitry modules. Unlike the defective Bobs, Forman has been extensively mapped and shows no killer tendencies."

Did they think their standard reply would placate him? Zeke's voice sharpened. "Two months? I waited a month for the boy toy you sent. I have critical deadlines to meet. Besides, this killer robot myth is a giant hoax."

"Your request is in the system, Dr. Landry," the voice soothed again. "In the interim, the Forman unit will assist you."

"Christ." He broke the com connection.

Across the lush fields of cordgrass, a gleaming white hovercraft approached the wharf. The ferry would dock soon. He needed time to assess the situation. He had none.

His sponsors pushed hard for conclusive results. Even with his three-hour sleep pattern, he couldn't finish the global hydrology computations before the International Water Summit. His uncle had promised skilled help. And now this sex toy had been assigned to him.

An unusual error for Uncle John. Zeke turned to study the robot. No way this pectoral wonder in a vivid pink shirt dotted with white palm trees knew a thing about science. As Zeke watched, the unit gave two passing women the once-over. An athletic male got the same treatment.

He was so screwed.

The publish-or-perish mentality ruled the research field. Once he missed his deadline, his sponsors would bail. Then what? Back to making his living as a fisherman in the dying sea?

He had a few minutes. Better make good use of them. He crossed to Forman. "Is light a particle or a wave?"

"Ah, good one, doc," Forman said. "Start me off with an easy chicken-or-the-egg question. As it happens, I know the answer to this. Both. Stick that in your pipe and smoke it."

"I don't smoke. And neither should anyone. It's bad for health and longevity. Not to mention illegal unless prescribed for medical reasons."

"Right. Medical reasons."

Zeke ignored the flirty wink that came his way, intent on his line of questioning. "Do rapidly shifting tectonic plates cause stronger earthquakes?"

"Yes, they do, though it depends on the fault."

Zeke felt a spark of hope. This robot's looks weren't his only asset. "What common nutrient deficiency caused sawgrass to be predominant in the Florida Everglades?"

"That would be phosphorus. Thanks to agricultural runoff and other inputs, that ecosystem has had incursions of cattails, duckweed, and algae blooms. Any more questions, Dr. Geek, or do you want us to continue working on our tans on this quaint wharf?"

"I don't appreciate your sense of humor."

"That's because you don't have one."

"So I've been told." Zeke managed a wry smile. "What are you? You look like a Gary but you sound like a Bob."

"I'm a prototype for robotic units. Every time there's a demand for a new A.I., they muck with my programming." Forman grinned. "Right now I'm in full nerd mode, but I can score us some action in a nanosecond. What do you think about the hottie blonde and the even hotter dark-skinned vixen with the beaded braids by the ticketing kiosk?"

Zeke's gaze shot over to the women in native orange robes. His second cousin and her mainland friend with a shrill voice. "God, no."

"Don't like girls? Got it. What about those two deckhands over there? They look like a ton of fun."

His throat tightened. "No *action* of any kind. I have work to do."

Forman blanched. "No wonder your sense of humor is gone. A guy needs action. Too much congestion down there rots your brain."

"My brain is fine." A facial muscle twitched, and Zeke clamped his hand on top of it. "If I decide to accept your help, and that's a big *if*, you have to tone it down several notches. We keep a low profile, understood?"

Forman leaned closer and spoke confidentially behind his hand. "So I'm in like Flynn?"

Zeke looked away. A stiff breeze swept across the ferry landing. The warm salt air bathed him with a sense of the inevitable, much like the landward march of seawater. With every inch the sea took, the water came closer to human structures and drowned the salt marsh that fed the bottom of the food chain.

The island hovercraft docked, and two dozen travelers spilled onto the platform. About half of them wore the traditional orange garb of island folk. Strangely, many of the faces were unfamiliar to him.

He had to make a decision about the robot. If he refused the A.I., he'd be back where he started, doing the work of three men. That wouldn't get the job done in time. He needed help. With a sigh, he resigned himself to the inevitable.

"We'll try this for a few days," he said. "Nothing permanent, mind you. This is a trial basis."

"Cool." Forman puffed out his chest. "I've never been on an island before."

"We'll be working around the clock. This is no R&R gig."

4

"Dr. Z, you said 'gig'! There's some fun in you after all."

Zeke sighed. "How much time is required to recharge your system each day?"

"I'm functional around the clock, but a daily one-hour rest cycle is optimal for my operating system."

"Got it. Let's go."

"Wait. What about my bags?"

"Bags? You're an A.I. unit, for Pete's sake. You have luggage?"

Forman pointed to the tower of brightly colored suitcases stacked by the loading dock. "Of course I do. Wardrobe is essential, and I knew there were no clothing outlets on the island."

"True. But you won't need more than a change of clothes, if that."

Forman drew himself up to his full height, two inches taller than Zeke. "My bags go with me, or I don't go."

Zeke swore. Why was good help so hard to find?

He flashed back to an argument he'd overheard between his parents many years ago regarding his accelerated education. After days of arguing, his father had allowed tutors for Zeke in their island home. He'd said it was important to know which battles to fight.

Zeke applied that lesson to the A.I.'s luggage. "Knock yourself out."

Forman beamed and hugged Zeke. "I knew you'd come around. We'll be a great team."

Zeke quickly disentangled himself, hearing the chortles from others on the platform. "No hugging."

Two

The hotel bellhop held out the thick yellow envelope. Jessie Stemford traced the bolded letters of her name and suite number.

Mystery mail.

Just like before.

Jessie accepted the envelope, noting the absence of a return address. Outwardly, she kept up her calm façade; inside, her nerves went on alert. More printouts? Who was her secretive benefactor?

She handed the wire-thin young man a double credit for his trouble. "Who gave this to you?"

"Guest Services, ma'am. A male guest asked that it be delivered to your suite."

She shivered. "He knew my room number?"

"Yes, ma'am."

Jessie thanked the man and locked the door, her thoughts in a tangle. How did this person know her Chicago location? Why had she been singled out? What did they expect?

The question that worried her more and more of late—was she in danger?

So far, that hadn't been the case. She hoped her luck held because she enjoyed reading the material. Curiosity overcame caution, and she ripped the envelope open. Official-looking documents spilled out. She sat at the desk and flipped through them, frowning at the bureaucratic gobbledygook. Why couldn't legislators say what they meant?

"Did I hear a knock on the door?" Her sister Beatrice waltzed into the room smelling like a rose garden, clad in a plush white robe with a thick towel wrapped turban-style around her head. "Oh. I see. More boring stuff. Translate it into regular talk, would ya? I've got a new melody knocking around in my head that needs some kickin' save-the-world lyrics."

"This will be a challenge, even for me. Some of these documents might as well be code. Who is sending us these packets? Should we trust information from an anonymous source?"

"Who cares?" Bea gestured broadly with both hands. "My career had no momentum until I started singing about the environment. Now my concerts sell out. Let's ride this eco-train until it runs out of steam. The world is in such a big mess, the people need a voice. Our voice. Protesting the workings of global power-brokers is great for our bank account. It gets us closer to our long-term goals of having the homes and families we've always wanted."

Jessie chewed on her bottom lip. She'd forsaken a life sciences career to anchor her pop star sister as she toured the world. They'd been through so much already. Their father's desertion. Their mother's drug-related death. The foster care system. Bea's passion for music and Jessie's passion for the environment carried them through the tough spots.

Together they'd climbed out of the pit of poverty.

Only to find success just as lethal.

Crazed fans were one thing; angry business collectives were another. They took stealth to a whole new level, luring you in with false promises when all the while their gazes were fixed on their personal agendas.

The system sucked.

Worse, it put the Stemford sisters in harm's way.

"What if those powerful people come after us?" Jessie asked. "What about the threatening messages you received?"

Bea waved her concern off. "That's the price of fame. If fans really love you, then there'll be folks who hate you, too. I'm not worried about a little hate mail."

"You should be. Those folks could be dangerous. Trouble can roll in here and crush us in a heartbeat. Maybe we should hire bodyguards for the rest of the tour."

"I love you, Jess, but you see trouble around every bend. Too bad the Font of Gaia is a myth. A double shot of the waters of life would fix you right up. Failing that miracle, you have to lighten up on the gloom and doom. I refuse to live my life looking over my shoulder for a disaster."

Incensed, Jessie surged to her feet and caught her younger sister's arm. Through the years, she'd been the parent to Bea's rebel. Bea's flip remark pushed Jessie back into her former parental role. "Trouble *is* around every bend. We're poisoning our air and water. How will future generations survive? What about our kids?"

Bea glanced pointedly at the restraining hand. "Far as I know, neither one of us is preggers. No worries there."

"That's not what I meant." Jessie blushed at her outburst and clasped her hands to her chest. "This is serious."

"Yep. It is. We're just babes crying in the wilderness." Bea's expressive face lit up. "'Babies in the Wilderness!' That's just the song title I needed. Thanks."

Bea rushed from the room, and Jessie stared at the thick sheaf of technical papers. The information they received always prompted Bea to write a save-the-world song. Not for the first time, Jessie wondered about their future. Would they create their own fate, or were they being manipulated down the road of no return?

Before the babies cried in the wilderness, someone had to hack a path through the jungle to put them there. What did that make the Stemford sisters?

Were they the jungle, the path, or the machete?

Three

"There's a soothing rhythm to their chanting," Forman observed from the doorway.

Pale fingers of dawn illuminated the silhouetted protestors outside Zeke's open bedroom window. He rubbed his face and glanced at the time. Another day. Another opportunity to find a solution to the hydrology problem he faced.

In the three days Forman had been with him, they'd rerun every computation. It would have taken him weeks to do that alone. Even so, the results hadn't changed. A significant amount of global fresh water had disappeared, but where did it go?

Yawning, he rose from his cot. "Nothing soothing about their message. Once they tire of saying 'go home,' we'll be treated to the ever-popular refrains of 'our island' and 'leave us alone.' Their creativity is sorely limited."

"Should they be saying 'Save our water, for our sons and daughters'?" Forman trilled the words to a haunting melody.

"That's good. Maybe you should join the protestors and lead the singing. You'd look right at home in an orange robe."

Forman snorted. "I might enjoy going tribal, but the lyrics I sang, they're from the lovely Queen Bea."

Zeke slipped on a pair of shorts. "What's she queen of?"

"Pop. Don't you know Queen Bea? She's so fab." Forman launched into another song about newly extinct animals.

Zeke groaned and raised a hand. "Hold up. I have a rule. No singing before breakfast."

Without missing a beat, Forman tossed Zeke an energy bar. Zeke snagged the bar and a coffee before settling into his office chair. He keyed up the data sequence compiled over the last three hours.

The result hadn't changed.

No matter how he approached the calculations, the world would run out of water during his lifetime. He didn't believe his results. Severe conservation measures had been implemented thirty years ago after global climate change caused rainfall to shift to the upper reaches of North America, bypassing most of the U.S.

Dangerous levels of atmospheric gasses had been reduced, but the damage had been done. Many populated areas now received less than 20 inches of rain annually. For places with clustered rainfall events, the infrequent supply of water caused desert conditions.

Between lower precipitation levels and the privatization of water rights, the general public had to pay out the nose for drinking water.

Worse, the level of water in subterranean, publicly held aquifers continued to subside. Drinking water had been rationed by price. Only the wealthy could afford "virgin" groundwater. The rest of the population drank recycled surface water. An acquired taste, for sure.

Water, water, where was the water?

The solution eluded him.

Popular opinion held that the missing water had been lost to space due to global warming, but no thinking scientist held that view. He believed the water remained on Earth, but he needed solid proof with statistical confidence levels. The water budget data—what were the chances of corrupt data?

He rang up his Uncle John on his office com unit. "The data sets you sent me. You're sure of their accuracy?"

Uncle John's image snapped into focus, his collar-length white hair mussed from sleeping. "Good morning, my boy. Nothing like a call at the crack of dawn to jump-start an old man's heart."

"Sorry. I forget you're a late riser." Zeke shot a repentant smile toward the com camera. "My calculations. They're not what we predicted, definitely not what the Institute wants to proclaim publicly. Therefore, the data must be corrupt."

"My source assured me the numbers were good." Uncle John coughed and cleared his throat. "I'll look into it and get back to you. By the way, I'm coming down there for a site visit soon. Can you pry yourself away from the lab for an evening?"

"I'm working on a tight deadline, sir."

"That's why you got the A.I. unit. To free yourself up. Your mother, God rest her sweet soul, would be shocked if she knew how one-dimensional your life had become. You need to find someone to share your life with. Someone who breaks you out of your workaholic mold. Your mom wanted a different life for you. One with a life outside the lab."

"I like my life just the way it is." A red light flashed on his com. "Another call coming in. Later, Uncle John." He flipped over to take the other call.

"Mandatory staff meeting at the lodge, 0630," Drue King, Institute site administrator, announced.

"Can't make it." Zeke barely spared a glance for the scowling matron on his vid screen.

"You said that for the last three meetings," she countered. "This is a required meeting. Come. Or I'll override your power draw from the Institute's energy grid."

"All right. You made your point. I'll be there." Irritated, Zeke hit the off button and caught Forman's eye. "Stay here while I go to the staff meeting. I'll be back in an hour."

"A meeting? With people?" Forman bounded to his feet. "You can't make me stay in this hellhole when there are people out there. I insist on coming. The calculation models won't miss us for a few minutes."

"I'd send you if I could." Zeke padded back to his quarters for a shirt. "You heard Drue. If I don't show up, she cuts our power."

Forman changed his shirt as well, selecting one that featured sunset colors and silhouetted couples. "I like a woman who plays hardball."

"She's too old for you."

"No one is too old for me. That's the beauty of my Gary programming module. I'm predisposed to find all adults hot, nerd boy."

"We agreed you'd turn off Gary programming while you worked for me."

"I agreed to tone it down while I worked with you. Big difference. The meeting is play time, and I'm ready to party."

Zeke sighed and thrust his feet into flip-flops. "Come on, then. Let me introduce you to the hottest senior citizen on Tama Island."

They padded outside into a wall of protestors. The group did not part to let them through. A thin man of undiluted African lineage with very dark skin blocked Zeke. "Go home." The man's tone reminded Zeke of a person scolding a disobedient dog.

Physical confrontations went against Zeke's low-profile policy. No matter how much he wanted to deck this guy, he couldn't. He turned to skirt the stranger. "I am home."

The man grabbed the front of Zeke's T-shirt. "Heed our warning and return to the mainland. The Institute goes against the laws of nature."

"Beat it." Forman edged forward, a cream-colored center sandwiched between the darker-skinned men.

Visitors to the island often assumed from Zeke's light brown coloration that he originated elsewhere, but they were mistaken. He'd been born and raised here by his black father and white mother. By now, people should have evolved past interracial prejudice, but distrust lingered like a festering sore.

"We have the right to protest," the thin man sneered. "Troubles of Biblical proportions will occur if scientists keep changing the genetic code. God's creation is sacrosanct."

Forman clamped a hand around the man's arm and squeezed. The man howled in pain, released Zeke, and stumbled backward. His companions quieted.

The A.I. unit strode toward the man. "Why don't you go home, fella?"

"He's not real," the man shouted. "Look at that gold collar. He's an A.I. unit. One of those killer robots. Run!"

Women shrieked. Orange-clad people shoved against each other, fleeing from Forman. The thin man melted into the thicket of shrubs.

Zeke tucked his leather thong necklace back under his shirt and joined Forman. "Thanks. Didn't know you had bodyguard training as well."

Forman flexed an arm, curling his buff bicep. "I have the full Brutus module on board. Do you require a bodyguard? I'm your guy."

"Looks like I've got one, whether I need it or not." Zeke nodded toward the distant lodge. "Come on, let's get this over with."

Four

The tall man cut the motor on the luxury yacht and studied the endless sea. He checked for service on his com. Nothing. He scanned the radar scope for blips indicating ship movement. Nothing again.

Perfect.

He swiveled in his captain's chair, facing his two younger companions sitting under the canopy. Each man wore a form-fitting swimsuit and nothing else. They'd left their shoes, shirts, sunglasses, and caps in the small transport at the anchorage.

Number One worshipped at the altar of self-preservation. He didn't get to his exalted position in the organization without taking security seriously. "Updates," he said.

Number Three leaned forward. "My people are in place. The operation is a go, sir."

One noticed the lightning-fast twitch in Number Two's cheek. Two resented Three's eagerness, which played right into his plans. Three displayed the right amount of initiative and naïveté to push Two to his maximum performance limits. He grinned at the absurdity of the Chameleon Society preferring these clandestine meetings and numeric aliases.

"The timing is as we discussed?" One asked.

Three nodded, bowing his head deferentially. "They will be released simultaneously, as you requested."

One nodded, glad of his cap and dark sunglasses. Kept the pups guessing. "Excellent work, Three."

Three preened under the praise, his ghostly blue eyes shining bright.

One visibly adjusted his head toward Two, though he had been watching the younger man covertly the entire time. "Your report, Two?"

"The explosives are being deployed. We are gaining ground on our target date."

"The unfortunate situation in Montana?"

Another small cheek tic. "Contained, sir. There's no way the

13

explosion can be traced to the Chameleons."

"You say that with one hundred percent certainty?"

"Absolutely."

Fool. "Good work."

"Sir, about the target date for Operation Earthquake." Two shifted in his seat. "If it were to slide a week, there would be less risk to our operatives."

One's hands curled into fists. With effort, he relaxed them. "Operatives are expendable, Two. The date stands."

"As you wish, sir."

One bowed his head in prayer, Two and Three following suit. "Glory will soon be ours."

Five

Jessie couldn't peel her eyes off the vid screen footage of Rio de Janeiro. The shock and terror on the faces of *People's Choice* newscasters Connor Bronson and Pauline Curran mirrored her own devastation.

Pauline burst into tears. "First they tell us travel might be limited, then they tell us all the stockpiles of food disappeared. Aliens stole our food."

"Not aliens, love." Connor patted her back. "Bugs did it."

"Bugs, aliens. What's the difference? They ripped us off. Exterminate them!"

The network cut to a commercial.

Tears blurred Jessie's vision. Her worst fears were a reality. She staggered to the lounger. After a few minutes, she found her voice. "My God. Oh my God. Bea. It's happening. It's really happening. And it's on every vid link."

Bea flounced into the hotel suite seating area in a cloud of flowery fragrance. "What now? Is that hunky Latin movie star selling milk again? Are intergalactic hunks breeding with fashion models?"

"No. It's bad." She wrapped her arms around her quaking middle. Her voice quivered, and she felt all of fourteen again. Alone. Afraid. And on the street. "So bad."

Bea joined Jessie on the lounger, hugging her. "You're scaring me, Sis."

"Everyone should be scared. This is big. Really big. Even worse than I'd guessed based on the data we've been receiving. My God. The food. It's gone. From the agridomes and the international stockpiles. Soldiers are moving food from stores to government facilities. World famine isn't in the future. It's right now."

"We're gonna run out of food?"

She wanted to reassure Bea that it would be okay, but she couldn't. Without a miracle, the people of Earth would starve. "Something happened in the agridomes last night. Something ate all the vegetation. The produce existed yesterday, and it's gone today. There's no more food."

"But there are stockpiles of food. Governments keep them. And seeds too. We can use the stockpiled food and grow more."

"It isn't that easy. Stockpiles are at an all-time low because of the chronic water shortage. Three seed repositories were checked this morning, and they're empty. All the seeds are gone. We don't have enough food. This is so terrible."

"It can't be that bad. Different governments have stockpiles. Someone has food and seed stock."

Jessie shuddered. She and Bea survived homelessness. Would they survive foodlessness? This time a kindly cop and social worker wouldn't take an interest in their welfare. This time they were on their own. Just like everyone else.

"Not according to what's coming out this morning." Her voice sounded so rational, so calm. Amazing.

Onscreen, Pauline the newscaster wept in great gulping sobs as her coanchor tried to soldier on with the bad news.

After muting the sound on the feed, Jessie spoke. "World leaders are astounded. Our president assures us we will survive, but if our nation has food and no one else does, we can't hoard it. There will be a war."

"How did this happen?" Bea asked.

"No one knows. The security cams didn't record any intrusions in the seed stockpiles or in the domes. People are saying this is the end of times. There's not enough food."

"Vids can be faked. They're sure this isn't a hoax?"

Jessie exhaled slowly. Once again she had to be the parent to Bea's child. They both had heard the same information. Why didn't Bea see this epic disaster clearly? Why couldn't Bea step up and take charge for once?

Grappling with the big picture, Jessie faced facts. This trouble encompassed the globe. It affected everyone. How could she best protect their interests? She needed a resource inventory. How much food lined the shelves of their pantry? Less than a month's supply.

Did they own any seeds to sow in a garden? No.

Her stomach knotted. "Look at these pictures. These are the actual domes. The fields are empty except for the hordes of insects. Hear the buzzing?"

"What insects would do that?"

"They say it's some kind of man-made locust."

"But overnight? Eating everything in the domes?"

"Scary."

Bea recoiled. "Will they get out and eat us?"

"Dunno. Connor and Pauline reported the domes have been sealed. If they fumigate the critters, they'll poison the soil. That's a risk they can't afford to take. The dome placements were optimized twenty years ago. With the water shortage, the rest of the world's soil is too arid. It took them a decade to bring that last dome online. We don't have enough food for this year, let alone ten years."

Bea sprang to her feet, her hands stabbing the air. "We've got money. Let's buy up extra food. We'll be okay."

"Too late." Jessie collapsed against the back of the lounger, too overwhelmed to pace about the room. "All food supplies have been confiscated by world governments. Rationing started this morning."

"Is this the end of the world? Will our unborn children have food?"

"Gosh. Children." Jessie curled into a tight ball. "Who brings kids into a dying world? The kid permit stamps will soar out of our price range. Our dreams of home and family will never come true at this rate."

Experience had taught the sisters to stick together, but they still longed for a traditional family. They wanted to marry men who were true. Men who understood the meaning of commitment. They'd seen too much of the other sort.

Bea stopped pacing and stood in front of Jessie. "Should we cancel the tour?"

"If travel is restricted, we might not have a choice. I know you don't want to disappoint your fans. I hope we can finish this series of concerts."

"Me, too. People need to hear our message. Now more than ever."

"I agree. Back to nature is the only way to survive. Genetic modifications are killing us. They're killing the world. We have to tell people. We have to make sure the word gets out."

Bea nodded soberly. "Got a new tune running around in my head anyway. We'll do it, Sis. We'll spread the word. As long as we're able."

Six

At the murmur of accented voices, Zeke hit a function key to clear his data screen. It wouldn't do for the visiting scientists to see his troubling computations. The Institute put out a glossy think-tank image to the world. He knew his role for today's dog and pony show.

With a few deft keyboard clicks, his slide show presentation of the last year rolled onto the larger vid screen, a total of thirty animated, politically correct graphics, courtesy of the Institute's tech support contractor.

He shrugged into his wrinkled lab coat. "Let me do all the talking. The sooner we get this tour group out of here, the sooner we can get back to work." *And the sooner I can think straight again.* Being around so many people wore him out.

"Killjoy." Forman's lab coat looked brand new, and the added pocket protector full of pens gave him the appearance of a geeky lab assistant. "Appearance" being the operative word for a Bob-smart helper with a Gary tendency for flirting and a Brutus propensity for protection.

Institute administrator Drue King crossed the threshold first, pink cheeked and nearly tongue-tied when she glanced at Forman. It irked Zeke that he knew she'd hooked up with Forman twice since their initial meeting several days ago. Drue had always acted like a prickly stepmother to him. He preferred to think of her in a matronly role instead of as a sex-starved female.

A gaggle of international scientists followed the chief administrator. This facility tour reflected the Institute's open-door policy to promote the cross-pollination of science. By fostering the open exchange of information through international borders, global issues, such as the ongoing water crisis, could be better managed.

Everyone crowded into Zeke's laboratory, and Drue King made introductions. "Dr. Landry uses the annex for his hydrologic data analysis. Dr. Landry, allow me to introduce our esteemed guests. Dr. Ming Li of China, Dr. Claudia Gruber of Austria, Dr. Cosma Rossi of Italy, Dr. Stephan Ivanov of Russia, and Dr. Gareth Davies of Great Britain."

The VIPs nodded as their names were called. The Austrian woman glared heatedly at the vid screen that showed what her country had lost; the others showed polite interest in the image. Zeke realized his opening slide struck the wrong note with Dr. Claudia Gruber.

A pastoral Alpine scene filled the screen above his head, the "before" scene when world-wide river flow had been plentiful and drinkable. The image exemplified the Institute's watchdog mentality, illustrating how naive the world had been before the Institute came on board with its esteemed international experts and global resource applications.

He'd inherited his elite stature when he became the late Dr. Hugh Mitchell's protégé. What he wouldn't give to be able to talk out today's water problem with his former mentor.

Instead, he launched into his spiel. "With the world's attention focused on our global food crisis, accurate monitoring of the world's drinking water supply is essential. Our computer modeling system tracks water usage and availability around the globe."

Dr. Li nodded politely, his bowl-cut dark hair framing his rounded face. "Your system data package? Comes to you how?"

Zeke knew for a fact that Dr. Li was fluent in six languages. Drue had confided in him earlier that the man had only been studying English for a few months. The man must be a quick study.

"Our data streams are encrypted from secure hosts," Zeke said. "We receive direct feeds from the One World Water Association."

"You . . . quality assurance? Veracity?"

"Good questions, Dr. Li," Zeke said. "Data is spot-checked and compared to benchmarked parameters. Outliers are flagged and investigated."

Dr. Li's almond-shaped eyes narrowed. "How you tell the other way? If too much good data?"

Zeke didn't miss the conspiratorial look between the Russian and the Austrian. "Our data analysis is handled by a complex software system customized for streaming data. A static data set would also red flag."

Dr. Rossi patted Dr. Li's back. The slender Italian towered over the shorter man. "Dr. Li and I share concerns that the international water supply has already been irreparably depleted and that the data streams from different international sectors have been corrupted."

Dr. Claudia Gruber's blonde head jerked up. "Dr. Li thinks to discredit my country so an emergency agridome will be built in China. Austria has as much right to that new placement as China—more because we don't have a dome."

"Economies of scale suggest it is less costly to have food growing near population centers." Dr. Rossi's condescending tone suggested that a female didn't have the mental capacity to grasp the complexity of the situation. That kind of thinking had gone out the door with the new millennium. What a dinosaur.

Dr. Gruber huffed out a breath. "What are you getting out of this, Rossi? Black market food rations? New koala bears for Rome's zoo? Italian leather all the way from China? Water and mineral rights from a secret consortium?"

"Ladies and gentlemen," Drue King started. "We can't solve the world's ills in this lab, however much we'd like to. Dr. Landry—"

"I need some air." Dr. Gruber stalked from the lab, with Dr. Stephan Ivanov on her heels.

Zeke completed his talk without further incident. The remaining scientists shook Zeke's hand and left.

"I apologize for Claudia." Dr. Gareth Davies hung back to explain. "Li and Rossi hope the new northern hemisphere dome will go to China."

Zeke shrugged. "I leave politics to others and focus on science."

"You don't fool me, boy." Gareth Davies playfully punched Zeke in the shoulder. "We want you to speak at the Global Water Federation's annual meeting in Paris next month."

"Thank you, but I can't accept. My schedule is full."

"Nonsense. All expenses will be paid. For two." Davies waggled his eyebrows.

Drue nodded encouragingly. "You should go, Zeke. It'll be great publicity for the Institute."

A blinding headache pulsed into Zeke's conscious thoughts. Paris. Flying. No way. "I'll consider it."

"Excellent." Drue ushered everyone out and closed the door.

Sweat broke out on Zeke's brow as he stared at nothing. His stomach ached. God. How could he get out of this? Drue would push him to attend the symposium. Her daughter lived in Paris, and this would give her an unexpected visit. "You going to Paris?" Forman hung up his lab coat on a hanger.

"Not if I can help it."

Forman bent over and clicked a few keys. "Here's the conference. And the list of speakers. Uh-oh. Dr. Marielle Janssen is on the list of speakers. She passed away two days ago. They want you to fill her shoes."

Zeke leaned in to read the information, but frantic thoughts threaded through the pounding in his head. Janssen had been a moderate from the Netherlands. How did they expect Zeke to replace a female politician? Playing funding roulette with the Institute taxed his free time. He didn't need to take it up a level. Besides, going high-profile went against the grain.

Keeping a low profile suited him. His parents lived by that rule, and he would, too.

Forman whooped like a kid. "Omigod! We *have* to go to Paris. Queen Bea is performing in Paris at the same time as this dull meeting. I have to see her in person. You have to meet her. That 'Babies in the Wilderness' song she just uploaded is so beautiful it makes me weep."

"Put it out of your mind. You're a lab assistant. I'm a scientist. We're too busy. We're not going to Paris."

"Yes, we are. You've got a photo album full of images of Paris in your hard drive."

"My parents visited Paris on their honeymoon, before air travel skyrocketed so that only the rich could afford it."

"You wanted to walk in their shoes?"

A fresh wave of grief struck him. It still took his breath away to think about his parents. Not a day went by that he didn't mourn their loss at sea. "I changed my mind. Besides, we're too busy, and it's too expensive."

"Not this trip. It's all expenses paid."

Zeke glumly studied his open lab door and the visiting scientists far across the courtyard. "Nothing's ever free."

Seven

Zeke slipped away from the lab just before sunset. The farther he biked from his lab, the easier he breathed. He loved science, but nature inspired his passion. He'd been offered the world to set up shop at Oxford, Harvard, and Stanford, among other prestigious universities. Corporations and think tanks wooed him regularly, but neither fortune nor fame had the draw of Tama Island.

The push and pull of tides had long guided his life, and he embraced this familiar diurnal rhythm. Without thought, he reached up to finger the necklace he wore and felt comforted.

A simple thing. No sparkling chain. No glittering jewel.

A bit of rock on a leather thong.

It had been his father's.

Winston Landry had rarely taken it off, but he'd done so on that fateful morning six months ago before he disappeared. Memories crowded in on Zeke. His mom. His dad. They'd encouraged him to think for himself and taught him the ways of the island.

From his mother, he'd acquired a keen intellect and an above-average IQ. From his father, he'd learned to hunt and fish. He'd also learned to live and to love, but loving left you vulnerable. Loving left you empty when love ended.

He leaned his bike against the lighthouse, sat on the sand beside the stone structure, and listened to the pounding surf. The world followed the same pulse, relentless in its desire to move forward.

Change happened. The water shortage proved that. Now the food disaster. What other ugliness did the world have in store for the future?

Were the doomsayers right?

Was the end of the world at hand?

Was the mythical Font of Gaia everyone's only hope?

Would aliens round up all the humans for their consumption?

"Thought I'd find you here." Angelika softened the last part of "here" to an *ah* sound.

Zeke startled at the sound of his second cousin's voice. Her dark skin set off her orange robes to great effect. As a kid, she'd rescued wounded birds and nursed orphan critters to adulthood. He'd created a water delivery system to her critter nursery that still flowed.

He clambered to his feet. "Angie." He glanced around the shadowed lane leading to the settlement where the island natives lived. "Your protestor friends with you?"

"Just me. Don't get up on my account."

He gestured toward the ground, the onshore breeze cooling his face. "Join me?"

She settled cross-legged onto the sand beside him. "It isn't easy, is it?"

"What do you mean?"

"Living in both worlds."

"Nothing about living is easy."

"You miss your parents?"

A dark wind howled inside of him. "Every day. They were special."

"They were. They believed in this place. They believed in you."

"I never realized how much I took them for granted. If I could go back in time, I'd tell them every day how much they mattered."

"They knew."

Her words hit him squarely between the eyes. Data shifted, faces blurred, but he couldn't gain perspective. "I didn't know. I'm supposed to be brilliant, but I missed the most important thing of all."

"Uncle Winston and Auntie Ruth lived in the moment. They lived for you, for this island. Now they're gone and the island is in trouble."

Her thoughts paralleled his thoughts. Was he that easy to read?

"What?" he asked.

"We're in trouble, Zeke. The world is coming here. The protestor who came after you today is gloating. Gabe Servalis thinks he got to you, that you're on the ropes now."

"He put his hand on me, but he didn't get to me, not in that sense. He's bad news, Angie. Maybe you should stay on the mainland with your grandmother for a while. Let someone else save the world for a bit."

"What I do is important."

"Of course it is. The world needs Angies who care so much their hearts are about to burst. Men like Gabe are driven by meanness.

23

They don't care who they hurt. Reaching their objectives is all that matters to them."

Angie fell silent. She smoothed her robe over her lap. She stared resolutely at the endless line of breakers crashing on the sand before them. "He says you're a puppet, that the Institute is pulling your strings, that you do bad science."

He'd had detractors before, that didn't bother him. But Angie. She'd always believed in him. Did she believe the troublemaker? "Where'd he get his PhD?"

"I'm serious, Zeke. Gabe and his pals are riling everyone up. The rest of us have always included your lab on our protest march because it's in the loop of Institute buildings, but we know you. You are honest and hardworking and a friend of the environment. But this Gabe, he's down there preaching in the settlement day and night, reciting the gospel of conspiracy plots and world revolutions. He says you're the problem, that you change the answers to suit the powerful. He's so adamant and angry, I'm afraid to stand up to him. My friends are, too."

Zeke's hand curled around a fistful of sand. "He's wrong about me. You know he's wrong. I'm trying to figure a way out of this water mess. Trouble is, the results I'm getting don't make sense. Something is wrong with the big picture. That's why I got the A.I. to help sort it out. My science is on point, but I have little confidence in the answers I'm getting. Gabe's right about one thing, though. Millions of people are relying on me. I've got to ensure my analysis is accurate."

"You need a break from it for a while." She nodded, warmth spilling into her soft voice. "A break would be good, Zeke. Take a trip. Canoe over to Blackbeard Island for a weekend campout. Have some fun. Then come back to it. The world won't end in a few days."

"I can't leave. I have to figure this out."

Her eyes gleamed as she patted his shoulder. "I know you do. That's why I love you like a brother. Saving the world is hard work."

Eight

The dawn of a new day brought Christmas morning expectations into Number One's heart. That nub of hope spiked into pure, undiluted joy when the words finally appeared on his wrist com. He'd waited a lifetime to see those words.

It is done.

One exhaled in sweet satisfaction. For years, he'd planned this assault and waited for his chance. The locusts had been the preemptive strike, but this medical disaster had been his baby from the start. Terminal cancer patients delivered the aerosol containers to highly populated areas around the globe. After the *Yersinia pestis* bacteria saturated the air, the couriers removed the empty containers. Not a single operative had been questioned.

From the comfort of his sealed fortress over the next week, he followed the world's descent into terror on the vid screen. He bypassed the tough-stance news stations, opting for the People's Choice entertainment team of Connor Bronson and Pauline Curran, who broadcast from their home.

The first day Pauline went bonkers in her kitchen as Connor tried to console her and transmit the bad news. From her quivering chin to her mascara-stained cheeks and shock-glazed eyes, Pauline's grief-ravaged face spoke volumes, One thought.

By late afternoon, Pauline and Connor sported gas masks on their patio to protect them from disease. Both wore provocative clothing, which displayed Pauline's ample breasts and Connor's manly chest. One saluted them with a glass of scotch.

Evening came, and Pauline and Connor appeared again, this time in their den.

"If you just turned on your com today," Pauline warned, "don't go outside. You could catch the plague."

Connor's hand covered hers. "The Great Plague, dollface. That's what they are calling this version of the bubonic plague."

"Why did this have to happen?" Pauline shrilled. "Why can't the plague leave us alone? What did we ever do to the plague?"

Connor's concerned expression never wavered. "Precisely. Bad enough food and water are in short supply. Now this prehistoric monster rises from the grave to grab us. We can't do anything except cling together."

Pauline stared right into the com camera. "Prove we're still alive. Make love to me."

One became aroused as Connor kissed Pauline's shirt off. Federal broadcast regulations still prohibited the video airing of sexual relations on broadband feeds, so the screen image flashed to various firework displays as the audio feed continued.

"Yeah, baby," One said, taking care of his personal needs. "Screw the world."

As days passed and reports worsened, One strutted about his lair with pride. Hundreds lay dying in the streets of Beijing. An emaciated, shivering man cradled his dead wife, dark lesions discoloring her skin and freckling his. In Calcutta, workers stacked bodies in ditches and covered them with scraps of whatever they could find. A worker fell in with the bodies, twitched, and died.

One gloated at the exquisite chaos.

It played out even better than he'd hoped.

The story repeated with fresh waves of horror in Madrid, London, Jakarta, Dallas, and Mexico City. Tens of thousands were estimated dead in each population center. Air and tube travel ceased worldwide. Medical workers around the globe clamored for One's plague vaccine and souped-up antibiotics.

"Come to papa," One said, as the urgent demand for meds drove the price of his product through the roof. The Chameleon Society held patents on the needed antibiotics through three companies. All purchases of the vaccine benefited their cause.

With a few keystrokes, One released a cargo container of antibiotics and vaccines, this time to London. Every day he "found" another stash of the desperately needed medication and vaccines, located strategically near the disease centers. Money poured into the Chameleon Society's coffers.

To One's delight, hysteria ruled.

In cities where the disease hadn't struck, shoppers fought for food and water. People refused to go to work. Looters broke into stores and stole what they wanted. Cop cars patrolled in rolling blockades.

One rubbed his hands together, the excitement almost too much to bear. Nobody had any idea that the world's recent ills had been orchestrated. They had no concept of a global organization with such an effective strike force.

Fresh food supplies were gone, the reserves hidden away. The plague had inflicted fear in the hearts of every nation, a suitable beginning for his campaign of terror.

The virulent disease had been created in a Chameleon laboratory and spread by valiant foot soldiers who gave their lives for the cause. Surprisingly, many cancer patients had volunteered for the deadly duty. Though he'd had to turn people away, he kept track of those who still wanted to die for his cause. Kamikaze soldiers were a valuable commodity. He held them in reserve in case heads of state failed to go along with the final plan. The Chameleon Society didn't tolerate dissension.

Pauline and Connor's broadcasts continued to entertain One. The bathroom broadcast won his heart.

"What's a Malthusian limit?" Pauline asked from the toilet. She wore a lacy peignoir on top and nothing at all on the bottom.

Over at the sink, Connor scraped a razor across his face. "I read about that. Some old dude name Thomas Malthus earned fifteen seconds of fame by saying the earth would fight back. That humans would overpopulate, causing the earth to purge itself of the infestation."

Pauline's face scrunched as her bowel moved. "So we're rotten sushi and the earth is having diarrhea?"

Connor grinned. "Something like that."

The toilet auto-flushed as Pauline stood. "Who put the earth in charge of anything? This is my planet, and I'm not going anywhere. Poop on them."

One laughed every time he replayed the segment, but he nearly crapped himself at their next day's broadcast from the hot tub. How dare they treat a precious topic in such a frivolous way?

"What would you do with everlasting life?" Connor asked a naked Pauline. Her breast tops crested the water level.

"Easy. I'd make sure you got it, too, and we'd hump like minks for all eternity."

"Fine idea. You think we should join the others searching for the Font of Gaia?"

Pauline's perky features reddened. "Gaia? You saying I like to sleep with girls? I thought we had something going here, that it was

27

more than bumping around on the bed and table and car and deck, and you know what I mean."

"Easy, love. Gaia is another name for the planet. The font is reputed to contain the very waters of creation. Whoever drinks of it shall have eternal life. It has nothing to do with our sex life."

"It would if you found that font for me. With everlasting life, you wouldn't age another day. Me either. My titties would never fall, your wood would never fail."

"You have the best titties on national news." Connor cupped one and displayed it proudly for the camera. "Come on, world. Cough up that font. What would network news be without perfect tits?"

"Fools," said One. Chameleons had searched for the font for over a century. One hurled a nearby vase of red roses at the hearth. The crystal shattered with a loud pop. "You can't have the font. It's mine to find, mine to control, mine to drink."

One's secure line flashed. He hurried to answer it, injecting subservience into his voice. "Yes, Master?"

"Delay the next phase. Another week is required."

The delay would make Two's week. His precious operatives would have more time to set the earthquake-inducing charges in place. "As you wish."

Nine

The medical tech wiped Zeke's arm with alcohol. Zeke winced at the sharp jab of the vaccination needle. "I don't need this. I'm not going anywhere."

Forman stood with his arms folded across his chest. "With world health in crisis, it's wise to prepare for every eventuality."

The injector pulsed vaccine into Zeke's arm like an angry hornet. "Easy for you to say. You don't have to get shot up with bug juice."

"Human diseases don't faze me. However, I have to be on guard against module failure, module failure, module failure—"

"Cut the crap, Forman." Zeke rolled his sleeve down and hopped off the exam table, ignoring the tightness in his arm muscle.

"We need to work on your sense of humor, boss man."

"Wrong. We need to figure out what's going on with the water numbers." They stepped outside into the sunlight, donned sunglasses, and strolled across the courtyard toward the distant lab.

"No protestors on the grounds today," Forman noted. "Where did they go?"

"Hope they went home to resume their normal lives."

"They're not all bad. And that Angelika? She's one prime female. I could spend all night getting to know her."

It bothered him that the robot had serviced Drue King. Zeke forced his coiled fingers to relax. Angie deserved better than a machine. "Leave my cousin alone."

Forman's face contorted as if he were distressed. "I meant no disrespect. She's a total babe."

"Angie wears her heart on her sleeve. I don't want her hurt."

"She's safe from me. If she crawls in my bed, I promise I'll climb right out."

"You don't sleep in a bed."

Forman grinned. "And I thought I could out-clever you today."

They strode across the Institute grounds, passing from blinding sunlight to the thick, shady canopy of mature live oaks. Birds chattered high overhead. Airy swags of Spanish moss trailed from the intertwined branches, adding to the dense shade.

Zeke welcomed the cooler air under the trees. Usually, being on Tama Island gave him a sense of well-being. Lately, he'd felt ill at ease on his home turf. Nothing concrete, just a little off. He wished he could travel back in time to a more peaceful era on the island.

"Thought anymore about us going to Paris to that geek summit and to hear the delectable Queen Bea?"

"Forget it," Zeke said. "People are dying all over the world. I'm staying on Tama Island. Couldn't go if I wanted to, with the travel moratorium."

"That'll be lifted soon."

Horrific images from the global network vids seared into Zeke's thoughts. So many dead. Gone forever. "The original bubonic plague had outbursts for decades after it first struck in Europe. No telling how long this strain will be active. I like being on this island, out of the mainstream germ pool. We're safe here."

"You're safe until the ferry starts up again, and then each arrival represents a potential disease vector. That's why the Institute director mandated the vaccinations. You are valuable property, one of their prized assets."

Zeke missed a step. "They don't own me."

Forman walked backward to speak with him. "You live, eat, and work in their labs. You have no social life, no family life, and no friends. All you have is me, a programmed research assistant, which they provide free of charge. Yeah, they own you."

The truth stung worse than his arm. Zeke shot back an offensive parry. "If you're so smart, why isn't my computerized projection in agreement with the data set?"

Forman pivoted and walked forward with Zeke, matching his prowling stride. "We've studied the analyses and verified the results. They don't follow earlier trends, and they certainly aren't logical. Potential sources of error exist in the process. The program itself could be flawed."

"There's nothing wrong with my program," Zeke growled. "I've triple-checked all sources of error."

"If it isn't the analysis, then it must be the data. Could the data itself be bad?"

"The data came through secured sources as per standard operating procedures. The same way earlier data sets were acquired.

Even so, I asked Uncle John to check it out." Zeke scratched his head. "The last data package is as sound as the earlier data."

"That narrows the field of inquiry down considerably." Forman laughed, the startling sound echoing through the shaded area. "If it isn't the programming or the data, then it has to be the investigator."

"Bull."

Ten

Jessie glared at the bathroom scale readout in disbelief. Two pounds up. How could that be? Water and food were rationed worldwide. Had been rationed for weeks.

Less food and more weight.

Not good.

Folks would say she'd hoarded food, holding out on those with greater need. They would say that's why the Stemford sisters had returned home to Richmond.

She hadn't taken more than her fair share. She and Bea ate the same tasteless food packs as everyone else. The obesity of her grandmother's generation repelled her.

"Bea, come here," she said. "I want to see how much you weigh."

Her sister obliged, with no zip to her step. "I can't write this morning, Sis. My head feels thick. I'm having trouble breathing."

The scale showed Bea had gained as well. Three pounds.

Bea stared open-mouthed at the readout. "Is it broken?"

"Something's broken, and I pray to high heaven that it's the scale." Jessie said. "Strip down, and let me look at your skin."

Bea's eyes widened. "Oh God, no. Not that. We've been so careful. We had the vaccine."

"The vaccine isn't foolproof." Jessie's heart fell into her shoes at the sight of a dark, circular lesion near her sister's groin. She swore under her breath. "You've got the new plague. Weight gain and clouded thinking are the first symptoms."

Bea bent double and wept. "I'm going to die. We're going to die."

"No we're not. We'll use the antibiotics I bought off the black market. We're not leaving this house until we're okay."

Their eyes met in the mirror. "I'm scared, Jess," Bea said in a small voice.

"Me, too."

Jessie gave Bea a handful of pills. "Take every last one of

these."

"So many?"

"I've been tracking the disease treatment in online forums. Folks who take vital-pack supplements with the meds do better. It ups our survival odds from fifty percent to seventy percent."

Jessie tossed back a handful of her own pills and prayed her proactive research would be enough to get them through this.

"You could leave. You could save yourself," Bea said.

"I'm gaining weight, too. We've been glued to each other for months. Both of us must have come in contact with a carrier. The world doesn't need another wave of contagion and hysteria. We'll stay here at home and ride it out."

"We're trapped by the disease."

Bea's eyes grew dreamy. Jessie recognized the symptoms of a song coming on. "That's it, Sis. Write about it. Do us proud."

As her sister wandered off to her keyboard, Jessie sagged against the bathroom counter. She'd done all she could. Would they survive?

Eleven

Data swirled through Zeke's head like a raging whirlpool, greedily sucking more and more of his consciousness into its dark maw. He resisted the urge to bang his head against his office wall, resisted the urge to run down to the beach and tune out the problem. Running wouldn't solve anything. Thinking would, but he needed a fresh approach.

In his head, he listed the facts about the missing water. Global water levels were certified by secure monitoring systems. Uncle John had verified the quality assurance measures on the data sets. On an individual level, those truths were inviolable. When taken as a whole, they didn't stand up to the harsh light of day.

They went against every scientific principle he'd ever learned.

As long as there were oceans, water would cycle through the atmosphere. With a deficit of surface water, the volume in other compartments of the model should increase by the same amount, but it hadn't.

He trusted his computer software.

He trusted his secure system.

He trusted the data source.

But he didn't believe the analysis.

He couldn't.

World water levels couldn't dissipate by forty percent in six months. He wouldn't endorse another water hoax. His late mentor at the university, international water expert Dr. Hugh Mitchell, had been tarred by the water controversy the first time around.

Mitchell and his physicist colleagues were positive the earth's magnetic field prevented water loss to outer space. However, other scientists, and Zeke used that term loosely, whipped folks into a frenzy with emotional extrapolations of gloom and doom. Amazingly, the public bought into the frenzy and accepted the concept of global water rationing in 2035.

To make matters worse, by 2030 Global Now, using its subsidiaries North American Water Works, Eurasian Springs, and

Worldwide Water, had bought up the water and mineral rights to most of the reserve aquifers on the planet. They'd focused on populated areas worldwide and the landmasses within the Arctic Circle: Canada, Greenland, Scandinavia, Russia, and Alaska.

With the majority of the world's precipitation now falling between 70 and 90 degrees latitude due to the planetwide weather shift, Global Now commanded a vast share of the world's water. The price they set for virgin groundwater bordered on criminal, but they'd crossed every *T* and dotted every *I* on their contracts. When sued by governments, Global had conceded enough to allow water monitoring equipment on some of their property.

Thirty years ago, powerful people brought the water crisis to a head, using bad science and greed to justify a political end. The ruse didn't fool Zeke. His mentor had it right all along. The water was here, on the planet, then and now. But even with real-time data from representative Global Now reservoirs added to the public-domain water, the numbers didn't add up.

Where had the water gone?

He needed to know. The world needed to know. He'd accepted this research position with the Institute, in part, to exonerate Dr. Mitchell, but the more water data he analyzed, the more confused the entire hydrology picture became. Numbers didn't lie, people lied. But who and how?

You couldn't break the hydrologic cycle.

His toes gripped and released the thongs of his flip-flops as he rolled the puzzle around in his mind. Maybe he'd gone about this all wrong. Maybe tallying the volume of water in various sectors of the water cycle to create a composite water inventory was the wrong approach.

Hmm. Interesting. Bad answers resulted from provided data on volume, displacement, and usage. What about the data he didn't have?

For the first time in weeks, he felt right, like he'd stumbled onto a truth.

About time.

According to his calculations, the missing water didn't reside in the underground water table. It hadn't augmented surficial water flows either. Lakes and ponds worldwide showed declines in water volume, but the data in central Asia came from a source that historically had monitoring glitches, which they refused to admit until they were called out on the lie.

"Forman, tap into the satellite cams and use stealth monitoring to assess volume at these Asian sites." He shot his assistant a list of places to spot check, reservoirs that had impermeable liners in their bottoms.

"On it, boss."

Zeke punched a few more keys, and the world map came up. He overlaid the underground reservoir template on the map. Next, he highlighted the places he'd asked Forman to verify. If they came back high, that would explain some of the difference in his projections.

Some but not all. Where could the missing water be?

"Thought anymore about Paris, boss?"

"What?" Zeke replayed Forman's question in his head. "Oh, Paris. I was iffy on that from the start. Then the plague hit. Paris is a no-go."

"Pauline and Connor, my fave newscasters, reported that the World Health Collective says it's safe for travel again. Disease incidence has sharply fallen. Besides, Paris had a low incidence of plague."

Irritated by the small talk, he brushed aside Forman's remarks. "I can't think about travel until I figure out what's happening to the world's water supply."

"Queen Bea will be in Paris."

"I thought she came down with the plague last week."

"According to her fan forum, she's on the mend. She wants to show the world that people are resilient, that the human race can thrive in adverse conditions. I really want to see her, boss."

"You go to Paris. Give my talk. I don't care to go."

"They want you. Your human words carry more weight."

His words shocked Zeke. "Are you saying they wouldn't believe an A.I. unit?"

Forman swiveled in his seat to face Zeke. "Would you?"

Many people had a bias against machines because they could be programmed to say and do anything. Zeke had refused an altitude-displacement implant because he didn't want any kind of machinery beneath his human skin. However, Forman was a cut above the average robot. "Hmm. I believe you, but then I know you."

"People have such an A.I. bias. It isn't fair. I'm as smart as any human. Smarter."

"Keep that to yourself. You don't want doomsayer fanatics tearing you limb from limb."

"That would be awful, but I would take a few of them out if they tried to destroy me."

Zeke's eyebrows rose at the flip remark. "Thought A.I.s were programmed to protect humans."

"I am a bodyguard. If pushed, I will protect my body."

"I'm stunned."

"Don't be. Supply realized their mistake with me. They should have deleted my differential programming instead of adding auxiliary modules. I'm one prototype they won't replicate. If you'd sent me back that first day we met, I'd have been decommissioned on the spot. Thank you for saving me from the garbage heap."

Inwardly appalled, Zeke shrugged off the compliment. "I didn't do anything."

"My processors were on the chopping block. Still are, if I mess up."

"I don't have a problem with you, Forman. Relax."

"Roger that."

Zeke studied his map. He hit another key and added the cities hardest hit by plague. Mexico City, Dallas, London, Madrid, Jakarta, Calcutta, Beijing. Highly populated areas. Over eight percent of the world's population eliminated in ten days.

On a whim, he added the agridomes wiped out by locusts three weeks ago. They were nowhere near the plague areas. They were widely spaced, with acute food shortages on every continent.

How odd. The incidents didn't follow the usual cluster pattern of data.

That anomaly bothered him.

Doomsayers on the vids were quick to claim the hand of God and to call upon the Font of Gaia for deliverance, but Zeke suspected God and Gaia had little to do with the world's current woes. This strategic targeting had politics and greed stamped all over it, just like the water crisis.

He hated politics and greed.

Foreigners asserted the U.S. had gotten off easy. The vaccine and antibiotics were already in med centers when the plague hit Texas. The larger U.S. agridomes had escaped the locust infestation. His gut tightened. Were American politicians behind this? Stranger things had happened throughout history.

"Sat data coming your way, boss."

Zeke saved the map and plugged the newly harvested data into his reservoir program. Net gain increased several percent in each case. He cracked a smile. He'd asked the right questions.

Missing water had been hidden in plain sight in isolated areas. He'd found it in surface impoundments, and the overage was so slight that it didn't alert the locals that water levels had risen substantially. Sneaky, to hide something out in the open like that.

Moments later, he had a quick and dirty analysis of the data. Much better, though seventy percent of the missing water remained unaccounted for.

What about the rest of it?

Where would someone stash sixty-eight thousand cubic kilometers of water?

How could that have been done without detection?

Who had done this?

Global Now?

Or had a new player taken control of the game?

Twelve

At the crisp rap on the lab door, Zeke's fingers spasmed on the keyboard. Nonsensical letters sprouted in the cell of his data-analysis program. He swore under his breath and deleted the excess characters.

"Who comes calling at midnight?" he growled.

"Want me to shoot 'em, boss?" Forman fired back as he hurried to answer the door, his sunny yellow shirt much too bright for the late hour.

"No shooting. Whatever they're selling, we don't want any. No interruptions."

"Got it."

With that, Forman exited the lab. Zeke heard a low murmur of voices, followed by the sound of multiple footsteps. He groaned his displeasure. "This better be a visit from God almighty, Forman, or you're fired."

"Don't blame the help, my boy," Uncle John quipped with a cheesy grin. His conservative business suit looked out of place on the island. "We've come a long way to see the pride of the Institute, Dr. Zeke Landry."

"Uncle John?" Zeke stumbled out of his chair, rubbed his beard stubble. "You should have called me from the landing. I would've met your boat."

"We came by private transport. Allow me to introduce a close personal friend and colleague, Rissa Porter."

A very pale woman with spiky white hair peeked around Uncle John's broad shoulder and waved. An albino, Zeke realized as he took in her barely blue eyes; her tall, model-thin body; and her ice-blue slack suit. If aliens ever came to Earth, they would not stand out as much as this pale, nearly ethereal female.

Zeke nodded and extended his hand. "Welcome, Rissa. Any friend of Uncle John's is a friend of mine. What can I do for you two? Is something wrong at the Institute?" Another thought flashed through his mind. "Did you book a place to stay? If not, you can bunk here at the lab with Forman and me, or we could open up my parents' place."

"No worries here. We've booked a room at the mansion. What do you say to Forman giving Rissa the lab tour and the two of us stepping outside for a chat?"

Zeke obeyed the steely command in Uncle John's voice. He caught Forman's eye. "Behave."

Outside, cooler air prevailed, brightened by honeysuckle and the salt breeze blowing in from the ocean. Stars twinkled overhead. Zeke automatically traced Orion's Belt and the Big Dipper as he waited for Uncle John to speak. He'd always thought of the stars as his friends.

"The A.I. unit—he's working out for you?" Uncle John asked, stopping next to Zeke.

"He isn't what I expected, but he has been useful."

"What about your results, Zeke? You ready to go on record with the state of the world's water supply?"

"Definitely not. The data set contains inaccuracies. We've extrapolated from satellite images and found water hidden in plain sight. Water is unaccounted for throughout the planet. Enough to cause concern and trigger worldwide panic. Any conclusion I make from this data installment would be erroneous and misleading."

"Our funding agents are anxious for the Institute to have a firm position on the global water picture. I can't hold them off any longer."

Zeke's back teeth ground together. He worked them apart. "We agreed I had until the International Water Summit. That's two weeks from now. I haven't missed the delivery deadline."

"No, but the board decided today they would be better situated for the summit with prepared position papers and talking points. They need your analysis immediately."

"It isn't ready."

"What does the data say?"

"The data points to a huge deficit in the drinking water supply."

"But?"

"We can't destroy water. It's here on the planet. Like I said, we've found excess water in places where it shouldn't be. The amount I uncovered disproves the loony-tunes theory that we've lost water to outer space. Something is going on here. Something big, only I can't prove it's a hoax. Yet."

Uncle John studied the distant stars for a long moment. "Are you saying we're not in a deficit? The water crisis is a hoax?"

"I can't say anything definitively. Not with this data set." He didn't like being pigeonholed. "My analysis is incomplete."

"What's your best guess?"

Estimation led to errors. Zeke considered ripping his hair out by the roots. "There's nothing to be gained by guessing. I'm reworking the data. We've only tonight discovered and started documenting the true water levels. This is big, Uncle John. The discrepancies are worldwide. Whoever is behind the data falsification has a very long reach."

Uncle John stilled. "What are you saying?"

"Someone keeps tightening the screws on humanity. The water shortage. The locusts in the agridomes. The global plague. Someone is benefitting from these scary situations. Someone has the whole world dancing on puppet strings. I don't know if Global Now is behind it or if another entity is poised for a power play."

"This is a contrived political ploy?"

Zeke didn't know how to take the excited edge in his uncle's tone. Plus, his uncle hadn't questioned his theory. Instead he'd gone right to the motivation. Zeke cleared his throat. "It wouldn't be the first time science justified a politician's agenda; only look at how water came to be rationed."

"Where's your proof of a conspiracy?"

"That's the maddening part. Other than the interpolated satellite data, I have no proof. We don't know how long the data stream has been corrupted. The entire monitoring project could be built on falsehoods."

Uncle John harrumphed. "Heads of state took action from your previous data summations. Global water amounts were reapportioned. You were wrong?"

"Someone manipulated the data, Uncle John. My analysis is only as good as the data."

Cold moonlight slid down Uncle John's face as he glanced skyward. "I have to have your final analysis in two days. Our sponsors are on record as saying they will pull the plug on your funding if we don't have anything tangible to show for the millions we've spent here."

"We've got plenty to show, but it's of limited value."

Uncle John shook his head, his silvery hair shining. "A

conspiracy of this scope is unthinkable."

"Improbable but not unlikely. Only remember how Global Now became the laughingstock of the world for twenty years as it bought up arctic water rights. Once weather patterns shifted, they were hailed as brilliant strategists."

After a few minutes of silent pacing, his uncle asked, "Have you mentioned your findings to anyone else?"

Zeke shook his head. "Only Forman's seen the data streams and the satellite data. No one else has access to my software."

"Don't tell anyone. We don't want this getting out. Rest assured the Institute will consider your new theory and closely monitor known terrorist groups for chatter."

"Thanks for believing me. I'd love to hand you a document with proof supporting my hypotheses. But until then, the conspiracy claim won't stand up in a court of law."

"Once the lawyers get a hold of this, the Institute will be blamed for the worldwide water shortage. You'll be tied up in global courts for the next ten years. We can't have that."

"That would not be good," Zeke said. "My altitude displacement issue has intensified with time. I'm miserable whenever I leave the island."

"You've given me a lot to think about tonight. Why don't we meet for breakfast at the Canteen in the morning?"

Glad for the brief reprieve, Zeke nodded. "I'll be there. What time?"

"Rissa and I are on a tight schedule and must leave after breakfast. Eight sound good to you?"

"Fake eggs at eight it is."

His uncle drew himself soldier-straight. "Zeke, if anything happens to me, my friend Asia Minor on the mainland will help you."

Uncle John and Asia had attended the same college and served in the same army unit. Afterward, Asia had moved from the big city to the Georgia coast and become a recluse, while John had migrated north to Washington, D.C. Even so, Zeke knew the men had been close friends for years.

"Got it, but nothing's going to happen to you."

"These are uncertain times. That's the only sure-fire thing. Remember that."

Thirteen

Researchers and technicians huddled over cups of coffee in the Canteen. Uncle John and Rissa sipped green tea, while Zeke worked on his second coffee. Beside him, Forman sipped water sparingly. Much easier to drain water from his fake gut, Zeke thought, eyeing with trepidation his snow-white scrambled eggs piled high on burnt toast.

Outside the open window, protesters in orange robes chanted "our island" as they waved palmetto fronds. In the distant tree canopy, birds vied for recognition, tweeting and twittering for all they were worth on this overcast, humid day.

"This grub isn't half bad," Uncle John said. He'd emptied his bowl of whole grain cereal and fresh fruit. Claiming a headache, Rissa had only picked at her plate.

Zeke choked down another bite of his fake eggs. "Coming from a man who enjoys grazing on sticks and berries, that is high praise."

"You've got a sweet setup here, Zeke. I'd hate to see you blow it."

Puzzled, Zeke leaned toward his uncle and dropped his voice. "Excuse me?"

"Blow it. You know, crap it up. Lose it. Lose your job."

"Is my job on the line?"

Uncle John clasped his hands together on the table. "Your job is at risk. Hell, everyone's job is at risk. Mine, too."

Zeke glanced at the nearby tables with growing concern. "Perhaps we should take this conversation to a more private location."

"No time for that. Our chopper will be here in ten minutes. Rissa and I talked at length about this last night, and I need to make sure you understand the stakes here."

"I'm about to be fired? And what's with the travel by chopper? You a big Institute muckety-muck now?"

"Things are in flux at the Institute. We've got to tread lightly. I'm no bigwig in the company, but Rissa is. I convinced her to fly down from D.C. to see that you were more than a budget line item."

Zeke glanced over at the pale, unsmiling woman. "You're here to fire me?"

Rissa shook her head. "The Institute doesn't fire anyone. I'm getting pressure from my superiors for results. Without it, funding will shift to another priority, and your project will remain on the books, unfunded."

The noise of the room receded as Zeke ruminated on the problem. If he didn't do what the Institute wanted, his funding would dry up. He would be forced to give up his lab. There would be no research position for him on Tama Island.

A dark vortex opened in the pit of his stomach. A mournful cry of a lost child sounded inside his head. Tama Island was his home. Nausea assailed him every time he left the island, and his displacement orientation severely limited his career options. Worse, the Institute controlled all of the jobs on the island.

He needed this job.

What would it cost him to keep his employer happy? "Will releasing a preliminary report satisfy the Institute's immediate concerns?"

"It might." Rissa sat back in her chair and glanced pointedly at Uncle John.

No one said anything. The silence ate at Zeke. "But?"

Uncle John cleared his throat softly. "It has to say the right thing."

Zeke's teeth clamped together. He replayed his uncle's words in his head, sure that he'd misunderstood. He hadn't. Cold sweat beaded in his hairline. He leaned toward his uncle. "You want me to shade my scientific analysis?"

"I promised my sister that I'd look after you if anything ever happened to her, Zeke. I can't do that if you go rogue on me."

"There's nothing rogue about the truth."

Rissa rose from her seat, settling her sunglasses firmly into place over her pale eyes. "If you gentlemen would excuse me, I need to step outside in the shade for some fresh air."

The men stood. "I would be happy to accompany you," Forman said.

"No need. I prefer to meditate alone before the flight," the pale woman said.

Zeke watched her go and sat down again. He pushed his cold

eggs around on his plate. Uncle John had him backed in a tight corner. Outrage simmered as the implications of following this course of action rolled in. He didn't lie. He wouldn't lie for the Institute.

Not now.

Not ever.

"I'm sorry." The bitter winds inside Zeke howled in his ears. He leveled his gaze at his uncle. "My job isn't worth my integrity. The Institute hired me because of my reputation. I won't compromise on that."

Uncle John helped himself to Zeke's meal, drank his coffee. "Compromise is the name of the game. If you make a stand here, the consequences will be dire."

His uncle held a hard line, but Zeke knew a thing or two about bargaining. "I'll issue a preliminary report. I'll even go on record saying the data analyzed suggests a water shortage, but my water cycle analysis will mention the data anomalies. I'll insist that the Institute perform an in-depth quality assurance of the data trail."

Uncle John's cheeks pinched in. Zeke braced for a blast of familial wisdom. The volume of protests outside droned louder and louder. A shot rang out, followed by a woman's scream. The Canteen quieted.

"Rissa!" Uncle John scrambled to his feet. Forman and Zeke bolted for the door. Zeke expected the worst, though he hoped he was mistaken.

The albino lay on the ground, her pale features marred by a crimson stain on her abdomen.

A champion swimmer as a boy, Zeke had also been a lifeguard. He checked Rissa's vital signs. Breathing, shallow. Heart rate, steady. Unconscious but alive.

"She's been shot. Someone call the medics," he shouted, placing his palm over the seeping wound.

Uncle John dropped to his knees on the sand beside Rissa and Zeke and took her limp hand. "Rissa! My God. No. Don't die on me, Riss."

"Give her some space, Uncle John. She's fighting for every breath." Zeke glanced at Forman. "Find out who did this."

Forman loped toward the orange-robed protestors. As one, they scattered, melting into the woodline. The A.I. unit followed.

"I never should've asked her to accompany me. I put her at risk by bringing her out of her protected environment," Uncle John said. "I shouldn't have let her out of my sight."

"You can't protect someone if they don't want it. Forman offered to accompany her, but she refused his company and protection."

"The stakes are sky high, Zeke. We have to toe the Institute line. I'd hoped it wouldn't come to this."

Zeke blinked. "You think the Institute did this? That her injury is related to my reluctance to send out a politically correct report? That's preposterous. Completely unjustified."

"When it comes to the people we're up against, scruples go out the window. Your parents learned a fatal lesson when they went against the prevailing wisdom. So did you, for that matter."

Zeke's head reeled. "Wait. Are you suggesting my parents were killed? That's outrageous."

"Be very careful. Powerful forces are at work here. Do the right thing. Send in that report by tonight, if possible."

Dark clouds billowed. The whir of chopper blades filled the sky. Sand swirled as the Institute helicopter landed not twenty feet from where they huddled on the sparse lawn.

A man wearing a flight suit sprinted across the lawn to Rissa. He checked her heart and lung function, as Zeke had done. "We need to airlift her to the Trauma Center in Savannah."

"Done," Uncle John said. "No need to wait for a hospital transport. We'll use the company helicopter."

A stretcher appeared, and the pilot and Zeke wheeled the albino on board the chopper. With a grim wave, Uncle John lifted off with Rissa on board.

Zeke protected his face against the swirl of sand during the takeoff. He watched the chopper until he could no longer see it.

Uncle John had a point. The stakes on Tama Island were indeed high.

His job hinged on toeing the party line.

His life could be at risk.

Worse, Uncle John believed his parents had been murdered six months ago for failing to follow company policy. Throughout his employment, Zeke had believed he worked for a think tank funded by endowments of free-thinkers of past ages. Now that mindset seemed excessively naïve.

Who funded the Institute?

Fourteen

Zeke ripped open the meal substitute pouch and chugged a big swig, grimacing at the chalky taste. The lighthouse's long shadow fell across his back, blocking the burnished rays of the setting sun.

An onshore breeze stirred his hair, and the ocean waves pulsed with nature's unrelenting rhythm. A white yacht gleamed offshore, a vibrant thumbnail-sized icon in a sweeping blue-green field of ocean.

His toes dug into the soft sand, seeking warmth and cover. He understood the marine ecosystem. Creatures followed the ebb and flow of the tides, eating their prey or being eaten by something bigger and faster.

He understood the natural water cycle, but that reliable paradigm had shifted through an external influence. Someone had removed a substantial volume of water from circulation. Had that someone keyed in on his water research? Had that someone targeted and killed his parents?

He'd never felt right about his parents' alleged drowning. Their bodies had never been found, only their small, empty boat drifting in the Gulf Stream current, far from their purported diving coordinates at Gray's Reef. He'd held out hope for a miracle for days, but as the weeks stretched past, his hope had vanished.

Winston Landry, ninth-generation islander, had lived quietly, helping others and respecting the beauty of nature. Dr. Ruth Landry had fallen in love with the island's favorite son during a research fellowship on Tama Island. Her marine tectonics expertise had earned her a twenty-year berth as the Institute's director of research at Tama Island before her retirement.

White and black, scientist and naturalist. Two very different peas in the same pod. She'd championed and facilitated the genetically altered microbes and fisheries stock to keep the dying ocean alive. He'd argued for natural selection as a more enduring criterion. The philosophical differences had made for an interesting home life.

But they'd been targeted.

A pit opened in his stomach. The air darkened with his thoughts. Anguish blinded him to all but the stabbing pain in his heart.

His parents.

Murdered.

He barred his arms against his chest and rocked slowly on the sand, his body wracked by dry sobs.

He should have done more, should have insisted on an extensive investigation. They were too experienced to have a rookie diving accident. He should have acted on his gut instinct.

Instead, he'd done nothing. He'd accepted the news and moved on.

Only it never felt right.

Now he knew why.

Overhead, a screeching gull wheeled in the empty sky. Zeke gulped in air and grieved with dry sobs. What a waste. His father had always kept a low profile, but his mother had lived for the Institute. Did the Institute have enemies?

Now Rissa had been injured on Tama Island, and for what? How did an Institute manager fit into the global water community? He'd never heard of her until she arrived with Uncle John the previous night.

He squirted the rest of the protein shake down his throat and pocketed the collapsed container. Nothing made any sense. There weren't enough data points. He needed connections to discern the pattern.

At movement in his peripheral vision, he startled. Friend or foe? He studied the advancing object. Person-shaped. Bright shirt. Large footprints in the sand. Forman.

"Found you." Forman dropped down beside Zeke on the beach.

"I'm not lost."

"You want the good news first or the bad?"

"I've had my fill of bad news for a while."

"Queen Bea recovered from the plague. It's a miracle."

Queen Bea? Zeke drew a blank. Then the connection surfaced in his thoughts. The pop star Forman admired. "Good for her."

"More than good. She'll be well enough to give her Atlanta concert tonight and her Paris concert in a few weeks."

"We aren't going to Paris."

"Never say never. It will come back to bite you in the butt."

"The probability of us going to Paris approaches zero in every regard."

"Queen Bea rallies the people. She is their voice. She will not be silenced."

No point in arguing with Forman about this. The A.I. unit was obsessed with the singer. "What's the bad news?"

"I can't locate the protestor who shot Rissa. I interviewed five people, and no one saw anything."

"Given the ganglike mentality of the protestors, we should have expected that. Having no answers provokes more questions. Who did this and why?"

"Dunno. Want the rest of it?"

"There's more?"

Forman nodded. "Your uncle and Rissa never arrived at the trauma center in Savannah—or any hospital, for that manner. They've vanished off the grid."

The pit in Zeke's stomach deepened. "They're missing?"

"Looks that way, though it's too soon to file a missing persons report."

"Where would they go?"

"That, Dr. Brilliant, is the right question."

If Uncle John needed help, Zeke wouldn't let him down. He'd move heaven and earth to find him. Politics and greed be hanged. No way would Zeke let every member of his family be exterminated like bugs. "We have to find them."

Fifteen

Flags snapped in the stiff sea breeze at the Tama Island ferry landing. Palm trees rustled along the shoreline. Snatches of conversation drifted over to them from the travelers who waited for the public transport. Zeke leaned in close to whisper, "Be discreet."

"Discreet is boring," Forman said.

Zeke frowned as the old-fashioned vehicles on Forman's magenta shirt cavorted in the wind. "I mean it. Keep your investigation low key, but find them."

"Got it. But I could run a hospital search from the island com trunk as easily as I could from the mainland."

"No. I don't want anyone on the island to know about your search. That's why I tweaked your com signature an hour ago, so the query wouldn't be traced back to us. I'm not sure who to trust, and I believe we have to maintain a low profile. You find a city info kiosk somewhere, someplace untraceable to run your people searches, and then get far away from it, you hear me?"

"I hear you, but I'm supposed to stay with you. I'm supposed to help with your work."

"Work's done for now. Uncle John insisted my top priority is to write that report. That's my focus for the next twenty-four hours. Yours is to find Uncle John."

"We'll finish the water analysis later?"

"Damn straight. I'll figure out what's going on with the world water supply, but first I have to get these Institute policy folks off our backs. They want doom and gloom? I'm their man."

"How will I contact you?"

"If you're not back by this time tomorrow, place a notice in the Atlanta classifieds. Give me a status on your lost cat."

"Gotcha. Deep spy mode."

A mother and daughter both dressed in island orange walked by holding hands. Zeke waited until they were out of earshot to speak again. "Look, I don't know what's going on, but these people play for keeps. You be careful and keep moving. Remember to stay low profile."

As the words came out of his mouth, he flashed back to a similar conversation he'd had with his parents when he'd gone off-island to school. Had they known of the evil out there when they told him to keep his head down? It would be easier if he could talk to them about his concerns. Too late for that now.

"Come with me," Forman said. "That way I can keep an eye on you."

"I need to stay here. The island is my home. Chances are Uncle John is fine, and you'll be back on the next shuttle."

"Want to know the odds of that?"

"Don't tell me. It makes me feel better to think that he's out there, safe and sound."

The whistle on the hovercraft blew twice, signaling boarding time. Forman hitched his over-the-shoulder bag into place. "Seems like I just arrived. You won't reroute me to Supply as soon as I'm underway, will you?"

"Hadn't thought of it. Should I?"

"We're a team. I'd like to continue with you—if you're happy with my work, that is."

What a strange thought for an A.I. unit. It was a machine, for goodness' sake. Machines shouldn't be sentimental or emotional. Just his luck to get a defective robot. "I'm happy enough, but right now, your job is to find Uncle John. Report back to me with his whereabouts."

"Gotcha." Forman strode off, melting into a group of women and children boarding the hovercraft ferry.

When the vessel pulled away, Zeke's hopes went with it. Times had changed, and he needed to catch up. Uncle John needed help. But he had to find him first.

To clear his head, he walked the mile and a half back to the lab. The September sun beat down on his shoulders as flies buzzed around his head. Seemed like with all the world's troubles, pests like flies and cockroaches would have been eradicated, but they thrived no matter what the conditions. Humans should be so lucky.

The world changed fast these days. Food and water had been rationed. Plague had been unleashed on the world. Doomsayers on the vids asserted that the end of the world approached.

The end of the world. What would it look like?

He couldn't wrap his brain around the concept. Especially since he knew water levels had been incorrectly reported. It wasn't a stretch to theorize someone had messed with the global food stores as well.

He'd write the report they wanted. That would allow him to stay put, which suited him. Every time he went off-island, he felt sick to his stomach. Living on Tama Island brought him health and solace.

He took a deep breath. Forman would find his uncle. The A.I. unit had proven to be intelligent and resourceful. Great qualities for an assistant. In this electronic age, no one was better suited than a robot to search databases and camera feeds for a person.

Zeke's lab came into view, as did a tall, lanky man in a white suit leaning against the locked door. His back teeth ground together. Now what?

The man strode forward to intercept him. "Dr. Landry, I'm Browning Charles from the Institute's Savannah offices."

He'd heard of Dr. Charles. Uncle John's bitter enemy. Zeke stopped moving. "What can I do for you, sir?"

"I need your lab."

Zeke mentally reeled at the man's presumption. "Pardon?"

"You heard me. I need this building. For my dolphin researchers."

"This is my laboratory."

"No one at the Institute knows how John Demery pulled the strings for you to get this prime space. It should have been mine five years ago. I've waited long enough. You can run your water computations anywhere, but my dolphin researchers need a home base. They have to commute back and forth to the mainland each day with their gear. That's ridiculous and extremely inefficient."

Was the dolphin research chief an opportunistic predator? Did he know Uncle John was missing? Zeke squared his shoulders. "I'm not vacating the premises, Dr. Charles."

Charles's face and neck turned bright red. "This isn't right. You're squatting on valuable real estate here."

"It would cost the Institute a fortune to move the customized electronics inside this building. I'm not going anywhere."

"We'll see about that."

Sixteen

The report wouldn't write itself. Zeke struggled with the words, couldn't point the finger of doom by citing comparable research projects, and decided to let the errant numbers speak for themselves. With that mindset, the chore aspect of the report eased.

He ginned up black-and-white graphics to display the data and interspersed them in the supporting text. When he finished, with caveats that the analysis was only as good as the data, he fired the report off electronically to the Institute's offices in Atlanta and D.C. He breathed easier than he had in weeks.

Now they'd get off his back.

The threats about yanking his funding would cease. Forman would return, and they would find the last seventy percent of the missing water. Drawing another deep breath, he realized how weary he was.

Bone tired.

He glanced over at Forman's empty console and sent up a silent prayer. *Please find my uncle. Please let Uncle John be all right.*

At two o'clock, he staggered to bed. Dreams hit him hard. Awful dreams of him falling and falling, the bottom of his stomach dropped to his knees. Something monstrous rose up from a shadowed pit. Tentacles of darkness reached for him. A soundless scream died in his throat.

Fear pulsed through him.

And guilt for all the things he'd left undone.

His time had expired.

He'd wasted his life.

Now this.

He would die.

Horribly.

Terrified, he startled awake in the dark room. Sweat beaded on his forehead, moistened his scalp. He closed his dry, cottony mouth and kicked aside his tangled sheets.

The nightmare had been the worst one in a series since his

parents died. Worse, in his dreams the water he loved so much seemed to be drowning him. Up until now, water provided a friendly, positive experience, but his friend had become a powerful foe.

He rubbed the sleep from his eyes, but his senses wouldn't settle. He felt off, in a very bad way. How long had he slept? He tapped the com screen beside his bed. Four in the morning.

Too early for him to be awake.

No wonder he couldn't think straight.

He needed another hour of sleep.

He closed his eyes, thinking to rest a bit longer, but his nerves wouldn't settle. A liter of adrenaline surged through his veins. Distant sounds worried at him, sounds that weren't of the night. Whooshing sounds. Crackling sounds.

Light flickered against his dark window. The queasiness in his stomach intensified. There should be no lights out there. Tama Island should be dark this time of night. He eased off his bed, peered out the narrow window.

His lungs stilled. The bright orange glow to the right could mean only one thing: fire. At the big house.

Sliding the window open, he inhaled thick smoke and heard the chanting cadence of the island protestors over by the Institute's administrative area. Connections formed.

The protestors caused the fire?

Pomp and grandeur didn't usually impress him, but the Tama Island landmark deserved better than this. He had to stop them.

"Floor lights on, twenty percent," he said.

A faint glow brightened the lower half of the room.

He threw on jeans and a T-shirt and was slipping on running shoes when the power winked out. The absolute silence in the lab chilled his blood. The backup generator should've kicked on by now.

"Lights on," he countered.

Nothing.

Not good.

Flames flickered in the mansion.

Protestors were on the Institute grounds.

Worse, they'd lost power.

Danger crackled like stray electricity.

He needed to get out of his lab. As long as he stayed under this roof, he'd be vulnerable. Quickly, he activated a disposable palm light and gathered a few treasures in a backpack. The framed picture of his parents. His wallet. His favorite hat. A jacket. Flip-flops. Water. Energy bars. A data reader. The portable data drive backup Forman had instituted for Zeke's analysis files.

With a last look around, he stepped out the back door and locked it behind him. Not that the lock would stop a fire, but it gave him a sense of security.

"Zeke!"

He turned to identify the whispered sound. Female. Behind him to the left. Glancing down, he saw that his choice of white shirt had been a mistake. Hard to melt into the shadows wearing white.

"Zeke! Over here! Hurry!"

He could run in the opposite direction or do as the woman said. Not many places to run on an island. Besides, she'd already made him. He hurried to her. "What?"

His cousin Angie hugged him before hauling him into the shadow of a palm tree. "Thank God you're okay."

"Why wouldn't I be okay? What's going on, Ang?"

"The protest got out of hand. The ringleader, Gabe, he's gone crazy. He's burning everything on the island. Security and the island fire department are already overwhelmed by the sheer number of fires. I've got to get you out of here. Where's your robot shadow?"

"Uncle John's vanished. I sent Forman to the mainland to look for him."

"Dear God. There's so much happening all at once. I'm sorry about Uncle John. Truly, I am." Angie paused to wipe her glistening face. "I'm even sorrier the protestors are torching everything the Institute owns. You're a target, Zeke. I heard Gabe talking about your lab. They're coming for you right after they finish the admin buildings. Gabe wants to destroy Forman and kill you."

Zeke blinked. "He said that?"

"He's a head case. No one can talk any sense into him tonight. He's a one-man destruction team."

"Think again. I heard multiple voices chanting. The others are with him."

"None of the island residents are in that mob. These are all off-island people doing the damage. That's why you and I are getting out of here."

"What? How?"

"For a smart person, you don't have a lot of walking-around

sense. Follow me."

"Angie. We can't leave. The island is our home."

"Right now it isn't. Right now something terrible is happening, and our only recourse is to run and hide. Bad people are here, Zeke. Bad people who are very dangerous."

He stopped, wanting to retrieve more pictures of his family, needing to have more of his data than the last analysis stream. "Everything I own is in that lab."

She grabbed his hand and took off. "Let it go. It's not worth your life."

Reluctantly, he allowed himself to be led away as he struggled to make sense of the facts. Off-island people were trashing the Institute. Uncle John had gone missing. Forman hunted for leads on the mainland. He and Angie were on the run.

"Where are we going?" he asked, hemming in his racing thoughts.

"You remember how to paddle a boat?"

He hadn't done that in years. "Sure."

"I've got a canoe for us. My grandfather's boat."

"I remember it."

"We can get off-island, but we'll have to work for it. The tide's running the wrong way."

If they weren't strong enough to buck the outgoing tide, they'd never make it to the mainland. Instead, they'd be swept out to sea, and no one would be the wiser. "Can't we wait a few hours until the tide turns?"

"No. We'd be too visible in the daylight. We have to go now."

They needed the cover of darkness to stay safe. Not twelve hours ago Forman had joked about stealth precautions, and now Zeke's survival depended on the unfortunate jest.

Stealth mode.

Would it save his life or be his undoing?

Seventeen

Zeke's shoulders throbbed.

His hands were raw from fighting the strong current and waves with his wooden paddle.

But thanks to his cousin's foresight, he'd survived.

As dawn's glow brightened the night sky, the thick cloud of black smoke over Tama Island intensified, confirming what he knew. The protestors had run rampant on the island last night. Like an invading army, they'd laid siege to their opponents' stronghold and burned it to the ground.

Hopefully, that was the extent of their furor. He prayed no raping or pillaging of the islanders had occurred. He shuddered at the barbaric thought.

"Not much farther now," Angie said.

She'd set a blistering pace across the sound. They'd battled wind and waves, but they'd made it. Now the marsh-lined tidewater creek sheltered them from the worst of the waves. The ebb of the tide had eased.

"Where are we headed?" Zeke asked. It had been a long time since he'd paddled so far. He'd memorized the creeks and bars like the other islanders had done, but his dated information hadn't helped. Through time the bars had shifted. He'd spent too much time with his head stuck in a book. For all the good that did him now.

"I have a friend on the mainland." Angie rested her paddle across the canoe for a moment. "Not long back he told me he knew the island protestors were getting ugly. He said his doors were always open, that I could stay there any time I needed a refuge. I'm holding him to that promise this morning."

"Who is it? Do I know him?"

"Asia will welcome you as well. He's been unhappy with the state of things on the island for some time."

"Asia?" There could be only one person who lived nearby with such an unusual name. "Uncle John's friend, the recluse?"

"They're about the same age. If they're friends, I can't say. I wouldn't say he's a recluse either, just highly focused on his work, like you."

"I've heard Uncle John speak of Asia Minor. He mentioned him as someone I could trust if I needed help. I'm glad to be headed his way."

The wind blew them into the muddy creek bank. Zeke and Angie used their paddles to push away from the thick cordgrass. Water lapped at the sides of the canoe.

"You doing all right?" Angie asked. "We were going pretty hard for over an hour."

"I feel like I could sleep for days. I'm beat." He yawned. "Thank you for having a plan, Angie. I'm not sure what I would have done if left to my own devices. Probably something stupid."

"There's no sense in that. It would be a waste of your talents to fight a thug like Gabe Servalis. His only talent is being able to incite a mob. I hope he moves on after this."

"I wish I could do the last couple of days over. I would've gone with Uncle John in that helicopter. I would have backed up my customized software programs offsite. I would've had Forman here to paddle the canoe."

"A.I.s are so much nicer now than they used to be, and your Forman is so fun-looking."

"Did he hit on you? I told him to leave you alone."

"He didn't bother me, but his attention wouldn't have been a bother. I think he would make a superb lover."

Zeke covered his ears. "Don't put that image in my head. I've never understood the sexual fascination people have with the robotic units. The whole concept of sex with a machine sounds contrived."

"Sex with a person isn't? At least with an A.I. you know you'll have personal satisfaction when all is said and done."

"You've been dating the wrong men, Angie."

"Perhaps, but I can't afford a night with an entertainment model. I'm intrigued you have one. You two spend a lot of time behind closed doors."

Zeke's paddle skidded across the top of the water as he heard the insinuation in her words. "We're not having sex."

"There's always a light on in the lab."

"We're working night and day to get the last data set analyzed. Luckily, I sent off my electronic report to the Institute a little before two this morning."

"Hmm."

"What?"

"Gabe woke everyone up a little after two ranting about how this was the hour. That we had to act now to destroy the Institute. Do you think there's a connection?"

"How could there be? How would he even know about my report?"

"How indeed?"

A solitary hawk winged through the cloudless sky, gliding effortlessly on a thermal current. Zeke's head filled with questions about the security of the Institute's trunk lines. Had someone gained unauthorized access? Did they know Gabe, the protestor?

They paddled in silence the rest of the way, running the bow up on a grassy bank. "You sure we're not on private property?" Zeke asked. "Some folks are very serious about their privacy. They also own very big dogs with lots of teeth."

"We're definitely on private property. Everything as far as you can see belongs to Asia. I think he's allergic to flesh-and-blood dogs."

"Must be nice to be so rich. Wonder how he affords all of this?"

"Family money, I think."

They secured the paddles inside the canoe, and then pulled the vessel under the cover of a large cedar tree on the shore. Angie struck out on the wide path that had been mowed through the thicket of natural vegetation. With the canopy overhead, a person could walk on this path and not be visible from above. Interesting.

A white-haired man with a cane approached through the open, nested tabby walls ringing the main house. With his proud bearing, he could have been nobility, but his casual, natural fiber clothing didn't fit the image of wealth and power.

Asia Minor was an intriguing puzzle.

"Angie! You came! Once I saw the smoke, I worried about you." The man held his arms wide, and Angie dashed into them.

"We had trouble on the island this morning," Angie said. "Gabe started burning down Institute-owned buildings. His followers helped him torch the island."

"There's a thick haze of smoke cloaking the island. Anyone hurt?"

"Not to my knowledge." She smiled shyly up at the man. "I hope you don't mind that I rescued my cousin."

"Not a problem, not at all." Asia extended his hand. "Asia Minor, son. Welcome."

Zeke nodded and shook his hand. The man's firm grip matched his hawk-sharp gaze. "Zeke Landry. I believe you knew my parents."

"Yes, I did, though their passing brought me sorrow." Asia's face relaxed a fraction. "Your uncle brags about you all the time. I'm delighted you're safely off Tama Island. Let's get you two some breakfast, some dry clothes, and a place to sack out. Come on up to the main house."

Zeke followed, not daring to trust in his good luck. He and Angie had survived the treacherous waterways, but how would they fare with Asia Minor?

Sink?

Or swim?

Eighteen

Pulse skittering, Jessie Stemford motioned her sister forward. "There's a sexy hunk at our door. An entertainment model, by the looks of him."

"Really?" Beatrice strolled across the hotel suite and glanced through the peephole. "He's a dreamboat, all right. What's he want with us?"

"Dunno." Jessie giggled. "Maybe a fan sent him."

"Should we let him in?"

"He doesn't look like a killer robot. A.I.s are supposed to protect mankind."

"Except for the Killer Bobs." Bea yawned and rubbed gloss over her lips. "I've always wanted to talk to a Gary, to find out what it's like to not be human, but it's late. I've already taken off my stage makeup."

"I've always wanted to meet a Gary, too." Jessie's face warmed. She'd spent all day grooming her sister for the show, being present for the show, and getting her back to the hotel room. Jessie wanted to do something to burst out of her structured support role, she wanted to do something for her. "For purely research purposes, of course. As a machine, he should have no expectations about your natural appearance."

"Good point. Ask him what he wants, but keep it short. I'm bushed after tonight's performance."

Jessie cracked the door to the first stop of the security bar. Enough space opened to see the robot and yet still have the door locks engaged. The gold of his ID necklace gleamed in the soft light. "May I help you?"

"Hey, beautiful. I'm here to see Queen Bea."

Jessie felt heat rising from her collar. Compliments didn't often come her way, but she liked them nonetheless. "Bea doesn't give interviews after her show. Come back for the group media interview tomorrow afternoon."

The unit clutched his hands to his chest and gazed rapturously at

Jessie. "I'm not with the press. I'm a fan. A huge fan. Please, I would give anything to meet Queen Bea in person."

"One moment, please." Jessie closed the door and fanned her face. She hurried over to the plush sofa where her sister sat with her feet propped up. "He called me beautiful."

Bea yawned again. "He's all yours, Sis."

"He came to see you. Didn't you hear him? He's a fan."

"Is that possible? Did someone program him to like my music?"

"It's a puzzle, isn't it?" Jessie beamed. "My vote is to let him in. Or should I grill him some more?"

"Open the door. Let him see the real me. If he goes berserk and kills us, that's on you."

"He seems too nice to kill anyone. I'm willing to take the risk of him being a killer robot." Jessie jogged across the carpet and opened the door. She tingled with excitement from head to toe. "Bea will see you now."

"You're a doll. Thank you so much." The unit walked gingerly as if he expected the floor to fall out from under him. His hand clapped over his mouth, and his knees nearly buckled when he entered the room where her sister sat. "I can't believe it. I'm in the same room as Queen Bea."

"Hello," Bea said. "Come on over and sit down. I don't have much energy after a show."

"Yes. Yes, of course." He sat in the chair directly across from her. Jessie sat down beside her sister, pen in hand.

"Who are you?" Bea asked.

"As you can tell from my lovely neckwear, I'm an A.I. unit named Forman."

"I see that," Bea said. "You see it, Jess?"

A robot that looked like a Gary but didn't act like one. Jessie's level of interest rose. "I do."

"Well then, Forman," Bea continued with a wave of her hand, "what can I do for you?"

He sighed with joy. "Your music is . . . inspired."

"Thank you," Bea said. "How is it that you have an appreciation for my music?"

He leaned forward, his smiling gaze fixed on Bea. "I've always adored your music. Your 'Babies in the Wilderness' struck such a chord with me. I can't get that song out of my head."

Bea sat up straighter, and her face glowed. "Thank you. I wrote that song in this Atlanta hotel not too long back."

"Where does the music come from? How do you compose the lyrics and the score?"

"The music comes to me. I know it sounds silly, but I wake up knowing what a song will sound like. Then a phrase catches in my brain and out pops the lyrics. Probably not what you wanted to hear."

"That's exactly what I wanted to hear. I'm so in awe of you. And you survived the plague. You're like a buoyant superstar. You're unsinkable."

"I'm plenty sinkable. The plague sucks, and if you quote a word of this to anyone, I'll know who leaked it. You will be off my A-list."

The unit's eyes widened. "I'm on your A-list?"

"My fans are important to me. Especially strong, virile men—er, robots. You can stop in to see me anytime you like."

The scientist in Jessie wanted answers. She tapped her pen on a pad of paper. "Mr. Forman, sir, I have a question for you."

"Okay."

"Do you like all music or just my sister's?"

"There's something about your sister's music that enchants me. I'm not deeply moved by other music. I know every tour stop you've ever made. I know how many fans came to each performance, which songs you sang in what order."

"Whoa." Bea drew her knees in tight to her stomach. "That's a little stalker creepy."

"Pardon, my queen. I didn't mean to scare you. I have a special cache in my processors just for you."

"I hope my next question doesn't offend you, Forman," Jessie said. "Were you programmed to like Bea's music?"

Forman's face went blank for about half a minute. "Nope. It's not a subroutine in my memory banks. There are no programs with her name on them, other than the ones I've initiated in the four months of my existence."

"Interesting." Jessie scribbled those facts down. "You're a valuable commodity. We've never met anyone like you before. How is it you happen to be here?"

"I'm in Atlanta tracking a missing person for my boss. When I tapped into the region's com system to initiate a wider search for him, I automatically ran a search for you. I knew you'd stayed here in the past. Sorry," he shrugged. "I'm sounding stalker-ish again, but I like knowing where you are. I'm such a huge fan. I had to meet you."

"Let me get this straight. You like music, but you love Bea's music," Jessie said. "You like knowing where my sister is, and you're looking for a missing person. Tell us about that."

"Can't. It's very hush-hush."

Bea's fingers started tapping on the sofa cushion in four-four time. "Really?"

Jessie groaned aloud. "Not now. You're too tired, Bea."

"What?" Forman's gaze swiveled between them. He focused on Bea's fingers and quivered with puppylike excitement. "Are we writing a song?"

"Don't know. Something about the way you just said hush-hush caught my attention. Keep talking."

"I can't talk about it. I'm sworn to secrecy."

She gestured with a hand, the other still tapping out a beat. "More."

"A friend is missing. A powerful friend and his lady vanished. It's very important that I find him."

"Why?" Jessie asked. "What does this friend have to do with anything?"

"He's the man behind the money."

Bea's eyes lit up. She reached for Jessie's notepad. Sighing, Jessie handed it over.

"What good is money when the world is dying?" Bea asked, scribbling fast.

"Exactly," Forman said. "Except the money pays for our research. Without it, no one would know what happened to the missing water."

"Whoa. What missing water?" Jessie asked, wishing she could take back her pad of paper. She got up, searched through a drawer, and came back with another pad.

"I've said too much already. Zeke will kill me."

"Zeke? He's a killer?"

"Dr. Geek is not a killer. He's brilliant. I'm currently detailed to his research program." He reached across and stilled Bea's pen. "Please don't sing about the missing water right now. Zeke has to write this report that neither of us believe in."

"Are we talking cover-up?" Jessie asked. "A huge government

conspiracy?"

"No way." He handed her Zeke's business card. "We're a small independent research facility on Tama Island off the coast of Georgia."

The hair on the back of Jessie's neck stirred as her stomach sank. "Tama Island?"

"You've heard of it?"

"Yeah. It's all over the news feeds. A big fire there."

Forman rose and grabbed Jessie's arm. "Show me."

"Easy, big guy. I'll flip on the com. They have aerial shots of the island and plumes of thick black smoke. How did you miss it?"

"I left the island at noon today. I mean yesterday, seeing as how it's morning now. Everything seemed fine when I left." He fiddled with his wrist com. "Come on, Zeke, pick up."

The vid screen flickered on. Newscasters Connor and Pauline joked about the falling property values of vacation homes on Tama Island. Dark helicopters whirled about the fiery island like vultures.

"Call me, dammit," Forman said to the wrist link before he signed off.

"Is swearing in your programming?" Jessie asked.

Forman strode over to the wall screen, transfixed by the images. "I can't believe this. What happened? I leave the island for a day, and the whole place falls apart. What's the world coming to?"

"You suspect arson?" Jessie asked.

"Damn straight. Zeke's in trouble. I've got to get back to him."

"Wait." Bea stood. "Is Zeke a good guy or a bad guy?"

"Zeke's the best, and he needs me. Ladies, please excuse me."

With that, the A.I. unit rushed from the room.

Jessie caught her sister's eye. "Very cool."

"No kidding. Some guys play for keeps." Bea's face went blank and then lit up. "That's it. 'Some Guys Play for Keeps.' That's my new title."

Jessie fingered the business card. "The only guy we've seen lately just went running out of here, and he isn't a real guy."

Bea chuckled knowingly. "He's real enough for me."

"He had it right. What's this world coming to?"

Nineteen

Zeke awoke to a pounding headache and a familiar wooziness. He must have been on the mainland. When he was a kid, his dad used to joke that he was a spaceman from a watery planet. There were times he wished the jest were true so at least there'd be a rational explanation for his displacement symptoms.

But there was nothing rational or logical about feeling so out of sorts whenever he left home. Worse, more than one medical professional thought he brought the symptoms on himself.

He wasn't a head case or an extraterrestrial.

The bed spun in a lazy circle. Groaning, he gripped the bedding to anchor himself. His eyes edged open to a strange setting. He jerked upright, holding his aching head. *Where am I?*

Dark wood and heavy floor-length drapes of gold accented the ornate furnishings instead of the more common white-on-white minimalist color scheme of homes today. Very old school, with museum-quality pieces. An older home, then. Belonging to an older man. A reclusive friend of his uncle's. Asia Minor.

Friendly territory, then. No worries. His fear ebbed, but the disorientation grew stronger. Meds. He needed his wrist band meds. Where was his bag?

"Lights, fifty percent. Curtains, open," Zeke said.

The lighting didn't change. The curtains didn't open. How retro. He stumbled to the window and tugged the fabric coverings to the side. Bright afternoon sunshine flooded the room, blinding him. "Yeouch!"

He thrust the drapes back into closed position. His stomach lurched, and he grabbed his belly. The off-island sickness usually didn't hit him this fast. He usually made it a day or two on the mainland without getting woozy.

With slitted eyes, he scoped the room. There. Near the foot of the bed. His bag. He grabbed it, found his wrist bands, and donned them. At least the blisters from paddling had healed. Why didn't his rapid healing ability work on this darned disorientation problem?

Life wasn't fair. Closing his eyes, he sagged into the soft bedding until his disorientation eased.

He tried to think restful, relaxing thoughts, but his uncertain situation intruded. How much damage had been done to his laboratory? Had Forman found Uncle John? What should he do next?

He had no answers, and he wouldn't find them in this low-tech bedroom. With that, he arose, dressed, slipped his bag over his shoulder, and went in search of his host. If there were answers out there, he wanted to find them.

Within moments of his stepping foot into the hall, two thick-chested dogs charged him. Robo pit bulls, by the look of them. He froze. When the dogs were three strides from him, a woman uttered a terse command in German, and they halted.

Zeke tore his gaze from the attack dogs to study the woman. A small brunette, compact in frame, fair in coloration, she wore white martial arts attire and a black belt. A gold ID necklace gleamed at her throat. An A.I unit. A Nola.

Not many of these assassination units left.

Curious.

"They won't harm you now." A sprinkling of European ennui seasoned Nola's husky voice.

Zeke glanced at the robotic dogs again. They didn't appear friendly, but he would overlook that as long as they didn't maim him. He hurried toward Nola.

"I'm looking for a cup of coffee," he said. "Can you direct me toward the kitchen?"

She nodded, serious and precise. "Go back past your room and down the stairs. Follow the main corridor until you can make a left. Mr. Minor is expecting you."

Zeke glanced back down the hall at the four-legged guard dogs. He dreaded passing them alone. "Can you call the dogs?"

Nola hissed out a guttural command, and the dogs padded silently to her. Zeke held his breath as they passed. Whatever Asia Minor guarded must be the equivalent of a national treasure. If he stayed here another night, he would not make the mistake of turning right out of his room. Not unless he wanted to be crushed by two robo dogs or gutted by a killer android.

"Thank you." He hurried away, noting more details of the dwelling as he went. Antique furnishings and dark colors gave the house a brooding, melancholy air, as if it had been long forgotten. As he descended the double-wide stairs, he caught the pleasing scent of coffee and followed his nose.

Asia Minor sat comfortably at an oversized table, an entire wall of vid screens flashing market news and world events. "Good afternoon, Dr. Landry." He gestured to a seat beside him and Zeke sat.

"Zeke, please. No need for formality. Thanks for your hospitality. It's nice to meet you after all these years."

"I'm delighted to have you as my guest. What can I get for you to eat or drink?"

"I'll start with coffee," Zeke said.

Asia spoke over his shoulder to a kitchen attendant. Moments later, coffee and a sandwich appeared before Zeke.

Zeke tasted the coffee. The rich dry roast eased the pounding in his head. "Thank you. This is the best cup of coffee I've ever had."

"I'm very particular about my coffee. Glad you like it." Asia glanced at Zeke's banded wrists. "Are you ill?"

"It's no big deal."

"Your uncle mentioned your spatial disorientation to me. I hope you don't mind my curiosity. My company designed those bands you wear. Are they effective?"

"Without them, I'd be island bound. The wrist bands allowed me to travel off-island for my education. Luckily, I found work on Tama Island so that I don't need to wear them daily. Speaking of the island, what is the extent of the damage?"

"The news is bad. Brace yourself." Asia nodded to the kitchen attendant. A vid screen mid-wall flickered to show multiple fires in the night sky. Newscasters Pauline and Connor wore dashing trench coats and stout boots and professed shock and awe by Zeke's lighthouse, and then the image changed to the fires again. The old mansion, ruined. The Institute, leveled. His lab, gone. Four people presumed dead.

A bone-numbing sense of devastation bore down on Zeke. He turned to his host. "I'm stunned. What a loss. Did they catch the protestor named Gabe Servalis?"

"The authorities have several protestors in custody, but not Servalis."

"That sociopath. I hope they catch him soon."

"His buddies said he didn't do it."

Zeke huffed out his disbelief. "Gabe led the protestors for weeks. Angie told me he started the fires. I believe her."

"The police will sort it out, of that I have no doubt."

No matter who sorted it out, the island still lost. The Institute lost. Zeke lost. "Where is Angie, anyway?"

"She left around noon. Said she wanted to be in Savannah in time to attend a friend's birthing. She left you a vid, and she told me everything that happened on the island."

"Oh." Zeke activated his wrist com for the message, but the screen stayed dark.

"Sorry. I have blockers in the walls," Asia said. "Only secure feeds routed through my scanners enter my home. Angie's vid is saved on my com system. Would you like to view it after you dine?"

"I would. I also need to contact my employers about my status. May I send an outbound message?"

"No problem, though I might offer a suggestion."

"What's that?"

"You're listed as missing and presumed dead."

"What?" Zeke rose. "We have to set the record straight. I need to call the authorities."

"Do we? Your uncle is missing. Your lab is gone. You might want to stay off the radar for a bit until we discover what's going on."

"I'll take that into consideration."

Twenty

Zeke whistled at the computer lab layout. "Mega cool setup, Asia. I'm impressed. You've got every widget on the planet in here several times over."

"I like to be prepared. Make yourself at home."

Zeke sat. The chair conformed to his shape, and the grid of vid screens loomed closer. "Is it voice activated?"

"Yes. Computer, recognize Zeke Landry."

"Hello, Zeke," a sultry woman's voice said.

"I know I'm in heaven now," Zeke said. "How'd you get Laurel Haywood, the most famous vid star of all time, to do your voice feed?"

Asia flashed an enigmatic smile. "Money talks."

"I'm definitely in the wrong profession. If I had a sweet workstation like this, I'd never leave it."

"My computer lab is at your disposal. I've set aside a section of core memory for you and given you access to routine functions. Feel free to use my equipment as you wish. I have pressing business matters to attend to in my upstairs office." With that, Asia departed.

The chair massaged Zeke's upper back, and he sighed with pleasure. "Computer, show me Angie's vid."

Angie's sleepy but excited face showed on the screen at eye level. "Zeke, I hope you don't mind me abandoning you. I heard that a friend in Savannah went into labor. Asia arranged transport for me, so I'm off. Take care of yourself, cuz."

The image flicked off. Zeke called up the fire vids again. They were every bit as horrifying the second time around. This time he listened to the entire broadcast.

Should he notify the Institute about his status? Or was Asia right about his life being in danger?

He pulled up the Institute page on the vid screen. Details and a vid about the island fires covered their home page as well. His face flashed on screen. A banner streamed underneath, "World-renowned scientist presumed dead in island tragedy."

They'd already written him off?

"Computer, locate A.I. unit Forman."

Moments later a feed showed an agitated Forman on the hovercraft dock. The swift response impressed Zeke. "Computer, open a link to Forman."

"Negative," the computer said. "The unit does not recognize us."

"Hail him again. Tell him I'm alive."

A blast of annoying static shot through the connection, and then Forman pivoted to avoid the ferry cam. "Zeke? That really you? I came back to the coast as soon as I heard about the fire."

"Reports of my death are greatly exaggerated. I'm staying out of sight for now. I'll shoot you my coordinates. Join me."

"Don't move. I'll arrange transpo and be right there."

The transmission flickered and went blank.

While he waited for Forman, Zeke surfed the news feeds, looking for information on his uncle, the albino woman, and the global water situation. He found nothing useful. In fact, other than his uncle's bio on the Institute home page, he barely existed on the world web. Curious, he checked two recent symposiums he knew his uncle had attended. No John Demery at either event.

Odd.

He searched for himself and found his talks, papers, and book listed in cyberspace. What was the deal with Uncle John?

The door opened behind him. Zeke whirled in the console chair to see Nola escorting Forman in.

"You made good time," Zeke said.

Forman pulled Zeke out of his chair and clapped him on the back. "I've been worried sick, buddy. Thought you'd returned to dust and ashes."

Embarrassed by the emotional display, Zeke disentangled himself and sat back down. "A.I. units worry?"

"This one does. How did you get here?"

"Angie and I paddled across the sound in the dead of night."

"The world believes you're dead, Zeke."

"I know. Asia suggested I stay dead for a while, for the sake of my family's longevity."

"I haven't met Asia Minor, but he makes a good point. You are the last of your line."

"Maybe. We don't know what happened to Uncle John. Unless

you found him?"

"No luck. John Demery and Rissa Porter are ghosts. I tried various com stations at libraries and hotels in Savannah and Atlanta and got nothing. We need another strategy."

"Asia has given me an all-access pass to his state-of-the-art computer lab. Maybe there's something in here that could help us refine the search."

"Do you wish me to interface with the computer?"

"Yes. Computer, recognize A.I. unit Forman."

"Hello, Forman."

"Hello, dollface. This is my lucky day." Forman sat in an adjacent console chair. "Full data stream. All feeds."

Forman's face shrouded in ice blue as the data stream arced through the air. A moment later, he leaned forward to address Zeke. "As I discovered in my earlier queries, there are no records of John Demery or Rissa Porter anywhere in the system. They vanished without a trace."

"There should be a record of Rissa's injury treatment in the med system. Wait. I have an idea. Check the cam feeds at the ferry dock and the Institute headquarters in D.C. There has to be an image of her somewhere."

"Processing." After a minute, Forman leaned back out. "Got her. It only took me six million images to locate her."

The albino's image flashed on Zeke's vid screen. "That's her, all right. What do we know about her?"

"Nothing. Her image isn't in the personnel databases."

"Try an image recognition search. Maybe she's turned up elsewhere without her identification."

Moments later, Forman crowed. "Got her. She's in a morgue in Baltimore."

"A morgue?" Zeke's heart stuttered. "Is Uncle John there?"

"No. Just Rissa. She is listed as a Jane Doe. Fatal gunshot wound. Found in a bad neighborhood."

"I'm sorry she didn't make it. I didn't realize the severity of her situation, especially since she received immediate medical care. Maybe good can come out of this. Her personal effects might lead us to Uncle John."

"How can we do that if you're dead?"

"Hmm. There must be a way. I'll ask Asia about it. Say, since we're temporarily without a home base, what do you say to downloading my data here?"

"The system has twelve levels of security. I can add another layer of data encryption to further protect your intellectual property."

Zeke fished his portable data drive out of his backpack. "I'd feel better if this stuff had a permanent home."

"You trust this guy?"

"Yes. He's been Uncle John's friend for years. Angie trusts him, too."

"Works for me." Forman manually connected the data drive and facilitated the transfer. He handed the drive to Zeke. "I prefer redundancy in data storage. We should stash your data storage hardware in another location."

"Good idea. And Forman?"

"Yeah?"

"I've made a decision. I don't want to be dead. Whatever this is, I want to face it head on. Being dead is too low-profile."

"You sure that's wise?"

"My family is in trouble. I won't hide or cower. If that puts me in harm's way, that's a risk I have to take."

Twenty-One

Palms rustled in the gentle morning breeze. Tropical birds twittered in the adjacent flowering foliage. A bow-tied waiter hurried across the terrace with a second round of Mimosas. Number One's bikini-clad companions, twin redheads, purred at his side inside the plush cabana.

Life was good, indeed.

Too bad paradise came with a time limit.

Over the past two weeks, he'd sold his holdings in West Coast resort sectors and realigned his portfolio to include construction companies and construction materials. No reason not to benefit financially from his insider knowledge. Money didn't solve the world's problems, but it talked in ways only the clever could grasp.

With wealth and victory in his global destabilization campaign, the Master's chair would belong to him. For years he'd had his eye on the prize. He'd played the game and the Master, and now he'd reap the reward.

His com unit beeped. A message from Two. Usually he took his business messages in private. However, with his goal so near at hand, he felt invincible.

He selected the text feed and read the words. *Installation complete.*

Team Two's explosives were in place. An unprecedented disaster would occur in California, one that would take a heavy toll on lives, disrupt transportation for years, and finally end the stranglehold the Americans had on the world's economy.

Best of all, the Master lived on the West Coast. One brimmed with enthusiasm. He'd staged a coup on the Society's turf, and it hadn't cost him anything.

This day kept getting better and better.

He entered a text response. *Await my go.*

One sipped his bubbly beverage in triumph. It was good to savor the moment when his plan came together. With the groundwork in place, the implementation and surge would soon command his time.

Meanwhile, he'd done the impossible. The motto of his organization had never been more apt. Glory would soon be his.

He predicted sweet victory, and he was ready to party. The performance-enhancing drug had worked its magic. He felt as hard as iron.

Time for fun.

He signaled for his cabana to be closed for privacy and beckoned the well-oiled twins. "Come to me, my pretties."

Twenty-Two

"Sure you want to play your hand this way?" Asia Minor asked from the shelter of his private conveyance.

Beyond their transpo, cameramen and reporters milled aimlessly near the portal for the tubes. There on the coast, the tubes started out aboveground and turned underground twenty miles inland. Too much salty groundwater near the coast—pumping it out of the tunnels would be prohibitively expensive.

Passersby slowed to gawk at the expensive conveyance as if an alien spaceship had landed in their midst. Zeke adjusted the pressure of his wrist bands, grateful for the extra pair of altitude-mediating bands Asia had given him. No telling how long it would take to find his uncle. No telling how long he'd have to be away from Tama Island.

"I'm sure I need to get on that tube," Zeke said. "Drue must have leaked my travel plans to the media."

"How inconsiderate," Asia said. "Your boss should be more discreet. My offer of private transport stands. I can get you to Baltimore without the hassle of the public tube station."

Forman scowled. "Drue King is the Institute's administrative chief. She is not Dr. Landry's boss."

Zeke gave a slight shake of his head, silencing Forman. He'd rather not reveal his chain of command at the Institute to an outsider. "We've imposed enough already, Asia. Thank you for your help."

He reached across the spacious vehicle and shook Asia's hand. "I don't know as I can repay the favor anytime soon, but I owe you."

"Glad to be of service. Drop by to see me when you head back this way. Tell John I've got a brand new bottle of his favorite whiskey."

"Will do." Zeke glanced over at Forman. "Ready?"

"Ready."

"Let's do this."

Forman exited the conveyance first; Zeke shadowed him, sunglasses in place to block the bright morning sun. He walked toward the tube at a normal pace, but Forman hurried along at a fast clip. Zeke refused to hurry after him. He didn't want to be seen as a black man running from his reckoning. He had nothing to hide.

"There he is!" someone cried.

Within seconds, reporters with microphones and bright lights surrounded Zeke. "Where were you?" a big-haired reporter asked.

"Staying with a friend." Zeke stared straight into the camera with a level gaze.

"Why didn't you come forward right away?"

"After paddling across the sound to the mainland during the night, I slept late in the day. I notified the authorities once I realized their error."

A reporter in bright clothing asked, "Did anyone else escape with you?"

"My cousin. We used her grandfather's canoe to leave the island."

"Where's your cousin now? Is she here?"

"She's in Savannah attending a friend's childbirth."

A sweating man with perfect teeth who wore a brown suit asked, "Is your lab a complete loss?"

"That's what they say."

"Where are you headed?"

"I'm taking some time off."

A serious brunette asked, "What about your research? Will the Institute still report your findings to the International Water Summit?"

"The Institute has my latest report. I transmitted it yesterday before the fire."

"The whole world wants to know what you discovered. Are we running out of water, Dr. Landry? Is this the water crisis of the '30s revisited?"

He paused for a deep breath. "Preliminary analysis of the data set revealed water losses in reservoirs. My assistant and I will continue the analysis once we have a new laboratory, but for now, we're slated to hop a tube for some R&R."

Zeke forged through the crowd, catching up to Forman. "Some bodyguard you are. You threw me to the wolves."

"You handled yourself pretty well there, Ace. Sure you haven't been holding press conferences every day of your life?"

They shoved their tickets into the reader. With a whoosh, the barrier partition opened to let them through. As soon as they passed, it sealed again. They followed the signs through the terminal to gate E-4, where they passed their tickets under another scanner and were admitted to a smaller waiting cube.

"I hate traveling in these worm burrows," Zeke said as they joined the other northbound travelers waiting for a double pod. "Ever since the government built these high-speed tubes in 2040 to save the atmosphere, we've had trouble with the underground reservoirs."

"The rationale behind the tunnel network is irrefutable," Forman said. "The tunnels saved the atmosphere."

"Perhaps," Zeke grudgingly admitted, "but the vibrations and fissures they produced during excavation allowed contamination of groundwater. Before you start arguing the other side of this debate, let me do us both a favor. I am not in the mood for such a pointless conversation. It's bad enough having to seal myself into a tiny capsule and letting a machine hurl me through space at speeds that will cause instant death if there's a mistake."

"Z-man, the odds of a pod mistake are infinitesimally small. Billions of people use the tube system every day with no ill effect."

Zeke kept his dark thoughts to himself. The closer he got to the platform, the more irrational and unsettled he felt. His fingers tightened on the ticket in his hand. *I'm doing this to find Uncle John. He'd come looking for me. I have to do this.*

Up ahead, a teen wearing an ear com sang softly along with her music. Forman grinned at Zeke. "You hear that?"

"The girl singing?"

"Yeah. That's one of my faves from Queen Bea. 'Babies in the Wilderness.'"

He couldn't deal with Forman's fixation on the pop sensation right now, not when he faced traveling in a tiny pod and ending up at a different altitude. He'd hoped to outgrow the spatial disorientation that occurred when he went off-island. If anything, it had intensified in recent years.

"We're not going to Paris, Forman."

"I figured you wouldn't change your mind. That's why I stopped off to see her in Atlanta."

The cheeky admission stunned Zeke. He chose his next words carefully. "You were supposed to be looking for my uncle."

"I did. I looked and looked, but the hotel data center I used to post my query revealed Queen Bea's presence onsite. I introduced myself, and we hit it off. She's as nice in person as she is on stage."

Zeke's gut churned. "You quit looking for my uncle to hang out with a singer?"

"Your uncle fell off the grid. You saw that when we were using Asia's computers. Someone took him, or he doesn't want to be found. Either way, we have our work cut out for us."

No way would he squeeze in a compact space with Forman right now. His A.I. unit clearly had an unknown agenda. About time he remembered that someone else had programmed the robot. He was a mechanical man. A machine who had disobeyed Zeke's direct orders to find Uncle John.

Had Forman tampered with the records and removed all mention of Uncle John?

The possibility rattled him.

Forman could rewrite history.

The double tube arrived. Acting on instinct, Zeke stepped aside, all the way over to the single tube line.

"Zeke?" Forman said.

"Go ahead. I've decided to go solo."

Forman stepped into the other line with Zeke and spoke under his breath. "Speaking as your assistant and sometimes bodyguard, this is a bad idea. We should travel together."

"The double pod is too cramped. I need time to think. I need privacy."

The line moved forward, a person at a time. Finally, pod SLA4893 opened for Zeke. He turned to Forman. "See you in Baltimore."

Forman nodded.

Zeke inserted his ticket in the pod, sealed the exterior and belted himself in the utilitarian seat. The light dimmed to a murky twilight as the pod zoomed through the tube. Since he disliked traveling, Zeke activated the anesthetic vapor. A fine mist saturated the air. Perversely, he held his breath as long as possible.

Who did Forman work for?

Twenty-Three

Zeke's mouth was cotton dry as he exited the tube ramp into the bustling terminal. He stumbled and grabbed the nanorod handrail to keep from falling. Between his pounding head and his woozy stomach, he hardly knew what to do.

His vision blurred.

His stomach lurched.

He gripped his tender belly. Was altitude illness to blame? Baltimore sat a hundred feet above sea level. That little amount shouldn't affect him so strongly. Maybe the anesthetic mist in the travel pod had overdosed him. That must be it. He should report the side effects to the Travel Authority here in Baltimore. But first he needed to find a bathroom. Squinting against the bright lights, he found the pictogram sign for the men's room and staggered into the antiseptic-laced chamber.

Where the hell was Forman?

A wave of acute nausea nearly knocked him off his feet. Midstride he changed course from the hand sanitizers to the commodes. Spasms wracked his body as his stomach emptied. The room tilted and spun.

God. He needed help. His illness had never been so debilitating before.

He heard someone enter and stop by the bank of sanitizers. "Forman? That you?"

An expectant, brittle silence filled the restroom.

Not Forman.

Trouble waited for him.

He should have tubed with the robot.

Darn his pride.

He waited a bit longer, hoping someone else would venture into the facility. His mother always said there was safety in numbers. Weak and miserable like this, he felt vulnerable.

Who waited for him?

Why couldn't he think straight?

How could he improve his situation?

His heart thumped in his throat. His clammy clothes stuck to his body. He couldn't hide in here forever. With altitude sickness, he had at most fifteen minutes before another wave of debilitating nausea struck.

He'd have to take his chances.

Besides, Landrys didn't hide.

They got the job done.

He pulled himself together and exited the cubicle. Two barrel-chested men waited by the sanitizers. They started toward him. He instinctively backed up.

A gun poked him in the back. "Don't move, worm ball."

"What do you want?" Zeke asked.

The man closest to him pointed a second weapon at him. It looked like a tranq gun.

Zeke's throat tightened. "My wallet's in my pocket. Take it."

Tranq Gun squeezed the trigger. "Night, night, Dr. Landry."

At the prick on his skin, Zeke ripped the dart out. Tranq Gun fired three more shots. The room blurred, and he tumbled straight into hell.

Twenty-Four

The room swam into view. Foggy shapes became recognizable. A large room. Lots of people. Bright overhead lights. Pale blue walls in a long corridor. Gleaming floors. The stench of unwashed bodies prevailed.

Zeke's unsteady stomach rolled.

At the insistent pressure to move forward, Zeke shook his throbbing head to clear it. He tried to rub his eyes, but his hands were constrained at his waist. Off balance, he stumbled to his knees.

"On your feet, pukeface," a uniformed man shouted in his ear.

Zeke thrashed on the floor like a mullet out of water. Cold sweat beaded in his tingling scalp, but he was hot everywhere else. If he could get his shirt off, he'd feel better. Except he couldn't. Neither his hands nor his feet were working as they should.

He glanced up at the man's elongated face, and it whirled like an oak leaf caught in an eddy. God. He was so cold. His ribs throbbed. A noise sounded in his throat.

"Christ. He's going to puke again." The officer moved away.

His gut compressed, and he heaved with all he had. Liquid splashed on the floor, splattered on his clothes. When it was over, someone yanked him to his feet. Somehow he managed to stand and breathe. A bright light flashed. Then another man, one that looked less fit than the others, fingerprinted him.

"Where am I?" he managed.

"You're at the police station. Headed for jail."

Zeke's head reeled. "Jail? For vomiting?"

The man's expression darkened. "Says here you have outstanding warrants for public urination and you robbed a young couple, threatened to harm their baby."

"There must be a mistake. I would never rob or hurt anyone. I would never pee in public. My mama taught me better than that."

"You should have listened to your mother, Mosby."

"Zeke. My name is Zeke."

The gloved processing clerk arched an eyebrow at him as he

wiped the fingerprint ink from Zeke's hands with a moist cloth. "You want to add giving a false name to your charges? Says right here your name is Joe Mosby. You've been in and out of jail ten times in recent years. I've processed you through here twice myself."

The sweats started again. Zeke braced as nausea shivered through him. If he could catnap for twenty minutes, he could reboot his brain.

"It's a mistake. My name is Zeke Landry. I'm from Georgia."

"Buddy, every career criminal that comes through here spins a hard luck story. Save it for someone who cares. Next."

Armed guards watched while Zeke and a handful of other prisoners stripped and showered. With water pounding in his face, Zeke felt halfway human again, but his thoughts wouldn't align. He glanced down at the whorls on his fingers, enthralled by the patterns. So many circles and grooves. Such an interesting maze to explore.

"Come on, Mosby. We don't have all day."

Zeke glanced up at the thickly muscled guard. The man's face expanded and contracted like a bellows. The comical sight tickled him. He laughed for all he was worth, spinning out of control until he gagged again. Vomited. He collapsed on the wet shower floor, hovering on the brink of darkness.

A guard nudged him with a booted foot and swore. "He's high on something. Stupid zoners. They should be jailed for hurting themselves. How'd he sneak controlled substances in here? Get a gurney in here to haul Mosby's sorry ass to the med ward."

As night swallowed him, he managed to whisper, "Zeke. My name is Zeke."

Twenty-Five

Compared to the serenity of coastal Georgia, the tube station in downtown Baltimore flexed like a living sea serpent, with people pulsing by Forman in writhing waves. Forman scanned the gate area. No sign of Zeke. Knowing the man's preference for keeping a low profile, Forman moved out of the pedestrian traffic to an observation point on the edge of the corridor.

With each face he scanned, his concern mounted. How did he lose Zeke?

His pod left before Forman's. His boss should have arrived first and waited. Forman hung back a few moments, scanning the new arrivals, hoping that the pods had somehow reversed order in transit.

Zeke Landry did not appear. He didn't answer his com.

Something was wrong.

Forman's core temp shot up half a degree. He'd screwed up. Again. Zeke had been upset with him about visiting Queen Bea. That's why he'd aborted the tandem pod plan.

He'd brought this on himself by impulsive actions and an even bigger mouth. Forman hung his head. No wonder Supply Central wanted to crush his processors. His actions weren't logical. Who wanted an irrational A.I. unit? Zeke was his last chance to prove his worth, and he'd failed. Miserably.

He brainstormed the scenarios. If Zeke diverted his pod during the trip, Forman was on his own. If Zeke arrived on schedule and abandoned Forman, Forman was on his own. If someone else diverted Zeke's pod for an unknown reason, Forman was still on his own.

On the off chance the last option was true, waiting here would seal his fate. He couldn't help Zeke if he was captured. With his affinity for mechanical processors, he could tap into the com system anywhere and access the pod transpo records. In contrast, searching those records here would almost certainly invite disaster.

With that in mind, Forman melted into the crowd, threading his way into the middle of a group of elderly tourists. Calling on his

Holmes disguise module, he stooped his posture, grayed his hair, shortened his stride. His bright shirt he buttoned all the way up, covering his A.I necklace, an act forbidden by international law.

He blended right in.

"I don't recall seeing you before," a wiry woman with a large sequined tote said.

"I joined the tour late," Forman said. He tuned in the conversations around him and found a topic. "How did you like the Liberty Bell in Philadelphia?"

"I expected something the size of the pyramids. They were a sight, let me tell you. My name's Blanche, by the way."

"Henry," Forman said. "Nice to meet you."

"I've been around the world three times, not easy to do in this economy." Blanche droned on and on. Forman listened attentively but kept a sharp eye out for Zeke. Four robo cops in gray body armor hurried past the tourists, heading toward the pod gate he'd just left. Forman averted his face from the robot police, grateful he'd realized the danger in time to plan his escape. Once they were safely past, he took stock of the situation again.

Zeke was missing. Termination agents were hurrying toward Forman's last location. Were they searching for him?

As the tour group traversed the station, Forman stayed put, conversing easily with his chatty companion. He spotted a souvenir kiosk and excused himself. "I'll catch up at the transpo stand. I need a crab souvenir for my niece," he told the woman.

"I'll save you a seat," she said.

At the kiosk, he picked up a tan jacket and an Orioles ball cap as well as a furry crab. Peering between snow globes and the T-shirts, he surveyed the other passengers in the terminal. No Zeke. He'd been afraid of that. He paid with untraceable credits. Still cloaked in his senior citizen disguise, he donned the garments and walked on the edge of the corridor, careful to keep his features concealed from cameras along the way.

A line of human sentries stood by the exit. Forman strode forward with purpose, unwilling for them to see his internal wavering. If he got picked up now, he wouldn't do Zeke any good.

The door opened, and Blanche waved him forward. "Come on, Henry. I made them wait for you."

Forman waved back and smiled at Blanche. Then he put his head down and marched past the sentries. Using wireless data streaming, he manipulated the transpo driver's electronic log to show his name on the manifest. Then they motored off to the waterfront. He tagged along with the tour for a few hours. When they stopped for lunch at the Inner Harbor, he left the group, saying he had made an arrangement to spend the rest of the day with his niece.

"You forgot your crab." Blanche held it out to him.

"So I did. Thank you, Blanche," Forman said. With that he hurried away, melting into the crowd of urban professionals and tourists. He popped into a cyber café and accessed the wireless network, careful to disguise his signature from the computer bots by accessing Zeke's concealment program. Local, regional, and national news feeds carried no mention of a tube accident or a missing scientist. Zeke's disappearance didn't make the headlines. The pod system database held no clues either.

With such a lack of data points, he believed Zeke had been kidnapped, diverted off the grid, and possibly killed. Forman shuddered and resolved to think positively. He had to believe Zeke lived. He had to analyze the facts.

Someone wanted Zeke out of the picture. They'd torched his lab, and he'd barely escaped with his life. Now his pod had vanished. Forman could step out of the shadows and alert the media to Zeke's disappearance, but that could get him decommissioned by the robo cops, or worse, captured and repurposed to be a bad guy.

Not worth the risk.

Protecting Zeke topped his primary directive queue.

He couldn't do that now that he'd lost his boss, but he could do what Zeke wanted him to do. He could find out more about the albino, which had been the point of coming to Baltimore. He headed to the city morgue.

Twenty-Six

Time blurred. Zeke became aware of unrelieved white walls, annoying machine beeps, crisp antiseptic, the irritating hum of industrial lighting, and the rigid steel handcuff that chained him in the railed bed.

Nightmares swam through bouts of nausea and vomiting. Images flashed in terrifying snips of color.

Two divers fighting a marauding shark.

Uncle John trapped in a small cage, sinking into black water.

Angie's face, pale and drawn with terror.

Forman being used for target practice.

None of it made any sense, and yet the alarming visions cycled through his head until nothingness overtook him. He awoke again some time later, aching and cold. A single bulb glowed overhead. Teeth chattering, he reached for the scratchy blanket lying next to him. After he warmed up, he drowsed again.

* * *

Someone punched his shoulder. "Wake up, puke. Food's here," a deep voice said.

Zeke's eyes opened. The room didn't spin, but the unfamiliar concrete block walls and over-ripe stench disoriented him just the same. "Where am I?"

"Prison, moron. Gas main busted at the jail, and the sheriff sent over a batch of prisoners." The large white man jerked his thumb toward the steel bars beyond the foot of Zeke's bunk. "Grub man is coming down the hall. If you don't stand up, you don't get breakfast. Get your sorry ass up or don't bitch about being hungry later. I got no tolerance for whiners. Killed the last one."

Zeke sat up fast, rubbed his dry eyes with his hands, tried to get his bearings. Signals from his body intruded in his thoughts. His ribs throbbed. His head ached. His throat constricted. His mouth tasted of bile. Gazing down, he saw he wore an orange shirt and pants. His feet were bare.

"Hurry up, fool. You're making me look bad."

Reacting to the growled threat, Zeke slid off the top bunk, his legs buckling on impact. His head banged on the cold tile floor. He moaned at this new pain.

"Get off my floor, Mosby."

Head throbbing, Zeke managed to get to his hands and knees. "My name's not Mosby."

"Don't matter. In here you're Joe Mosby."

He heard the squeak of wheels, the murmur of voices. He grabbed the bars and made it to his feet. Barely. Following terse commands from his cellmate, he accepted the wrapped breakfast sandwich and a carton of milk.

He glanced around. No chair or table. The top bunk soared to Mount Everest height. He looked longingly at the lower bunk. "May I sit on your bed?"

"Hell no."

Zeke sat on the cold floor. Opened the sandwich. A rubbery fried egg on two slices of burnt white bread. His stomach churned, and he lowered the offensive food to his lap. God, what he wouldn't give for a cup of hot tea. Or ginger ale.

"Can't be picky in here. Eat up."

The smell of fried grease and burnt bread clogged his nostrils. Gagging, he lunged for the toilet. Nothing came out as he wretched. Nothing left inside.

He slid to the floor, miserable.

"You breathe on your sammich?" the large man asked.

"No."

"Can I eat it?"

"Take it."

"Thanks." The man lumbered over and picked up the sandwich off the floor. He tossed Zeke a piece of the bread crust. "Eat this."

Zeke caught it. "I feel like death warmed over."

"You smell like it, too."

He eyed the crust and worked up the nerve to take a small bite. "What's your name?"

"Severnius Murray. But everybody calls me Tank."

"Where am I, Tank?"

"I done told you. Prison."

"I'm in a Baltimore prison?"

"Man, you are zoned out. This here's Denver. You're in Colorado."

Denver. Mile high city. No wonder he felt so bad. He was a mile above sea level. "I have altitude sickness. Did I come in with wrist bands?"

"You came in with the clothes on your back, same as the rest of us."

Zeke's hand went to where his father's necklace should have been and came up empty. "Where's my stuff?"

"Personal possessions are returned upon release. Unless you were stupid enough to have guns or drugs on you when they caught you. If so, you can kiss that stash goodbye."

"Denver. How did I get to Denver? I tubed to Baltimore from coastal Georgia because my uncle disappeared."

Tank jammed an index finger in each ear. "La la la. Don't wanna hear it. Don't tell me crap like that. I'm a short timer. I'm gonna get out of here next week. Unless you mess it up for me. And if you do that, I'll kill you with my bare hands."

Zeke clutched his stomach, wincing at his sore ribs. "This is messed up."

Tank took his fingers out of his ears. "You say something?"

"No."

"Good. You catch on quick."

"How do things work in here?"

Tank nodded. "What you wanna know?"

"The routine. Meals. Showers. Lawyers. That stuff."

"You just got here so you ain't gonna see no lawyer for a while. Shower is tomorrow, but I wouldn't be anxious for a shower if I was you. Big Mike said he owns the next new guy. Big Mike's trouble."

Fear stalked across his mind and as it took a dip, Zeke's bravado faltered. "No one owns me. That's ridiculous."

"Big Mike gets what he wants. You're his new butt boy. This time tomorrow, you'll be wearing his pink bow in your dark brown hair."

Terror clawed up Zeke's throat. "No way. I refuse."

"Refuse all you like, Mosby. I'm telling you how it is."

"My name's Zeke Landry. Not Mosby."

"Shut up about the name. You got to go along to get along."

"That's dumb. That how you landed here? Going along with a really bad idea?"

Tank laughed, a deep guffaw. "Something like that."

"Brains are what works in this world," Zeke asserted. Now if he could just get his brain to work, that'd be saying something.

"Brains got you in here."

Zeke nodded sagely at the irrefutable wisdom. Someone went to a lot of trouble to secrete him in here, in the worst possible place for his altitude condition. "That's a fact."

"What you gonna do?"

The answer smoldered in Zeke's belly. "I'm gonna out-brain them."

Twenty-Seven

The cop uniform in the second locker fit great. Forman buttoned it up, affected a police swagger, and hopped the elevator down to the city morgue. He identified the middle-aged medical examiner by sight from the personnel records he'd previously accessed.

"Dr. Brusher?"

The M.E. looked up from his desk. "Yes?"

Forman bobbed his head, quite pleased with the darker color he'd turned his short hair. "Officer Thomas. Mrs. Grancy from admin asked me to stop in here. A virus infected her personal leave database. She needs us to stop in and refresh our annual leave requests. There's no rush, but those who get their requests in first will be given preference."

A wide-eyed look of panic crossed Brusher's face. He shot to his feet. "My wife will kill me if I can't get off in November. We've had that beach place booked for Thanksgiving since last year."

"Know what you mean. I already got my request back in the system. Got a family thing next month myself."

"I'll shoot her a quick com message."

"Suit yourself." Forman gave a lazy shrug. "But if there's another hitch in the system and she doesn't receive it, you'll be stuck here looking at stiffs while your family eats turkey at the shore."

"Good point. I'll run right up there."

"I'm right behind you, buddy. Just need to hit the head. More privacy down here."

Brusher left, and Forman hid in the bathroom until he heard the elevator door close. Then he hurried to Brusher's console and accessed the autopsy record for Rissa Porter. According to the file, Clarissa Porter lived at 28570 Beacon Street. Cause of death, a gunshot wound to the temple. Date of death, two days ago.

No mention of a gut shot. Odd. He'd heard the shot that felled her. He'd seen the blood on her torso. Had he made a mistake? Was this the right Rissa Porter?

Forman downloaded her info from the com port. He probably

had five minutes tops before Brusher came looking for him. He located Rissa's berth in the cold storage unit, opened it. The albino pigmentation and physical features of the woman on the tray matched the Rissa Porter he'd met.

He pulled the sheet down and touched her cold abdomen.

No gunshot wound down there.

Curious.

Why had the woman faked an injury on the island? To draw Zeke's uncle off the island? Something was very wrong here.

His internal alarm chimed. He was short on time. With swift motions, he stashed Rissa back inside and bolted toward the stairs. He heard the ding of the elevator as he opened the door to the stairwell. Carefully he shut the door, avoiding the snick of the door latch.

He returned the uniform and slipped out of the building. A short tube ride later he was on Beacon Street. The modest brownstone sat in a quiet neighborhood. He found a good vantage point and watched her house.

By midafternoon, there'd been no activity in her house and both of her next-door neighbors had stepped out. The sky darkened. Great, a thunderstorm. Though with less moisture at this latitude, thunderstorms were mostly a light and sound show. Very little moisture fell from the sky these days, but humans still feared storms. He could use that.

If they stayed indoors, he had a better chance of avoiding detection. He hurried up the steps, deactivated the electronic lock, and stepped inside. The kitchen cabinets were empty. Indentations in the vacuumed bedroom carpet suggested previous furniture placement. In the bathroom, no towels, no toiletries. No one lived here.

How long had this place had been vacant? According to her autopsy report, Rissa had been dead two days. Given the barren state of her home, she didn't live here. Or else someone moved quickly to eradicate traces of her life.

Either possibility raised a disturbing question.

Who was Rissa Porter?

Twenty-Eight

Queen Bea launched into an encore. She loved performing, loved the sexy surge of energy from her fans. "Where will we lay our sweet heads? Upon mossy beds? What will fill the hunger in our hearts?"

As the packed theater sang along with her, she gazed out at the happy faces. Her music meant something. It had to, for all these people to take time out of their lives to physically be here and share this moment.

She strutted in front of the cameras again, flipping her royal blue cape over her bare shoulder. This part of her Mexico City show fed live to the Save the World fundraiser simultaneously staged in London, L.A., and Tel Aviv. International music stars had joined ranks to help those who'd lost so much.

"We are all babies in the wilderness." The bright stage lights splintered into a thousand points of light as she belted out the chorus. Blindly, she reached for the mike stand. Missed.

An intense pain shot through her heart, stealing her breath. The world spun off its axis, and she staggered forward, plunging headfirst off the stage.

* * *

Jessie cupped her sister's limp hand. Her sister was in there, somewhere, she had to be. "Don't you die on me, Beatrice Stemford. I'm counting on you. Remember that house by the sea we always wanted to buy? I can't live there by myself. That's going to be our house, so you fight this thing. You hear me? You dig in and fight."

Tears misted Jessie's vision. They'd been through so much together. Bea couldn't die now. She couldn't. "The jury's still out on unconscious people being able to hear their loved ones, but I believe with all my heart that you can hear me, Sis. Fight this thing. Come back to me. We're a team, remember? We always said once we found the perfect guys, we'd live right next to each other so that we could see each other every day of our lives.

"He's out there, Bea, I know he is. Your Mr. Right is waiting for you to find him. And when we find your fella, mine will be there too, just like we dreamed it. We deserve a happy ever after, but you have to fight for it. I know you can do it."

"Senorita?"

Jessie glanced up at the touch to her shoulder. "Yes?"

"You must leave her now to rest."

"She needs me."

"She feels your love. But visits must be short. You can come again in four hours."

Jessie gave Bea's hand a gentle squeeze. "They're kicking me out for now, but I'll be back before you know it. I love you, Sis."

She walked out into the waiting room where Bea's band members milled around. The drummer gazed up expectantly. Jessie shook her head.

Tears filled her eyes. She chewed on her trembling lip. It had been twenty-four hours since Bea collapsed onstage. Twenty-four hours of wishing, hoping, and praying. The entire world waited for Queen Bea to wake up, but exhaustion had taken a heavy toll. Worse, the doctors wouldn't give Jessie a straight answer.

Just like when Mom died. Nobody would tell her anything when her mom was sick in the hospital. Then her mom had the coronary, and it was too late to say goodbye.

Way too late.

Band members held her as she cried for her sister, the last of her family, and the best part of her.

How could she go on without Bea?

Twenty-Nine

"You punch like a girl. Put power in it," Tank said.

"If I had power, I'd use it." Zeke ignored the trembling in his rubbery legs and nodded at his hulking cellmate. "Show me again."

Tank pummeled the pillow they'd rigged to hang down from Zeke's bunk. His arms looked like mechanical pistons from historical vids. Zeke tried to imitate the trajectory of the fluid, powerful swings. Afterward he shook his aching fists and looked to his fight trainer for advice.

"Better," Tank said. "Needs oomph."

Zeke tried a few more punches and wished he'd studied self-defense in college. Not that he'd had any intention of ever landing in jail, much less prison. He still didn't understand the how of it, but he couldn't lie down and take it. He had to do something. He had to fight back.

Fortunately, Tank offered to help fill the void of his formal education. "What else do I need to know to defend myself?" Zeke asked.

"If the guy beating you up is bigger and stronger, you have to be fast," Tank said. "Lash out at weak points—the groin, the eyes, the knees. The only thing that counts in a fight is who wins. Everything in the room is a weapon. Attack the target where he's weakest. By the way, you look terrible."

Zeke wiped sweat from his brow. He shook all over. Between the altitude sickness and dry heaves for two days straight, he felt weak. Conversely, Tank had enjoyed double rations for the same amount of time and had repaid him by keeping Big Mike off him in the showers.

Which had led to Zeke's big plan.

He would get in a fight with Big Mike out in the prison yard, take a dive, and Tank would demand that he be taken to the med unit. Given his bad shape, he would be hospitalized for several days, during which time he'd find a way to send Forman a message through the med com.

He gripped the end of the steel bunk bed, the cold metal soothing the sting in his fists. If this worked, he'd owe Tank big time. "Keep your nose clean when you get out. If you get bored with Colorado, look me up in coastal Georgia. Zeke Landry on Tama Island. I'll make sure you get a fresh start."

Tank snorted. "Ex-cons never get a fair shake. We take what comes along. I'm hoping to befriend big-butted women who want my stud services. That's my dream job. God, I love me a big-butted woman."

"I can get you a job where I live. You'd like island life very much. The slower rhythms, the beautiful women, the gentle salt breezes."

"Man, don't be filling my head with cotton candy dreams. I ain't never seen the ocean, and I ain't likely to travel across the country when I don't have a single credit to my name."

"I know people. Trust me on this."

"Trust? I don't trust anybody. Just myself. Besides, you've got a dumb plan. They come down hard on fighters in here. If you survive, you'll be tossed in isolation for weeks. And I done told you about that name stuff. Now your other name is stuck in my head."

"Good. I appreciate what you've done for me in here. I'll return the favor on the outside."

"I still say it's a dumb stunt to pick a fight with Big Mike. I got into it with him once and got whupped."

"That's what I'm counting on. Get help before he breaks me in half."

"I could clock you in here. Same result."

"Yeah, but that would mess up your release. This way we both achieve our objectives. I get access to the med com, and you get your freedom on time."

A bell clanged down the hall, and the cells opened. Zeke knew the drill after several days. Walk single file past the guards. Stand in a walled courtyard with his entire cell block. Reverse the process twenty minutes later. Some guys hit the shade along the western wall. Others reveled in the bright light of day. Still others ran laps around the perimeter.

His odds of surviving this place sucked. The guards didn't believe he'd been railroaded. He'd requested a lawyer, even filled out forms. Nothing had come of it. Hence his desperate plan. With any luck, he'd land at least one punch before he got flattened.

He stopped walking and placed one hand on the warm concrete wall. Tank drifted farther along, talking to another inmate. One of Big Mike's toadies, the guy about his height and build, bumped into him seconds later.

"Didn't see you there," Denny said.

"Open your eyes," Zeke shot back. "I'm standing right here."

Denny shoved Zeke against the wall. "Not for long."

Zeke sidestepped the man's punch, landed a flurry of hits on the guy's unprotected gut. The shocked expression on Denny's face energized Zeke. Nothing to this fighting stuff.

He could do this.

Denny's buddy, Wayne, charged over, fists raised high. "You're going down, little man. Nobody hurts Denny but me."

Wayne had him by four inches. Zeke quickly replayed Tank's fight instructions. *Be quick. Move your feet. Use anything and everything as a weapon.* He couldn't out-hit this guy.

With that thought, he crouched and launched himself headfirst at Wayne's groin. Wayne shrieked in pain and pummeled his ears. Both of them hit the concrete pad hard.

Be quick, Zeke thought. *Be quick or die.*

He rolled off Wayne and stared into the double barrel of Big Mike's fists. He had enough agility to dodge the first few blows. Men clustered around them. Violence tainted the air he breathed.

Zeke didn't want to fight anyone, least of all a man who could kill him with his bare hands, but this was his ticket, the only one he had to punch.

Focus, Landry. Get a few licks in so this guy respects you. Otherwise, life in prison will be hell.

His gaze snagged on Big Mike's dark eyes. Meanness there. Nothing but ugliness and a crushing desire to hurt others. Big Mike wouldn't regret killing him.

He dodged another jab and careened into the crowd. They shoved him back toward Big Mike. Fists flailed. Zeke took a punch on the chin. It stunned him. His hands dropped. Big Mike pummeled his torso.

Each stroke took a toll. He ached and wanted to curl up into a ball, but he watched for a chance. He'd probably get only one. Out of the corner of his eye he saw Tank trying to break through the ring of people. Then the world narrowed to a pinpoint of light as another of Big Mike's punches grazed his head. He tasted blood.

If not for the wall of inmates behind him, he would have fallen. They shoved him forward again. Instinctively, he curled into a ball and launched himself at Big Mike, hands by his head. He heard raucous laughter as Big Mike sidestepped his clumsy move.

But Big Mike made a mistake. He looked at the crowd and waved his arms in victory. Zeke socked Big Mike in the side with a left jab as he hurled past. He heard the man's startled intake of breath as he lay on the concrete. Then Zeke got the daylights kicked out of him. Sound and vision blurred under the weight of mounting pain.

"Stop!" Tank said. "Get the guard. This man is hurt."

Zeke sank the last few inches into oblivion.

Thirty

Angry waves of pain crashed over Zeke. Just when it seemed safe to surface, another one careened into him, flattening him. He tried to surface again and again, only to be thrashed each time by a powerful hydraulic. Defeated, he floated under the water's surface and gazed upward at the flickering orb of light. Longing filled him. He wanted to touch the light, to feel its radiance on his cold skin.

But he couldn't swim.

Couldn't move his arms or legs.

They were too heavy.

Another wave rolled him facedown.

He sank into a cold, dark place.

Dreams came. Funhouse images of his parents, of his uncle, distorted by odd mirrors. They stretched so thin they disappeared. Dismay filled him. Come back!

He heard deep voices he didn't recognize. A guy named Joe was in trouble. Joe who? Where was he? What was this place?

His arm felt cold. So very cold. He shook all over with the cold. Tried to move his arm. He moaned as pain knifed through him. The voices came again. Then gray oblivion.

He floated on a mild current, bobbing like a fishing cork on its glassy surface. Shadows receded. Light beckoned beyond his closed eyelids. Don't let them see you're awake, he thought. Not until you know what's going on.

Keep a low profile.

His father had taught him that. No matter what, Winston Landry had said, keep a low profile. It doesn't pay to draw attention to yourself, son. Not when you have an important job to do.

A job? He had an important job?

Zeke struggled to make sense of his situation. He belonged on Tama Island. He needed to go home. He'd be safe there.

Safe.

He needed to find safety.

Alone in the room, he slitted his eyes open. Bright lights shone down from overhead on sterile walls. Machines beeped to his right. A hospital? Was he sick? His gaze circled the narrow room to a transom window near the ceiling with bars on it.

Bars.

Prison bars.

He was in prison.

His pulse spiked. He had to get out of here.

But his arm wouldn't budge. A steel cuff secured him to the bed. He struggled and wept. "No. I'm needed. This can't be." Machines alarmed as he thrashed. Pain lanced through his head, his chest, his leg. Men in white coats appeared.

"It's okay, Joe. You're gonna be okay," the white-haired man said, injecting something into his IV.

Zeke struggled all the more, yanking on his bound arm. "Let me out! I don't belong here."

Faces blurred, and his thoughts clouded. He drifted in and out of consciousness, sure of three things. He hurt. He'd been chained like a junkyard dog. He had to get out of here.

Understanding dawned slowly. He'd picked a fight on purpose. To access a com link in the med unit. He needed to send Forman an encrypted message. He drew inside himself, focusing on the content of that message.

His chance arrived two sleep cycles later. A medic accidentally left a com tablet in the room. Zeke drew from his reserves and sat up on the narrow bed. It galled him that he needed the rails to help him sit up. How long had he been chained to this bed?

But his big plan backfired. The com tablet on the counter weighed too much to pick up one-handed. He glanced around for a tool to draw it closer. Not much there. Sheets, blanket, pillow, and Zeke.

The bedding might help.

He kicked aside the covers and pulled the sheet free from the thin mattress. Knotting a corner of the sheet to an ankle and holding the other edge, he twisted it until it thinned like a rope. He positioned his feet near the com tablet and tried to lasso it with a loop of sheet. The sheet fell short. Drawing back, he curled his legs to the side again. The sheet brushed over one corner of the tablet.

So close.

Three more tries, and he had it. He untied the sheet from his ankle and reeled the tablet in with both hands. Listening carefully for sounds of an approach, he activated the com and streamed through several menus to find an outlet. Sure enough, the tech had an unauthorized personal account that he accessed on the sly.

Bingo. That was exactly what he needed.

Moments later, Zeke accessed Queen Bea's fan forum and addressed a message to "Bea fan." He hoped Forman would remember the lost cat ad they'd agreed upon as a status indication when Forman went to Atlanta.

How's it hanging, buddy? I'm a mile high. Can't say as I've ever been so far from home before. But there's nothing like a cuppa Joe to remind me of our island breezes and our water problem. Mosby I've been getting knocked around a bit, which is exzekely what you warned me about. Nuttin' like a few bars and some hard knocks to break you down, ya know? I axe you this. When you comin' out west to see me? I miss you and my lost cat, and that's hard for a black man to say. Keepin' it real.
Island Boy

He sent the post and maneuvered the com tablet back on the counter. With effort, he tucked the sheet and blanket back around his legs. Though his shakes returned, they were a small price to pay for his freedom.

If Forman was out there, he'd check Queen Bea's fan forums. Zeke had no doubt about that. His rescue plan hinged on an artificial life form, but there was no one else. Uncle John or his parents would search for him without question, but his parents were dead, his uncle missing.

Would Forman search for him?

The A.I. unit had already gone off script while supposedly searching for Zeke's uncle. He could be anywhere, doing anything.

He heard footsteps in the hall. Pretending to doze, he saw the tech snag the com link and hurry out of the room.

He'd done what he could.

Now he waited.

Thirty-One

The next day, Forman adopted his senior citizen persona to enter the Frederick County, Maryland, public library. His khaki pants and white short-sleeved shirt were so low profile, Zeke would be proud of him. A jaunty ascot covered his required ID necklace. He'd hitched a ride there in an executive transport, being careful to avoid all cams and checkpoints along transpo routes on the sixty-mile trip west.

The albino yielded no leads, John Demery had gone to ground, and now he'd lost Zeke.

If Supply learned of his failures he'd be decommissioned for sure, but he'd fix this mess, one way or the other. With the lead to Rissa being a dead end, he had no leads to point him toward Zeke's uncle. He'd searched extensively for John Demery for two days and found nothing. Finding Zeke moved to his top priority.

People didn't disappear without a trace. There had to be a record of Zeke's travel somewhere.

He selected a com station in the deserted reference section. With ease, he navigated through the institution's filters and firewalls. First he checked the route of Zeke's pod on the day Zeke disappeared. Odd. There was no record of a pod SLA4893. He went deeper in the transpo files, checking the individual tube cams. He traced the pod to Atlanta, then to Memphis and Oklahoma City. He checked Santa Fe, Denver, Phoenix, Cheyenne, and other more westerly cities and came up with nothing.

The pod went west initially. So he'd head west.

Out of habit, he skimmed the news feed for Queen Bea. She'd left the hospital now and was mending from her Mexico City collapse. Her tour stops for the next two months had been canceled.

Should he send virtual flowers? He cruised through the forums to see what her other fans were saying and doing. One post addressed to "Bea fan" riveted his attention. He read the text twice and stored it in his memory.

Island boy. With a lost cat and a water problem. The lost cat rang a bell. Zeke. It had to be Zeke. He'd sent a coded message.

His boss needed help out west.

Finally.

Something to go on.

He deleted his queries on the machine and skirted the library stacks to exit the facility. He'd nearly made it to the door when he noticed the line of black vehicles outside and the sleek neutralizer robots in dark suits.

Oh no.

They were here.

They'd found him.

How?

Hide.

He had to hide.

They were looking for a Gary. They had to be. Only his programmer knew of his Holmes module, which allowed him to alter his physical appearance. He melted into the library, aging more, adding a spinal hump and a limp, settling on the floor between two young mothers with toddlers and babies.

One toddler walked over and handed him a squishy palm-sized ball. He nodded politely. "Thanks."

The boy sat in front of Forman and stuck a pudgy thumb in his mouth.

Forman listened to a story being read aloud, but he noticed the robot police searching the facility. When they came close, Forman leaned over to whisper to the young woman next to him, who held a slumbering infant in her arms. "Your son reminds me of my grandson. I'm going to see him next month. This is his favorite bedtime story."

She favored him with a smile. "That's so nice."

Forman nodded. He felt the robots' critical gazes pass over the group and dismiss the entire lot. If he had a heart it would have been racing. He'd heard about the elite robot police. They didn't merely take you apart. They destroyed all your components, never to be recycled again.

It was a fate worse than death.

Plus, folks were so sensitive about killer robots since the problem with the Bobs, any mention of a defective robot at Supply Central led to a purge of all records regarding that model. He didn't want that. He wanted to leave a lasting legacy, to have made a difference.

All he'd done so far was to screw up.

That was about to change.

He'd find Zeke, and they'd figure this out. Between the two of them, they had enough brainpower to light up a city.

He hoped that would be enough.

Thirty-Two

A gray sedan pulled into the abandoned Los Angeles warehouse where One waited. He engaged the vehicle's electronic jammer and the building's security field. Covering his tracks was desired and expedient in a Darwinian organization like the Chameleon Society.

Two exited his vehicle and sauntered across to One's black SUV. One noted the confidence and arrogance in the man's stride. No question in his mind. Two was a problem.

Only when Two tapped lightly on the passenger window did One lower it a fraction of the way. He did not unlock the door. He studied his protégé through wraparound sunglasses. One's blonde wig, nose overlay, and fake bad teeth concealed his facial features, a necessary tactic for anonymity.

"You're late," he said.

Two leaned down to peer in the window opening. "Traffic on the five."

One's lips thinned. Two hadn't earned the right to be so smug. Not yet. As the silence lengthened, Two's steady gaze faltered. One breathed easier. Yes. Two still had pressure points to push. And push he would.

"Status," One said.

"We've got destabilizers injected at key points along the New Madrid, Ramapo, Hayward, and San Andreas faults. Once the temperature and pressure differentials reach a critical point, the tectonic plates will respond."

"You're certain of the science? It will hurt our cause if we ruin the atmosphere."

"The science is rock solid, plus small-scale trials confirmed the results. The earth will quake, guaranteed. The air won't be harmed."

"This procedure has never been done before." One studied his fingernails as if he thought the matter inconsequential. Everything depended on this. One planned to ride this stroke of genius all the way to the Master's chair.

Out with the old. In with the new. Operatives were expendable, the Master included.

Two preened. "Until now, no one has ever had this assemblage of brilliant scientists and engineers together working to 'prevent' earthquakes by lessening the tension building up in the tectonic plates. We made this happen by creating an interdisciplinary research center."

"Your elite team doesn't suspect you've adapted the process? They don't know about the deployment?"

"They're completely in the dark. They will truthfully claim no foreknowledge of the catastrophic events. As you suggested, it will appear a midlevel employee sold the proprietary technology to a foreign intelligence agency."

"And your installers?"

"In the dark as well. They'll be eliminated tonight."

"Well done." The plan sounded good, but Two had promised before and failed to deliver. He was lucky to have a second chance. One's contemporaries would have killed Two at his first screw up. But One had more than a short-term goal in mind. Two had the means to make his long-term goal happen. "And the timeline?"

"The blasts will be remotely triggered, sir. Exactly as you said."

One nodded, allowed a whisper of a smile on his face. It would happen. A dream come true. "Good time to leave California."

"I've got a rabbit hole. I don't want to be too far away from my scientists when the tremors start. They trust me implicitly. I will appear as shocked and horrified as they are. You can count on me, sir."

Could he?

Not likely.

Once Two tasted success, he'd crave more. One had dealt with his type before. This wasn't his first go-around in the snake pit. Time to bring the man's ego down a notch. Minions worked much better with the threat of competition.

"Three's infection campaign was masterful. Using terminal cancer patients to disperse the disease was a stroke of pure genius. He's also in line for the promotion."

Two's features contorted. His fingers coiled around the rim of the glass window. "My earthquakes will wreak more havoc than those measly little epicenters of disease. Forget about him. That promotion will be mine."

One's voice sharpened. "It's yours to win or lose."

Thirty-Three

"Take it easy, Sis." Jessie Stemford hurried across the room to assist her staggering sister. "I've got you. Where are we headed?"

"Nowhere." Bea's feet stopped moving. "I'm sick and tired of being coddled. You're driving me nuts. I want my life back. I want the freedom to do what I want, when I want."

Jessie maneuvered her to the living room sofa, and they both sat down. "In that case, you need to change careers. As a pop star, folks want to know every little detail about you. People speculate and discuss how many times you go to the bathroom each day."

"People need to get a life and leave me alone. It isn't too much to ask, is it? That I can do my own thing for a while?"

"Nobody can get in here. Not with the security detail we hired. You're completely safe."

"I'm a prisoner in my own house, and you're making it worse."

"You scared me, Bea. I almost lost you."

"But you didn't lose me. I collapsed a week ago. I'm fine now. I could perform a concert tonight."

"You could, but you won't. Doctor's orders, remember? She said you took on too much too soon. Your body couldn't cope with such a grueling pace after the plague. That's why the exhaustion hit you so hard."

"I got that. I'd have to be dumb to miss that point, but I'm going stir crazy here. I want to do something. I want to be somewhere else. Like Paris. Weren't we supposed to be in Paris this week?"

"Paris will still be there later on. We'll reschedule the tour when you're healthy again. We have to take two months off. Do something different. Catch up on vids. Take up a new form of exercise. Get creative with our food rations. Read a book. Work a puzzle. Relax."

"Grrr. I don't know how to relax. And those activities you mentioned, those are things you want to do. I want new tattoos, new shoes, international shopping, fast rides at midnight, wild sex under a full moon." Bea gazed pointedly at her sister. "I don't want to be stuck in the 'burbs of Richmond, Virginia."

"You make this sound like a bad place. We chose this house, this neighborhood. We wanted the best school district for our kids, remember?"

Bea's sigh carried the weight of the world. "Got no kids. Got no husband. Got no prospects in either direction. Maybe we should order up some guys—you know, like pizza. That would be fun."

Memories rushed into Jessie's head. If not for the cop she'd propositioned when they'd run out of money years ago, she'd be a career prostitute by now. Likely Bea would've fallen down that slippery slope as well. The cop had understood their situation and helped them.

"We're not calling prostitutes," Jessie said adamantly. "You know how I feel about that."

"Yeah. I do." Bea shot her sister a guilty look. "Sorry to push your buttons. I don't know what to do with myself. I can't go anywhere. I can't do anything."

"Write a song. You love doing that."

"I've got nothing to write about. Nothing good, anyway. Who wants to hear 'woe is me' songs? Poor, pitiful Bea. She's stuck at home because she can't take care of herself. My world has shrunk to me, myself, and I."

Jessie laughed. "I don't agree. There should be a song in there somewhere."

At the knock on the door, Jessie rose. "I'll see who it is."

"If it is living, breathing, and male, let him in. I need more stimulation."

"Be careful what you ask for." Jessie checked the peephole, recognized the bodyguard she'd hired, and opened the door. "Yes?"

The muscular female waved a thick envelope at Jessie. "A courier left this at the gates. I checked it out, and it appears to be a lot of loose papers."

Jessie took the envelope. At the sight of familiar block letters of her name, a chill snaked down her spine. Excitement chased after the chill. Her secret informant had struck again. "Thanks."

"How is Queen Bea today?" the guard asked.

"I already had a bowel movement," Bea hollered from the living room. "And I'm about to drink one third of my daily water ration."

"Sorry," Jessie said. "She's getting a little stir crazy. Everything else all right outside?"

"It's quiet. No media. No fans."

"Good. That's what we want." Jessie turned to go, thought the better of it and turned back. "What did the courier look like?"

"He was a young man on a bicycle. Thin build. Well spoken. From the Richmond Cruisers Courier Agency. Should I follow up with them?"

He'd check out as clueless, like the other couriers. "No need. Thanks."

Jessie closed the door and hurried back to the sofa. "Look, Bea. You asked for excitement. Here it is."

Bea shivered and reached for a throw blanket. "I didn't mind when we got the packets at hotels on tour, but this guy knows where we live. Don't you find that creepy?"

"What's creepy is the content we receive. Someone is directly responsible for this bad stuff that keeps happening to the entire world. I don't believe the doomsayers have it right. God isn't punishing us. If it truly is the end of the world, someone or something is helping things along. This is a giant conspiracy."

"The end of the world. Puts my stir craziness in perspective, doesn't it?"

"We're all a little bit crazy. That's how people are wired." Jessie dumped the papers in her lap, and a picture spilled out. She picked it up and studied it front and back. "Who's this?"

Bea gazed at the photo of the older man with collar-length white hair and a broad forehead. "Never seen that guy in my life."

"Me neither." Jessie set the picture aside and skimmed the pages of technical text. "Looks like more of the same. Projections of population growth along with insufficient food and water. Hard times are coming."

"Don't get me wrong—because this is going to sound heartless—but with the plague deaths, you'd think we'd have enough resources to feed everyone."

"Not as many died as you think. Not even a million people."

"Really? Seemed like the plague hit everywhere."

"I followed the summary reports on the news feeds. Dense population areas were hit, almost as if they were targeted. And some cities were lucky enough to get vaccines or antibiotics in time."

"So if we'd stayed home, we'd have missed it?"

"Looks that way, but what's done is done. Now we have to figure out what to do with this data and this bad guy. Is this the end of the world as we know it?"

Bea's eyes widened. Then she laughed. "Catchy line. The end of the world as we know it. I've heard that lyric before, but I can do something fresh with it."

"You write us a new song. I'm going to decipher the science here and see if I can't figure out what we should do next."

While Bea jotted down lyrics on a pad of paper, Jessie read the stack of papers. In most of the documents, a certain John Demery spoke out against attempts to legislate more food and water for people. He made incriminatory statements about the plague, too.

Jessie resisted leaping to the obvious conclusion. Surely one man wasn't behind everything? She took her time and read the materials again. Nope. Right the first time.

John Demery had masterminded this world terror. He wanted to unite the world into one government.

Jessie's stomach rolled. This dictatorial guy wanted to control everything. He hid behind a thin curtain of science. She had to warn people. She had to act on this new information.

According to one document, Demery would be in Los Angeles in a week.

"I'm going to California." Jessie waved the man's picture at her sister. "I'm going to find this John Demery and expose his traitorous ways."

"Not without me," Bea said. "If you go to California, I'm coming along."

"You need to rest. But I could go. I wouldn't be gone long. You'd be fine here."

"Can't let you do that. It might be dangerous. I need you."

"And I need to do this."

"How about a compromise? I'm getting stronger every day. We could wait to travel the day before his event. When is he speaking?"

Jessie sighed. Bea was going to have her way. If Jessie didn't acquiesce, a lot of yelling would commence. Her head pounded just thinking of Bea's bad mood. "Seven days from now."

"Then we'll travel on day six, even if you have to haul me in a hover chair. The Stemford sisters are on the case."

Even if Bea wasn't up to par, Jessie could get her out of Los Angeles and stash her in a five-star hotel. She'd certainly taken care of Bea at hotels all over the world in the past. "God help us both."

Thirty-Four

The warm, dark womb writhed and pulsed. Zeke felt himself forcibly expelled, thrust into a cold and tight canal and knowing it was death to linger there. A soundless scream ripped from his throat.

No! This was not the end.

He wouldn't let it be over.

He couldn't give up.

Not while there was a breath in his body.

Kicking and stroking through a thick soup of pain, he fought his way forward. His heart rhythm stuttered and warped into another universe. Bright light dawned, blinding him. Confused, he tried to shield his eyes. Couldn't.

The wrong place. He'd come to the wrong place. He had to get out of here. To hide before they came back. He had to go.

The room spun. The light shattered into a kaleidoscope of streaking points, his own private meteor shower. Disoriented, he sought a landmark and found none.

Why couldn't he see?

From his subconscious, he heard the distant voice of his father. "Dark times will come, son," he'd said. "Times you can't even imagine. Dig deep to find yourself when the world comes apart. Dig deep and hold on to who you are and what you are. Trust your instincts and your need to be near water."

"I'm Zeke Landry," he shouted into the void. "Dr. Zechariah Landry. The son of Winston and Ruth Landry. I live on Tama Island."

He clung to his identity. Pain radiated from his temple. His jaw. His ribs. His back. His left hand. His knees.

Pain he understood. It throbbed like the constant pulse of the sea. A living organism, a worm of agony burrowing under his skin. The need to hide intensified. He couldn't fight them again. He was too weak. Too broken to find cover.

The spinning subsided.

The light stabilized into a soft glow.

It was only him and the light. He edged closer.

Sounds crept into his mind. Institutional hums of beeping machines, soft-soled shoes traversing waxed floors, fingers tapping a data entry port. He gasped in a lungful of antiseptic-smelling air.

Med unit.

He blinked against the knowledge. Tried to sit up. His arm caught and held. Reality pulsed like a stinging hornet. Not just a med unit.

The prison med unit.

Wide eyed, he stared around the room. Three men and a woman wearing white lab coats stared right back. He studied their faces. Strangers. His guard went up. "We don't speak to strangers," his father had said. "Protect your privacy at all costs."

"He's awake," the man with a full head of thick gray hair said.

"Vitals aren't stable," the dark-skinned woman said. "His physiology is nonstandard."

"So?" the man said. "Is he one of those machine hybrids?"

"No machine parts in him. His 'normal' is a little different from most people, that's all."

"Good enough for me. Can you hear me?" The bald man leaned in, his breath a dense cloud of garlic-laced spearmint. "Tell me about the keystone. Nod your head if you can hear me."

Zeke stilled. These people wanted something from him. Chills wracked his body. His teeth clattered. His skin felt too tight. He had to get out of there. He needed to be around water. He needed to be on Tama Island. Sweat dripped from his brow. Muscles contracted in his abdomen. He vomited on the bald man.

"Christ almighty, that stinks," Baldie said. "Get someone in here to clean up the mess. Did you give him too much stimulant?"

"It's not the drug." The woman's fingers flew over the com keyboard. "He has altitude sickness. Without wrist band meds or anti-nausea meds, he has repetitive vomiting cycles."

"Put the wrist bands on him for starters," Baldie said. "He's no good to us like this."

Machines rang.

Voices blurred.

Zeke sank back to the dark place.

A single thought prevailed.

What keystone?

Thirty-Five

Forman traveled in transpo unit cargo holds across the Midwest. He alighted in Columbus, Ohio, and found another untraceable com, learning that Zeke had a roommate in his prison cell, one who'd been released. He arranged for three floral leis to be delivered to one Severnius "Tank" Murray. Since Zeke had mentioned the island in his message from prison, Forman hoped he'd mentioned his home to his roommate. "Enjoy some island time, Your Friend," he wrote for the accompanying tag.

In Springfield, Illinois, he found an open com link at a cyber café. Working quickly, he hacked the Denver police department and voided the charges against Joe Mosby. He found prints from a dead civil servant and attached them to Mosby's file. He changed the blood type in Mosby's file to be O-negative. Zeke was A-positive.

Disguised as a retired farmer in faded jeans and a straw cowboy hat, Forman entered a Topeka, Kansas, library. With a few deft strokes, he wormed his way into the Colorado prison system matrix, learning that Zeke lay in the med unit. He winced at the injury write-up. "Hang on. I'm coming, buddy," he said under his breath. With a few keystrokes, he changed Zeke's med prescription to a high-energy, high-healing nanite blend and ordered a time-released skin patch of altitude-sickness drug.

He could tap into the room feed to see Zeke, but his intrusion might alert the enemy. That would not be good. Instead, he wrote orders to keep Zeke in the med unit for observation. He signed the prison doctor's name to the new orders. Traveling across town to a fancy hotel, he entered as a guest, sporting a jaunty hat. A grinning bellhop opened doors for him. The ground shook, and Forman read the surprise and terror on the young man's face.

"That's unusual," Forman said when the tremor ceased.

"Been a crazy day," the bellhop said. "My mom doesn't believe the doomsayers, says the world isn't ending. What do you think?"

"Definitely not the end of the world," Forman said. "Mother Nature is having a small hiccup. That's all."

"Good to hear."

Forman tipped the boy for his service and hurried through the plush lobby. Reading the signs on the wall, he headed for the administration area and found a com link in an empty office. In a few clicks of the keyboard, he searched the Denver newspapers for an ambulance-chasing attorney who enjoyed the limelight. Martin Lopez met his requirements. Forman made the call.

"This is Griffin Hayes." Forman modulated his voice to sound harried and frantic. "My nephew, Zeke Landry, is being held at the Denver Correctional Facility on trumped-up charges. I want you to get him out and sue the city. Sue the police force, too."

"Trumped-up charges?" Interest energized Lopez's voice.

"The boy was traveling out here to see me in Topeka, got in the wrong tube, and ended up in Denver. He got mugged and lost his altitude-sickness wristbands. Sick as a dog, the cops arrested him and mistook him for a career criminal. He's all beat up. My sister is furious, and I need help to fix this. I need a smart lawyer."

"I'm your man. What about my fee?"

"I'll transfer twenty thousand credits to your account today if you'll take the case. Once you sue the city and the cops, we'll split the take fifty-fifty. We want our boy back."

"Done. Hang on, and I'll put my associate on the com. Give her the details, and we'll get right on it. If everything is as you say, I should have your boy out in a day or two, tops."

"Wonderful."

After Forman finished with the gum-snapping associate, he did some creative banking and paid the lawyer. Then he changed his appearance to resemble the helpful bellhop. He palmed a master key from the front desk, located a luggage trolley, and rode the elevator to the ninth floor. As he pushed the trolley down the hall, he noted a couple exiting room 921.

He waited until the elevator closed behind them and entered their room. On their private com system, he scanned news feeds for mention of John Demery. Nothing. He tried another source. There. He reread the last line. Demery would speak in Los Angeles before the Citizens Against Global Unification in two days.

He felt no satisfaction. Instead, more questions arose.

How did Zeke's uncle get to California?

Who were the Citizens Against Global Unification?

Thirty-Six

Zeke clung to the armrests of the wheelchair and regarded the twitchy man on the other side of the glass. He felt better, but the adhesive patch on his neck worried him. What had been done to him? "My uncle sent you?"

"Yes. Griffin Hayes, your uncle." Martin Lopez sat a little straighter. "He said there has been a gross miscarriage of justice in your case, and I agree."

The lawyer's words were clear, but their content puzzled him. Zeke resisted the urge to tug his ear. He'd heard correctly. He had a lawyer, which was good, but he'd never heard of Griffin Hayes.

His brain began structuring an array of people who might be Griffin Hayes. *Please be Forman,* he hoped. *Or Uncle John. Or Angie. Or someone from the Institute.*

But when it came right down to it, as long as Hayes shared the same goal of springing him from this nightmare, he wouldn't deny the kinship. Whatever the cost, he'd pay it.

Zeke leaned close to the window. "You can get me out of here?"

"I filed release documents with the court system, Dr. Landry."

He savored the news like a hawk gliding on a thermal. He'd be getting out of this hellhole. "Thank you," he managed.

"I've filed wrongful-imprisonment papers and false-arrest suits against the police force. There's also the question of due process. Do you remember going before a judge when you were arrested?"

"I don't remember any judge. I got off the tube sick as a dog, then I woke up in prison. I have no memory of anything in between."

"I requested the records of your hearing, but they've vanished. The logs, the vid feeds, the police evidence—they're all gone. The judge who heard your case had a heart attack this morning and is not expected to live. You following me? This is big. A huge cover-up. We're gonna make a bundle."

"Someone needs to pay, that's for sure, but I want out of here first. How soon can you spring me?"

"It would've been today, except for that judge's heart attack.

That outage left the circuit short-handed, and the criminal cases are backed up."

"You're saying I'll walk out of here tomorrow?"

"I'm not sure about the walking part, but you'll be released."

"What about this Mosby stuff?"

"What about it?"

"Who is Mosby? Why do they think I'm him?"

"Not sure exactly. The best my associate can figure is that a computer glitch matched your fingerprints with Mosby's name."

"I won't have a criminal record?"

"Nope. Your record will be wiped clean."

Gratitude unfurled in his heart, a bright flag on a stiff morning breeze. He would be free. He could walk freely, choose where he wanted to go, when he wanted to eat. He wouldn't have to constantly look over his shoulder. And he could get the hell away from this altitude.

The new wristbands had helped. So had the shot the prison doctor had given him that morning. He felt halfway human. Except for the bruises, aches, and pains. And that odd patch on his neck. He wouldn't have any of those if he hadn't been in prison.

He'd lost personal freedoms, lost his identity, and nearly lost his life. For what?

Uncensored words boiled out of his mouth, a boiling stew pot of profanity that shocked even him. When he ran dry, he stared at his hands until he regained control of his emotions. "I lost five days of my life because of a computer glitch?"

"Bottle up that rage, Landry. We'll need it for the jury. I've received copies of your medical reports, and we have photos of your injuries. This case is a slam dunk, but we can milk it for big money. You and I are going to be rich. Your uncle, too. Hayes fronted the money for my services."

His mysterious uncle again. "Is he here? My uncle, I mean. Is he here?"

"Said he doesn't like prisons and that you'd understand. He has a friend on standby to pick you up tomorrow. I'll have transportation as well."

Zeke didn't know what tomorrow would bring, what his alleged uncle or his uncle's friend might want. One thing was certain—it had to be a lot better than the Denver Correctional Facility.

Thirty-Seven

Forman pounded on the apartment door. From nearby rooms, people yelled, babies cried, vid feeds blared. The walls in the dive were a joke.

The weight of the world tugged on his shoulders. He hadn't powered down since leaving Tama Island, hadn't felt safe enough to leave himself that vulnerable. If he didn't recharge soon, he'd hit massive systems failure.

Which wouldn't help Zeke or him.

He banged on the door again, harder. From inside, he heard the metallic creak of bedsprings, the sound of heavy footsteps.

"This better be the end of the world," a man behind the door said. "Who the hell is it?"

"I need to talk to you," Forman said to the closed door. "About a mutual friend who lives on an island."

"Go away. I don't want no trouble."

"I need your help, Severnius Murray. Zeke needs your help."

The door opened slightly. "Good God almighty. I ain't been out of the joint for three days and now this. How'd you find me, anyway?"

His disguise as an unthreatening old man held up to close scrutiny. Otherwise, this big man never would have chanced opening the door to him. Little did the ex-con know that Forman could bust open every door in the place with minimal effort. "I'm good at finding things. May we talk inside where it's more private?"

With a covert look at the empty hall, Murray waved him in. "Not much private in this cracker box. The walls are wafer thin. But come on in, whoever you are."

"Call me Griffin Hayes. The less you know about me, the better."

"No kidding. Why'd you tap me?"

"You shared a cell with my friend Zeke."

"Keep your voice down, man. Sound really carries in here. My sister's landlord finds out she's got an ex-con in here, and we're both out on our asses."

"Zeke's getting out tomorrow. I need someone to pick him up. Can I count on you?"

"I'm not going near that place. I'm on parole. Not supposed to associate with ex-cons either. Why don't you get him?"

"I can't take the chance of being recognized, and there's a cam at the prison gate. That's why I need you. I'll help with your disguise."

"No way. I got to get me a job and start earning some money."

"I'll pay you. Good money, too."

"How much?"

"Five thousand credits, after you deliver Zeke to me."

"Nope. I don't work that way. I need some whatchamacallit . . . earnest money. Yeah. I need good faith money up front."

Forman pulled out a card with one thousand credits on it. "Take this. A thousand right now. The rest upon delivery."

Severnius pocketed the money. His smile exposed a full set of crooked teeth. "Now we're talking. What's the plan?"

Forman laid out the car rental, the route, and the destination, careful to keep the instructions simple. "You got it, Severnius?"

"Yeah, I'm no dummy. And the name is Tank. Only my mother calls me Severnius, and you definitely ain't my mother."

"Okay, Tank. I'm counting on you. Zeke is counting on you."

"He got a bum rap. They treated him like a con. I bet he's gonna sue the pants off of everyone involved. I'd like a piece of that action."

"His lawyer, Martin Lopez, will handle the lawsuit. Lopez will be there tomorrow as well. Make sure you get Zeke in your car. Bring him to me."

Tank's head bobbed. "How'd you do that?"

Forman stilled. "Do what?"

"Make your white hair have black stripes in it for a second. That's an awesome trick. You're like a walking zebra. Very cool."

Not cool at all. His control was slipping. "It's the lighting in here. Shadows. That sort of thing. Look, I have to go. Contact me if there's any deviation in the plan. And remember what I said."

"What's that?"

"I'm very good at finding people. Double-cross me, and it will be ugly."

Thirty-Eight

Zeke's pace slowed. As much as he craved freedom, he dreaded running the gauntlet of reporters waiting outside the prison gates. He scanned the faces of those assembled beyond the chain-link barricade, hoping for a familiar face.

A twitchy man stood by the voluptuous reporter with big hair. Martin Lopez, his lawyer. Martin beckoned Zeke forward.

He scanned the crowd one more time, hoping against hope to see Forman, but there were no bronzed sex machines lighting up the parking lot. Now what?

Lights flashed. His hands tightened on the sack of his clothing. His shirt was dirty and ripped, his pants were stained. The socks he'd thrown out, but he'd worn the athletic shoes. And his father's necklace. Unconsciously, his hand strayed to that necklace, a triangular bit of rock on a rawhide tie.

Certainly not worth much in the eyes of the world, but to him, it felt like he'd gotten an important chunk of his life back. This tangible connection to his late father helped him feel centered, as if he were finally on the right track.

His backpack with his encrypted data drive was missing, but right now he cared less about his work than his freedom. All he wanted was to go home to Tama Island and never set foot off it again. Even if his island had been burned and was infested with protestors, it was still home.

"Make way. Let him through," Martin Lopez said.

Microphones appeared before Zeke's face. Cameras rolled. People crowded closer, except for one person standing near a retired cop car. A mountain of a man wore a cowboy hat, a fringed leather jacket, and jeans. The man acknowledged Zeke's perusal with a tip of his hat. He looked familiar and yet Zeke couldn't place him.

The voluptuous blonde jostled forward and shoved her shiny microphone almost in his teeth. "Will you file suit of wrongful imprisonment immediately, Dr. Landry?"

"Legal matters will be handled by my attorney, Martin Lopez,"

Zeke said.

"We understand that you were mistakenly thought to be a criminal named Joe Mosby," a tanned man with a sharp blade of a nose said. "How do you feel about the mix-up in the computer database?"

"Computers were created by people. They aren't perfect."

He gazed over the crowd at the hulking cowboy. The man smiled, exposing a mouthful of crooked teeth. He knew the man. Tank, his former cellmate. In disguise. Tank nodded toward the dusty vehicle he leaned against.

He expected Zeke to leave here with him?

Should he do that?

Wouldn't it be safer to go with the lawyer that his fake uncle had arranged?

Decisions.

Fatigue made him feel as if he were slogging through chest-high water, but he couldn't collapse now. Not in front of these cameras. Whoever had it in for him might be watching. He wouldn't give them the satisfaction of seeing him broken. The bruises on his face spoke loudly enough.

A dark-skinned man with curly hair hurled a question at Zeke. "Would you care to comment on the conditions inside the prison?"

"No. I would not."

An Asian woman muscled her way forward. "What is the first thing you plan to do now that you're free?"

His immediate plan was to get as far away from prison as he could run. Not that he would say that on vid feeds. "I want to sleep without buzzers and alarms and guards. My immediate plans involve plenty of rest."

"But what about your robot companion?" a svelte senior asked. "What happened to him?"

"I appreciate the interest in my situation, and I hope I can answer your questions better once I've rested. Right now, I'm interested in seeing prison in my rearview mirror."

That brought a chuckle from the reporters and set his lawyer to twitching. "Please direct all future inquiries about Dr. Landry to my Denver office," Lopez said. "Excuse us."

Zeke allowed Lopez to escort him through the boiling clot of news people, but as he neared the lawyer's sedan-shaped hovercraft, Tank drove up.

Inside Zeke's head, questions streamed like a news-feed banner. Lawyer or cellmate? Lopez or Tank? Freedom or entrapment?

Lopez opened the door of the luxury vehicle for him. "Let's go."

The vibe from the conveyance felt wrong. Off. The hair on the back of his neck stirred. Zeke took a step back, glanced at Tank's transpo.

He had nothing to go on but a feeling. No facts. No computer analysis of mountains of data. Just his gut. His gut told him not to get into the lawyer's vehicle. In the absence of logic, that internal warning counted for a lot.

"I'm hitching a ride with a friend, Lopez. I'll be in touch."

"Wait! Decisions must be made. We must talk strategy."

"I'll leave the strategy to you. Right now, I want to spend time with my friend."

Conscious of the news people watching, Zeke strode purposefully toward Tank's sedan. He opened the door and sat facing forward. "Tell me I made the right choice."

"You made the only choice. If you'd gotten in the car with that ambulance chaser, my cover would have been blown. My instructions were to make sure you left with me. I coulda busted that slimy lawyer, easy, but I didn't want to violate my parole on the prison camera."

"How come you're here?"

"An old dude hired me to pick you up. Said he was your friend."

"What did he look like?"

"An old dude," Tank said. "He had this neat trick with his hair. It changed colors."

Impossible. Or was it? "Where are we going?"

"A safe house. No, wait. That's not what your friend said. He said to tell you we were keeping a low profile."

Zeke let out the breath he'd been holding. Low profile—that he understood. "Thank God."

"God had nothing to do with it. I'm getting paid good money to haul your skinny ass away from the vultures."

"What about your golden freedom? That going well?"

"Not so much. My girlfriend hauled ass. No one hires ex-cons, so I'm mooching off my sister. But I'm not in jail. And I haven't killed anyone. Yet."

Thirty-Nine

Zeke rubbed his neck and gazed at the twilight-shadowed mine shaft with trepidation. Despite his intention to stay awake, he'd slept in the vehicle, only to be awakened by Tank's crazy driving. "Remind me to never ride with you again."

"I'm a good driver," Tank said. "We're here in one piece, aren't we?"

"I lost my stomach about six turns ago. You drive like a maniac."

"I had to make sure no one was following us."

"They didn't have to physically follow us. They can track us from the sats and cams. There truly are very few places a person can hide on the surface and not be found."

"Good. You're thinking like a bad guy. Which is why Mr. Hayes directed us to the Boulder-Weld coal field."

Zeke knew the term from his prior study of the area's underground aquifer. "We're northwest of Denver?"

"Yep. He said you were smart."

So smart he'd been sitting in prison for the last five days.

Tank pressed a button on his com and a hydraulic door closed behind them, sealing them inside. *Like a tomb,* Zeke thought. Great. He'd traded one kind of confinement for another.

"Now what?" he asked.

"I show you the way to find Mr. Hayes."

"You're not coming?"

"Nope. I don't want to know what you two are up to. If I don't follow his directions to the letter, I won't get the rest of my money. I need the money, bad."

The ground rumbled and the transpo shook. Dust rained down around them, and Zeke automatically covered his mouth and nose with his shirttail. Great. An earthquake and he was in a mine shaft.

Tank laughed at him, choked on the dust, and covered his breathing zone as well. "Let's get out of here."

"Agreed."

The door mechanism wouldn't activate. Then the lights flickered out. The shaft plunged into inky darkness. Only a thin seam of daylight showed beneath the rear door.

Tank slammed his fist into the transpo instrument panel. "I survived prison, and now I'm gonna die in a hole in the ground? That ain't right."

Zeke had the same thought, and then the ground shook again, bouncing the transpo inside the shaft like a kid's soccer ball. Wood creaked and splintered in the darkness. Zeke could hear things falling. Would he be trapped inside this small vehicle? How long would the air hold out? Not long with the two of them breathing so heavily.

He clung to his molded seat. This would be a good time to pray, but he believed in science and nature, not dogma. He touched his father's necklace in the dark and wished to come through this ordeal safely.

The tremors eased, though Zeke's stomach contracted like an accordion. He might erupt any second now. That would be ugly. He dug deep, trusting in the power of positive thinking. *I will not throw up.*

"What's that?" Tank asked.

"What?" Tank's question startled Zeke out of his gloomy thoughts. He swiveled his head around. There, off to the right. A faint light flickered in the darkness. It bobbed as if it were moving. "I see it. What is it?"

"You ever watch horror flicks?" Tank asked.

"No. What's that have to do with anything?"

"This is exactly where the monster would come out of the center of the earth to eat the people. God only knows what monsters these tremors unleashed from the deep. Maybe it opened a portal to an alternate universe and an alien is after us."

"There's no such thing as monsters, and I highly doubt an alien would use an earthquake to fuel his travel. Too unpredictable."

"Shows what little you know."

The light intensified as it neared. Zeke noticed it bobbed about head high. "There's no scientific proof of monsters. However, some people act in awful ways that make them monsters."

"Might be a ghost. I bet a lot of people died in this place before they shut it down. Surely you believe in ghosts."

"I believe in the documented energy fields found in the area of suspected ghosts. That's about it."

"Man, you got to get out more. That's the craziest, pansy-ass bullshit I've ever heard. Ghosts are real. My sister talks to my dead grandma all the time."

"She does?" As illogical as Tank's statement had been, the idea of talking to his parents appealed to Zeke. Had prison opened his mind? He considered contacting Tank's sister as the light continued toward them. Through the murky air, it appeared to be a single light coming their way. Hopefully that translated to one person. He balled up his fists and waited. "I might have a job for her."

"If we survive this."

"We're gonna survive. Trust me."

"I don't trust nobody."

The light stopped near Zeke's window. He heard the screech of rocks and timbers sliding across the floor. Zeke's door opened.

"Come with me," the soot-covered man said. "Keep your nose and mouth covered."

Zeke regarded the older man. Something about the man's face tugged at his memory, but he couldn't place him. "Who are you?"

Tank pushed Zeke toward the stranger. "That's Griffin Hayes, the man who hired me. Let's get out of here."

"I'm a friend, Dr. Landry." Hayes tugged on Zeke's arm.

With Tank pushing and Hayes pulling, Zeke had no choice in the matter. Hayes extracted him from the transpo unit, and then manually opened the mine shaft door. Sunlight poured in, blinding Zeke temporarily.

Gauging by the size of the door, Zeke knew Hayes could be no mere human. More likely an A.I. unit. But was he Forman?

Forty

Thick dust followed them out of the mine shaft. Blinking against the bright light, Zeke sucked in a big breath of the black stuff and wished he hadn't. Coughing, he stumbled and would have fallen except for Griffin Hayes.

Through the bone-wracking spasms, he noticed Hayes had left Tank behind. Zeke stopped at a scraggly tree, away from the dust dispersal pattern. Hayes returned to the mine shaft.

Zeke clung to the tree, wracked by respiratory hitches. Stomach heaving, he fell to his knees. Nothing in there to come up, but he couldn't stop the dry heaves. The horizon whirled, his internal thermostat flashed between hot and cold, and his skin tingled.

Finally, the nausea storm eased, and he slumped against the tree. His ribs ached again. His jaw hurt. The abrasions on his knuckles bled.

His parched throat longed for moisture. What he wouldn't give for a sip of water. Hell, why stop there? Why not wish for a day's food and water rations? He pushed his matted hair back from his brow. At least he had fresh air to breathe. After being trapped in the mine, fresh air ranked up there with food and water.

Hayes reappeared and assisted Tank over to Zeke's location. Tank collapsed on the ground beside Zeke, coughing. Hayes pulled two water bottles out of his canvas shoulder sack and handed them out. Hayes didn't take a bottle for himself, Zeke noticed.

Definitely an A.I., Zeke concluded. But he didn't look or sound like Forman. Same general height but older in appearance.

"Better?" Hayes asked.

Zeke drank slowly, not wanting to rile up his volatile stomach. "Yes."

"That was mag," Tank said. "You emerged out of the dark like a superhero."

"Be honest. You thought he might be a ghost, a monster, or an alien," Zeke said.

"You're safe here," Hayes said.

"What happened?" Zeke rubbed his stubbled face. "Felt like an earthquake."

Hayes tipped his head to one side like an inquisitive parrot. "You're correct, Dr. Landry. Tremors shook the country today. Some more violent than others."

"That's a lot of seismic activity. I bet the vid meteorologists are beside themselves with glee. How is that even possible?"

The A.I unit shot Zeke a warning look. He didn't want Zeke to talk about the tremors? What did the earthquakes have to do with his troubles?

"Why'd you direct us to a coal mine?" Tank asked. "We nearly died."

"There had not been any seismic activity in this area in over fifty years when I selected the meet location. I'm as surprised as you are."

"This sucks," Tank said. "Our ride is trashed. We've got black dust all over us. Worse, nobody knows we're up here."

"That is precisely the point, Mr. Murray," Hayes said. "No one knows we are here."

Tank studied Hayes. "You're doing that trick with your hair again. First it's dark, and then it's striped. That's so rad."

"I require a rest period," Hayes said. "It has been nearly a week since I timed out."

"Man, that's some serious insomnia. You should take something. Zoners work. Booze, too. Do 'em together, and you'll sleep like the dead. Just kick back, and we'll hang tight."

Hayes turned to Zeke. "You give me your word that you will remain here?"

Zeke shrugged. "Got nowhere else to go."

"I've prepared a rest location for myself inside. However, in light of these tremors, it may be unsafe for you to return to the mine. I suggest you wait outside until I recharge." He lowered the bag from his shoulder. "There's food and more water in here."

Tank reached for the bag. Hayes held onto it. "The rations must be shared equally," Hayes said. "Is that understood?"

"Got it," Tank said. "Now will you give me the grub bag? I'm starved."

Hayes held Zeke with a stern look. "Normally I'd only rest for an hour, but I require a longer recharge period for maximum performance. Do you understand?"

Hayes's eyes changed from brown to blue as Zeke watched. Along with the strange striped hair, this A.I. had a changeable appearance. Interesting. What kind of A.I. did that? He'd never heard of such a thing.

If Hayes was Forman, he must have a good reason for maintaining his disguise, even though they were allegedly safe here in the mine area.

"I can't speak for Tank, but I'll be here," Zeke said.

Tank unsealed a ration pack. "What about my money?"

"You'll have it this evening." With that, the A.I. strolled back into the mine.

Zeke reached into the food bag for a ration pack. Ideas spun wildly in his head, but he couldn't string them together to form a credible hypothesis. He needed food and rest as well.

"That is one weird dude," Tank said.

"He's an A.I.," Zeke said.

"You're kidding me. He looked as real as you and me."

Zeke shrugged and bit into his food bar. It tasted vaguely like chicken with mashed vegetables. Turnips, maybe.

"What about that neck thing they're supposed to wear?" Tank asked. "I didn't see one of those gold identification necklaces."

"Hard to know if he has one. He wore a turtleneck."

"Isn't it against the A.I. directive for them to be concealed?"

"Got a feeling this one bends the rules a bit."

"So we're stuck in the middle of nowhere at the mercy of a rule-breaking robot? That don't worry you?"

"Not nearly as much as being in prison for five days. Funny how life experiences change your perspective."

"I heard something bad in the news about those robots." Tank snapped his fingers rapid-fire as if that would trigger a memory.

Zeke decided to have some fun. "You talking about the killer robots? The ones that shot people?"

"Yes." Tank leapt to his feet. "Shit-a-ree, we've been captured by a killer robot. We gotta get outta here."

"We're not being held against our will. Hayes freed us from the collapsed mine and provided us with food and water. If you want to leave, head on down the mountain. I'll wait here as long as it takes."

Tank looked down the road wistfully and then he glanced toward the mine. "He's still got my money."

"There is that."

Forty-One

Heart thumping erratically, Jessie clutched her validated transpo ticket and waited, along with her sister, in the thronged Richmond tube station. Travelers milled around their island of stillness, waiting until their transpo signaled them to move toward the loading platform.

Should she have hired bodyguards for the trip west? Was Bea's disguise protection enough?

Her pulse jumped. Had she jeopardized their future?

Stop that, she chided. Taking no action would be worse for the world; it might change everyone's future. Her dream of a future included a husband and children. She wanted that dream very much. She wanted it for Bea, too.

Her lips pressed together tightly. After being sequestered with Bea for days, being out here in the thick of life worried her. What she wouldn't give for a solitary walk in the woods. But woods were a luxury only the ultrarich could afford.

In the center of the terminal, a cluster of white-robed, shaved-head doomsayers urged death to all who sought the Font of Gaia, insisting that eternal youthfulness would fatally strain the planet's resources. They warned against the ongoing alien invasion, claiming people would soon be eliminated. A siren blared and a stick-thin teen spurted through the travelers, two cops on his tail.

Basically, it was the same circus anyone encountered when using mass transit.

"I've missed this wonderful chaos. I adore traveling." Clutching a doomsayer pamphlet, Bea twirled in a tight circle, red flags in her cheeks. Her trademark long blonde hair was hidden underneath a wig of black dreadlocks. She wore retro street clothes and dark brown contacts, with her skin tone disguised by dark makeup. "Doesn't this place give off the best vibes?"

"If you say so." Jessie's grip tightened on the shoulder straps of her carry sack. She'd packed the last set of documents and John Demery's picture. Too much rode on this. She could go to the cops now, but from living with a pop star, she knew that exposing him at the conference would create more media attention.

"Loosen up, Jess. Feel the pulse of the people."

"Someone out there is watching us and tracking us. I want to stop them right now. I've never liked waiting. The sooner we get to California, the better."

"You ever wonder if the doomies are right?"

"No way. If aliens walked among us, why would the doomsayers be the voice of truth? I don't buy it for a minute."

"But aliens could be here, and we wouldn't know."

"Sure, and NASA would've missed seeing their spaceship? Come on, Sis. Get with the program. The doomies are panhandlers who make a living out of telling lies. I don't believe aliens are walking the earth, and I don't believe the Font of Gaia exists. I believe in people. I believe in what I know and what I see."

"Arrgh. You're such a realist. You need to release some of that tension before we hop into a pod. Want me to score us some zoners from the druggies camped out near the restrooms?"

"No. Nothing illegal. We have to blindside Demery. I can't do that under the influence of a drug. And besides, we can't take the risk those druggies aren't cops running a sting here in the terminal. Let's try to blend in. We can watch the news feed."

"Yeah, like that slop isn't a natural downer. How often do they show good news on the feed? Why don't they have stories about puppies and birthdays instead of food shortages and water rationing?"

"Bad news sells. Good news won't hold people's attention for long."

"That's seriously wrong, Jess. The world is upside down in its thinking."

Jessie ignored Bea and watched the news feed. One network discussed the food shortage. Since the disaster, scientists had studied the locusts and pronounced them to be bioengineered. The fresh food shortage had been credited to bioterrorists.

Jessie shook her head. "What a waste. Someone did this on purpose. Someone thought we'd start another world war over food. We're smarter than that."

"The world is full of crazies," Bea added. "We need to make sure their message of hatred isn't the only voice that's heard."

"Righto. The John Demerys of the world will be held

accountable for their actions. No more working behind the scenes. His days of evil deeds are nearly over."

They fell silent as the next story aired about tremors in the San Francisco area. None of them topped magnitude 3.0. Despite all the quakes in the area, no buildings collapsed. It was business as usual in California, except for the widespread tremors.

"Tremors?" Bea's eyebrows rose as the news segment ended. "Will they affect the tubes? Is it safe to travel? Should we cancel our trip?"

"Can't delay. We're on a tight timeline. Besides, California has tremors all the time and their tubes work fine." Another story flicked on and held Jessie's attention. "There's that scientist guy. Zeke Landry. Can you believe what happened to him? He's had the luck of Job. First the fire, and then an identity mix-up lands him in prison."

"He is lucky to survive prison," Bea said. "He could've been killed."

Jessie stared at the bruised man on the screen in rapt fascination. "I'm interested in his water research. I'd love to talk shop with him."

"Good luck with that," Bea said. "He said he's going home to lick his wounds."

"What home? He lived at his lab until protestors torched it last week. He's a magnet for trouble. Poor thing."

"Going soft on me, Sis?" Bea asked. "Losing it over a science nerd?"

"This guy's got something I want."

"He does? Are you going to let him give it to ya?"

Appalled at the idea of intimacy with a stranger, Jessie tore her gaze from the vid screen. "Not like that. Get your mind out of the gutter. I'm interested in his brain." She stood taller. "His science. I'm interested in his science."

"Gosh, I dunno, Jess—seems to me that's an understatement. I've never seen you so flustered, and you've never even met this guy."

"His name is familiar, though. I'm trying to remember how I've heard of him. Oh, wait a minute. That A.I. unit in Atlanta. He said he worked for a man named Zeke, then he freaked when he saw the trouble on Tama Island. His boss must be Dr. Zeke Landry. Do you remember seeing the robot after your concert?"

"I remember dreamy Forman."

"Forman? Yes. That's his name. Forman has a major crush on you."

"You know what would be way cool? If we met up with them on our way to California. That way we could hang out with two very cool guys."

"Slim chance of that. We're going west along a southerly route. When he's released, he'll head east and south. There's an outside chance our tubes might cross in the darkness of the tunnel, but that's about it."

"Too bad for us. I'd enjoy something a little more personal. Something sexy and intimate."

Jessie blushed down to her pink toenails. "That's outrageous. I've never met Dr. Landry, and you barely know Forman." She leaned in close. "We're trying to save the world, and you want to cavort with a robot?"

"Nobody said saving the world had to be boring."

"Stay home if you're bored."

"No way. Stemford sisters stick together. I'm not blind to all that you've given up for me. You want to save the world. I'm here for you."

As Jessie blinked back her tears, the ticket vibrated. "Time to go."

Forty-Two

Zeke startled awake. Thousands of friendly stars filled the sky overhead, along with most of a radiant moon. He sat up slowly, gazing uncertainly at the silvery mountain ridge and the snoring giant beside him.

Was this a dream?

Cold. He was cold. He reached down and touched the rocky ground. It was solid. He smelled the pungent scent of the pine behind him.

Not a dream. Reality.

How strange.

The gentle waves of Tama Island beckoned. Home. Yes. He wanted to go home. But his parents were dead. His lab had been torched. His uncle had vanished.

Memory returned full force.

Prison. He'd been in a fight.

He'd been released. Tank had brought him here to meet with an A.I. unit. An earthquake had trapped them in a coal mine. The A.I. had saved them and then returned to the mine to power down.

If it was Forman, he'd been operating around the clock since Zeke disappeared. Going by Forman's earlier statement of needing an hour offline each day meant he needed at least five hours of uninterrupted rest to recharge, maybe more.

Boy, what he wouldn't give for a cup of hot coffee right now. The nearest coffee shop must have been miles away, but with no transportation, it might as well have been on Pluto. He shivered again, the trembling motion activating the aches and pains in his bruised ribs. He needed heat.

He could share body heat with Tank. But his former cellmate was a stranger, one who had committed a violent crime in the past. Not a good plan. Wait. He had a change of clothes in the transpo. Gingerly, he rose to his feet, stretched the tension from his shoulders. He approached the mine with slow steps.

Would there be another series of tremors?

He weighed his options. Hypothermia could kill as easily as a mine cave-in. He needed to maintain his core temperature to make good decisions. With that thought, he moved forward, easing through the rubble in the darkness. Found the transpo. Yanked a door open. Got his clothes. Put them on.

In a few moments, he stopped shivering. It would be safer to spend the rest of the night in the transpo unit. His body heat would warm the small space. He sat back in the vehicle, closed the door.

Should he go get Tank?

In a minute. He'd do it in a minute.

His eyelids drifted shut.

* * *

The door opened, and the vehicle rocked as a person slid into the seat beside Zeke. He opened his eyes to thin daylight and a familiar face. His smile bubbled up from deep inside. "Forman! I'm happy to see you."

"You still look a bit rough," Forman said.

"Prison will do that to a man. What happened to us?"

"Someone went to a lot of trouble to take you out of the picture."

"I got that. Why? It doesn't make any sense. I'm no threat to anyone. My water projections aren't the Holy Grail. There are other water experts out there. I don't get it."

"We need to use that brain of yours to ferret out the source of the threat. Once we understand what they want, we'll be on track to learn who they are."

"My brain has been occupied with staying alive." Realization sank in. It was morning. He'd slept most of the night in the car. Guilt constricted his airways. He reached for the door lever. "Tank. I meant to bring him in here last night, but I fell asleep."

Forman raised a cautionary hand. "I checked him just now. His core temp is stable. I didn't factor into account your injuries and reduced body mass when I asked you to wait outside for me. I nearly failed you again."

At the robot's downcast expression, remorse swamped Zeke. Forman had not stopped looking for him for the past five days. That was more than he expected from a human, much less a robot. "I'm fine. We're fine. Fill me in on what happened to you. And how'd you do that appearance alteration?"

"Slick trick, eh? Let me start from the top. I arrived in Baltimore as planned. Nearly got nabbed by the robo cops at the transpo station. You were a no-show. Not only that, your trip record didn't exist. This isn't a random malfunction, Zeke. We're dealing with a highly organized group here, one that has access to law enforcement, the coms, judges, you name it."

Someone orchestrated his incarceration? That truth warbled like an old-fashioned air raid siren in his thoughts, alternately chilling and heating him. Someone wrecked his life. On purpose.

"They know a lot about me," he said slowly. "With my altitude intolerance, Colorado was a diabolical choice for disabling me."

"Don't give them too much credit," Forman said. "Your med history is in the human registry database. Anyone with the right access codes can view the file. You were the brilliant one. That clever message on Queen Bea's fan page rocked. They've got to be wondering how I found you."

He stared down at his coal-blackened hands. He'd still be behind bars if not for this robot. He raised his gaze to meet Forman's. "I couldn't have done it without you. Thank you. From the bottom of my heart."

Forman blinked in what looked suspiciously like a display of emotion. "I'm supposed to help you. No single pod rides from here on out. We take a tandem pod, or we don't go. Got it?"

"I'm claustrophobic."

"They knew that. We have to vary our behavior patterns to avoid detection. We'll deal with your issues. That time-release med patch working out for you?"

Zeke nodded. "I feel much better. My mom suggested patches and implants years ago, but I refused. I didn't want anything man-made under my skin. I should have listened to her because I felt crappy for years due to my own stubbornness. But how'd you arrange it?"

"Hacked into the prison records. Put the order through on the authority of the head medic. You've got a month's supply of the drug in the patch. If you hate having the meds in your system, I can remove it."

"I need to function at a high level, so I'll keep it for now." He drew in a full breath and considered his options. His injuries would heal in time, but time wasn't on their side. Their opponent made up the rules of this game. "To recap, someone powerful wants me out of the way. Is it because we're searching for Uncle John?"

"My analysis indicates that's the most probable scenario."

"Why? Do they think we'll find him?"

Forman snorted. "They sent you clear across the country, changed your identity, and locked you up in prison. You are a big threat to them."

"I don't get it. Uncle John is a midlevel manager at the Institute. What's so earth-shattering about that?"

"Working on it, boss. His albino friend, she's definitely dead. I found her in the Baltimore morgue. Her quarters were a sham. No one lived there. Logically, it follows that she was a sham. Someone with deep, dark secrets. Someone involved in this conspiracy."

"Who was she? What was she?"

"It's likely she played one side against the other. When she became a liability, they killed her."

Puzzle pieces fell into place. "Rissa spied on the Institute?"

"It's the most plausible scenario. She faked her injury on the island. She died of a gunshot wound to the head, not an abdominal wound."

"The Institute doesn't murder its employees for nonperformance. She would have had her funding pulled if she messed up at the Institute. Her killer must work for the other side. Who doesn't want the Institute to succeed? We're a group of scientists, thinkers, and researchers. I can't conceive of a think tank having enemies, can you?"

"I have no data that supports that theory at present. But that's not to say it isn't possible. Anything is possible."

There had to be a loose end. "The medic on the chopper. Did you trace him?"

"Negative. There's no record of that chopper ride. No flight plan. No flight crew. The records were scrubbed. It's the craziest thing. But that isn't the half of it. I've been recalled, Zeke. Robo cops swarm locations where I access the net. I'm virtual poison. Every time I tap into the com system, they find me. I traveled to Colorado in cargo containers and in disguise."

"I'm stunned," Zeke said. "We must be scaring the tar out of someone. If only we knew who they were or where they were, we could return the favor."

His statements didn't reassure either of them. How could they? A powerful group wanted to terminate them. As long as he had breath in his body, he'd fight his faceless enemy. Nobody messed with a Landry. Nobody messed with his A.I. unit. They were a powerful analytical team. About time he made a few offensive moves.

"I can change your com footprint completely, given enough time and equipment. Even though I altered your sig before, I didn't change it very much. I need you to be able to access the net without raising red flags. Good thing I've always enjoyed cybertronics. I nearly majored in it in grad school, but water dynamics is my passion."

"Excellent. I'm glad I pulled you out of the slammer."

"About the disguise thing—is that unlimited? Can you be anybody?"

"I have several personas in my appearance module. My ability to hold the disguise for long periods is limited. When I pushed the bounds of my operating envelope, my altered appearance destabilized. I can't maintain it more than an hour or so at a time."

"Which appearance is your true form? The Gary look?"

"Yes. My current mode requires no concerted effort to project."

"I'm blown away. How many A.I.s have this disguise capability?"

"As a prototype unit, I am unique in that regard. A.I. Central tried out different modules within my system. I have the capability of four simultaneous units—the Gary, the Bob, the Brutus, and the Holmes—but Central is unaware of my cumulative programming. According to my records at Central, even though I resemble a Gary, I've got a Bob brain."

"Interesting. You're a secret weapon. Who knows besides me?"

Forman shrugged. "At least one person knows. The person who created the embedded subroutines to link the various processors."

"You don't know who that is?"

"There's a void in my processors in that area. I've approached it a myriad of ways trying to reestablish the data, but I can't recover the information. Someone made me this way. And there's something else."

"Yes?"

"I'm programmed to protect you at any cost. The command prompts are threaded into every layer of my processing modules."

"Wow."

"Yeah. Double wow. Somebody big is after you. And somebody else gave you the most advanced, powerful robot in the world to be your sidekick. We're talking major showdown potential here. The *Gunfight at the O.K. Corral* meets *The Terminator*."

The absurdity of him waging a gunfight drew a bark of laughter from Zeke. "Get real."

"For a smart guy, you're not appreciating how much trouble we're in. What's our plan?"

He couldn't make a plan without analyzing the facts. He'd traveled far from home and found trouble. Uncle John had vanished. A powerful enemy wanted to keep Zeke offline permanently.

How simple his old problems seemed. What he wouldn't give to go back to that peaceful, idyllic existence on Tama Island and study data trends.

Weariness bowed his shoulders. "I don't want a showdown with anyone. I've been trained to keep a low profile, to not draw attention to myself. I want to do what we set out to do: find Uncle John and go home."

"I figured you'd say that. I have a lead on John Demery."

Forty-Three

Forman produced another vehicle from the throat of the mine shaft, a four-seater comfortable for two but a squeeze for more, especially one Tank-sized. The ride back to Denver took forever, because of the heavy traffic on the two-lane road.

Zeke switched on the com and learned tremors had destroyed many tube systems. The nation had begun repairing the major tube routes to keep trade lanes open. Hence, the extra vehicular traffic on the local roads in the troubled areas.

They stopped at a roadside café, presented their fake IDs, and accepted their daily food and water rations. Zeke also squared things by com with his lawyer, instructing him to continue with the lawsuit. He didn't need the money, but he'd be damned if he'd let these people steamroller over him. Meanwhile, Forman, with his com signature disguised, surfed online while Zeke and Tank ate.

"Whatcha got?" Zeke asked when they were once more underway.

"Cross-country travel is restricted by level of urgency," Forman said. "But the conference in Los Angeles is still commencing tomorrow. We will travel west as planned."

"L.A.?" Tank asked. "We're going to L.A.?"

"You're staying in Denver," Forman said. "I've paid you for your service. There's no reason for you to tag along."

"Maybe I want to come. Maybe I'd like to hang with my pal Zeke here."

Forman shook his head. "Not happening, big guy. Zeke is my first priority. I couldn't protect you if we ran into a dangerous situation."

Tank tsked. "I don't need protection, old man. I am the protection. I learned all kinds of moves in prison. Besides, I've been looking for a bodyguard position, and this is gig is perfect. It beats the devil out of being a nightclub bouncer."

"I'm his bodyguard," Forman said.

"What you think, Z?" Tank asked. "Can I come with you guys?

For old times' sake?"

"Forman is right," Zeke said. "Staying with us is dangerous. Go home to your family."

Tank loomed large in the rearview mirror. "Ain't got nobody wants to see me. Can't get a job because of the ex-con thing, everybody knows that, so why even look? You're my best shot at making a positive change in my life."

"This could end badly. These people changed my identity and stuck me in prison, and I didn't do anything wrong except breathe." Cars zipped past them on the narrow road. Zeke tried to run probabilities in his head, but between the bouncing on the rough road and Tank's hot breath on his neck, his thoughts wouldn't settle. "I don't want to be responsible for anyone else."

"You promised me a visit to Tama Island," Tank insisted. "I want to see this island home of yours."

"It isn't a home to anyone right now, thanks to the fire. These people ruined my life and my home. Are you sure you want to invite this level of scrutiny?"

"My life isn't worth a plugged nickel. If I lose it in pursuit of a worthy cause like helping you fight bad guys, then the Almighty might forget the whole murder thing I got on my permanent record."

"About that," Zeke said. His stomach knotted. He didn't want to ask this question, but if Tank came with them, he wanted to know the truth. "Who did you kill and why?"

Tank seemed to fill up the entire back of the transpo. "It makes me angry to talk about it."

"Tough. Tell me the truth."

"All right, then. A pimp came after my mom, wanted her to go into his service. She refused. He beat the crap out of her, and she died. I killed him. And I'm not sorry one bit."

"I can see that," Zeke said after a few beats of silence. "How do I know you won't try to kill me?"

"If I'd'a wanted you dead, you wouldn't be sucking up my air in this tiny tin can. One murder is my lifetime limit. I got enough bad karma now. Don't need no more. Tell me about L.A."

"The less you know, the better," Forman said. "I haven't decided if you're coming."

"It ain't up to you, machine head." Tank punched Forman on the shoulder, causing the transpo to swerve. "Z does the deciding here. I've been watching you two. He's your boss, not the other way around."

"You want to sling names, jumbotron?" Forman asked. "You're one huge pain in the ass. You moronic, loudmouthed, asinine, useless bag of hot air. You're no more a bodyguard than the man in the moon."

"Yeah? That the best you got? One good rain and your circuits will be scrambled and—"

"Enough." Zeke rubbed his temples. "We've got enough trouble. No need to invite more. If Tank wants to come along, that's on him. I don't mind. He knows the risk."

"I'm in. I always wanted to see L.A. They got the Hollywood sign and everything." Tank held his silence for a blessed moment. "How we gonna get there if the tubes are zonked? You got the credits to call up a chopper?"

Zeke recoiled. Definitely not low profile. "No chopper. We'll find a tube that's been repaired and use that. The tremors have ceased for now."

Tank leaned forward in his seat, straining the safety strap. "Will we wear disguises?"

"Yes," Forman said at the same time Zeke said "No."

Forman shot Zeke a look. "We can't risk them coming after us."

"Cool." Tank pretended to point and fire a weapon sideways, gangsta style. "I always wanted to be a cop with a really big gun."

"Not feasible." Forman grimaced. "They'd pick up on the gun right away. I'll think of something better."

Tank settled back in his seat and examined his fingernails. "Make it a good disguise. Nothing drippy. I don't want to be embarrassed by my costume."

"Define drippy," Forman said as they rumbled through a tight turn.

"Drippy. Like all stupid. Like something no man in his right mind would wear."

Forman grinned. "I've got just the thing."

Zeke groaned. "I hate it when he sounds so cocky."

Forty-Four

Jessie Stemford clung to her seat restraints as the pod altitude shifted suddenly. Her stomach clenched at the jarring motion. Fear curled through her, a twisting vine of worry that choked the air from her lungs. Would her boast about tunnel safety cost them their lives?

She strained to see her sister's ashen face in the dim twilight of their pod and then wished she hadn't. Jessie wanted to reassure her sister that everything would be all right, but she didn't believe it. No matter how you looked at it, traveling one hundred miles an hour underground during an earthquake was risky. Sweat trickled down her spine, dampened her palms.

Bea's prayer beads clicked and clacked. Lucky her, to find a measure of solace in this mess. Jessie's hands fisted on the webbed harness as coulda-wouldas danced through her head.

They'd be safe at home in Richmond if not for Jessie's hasty decision to travel across the country. Only a fool would hop in an underground tube when the ground trembled. But she'd been swayed by her sense of justice. Exposing Demery had blinded her to reason. Her rash act had plunged her into a dangerous situation. And her sister had come along for the ride.

She'd always been the strong one, the steady one, the voice of reason. Lately, she'd been stupid. Reckless. Destructive, even.

Like their mom.

No, they'd never had a mom.

Stacy Stemford had never been a true mother to them. Sure, she'd given them life, but that was about it. She'd lived from fix to fix, trading their government-issued food supplement credits for drugs, leaving Jessie and Bea to fend for themselves.

They'd survived neglect, being orphaned, life on the streets, and the cutthroat entertainment business. Would they face more challenges in life, or was this the bitter end? *Can't think about that.*

Think positively.

Neither she nor Bea acted like their mother.

That was positive.

Haring off on this cross-country adventure was over the top—self-indulgent, even. Like something her mom would do. Jessie shuddered. Maybe she had a bit of Stacy in her.

The pod lurched again.

They were going to die. If they were lucky, it would be quick. If not, they'd be buried alive under tons of barren earth. What would run out first, air or water? They had their water rations for the day in the pod with them, but no other food staples.

Just as well. Lingering death didn't suit her. She had a family to start. She wanted to make a difference in the world, to make her life count for something. And Bea had more songs to write and sing.

Reason whispered through the thicket of worry. Reason insisted Demery would continue to do bad things. Reason shouted it was better to live and fight another day.

Exposing Demery waned in importance. He wasn't worth the lives of the Stemford sisters.

Jessie's fingers flew over the com console. According to the nav map, they were still east of St. Louis. She reprogrammed the pod to stop at St. Louis, the nearest debarkation point.

"Why are we slowing down?" Bea's eyes flared wide with fear in the twilight inside the tandem pod.

"Change in plan," Jessie said. "I'm getting us out of this worm burrow. We're stopping in St. Louis."

"I don't understand. What about L.A.? What about the bad guy?"

"The bad guy gets a reprieve."

The pod remotely shifted out of the upper express lane to the slower lane down below, nudging into midlevel traffic in Missouri. Jessie breathed easier. "I apologize for putting us in danger. After we're topside, I'll come up with a new plan."

"What? Why? How? We couldn't get air travel vouchers for this trip. How are we gonna get out of St. Louis without using the tube?"

"I don't know. My gut is telling me to get out of here. Demery can wait. I want him bad, Sis, but not at that cost. The tremors will subside, and then the tubes will be safe again. Meanwhile, we'll have a mini-vacation in St. Louis."

Bea looked thoughtful. "I could give a concert here and donate the proceeds to a relief fund. I've got new lyrics bouncing around in my head. Something about another crappy tomorrow."

"Great lyric. Everyone hates crappy tomorrows." The pod

slowed to a mere crawl as they descended to the lowest local level. Jessie breathed fully, confident of her decision. "The doctor told you to rest for three months, but that much time hasn't passed since your collapse. Even though you're stronger, performing takes too much out of you. Not much point in burning out this early in your career."

"Our lives shouldn't all be about what's best for me. That's why I came on this trip. So you could see I'm here for you."

"I never doubted that."

"It isn't right that I get so much attention, that you put your life on hold for me. But I couldn't do what I do without you. You're my anchor."

"It's okay. I'm not going anywhere. I want to be a part of your life, but I need to get this Demery guy. Just not today. Today, I want to live."

The pod banged into the one in front, jolting them both. The safety cradles engaged around their heads at the abrupt deceleration. Around them metal screeched. Loud explosions sounded. The ground rumbled. Darkness filled the pod as the nav system winked out.

Jessie fumbled for Bea's hand as the pod jostled around. "Hold on, Sis."

"What happened?" Bea whispered.

"Dunno. But I'm hoping for the best."

Something crashed into their pod, jolting them apart.

Bea whimpered in her seat. Jessie screamed silently, unable to utter a sound. *God, please let us live. I promise to take better care of my sister. I promise to be a better person. I will do anything if you just let us live.*

The ground shook. Objects struck their pod.

Jessie squeezed her eyes shut, not wanting to know what was happening and yet needing to know. More metal screeched. More objects hit their pod. Something large rammed into the back section. Sparks flew. A cloud of dust rained into the pod.

Bea screamed an octave above her normal range. "Are we dead? Is this the end?"

They were still alive. Jessie wiggled her fingers and toes. Everything seemed to be working. "Bea? Are you hurt? Is anything on top of you?"

"My foot," she sobbed. "I can't move it."

"Does it hurt?"

"No. There's no pain. But I'm caught."

"Hang tight a minute. I think the entire pod system shut down. We're better off staying strapped in our seats for a few minutes."

"I'm scared."

"Me, too. Keep your hands tucked inside the safety cradle for now. It's our best bet."

The ground rumbled again. The pod slid back and forth, whamming into the narrow confines of the tunnel. The tremors subsided. For a moment, Jessie's heartbeat deafened her. Then the screaming started. Behind them. In front of them. Above them.

"Jessie?" Bea's voice quivered.

"I'm here. How's your foot?"

"It's free now, but it throbs."

"We can work with that. Take an inventory to see if everything else is okay. I'm rebooting the com to call for help."

Jessie reached for the com panel in utter darkness. She pictured the console, worked her way down to the "engage" button, and pressed it. Nothing. No light. No power. Only darkness. She pushed all the buttons, flicked the emergency toggle. No response.

Her hopes sank. They were alive, but for how long? Moisture dripped down her face, running over her eyes. She rubbed it away, feeling the dampness on her fingers. Had she injured her head? Couldn't think about that now. Had to get out of there.

She pushed at the pod's door. It didn't budge.

"The com's out. My door's stuck," Jessie said. "What about your side? Can you pop the escape hatch?"

"Where is it?" Bea asked.

Jessie heard the rustle of clothing as her sister searched. "Near your right knee."

"I can't see anything. How am I gonna find it?"

"It's there. Keep searching. If you want, I can unstrap and try to reach across you."

"No. I can do it. Just give me a few. And turn on the lights while you're at it."

"I would if I could." Jessie swiped at the moisture on her face again. Definitely not sweat. Not good. She heard Bea unclick her straps, and then the pod wobbled as Bea banged on the side of it. "Any luck?"

"Only the bad kind. I found the hatch, but it won't open. We're stuck."

Stuck.

And bleeding.

Think, Jessie.

She had to stop the blood flow. Gingerly she felt her head. There. In her hairline, above her left eye. A scalp wound, then. They bled a lot. She needed to apply pressure. Her cloth belt. The pod rocked as she removed the belt from her waist.

"Jess?"

"I'm okay. Doing a little inventorying of my own."

"Did you hear what I said? We're stuck."

"We're alive. We've got water. And we've got to hope someone will find us."

Forty-Five

Zeke, Tank, and Forman threaded their way through the crowded St. Louis tube terminal. People milled around, going nowhere. Zeke wondered how many other travelers had been diverted to St. Louis. Even though Forman had gotten them in the Denver tube system with fake IDs, Zeke worried they'd been discovered, especially when they ended up in the wrong place.

St. Louis was a far cry from Los Angeles.

Would the militia swoop out of nowhere and haul him to another secret lair for more torture? And what the heck was a keystone? The men in the prison hospital had demanded its location from Zeke, but he couldn't tell them anything about it. There were no keystones on Tama Island. None of this intense interest in his life made any sense.

He tried to appear calm, but his bulky sweatshirt seemed absurd in these mild temperatures. "I feel like a street thug wearing this hood over a ball cap."

"That's why it's called a disguise," Forman said. He'd altered his appearance into an old guy persona, complete with a fedora and a shiny cane. All three of them sported ebony skin, courtesy of the makeup Forman had procured and the robot's adaptive ability. Three black brothers on a journey. Truth and yet a lie.

"At least you're not wearing a dress like me," Tank said. "I'm roasting alive under this heavy thing."

Forman managed to walk with a limp and yet cover a large amount of ground with each stride. "You're wearing a priest's cassock, not a dress. And you promised not to complain."

"That was before I knew you were going to stick me in a dress."

"Camera at three o'clock, Zeke. Turn your head like you're talking to Father Tank. The disguises will only fool the naked eye, not the facial recognition software in the cams."

"Gotcha."

The ground shook, and the lights flickered. Zeke fought for his stance. "What the—?"

"Crap," Tank said. "All the departure lines went from standby to closed. No way we're getting to L.A. anytime soon. Bad enough we got rerouted to St. Louis. We'll never make the West Coast at this rate."

"With so many people milling around, others were rerouted to St. Louis, too. Not just us." Forman cocked his head to the side. "More tremors are imminent. It will take us too long to get outside. We need a doorway."

"How does he know about the tremors?" Tank asked.

"He knows things." Zeke kept his gaze on the floor. "Which way?"

"Left. And hurry. There's an arrival port archway twenty paces away, due left."

Zeke hurried. When the buzzing started, he ran the last six steps. Forman dashed in behind him, then Tank.

Everything shifted. Disoriented by the crazy up-and-down motion along with the side-to-side swaying, Zeke clung to Forman, Tank clung to Zeke. His stomach lurched as the vibrations intensified. Lights flickered on and off, and then stayed off. Nearby a woman called loudly for Hector, over and over again. Others screamed. Glass shattered.

Earthquakes suck, Zeke thought. Loud pops of sound exploded up the arrival passageway. Metal grated on metal.

Gradually the shaking subsided. "Wait," Forman said. "My sensors tell me an aftershock is coming. Is everyone unharmed?"

Tank keened a monosyllabic "ohhhh."

"I'm okay," Zeke said. "How much time passed?"

"A minute twenty. This one will be shorter in duration."

As if on cue, the ground slid back and forth, but the intensity had lessened. Zeke's stomach shot up to his throat and back. He released the breath he'd been holding, unflexed his knees. High overhead, emergency lights flicked on, providing minimal illumination.

The volume of noise dropped a few decibels, and then picked back up as people tried to use their coms to no avail.

"Stay here," Forman said.

Zeke watched the A.I. unit walk toward a bare wall. He opened it and exposed electronic circuitry.

"What's he doing?" Tank asked.

"Gathering information." Or at least that's what Zeke would do if he spoke machine. He didn't need a news feed to know they weren't getting out of there via tunnel pod. Engineers would have to assess the tunnels after the quakes before they could be used again, which left them needing an alternate route out of St. Louis. Them and several thousand others.

"Man, I thought the mine shaft quake sucked," Tank said. "It was a kiddie ride compared to this one."

The security cams were probably offline with the rest of the power. Zeke risked a glance around the terminal. "Looks like folks are mostly okay in here. I don't think those in the tunnels made out so well."

Tank stepped out of the shelter of the archway, surveying the area. "It could've been us in the tubes. We'd be worm food by now. The quake missed us, what, by ten minutes?"

"Just about."

"Hey, there's a priest!" someone shouted.

"Uh oh," Tank said. "Busted. What should I do?"

Zeke glanced over at Forman, who remained plugged into the wall. "We can't leave without Forman. Stall for time. Go along with them."

"Lead us in prayer," a distraught woman begged. "Please. Help us offer thanks for being spared."

Tank raised his hands in a cross between a victory salute and an "I surrender" gesture. People swarmed to his side. "Come and listen, my brethren. Listen to Father Tanqueray's sweet words of prayer. We are all so blessed to be here, to be whole and free. Thank you, Jesus, for spilling your precious blood that we might be saved, for sending your eternal light into this dark world of sin and terror."

A man shouted "Amen," followed by other echoes of praise.

Zeke stepped back from the throng, awed at Tank's seeming ease with the role of spiritual leader. Not your ordinary convicted murderer. The man had surprising depth.

Forman strode over to him. "We've got a slight problem. Only the pods from Denver in a twelve-hour window were diverted to St. Louis. None of the other westerly bound traffic got shunted here."

Zeke processed that information, distrusting the obvious conclusion. "You think we were sent here on purpose?"

"I do."

"That makes no sense. No one knew about the earthquake here in St. Louis before it happened. Right?"

"Seismic pressure in the region didn't increase prior to the quake. Nor are there any active volcanoes nearby. Therefore, this wasn't a natural process. It's reasonable to assume the earthquakes stem from a man-made cause."

"Is that possible?" Zeke's marrow chilled. "You're saying this disaster is because of us? Because of me?"

"Yes."

The entire room began singing "Amazing Grace." Father Tank walked around hugging people.

"There's a complication," Forman said. "I need to go into the tunnel to check the pods there."

"What? Why?"

"Pod 45JC04 contains valuable cargo. I must retrieve it, but I can't leave you alone up here. Therefore, you must come with me. We have five minutes until the next aftershock."

"We're headed into the tunnels? Bad idea, Forman. No telling how destabilized those conduits are. Even without another quake, the tubes could collapse."

"I can't leave without finding that pod. Trust me." With that, Forman whirled on his heel, planted his cane to match his stride and hustled down the dark corridor.

"Wait. I'm coming. What could be so valuable that you'd risk both our necks?"

"Queen Bea is down here. I must save her."

Forty-Six

Number One stood before the Grand Canyon and marveled. Pictures didn't capture the essence of the place. With the sun high overhead, the distant walls seemed painted by a powerful brush, sweeping strokes of earth tones so masterfully wrought that it took his breath away.

He recorded the scenery with his wrist com and wandered over to a less crowded vista, where a solitary man stared out into the void. Tension emanated from the slender man like heat waves from desert sand. The man raised an old-fashioned camera to his face, presumably to photograph the canyon.

One closed the gap at that moment, stopping behind his protégé. "We have a problem."

"I saw." As previously instructed, Three didn't turn around. He snapped another picture of the sweeping panorama. "Two's face is all over the vid feeds."

One angled his wrist com to capture Three's supreme agitation. "His pretense of horror over the earthquakes is such an obvious ruse. It's a matter of time until his story falls apart."

Three's body stiffened. "Dr. Ira Cranfield-Meyers knows what we look like. He can identify us."

"Yes, he can. We must not let that happen. I recommend we go to ground for the foreseeable future."

"But we've worked so hard to put the plan in place. For him to jeopardize everything we've worked for is a travesty. He's forgotten his place as an expendable operative."

"Not once during Two's recruitment or training did he veer so sharply off script. I'm angered by his deception. He believes people will buy his victim pretense. Anyone who hears his thin lies will discern the truth."

"He's a liability."

"Agreed. When he self-destructs, he will take us with him. He must be stopped. But eliminating Two at this point will raise unwanted questions."

Three swore vigorously. "I know a way to kill him. A medical poison that is untraceable. A permanent way to neutralize the threat to us and the organization. We must think of the greater good. Sacrifices have to be made."

Deep inside, One gloated. Like leading a lamb to slaughter. He'd had his eye on this disciple for a long time, knew which buttons to push for maximum effect. Three was ambitious. Greedy, too. He'd hated his rival from the beginning. Putting two glory hounds in a tight box had paid off. Three would remove Two at no cost to him.

Perfect strategy. "Make it happen."

* * *

One paid the exorbitant price for the chopper ride around the canyon. While airborne, he surreptitiously sent a signal through his com to a relay station, which forwarded the signal through a maze of circuitry around the world. With that, he leaned forward to watch the show. Down below, canyon walls sheared off and crumpled with the precision of Fourth of July fireworks. Poetry in motion.

"Good God." The copter pilot activated his under-chopper cam. "You seeing this, ground control?"

Rough static filled the airwaves.

"Come in, ground control," the pilot urged.

One held his peace. He'd placed these charges himself in selected canyon walls and at the airstrip after studying Two's detailed schematics of several blast sites. Not a problem to replicate. He'd rather enjoyed getting back into the field. Victory was at hand. Two had given him the means to cripple the tunnel transportation system; Three had heightened world panic with the bioengineered plague. Now Three would get rid of Two.

He'd engineered the food and water shortages. Those outages would forge new alliances and destroy weak governments. In the new world, the Chameleons would rule. The less fortunate would live to serve them. The time-tested model had worked well throughout history. Only in modern times had democracy muddied the waters.

The chopper circled around to the airstrip. Buckled pavement and crumpled buildings dominated their field of vision. One fought hard to keep a smile off his face. He did good work.

"Look at that. The quake took out the airfield. I hope Lonnie and Liv got out safely," the pilot said. "We need another landing site."

"Wait. This entire area looks unstable. It might even be the epicenter of the destruction. I'm unwilling to chance that an aftershock won't hit once we're on the ground. I'll make it worth your while to fly me to Vegas."

"Vegas?" The pilot checked his gauges. "I have enough fuel. What do you have in mind?"

"Five thousand credits extra. Will you do it?"

"Done."

* * *

Later that evening, One found solitude in the dark Nevada desert. He leaned against his transpo and waited. Tonight the desert held its breath. Even the wild ones respected that Mother Nature had met her match. Overhead, stars twinkled in the dark sky.

The call came at midnight.

"Yes, Master?" One said.

"Your right-hand man is a problem. I want him gone."

"I anticipated your request. Plans are in motion to remove him."

"The new order will need brilliant scientists."

"The new order only needs his intellectual property. I have it."

The Master chuckled. "Excellent work, One."

One preened under the glowing praise. "Thank you, sir."

"About our other problem—any word on that?"

"We routed him to St. Louis. However, several tunnels collapsed there due to the tremors. Thousands are dead, but he isn't listed among the deceased. His A.I. will send out a homing beacon if he is trapped below the surface."

"I want Landry alive."

"I understand. Odds are very high that he is alive. The A.I. unit is with him, and another man."

"Can't you track the A.I. through telemetry?"

"This A.I. prototype lacks certain standard features. But we can track him when he plugs into the info grid, as he did in Denver and again in St. Louis after we diverted his pod."

"He did? Which files did he access?"

"The transportation log, the passenger manifests, and the extended weather forecast for the country."

"Our person of interest hasn't put it together yet?"

"No. His only interest is finding his relative."

"Who we said would be in L.A."

"But who is near St. Louis."

"Once we have them together, we'll play one off the other until we have the answers we need. With the keystone, the prize will be ours."

"Yes, Master," One acknowledged humbly.

The transmission ended and One let out the belly laugh he'd been holding inside. His eyes were on the prize. The Font of Gaia would be his. As would the Master's chair.

Time for a new world order.

Operatives at all levels were expendable.

Forty-Seven

Five minutes. Zeke sprinted through the twilight of the downhill pedestrian ramp, zigging around dazed survivors and trying to keep the A.I. unit in sight. Forman had reverted to his true appearance of a bronzed Adonis, though he still carried the cane.

Probably to conserve energy. Or maybe not. The robot had it bad for Queen Bea. Most likely he wanted to make a good impression. Studly, bronzed man to the rescue instead of a limping senior citizen. Yeah, like that would make the girl forget his robotic nature.

The closer Zeke came to the lowest level, the harder it was to breathe. In the dim emergency lighting, he vaulted the twisted metal and concrete chunks on the floor, ignoring the jarring of his bruised ribs.

As the carnage of the wrecked pods came into full view, he skidded to a halt. Horror etched his dust-clogged lungs. Destination ports like this were accessible to the bottom two layers of traffic. Pods in the express traffic lane couldn't exit here. Ordinarily, steel-reinforced concrete conduits and six feet of earth separated each level.

One large opening remained. Catastrophic engineering failures had occurred. Worse, without infrastructure, the whole tunnel could collapse with the slightest provocation.

Zeke's survival instinct urged him to turn and run, but people were trapped down here. Adrenaline surged. Five minutes. He had five minutes before the next quake.

Forman climbed on the wrecked pods, ripping them open, freeing people. Zeke assisted survivors to their feet, directed them to the pedestrian corridor, urged them to hurry. Women wept loudly. Men gazed at him mutely. Children clung to their parents.

Beside him, two men helped a shrieking pregnant woman out of a pod. Zeke checked the next tandem pod. Two dead inside. His gut tightened, but he kept moving.

He sliced his hand on a ripped hatch, but the little girl inside handed him her teddy bear as she climbed out. An older girl followed.

"That way," he said, pointing to the exit. "Hurry. An aftershock is coming."

The older girl nodded, and they took off at a run.

Zeke forgot and drew in a lungful of air. Coughing, he lost his balance and leaned against a jumble of pods for support. Lightened of their human loads, two upper pods slid to the side and another pod appeared. Zeke read the call numbers twice. Pod 45JC04.

"Forman!" he yelled. "I've got the pod. They were buried underneath the others."

The A.I. unit sprinted back to Zeke's location.

Noise sounded from inside the dented pod. Female noise.

"Help is here," Zeke yelled. "We're going to get you out of the pod."

He heard a muffled response as Forman dropped down into the pod jumble. "Don't see the escape hatch," Zeke said.

"It's on the underside. Help me move these other pods."

They cleared debris away from Bea's pod. A large chunk of concrete rested on the rear of the pod. Even with Forman's enhanced strength, the concrete wouldn't budge. Seconds of his life ticked away. The door wouldn't budge. They couldn't access the escape hatch. How could they rescue Bea?

"Move away from the left side," Forman shouted quite close to the pod. "I'm going to tear a hole in the pod wall."

With that, Forman drew his fist back and punched the pod. The nanomere-infused material held. He swore and punched again. Thud after thud, he beat the side of the pod.

Zeke touched his father's necklace. His fists couldn't take a beating like that. Not without breaking every bone in his hand. Powerless, he could only watch.

The artificial skin on Forman's right hand peeled and curled from the knuckles. Titanium showed through the ripped places. The ground rumbled, shafting a dagger of fear through Zeke's heart. He caught Forman's arm. "It isn't safe. We have to go."

Forman shook him off. "I've almost got this."

Around them, screams intensified. Images of bloody people, of dead people filled Zeke's mind. Needing to do something, he grabbed Forman's cane and bashed the pod. The access port seam gave slightly. They hit it until a crack appeared. Forman pried it open.

"Hurry," Forman said, reaching down inside the pod toward the two occupants.

"Forman. Omigod. It's you. Thank goodness you're here. Bea's hurt," a blonde woman said as her head emerged through the opening. She shoved a carry sack out on top of the pod. "Her right foot is injured."

"I'll get her, Jessie." Forman lifted her out and passed her back to Zeke.

Heart racing, Zeke helped the woman to the platform. "Zeke Landry, ma'am. Can you run?"

She shrugged the carry sack onto her shoulder. "I'm Jessie Stemford, and I won't leave without my sister."

"Forman will carry her out of here. Trust me, he won't leave without her, and an A.I. can run much faster than we can. We have to leave right now."

"Why?"

The ground shook again, another slow rumble. Dread filled Jessie's eyes.

Zeke grabbed hold of her hand and tugged her forward. "That's why. Run if you want to live."

They dashed up the inclined corridor, skirting walkers and sitters, running faster with each step they took. "Everyone, hurry!" Zeke shouted to all they passed. "Another quake is coming."

Forman sprinted past them midway up the ramp, Bea cradled in his arms. After that, Jessie stopped looking over her shoulder.

The ground slid sideways and up and down. Metal screeched. Loud thuds sounded below. Zeke and Jessie stumbled and fell. Zeke caught Jessie's hand again. "Can you continue?"

Her pale face tightened, but she nodded.

He headed for the safety of the arch, stopping beside Forman, Bea, and Tank. Others from the corridor streamed past into the domed terminal.

"Everyone okay?" Zeke fought for his breath.

"Peachy," Father Tank said. "I thought you guys abandoned me to die alone. Instead, you were out scoring chicks. Where's mine, Brother Forman?"

Forman's arms tightened around Bea. "Get your own girl."

Zeke released Jessie's hand and turned to the beaming A.I. unit. "You can put her down now."

"Don't wanna," Forman said. "She has a hurt foot."

"Bea?" Jessie asked.

"I'm fine." Bea sighed dreamily. "Finest kind."

With that, the entire terminal jolted. Machinery shrilled. Down below, booms sounded. Explosions. The emergency lights flickered. A noxious cloud of black dust rolled up the corridor they'd just traversed.

Jessie huddled against Zeke. Tank hugged them both. Continued aftershocks could destabilize the terminal. But tunnels beehived the entire area. Even if they went outside, they could still be in serious danger.

Breathless, Zeke met Forman's level gaze. The tunnel system below them had collapsed. If they hadn't pulled Bea and Jessie out of the wreckage moments ago, the women would be dead.

"That's the last aftershock for now," Forman said. "It's safe to move around."

"How do you know that?" Bea asked.

"Your boy's got technology coming out of his wazoo," Tank quipped. "He's a walking weather station."

"He's my hero," Bea said. "I'd love him even if he was a bus station."

Jessie stirred and pulled away. "What do we do now?"

Zeke sucked in a shallow breath. "Now we find a place to stay and figure out why someone wants me dead."

Forty-Eight

Jessie sank down on the butter-soft leather sofa with heartfelt relief. The pounding in her head had eased, but the agonizing screams from the pod tunnel would be etched in her memory forever. She hadn't known how bad it could be until they'd been trapped.

Her hands shook. What a close call in the tunnels. She and Bea could be dead. They should be dead, except for the A.I. unit who had taken a fancy to her sister.

She was grateful. So grateful.

But more than a little wary and suspicious. People did things for a reason. But A.I.s weren't human. They were machines programmed to act a certain way. She'd never heard of an entertainment robot acting so heroically. It shouldn't have been possible.

She had only to look at Forman's ripped hands to see his metallic parts. Once upon a time, she'd looked into getting her sister a Brutus bodyguard A.I., but she rejected the idea because she didn't fancy sharing their living quarters with a machine.

Why had Forman endangered himself and Zeke to save them?

Was their rescue related to the secret information they'd been receiving? Had someone programmed Forman to save them? And if so, why?

She had to stay vigilant, to keep her head on straight, because Bea had lost hers.

Her sister limped about the spacious living compartment in childlike wonder and gazed adoringly at her new hero. "How did you arrange this rental?"

Forman shoved his ruined hands in his pockets. "I tapped into the net at the pod station and made the arrangement."

"When?"

"When I scanned the info feeds, prior to the aftermath quakes. That's how I learned you two were down below."

"I'm glad you did." Bea found a seat and propped up her right leg. "I'm forever grateful for your act of kindness."

Tank lumbered out of the kitchen area, black market beer in hand. "The fridge and pantry are loaded with food. Black market stuff. What about a celebration?"

"We shouldn't," Jessie said, worry tightening her voice. "It isn't our food. The rental agency could press charges. We could go to prison for stealing their food."

"Too late." Tank raised the beer bottle to his lips. Jessie would have been shocked by his action if he really were a priest, but his clerical disguise and dark makeup had been explained to her on the taxi ride there. "I already raided the larder."

"No worries," Forman said. "The supplies are part of the rental. Help yourselves."

"I've never heard of that, but I don't care," Bea said. "I'm going to pig out and crash. Who's with me?"

"I'm with you, baby," Tank said. "We're on the same wavelength."

Zeke caught Jessie's eye and rose. "I'll get you something. Rest."

She nodded, wondering about the man who'd helped to save her life. He looked like no scientist she'd ever known. From his light brown skin to his shaggy haircut, intense brown eyes, and lanky physique, Zeke Landry's contradictions intrigued her.

Another chill zipped down her spine, icing her blood. She'd nearly died today. Her trembling hands raised to her face, cupping her cheeks.

Forman wrapped her in a soft blanket and sat down across from her on the coffee table. "It's starting to hit you now."

Jessie's teeth chattered. "What is?"

"Shock. You endured a terrible ordeal today."

"Don't remind me." Her words sounded waspish to her ears. "Sorry. Thank you for saving us. I can't express the depth of my gratitude. Bea and I are in your debt."

"You are family," he said.

"Yes, we're sisters."

"Why were you headed west?"

His tone was light, no different than his other words, but Jessie sensed an undercurrent to the question. "We had business in L.A."

"As did we. Through a system glitch, our pod ended up in St. Louis."

"When the tremors started, I wanted out of the tunnel system.

159

St. Louis was the nearest exit."

"A logical move. The tunnels west of St. Louis collapsed during the quake. If you'd kept to your original itinerary, your probability of survival would've been greatly reduced."

"Strange. Neither of us meant to be in St. Louis, and yet here we are."

Zeke returned with a tray of hot tea and cookies. "Thanks." She marveled at how comforting the heated cup felt in her cold hands. "That's just what I needed."

"I overheard the last part of your conversation with Forman," Zeke said. "Both of us ended up in St. Louis, and yet had L.A. as a destination. What are the odds of that?"

"One in two million, fifty thousand," Forman said, straight-faced.

"Odds?" Bea limped back in with a plate full of cheese and crackers. "Are we going to Vegas?"

"Vegas?" Tank carried an open bag of chips and a six-pack of beer. "Hoo-doggies. I love Vegas. When do we leave?"

"We're not going anywhere right now," Zeke said. "We need to figure this out. What does St. Louis have to do with anything?"

Jessie nodded. "That is a very good question."

"If you don't mind my asking," Zeke said, pausing to put his teacup down, "what was your business in Los Angeles?"

Her stomach knotted. "Personal."

"Mine, too. I'm trying to find my uncle. He's been missing for over a week."

"We're going to rat out a bad guy," Bea said. "Tell him, Jess."

"It's complicated," Jessie said, not knowing where to start, not knowing if she should say anything.

Zeke settled back into the sofa. "I've got time."

"Well," Jessie gathered her nerves. "You may not believe this, but for nearly two years, we've been getting classified, technical documents from a mole in the government."

"Documents?" Forman leaned forward. "What kind of documents?"

"Geeky stuff," Bea explained. "Jessie read it all, turned it into English, and I wrote songs about it. Very inspirational."

Forman turned to Bea. "Geek-speak into English. That's got to be 'Babies in the Wilderness,' right?"

Bea grinned. "Yep. 'Storms of Life.' 'Food for Thought.' 'Here

Today, Gone Tomorrow.' And many more hit songs."

"I don't understand," Zeke said. "Translate this into geek-speak for me."

Jessie cleared her throat. "I have a science background, enough to get the gist of the documents. Bea and I talked about the natural disasters indicated, the water shortage, the food shortage, the plague. We knew about these things before they happened. That foreknowledge saved our lives."

"But not the earthquakes?"

"Nope. That one blindsided us."

"Hmm." Zeke rubbed his square jaw. The dusty bandage on his neck strained at the motion. "Your leak must have gotten plugged before the earthquakes started."

"Could be."

"The media claims the food shortage stemmed from terrorists who bioengineered the locusts," Zeke said. "If your mole knew about the incidents before they happened, is he a fed with an agenda or a terrorist?"

Jessie's quivering stomach sank. Silence pinged in her ears. No matter how she looked at it, the Stemford sisters had been used.

Zeke propped his feet on the coffee table. "I believe these incidents are related. Each disaster pits neighbor against neighbor. It doesn't feel spontaneous. This took years, maybe even decades to orchestrate."

Tank lowered his beer and whistled. "That's some conspiracy theory."

"There have been rumors of international confederates through time," Forman said. "A well-known example is the Bramington Group that meets yearly."

"Holy cow," Jessie said. "Is an axis of evil taking over the world?"

"It's within the realm of possibilities," Zeke said.

"Our world is doomed?" Bea hugged herself tightly.

"We haven't hit mass chaos or hysteria yet, though we were close to it in the pod station," Zeke observed. "Exposing the group is the only way to reduce the threat. I have water discrepancy data I can release to the press. That should shine a light on some dark places."

Jessie drew in a shaky breath. "Sounds good. I always thought it too much of a coincidence that the vaccine and meds showed up in plentiful supply near the plague infection centers. The bad guys made money hand over fist every time they manipulated us with terror."

"Perhaps we can get out in front of this if we pool our information," Zeke said. "What's the name of your guy in L.A.?"

Jessie didn't want to answer. Revealing his name weakened her position. She shook her head.

"Tell him, Jess," Bea urged, drawing near.

"Are you worried we would reveal your secret to the media?" Forman asked. "Don't be. Your secret is safe with us."

The air stilled in the room. Jessie took a deep breath. "The man behind all the pain and destruction of late is speaking at a symposium in Los Angeles. His name is John Demery."

Forty-Nine

"You're wrong!" Zeke shoved away from the sofa and strode over to the vid wall. White noise trumpeted in his ears. "John Demery is a highly decorated Marine, a man of impeccable integrity. He's a valued Institute employee."

"So what?" Jessie countered. "He's a paper pusher gone bad. Big hairy deal."

"I don't believe you." The pressure in his temples increased until Zeke thought his head might explode. "This is not right."

"Easy, big guy," Forman said from the kitchen doorway. "Let's hear her out."

"She's making this up." The roaring in Zeke's ears intensified.

"No. I'm not," Jessie said. "I have proof."

"Impossible," Zeke asserted.

Bea lunged up from her chair and put her weight on her hurt foot. She yelped in pain. Then she shot Zeke a death glare. "Quit yelling at my sister. She's done nothing to you."

"Chill, Z," Tank said. "You didn't get this upset when Big Mike wanted to date you or when we were trapped in the coal mine."

Jessie's accusation of treason rankled. Zeke's fist ground into the palm of his left hand. Ever since his parents died, he'd felt off-keel. At work, the deadlines had increased in frequency and urgency. He'd even written that stupid water report Uncle John had demanded to save his Institute job. But his efforts to stay the course had been for naught. His lab and his home had been burnt to the ground. His very identity had been stolen from him.

He'd lost everything.

Everything, dammit.

He glanced around the spacious room. They stared at him in fright. Bad enough he'd scared the women, but Tank and Forman looked edgy, too.

His differences weren't the issue here. They needed unity and cohesion. For most of his life, he'd sensed he didn't belong; for his new friends to look at him with distrust brought those inadequacies to the forefront of his mind.

He took a deep breath, tried to find a calm place. Failed.

The awkward silence ate at him. He cleared his throat. "I'm sorry for raising my voice. I am. But I'm not sorry for what I said. I don't believe you. I can't believe you."

"Show him the files, Jessie," Bea said. "Once he sees that man's name all over the documents, he'll eat a big helping of crow."

Jessie waved toward the entry way but didn't rise from the sofa where she huddled in a blanket. "My carry sack is by the door. I brought images of the documents with me. Demery's name is everywhere."

Forman fetched the bag and handed it to Jessie. Those papers contained lies, Zeke thought. They had to be lies.

Jessie pulled a rectangular object from her bag. "Here's my data reader. I'll pull up the access menu. I've been getting these files for nearly two years, but Demery's name just surfaced in them. The tone of the reports is consistent throughout. I believe Demery wrote them all."

Zeke stalked across the room and took the pink polka-dotted reader from her. As she'd stated, there were hundreds of files listed. Because she said Demery's name appeared recently, he started there and worked backward. His uncle, or someone with his uncle's name, worked for the government, not the Institute.

But the phrasing and ideas were very familiar. Oftentimes when Uncle John came down for the weekend, they'd sit around, have a few beers, and shoot the breeze with other researchers, talking about how things would operate in a perfect world.

His blood chilled.

"This doesn't make sense," he said. "The John Demery I know doesn't work for the government. He's a midlevel manager for the Institute. That's his full-time job."

"Maybe there are two John Demerys," Jessie suggested in a soft voice.

"Thanks for that concession." He shot her a wry smile. "I appreciate the easy out, but I recognize the mindset in these later documents. It's him all right."

"World leaders endorsed water rationing because of him," Jessie said. "He writes about the plague, too. Reading between the lines, he created this modern strain and infected people."

Zeke held up the reader. "I don't believe that's the case. My

Uncle John cares deeply about people and the world."

"What?" Jessie's blanket slipped a bit. "Your uncle? John Demery is your relative?"

"He's my mother's brother. I know his entire employment history, and at no time has he worked for the government. He's a manager for a private research consortium."

Her face tightened. "Then he lied to you. He's living a lie."

"No way. He is a man of integrity and honor."

"Your A.I. unit could plug into the grid and prove my point," Jessie insisted.

"Too risky. We need to keep a low profile to maintain our anonymity here. Documents can be altered. After being incarcerated under someone else's name, I don't trust the integrity of electronic records."

"Where does that leave us?"

"That leaves me searching for my uncle. He's been missing for over a week. And his coworker is dead in a Baltimore morgue."

"I'm searching for him, too," said Jessie. "I plan to expose him for the liar he is."

"My uncle is innocent of wrongdoing," Zeke snarled at her.

Jessie snarled right back. "John Demery is raping the earth, and I'll prove it."

Fifty

With growing impatience, One flipped through the news reports. Not even the titillating broadcast of scantily clothed Connor and Pauline, the People's Choice newscasters, held his attention. On the vid feeds, experts struggled to explain the relative calmness in the San Andreas area given the other seismic activity in the U.S. They gloated that California should have triggered minor earthquakes to settle things down on the fault line years ago.

In contrast, pressure rose at a critical rate at Yellowstone. Old Faithful rumbled and belched, like Mount St. Helens had done prior to blowing its top. Scientists worldwide were putting their heads together to prevent the dawning of another ice age, such as what might happen if Yellowstone erupted and a blanket of dust in the stratosphere blocked the sun's rays.

Another screw up for Two.

Furious, One silenced the screens and paced his soundproof, high-tech lair. The sleek lines and Oriental-inspired austerity did nothing to soothe the savage rage unleashed in his bloodstream. He'd been so close to having it all. So damn close. After years of planning, years of sowing dissention in the Chameleon Society and leading a double life, he'd nearly pulled off the coup of the century.

Two had ruined everything. He'd sworn that the seismic effects would be localized. That the earthquake disaster could be contained and minimized. St. Louis hadn't been hit hard enough, California had escaped disaster, and now a volcanic eruption seemed imminent. A colossal disappointment on all fronts.

Worse, Palm Springs, California had escaped unscathed.

The Master lived.

One bellowed his outrage. The release felt great, so he yelled again.

Blood pumping, he stalked over to the bar, poured out two fingers of scotch, and belted it down. The frost in his veins melted. If he hadn't already ordered Two's execution, he'd attend to it personally today. Ira Cranfield-Meyers was living on borrowed time.

His com beeped.

"Yes?"

"Sir," his security chief said. "A man at the front gate is demanding entry."

"A moment."

He flipped over to view the feed from the gate. Two's grim face stared straight into the camera. One recoiled. How dare he come here?

His fingers itched to strangle the life out of Two, but Three had promised an untraceable medical death.

He should turn the fool away, but Two could blow his cover. Had he spoken to the authorities about Operation Earthquake?

One couldn't take that chance. He hadn't gotten this far by allowing his emotions to govern him. He'd hear Two out. Then he'd take out the trash.

"Park his vehicle inside the west garage," One said. "Escort him to the pool house. Standard meeting rules apply. He'll need a man's size large swimsuit."

"Yes, sir."

Interesting offensive gambit, One thought. Two had nothing to gain and everything to lose by invading One's personal space. Spiderlike, he remotely watched his team prepare his visitor. If Two thought to transmit their private conversation to anyone, he'd be sorely disappointed. The pool house contained enough high-tech gadgetry to scramble any signal, except for the open line to the big house.

Once his team had finished and Two waited alone in the deceptively bright room, One sent a life-size hologram of only his head to the room. He purposefully materialized in front of where Two sat on the blue-and-white striped chair.

Two jerked visibly. "You startled me."

One held his tongue, staring at the man who'd thwarted his plans. Two's Adam's apple bobbed repeatedly.

"Aren't you going to say anything?" Two asked.

"You are in violation of our agreement," One responded. He gloated inwardly that his tone sounded so level, so calm. "We are to have no direct contact unless I initiate it."

"I've had enough of your top-secret rules. Show yourself. Your real self, Senator. I won't talk to a projection."

"I give the orders here."

Two stood and punched his fist through the hologram. The image wavered and then rematerialized.

"I should've known you wouldn't play fair," Two said. "You're always throwing Three in my face. That weasel undermined my work. He set me up for failure."

One maintained his rigid facial mask, but his thoughts whirled. "Blaming others for your mistakes doesn't cut it. Chameleons take full responsibility for their successes and failures."

"The imploders we placed in the San Andreas fault line are gone. Someone stole them, and it wasn't my people. I suspect they are in place near Yellowstone National Park. I'd send a team to retrieve them, but every news station in the world is sniffing around that old dog, hoping for the story of a lifetime before we all go the way of the dinosaurs."

"Inciting Yellowstone to erupt would be very bad for humanity. I suggest you stop it from happening."

"Can't. Feds are watching me night and day. You wouldn't believe what I did to ditch my tail to get here today. I performed my task as ordered, and someone's undone it. Only an insider would recognize the equipment. My hand-picked team is loyal to me. Someone breached my security."

"I suggest you put your house in order."

"My house is fine. I'm telling you the leak is at your end."

A cold sweat broke out on One's body. Exactly two individuals besides himself knew what Two had attempted: Three and the Master. He trusted Three not to betray him. But the Master? Had he sensed One's plot to unseat him?

"Interesting claim," One countered.

"Bull. It's the truth. I have no reason to jeopardize my own mission. I want world stability. I want my children to inherit a better world than today, a world without constant fear of pestilence, terrorists, and famine. I'd take the blame if I'd screwed up. I didn't. Who else knew about our plan?"

Sensors in the room registered that he spoke the truth. Worry mushroomed inside of One, thick and pungent. How much did the Master know?

All he had to do was flick a switch and the pool house would flood with carbon monoxide. Two's fate hung in the palm of his hands.

"Only one person beyond our cell knew of our intent, and he

didn't know the details."

"No way am I going down for this. I heightened security at the lab and at home after the disaster. Imagine my surprise when my staff identified a lethal toxin in my latest supply of coffee beans. If you tried to take me out, you made a big mistake."

This upstart was so done. One remotely opened the gas valve to the pool house. He couldn't take any more of this drivel. His problem transcended Two if the Master knew of his scheme.

"We pay the price for our mistakes," One said.

"Kill me, and you'll kill your precious Three as well."

One leaned forward, his eyes drilling into Two's. "What's that?"

"You heard me. I've got Three. Plus, I know who you are and where you live. Cross me, and you'll find yourself in a snake pit like no other."

One killed the poison gas feed to the pool house and piped fresh oxygen to his upstart subordinate. "You have my attention."

Fifty-One

Zeke poked his head into the twilight-shrouded office where Forman sat before the streaming com station. Two hours ago, he'd shut Forman down. Using crude tools and kitchen cutlery, he'd tweaked Forman's com signal and removed his bounce-back ID. Now Forman searched at will on the rental house com system without fear of attracting unwanted attention.

"Find anything?" Zeke's pride of accomplishment at rescripting Forman's e-signature had long faded. He leaned against the doorway, wanting to appear casual, yet unable to kick the sense of urgency that possessed him.

Forman's fingers blurred over the keyboard. "I'm multitasking by searching for information and leaking your water data all over the world, but this retro setup would make a snail on holiday look like a space rocket. Go bug your girlfriend."

Annoyed, Zeke worked his back teeth apart. "Jessie isn't my anything. She thinks Uncle John is a terrorist, for God's sake."

"You look at her the right way, and she'd hop in the sack with you."

"If anything, we have an adversarial relationship. She's not after my bod. She wants to discredit my uncle. Where do you get this stuff?"

"Straight from my Gary entertainment module. Trust me, I'm an expert on people who want to have sex. She wants you, bro."

Zeke started to leave, changed his mind, and rounded on Forman. "You're way off base on this. Sideline the sex talk, and that's an order. Focus on finding Uncle John. Surely, you've found something by now."

"I've screened billions of info cubes, but nothing is relevant. I'm combing news feeds, weather feeds, and com transitions as we speak."

"No mention of Uncle John?"

"None. Although, curiously, his L.A. meeting was canceled this evening due to seismic activity."

"He might not even be on the West Coast?"

"He's in the wind. That's why I'm surfing the airwaves."

Zeke ran several options through his head. "His identity isn't active?"

"Nope."

"His credit status remains unchanged?"

Forman tapped a few keys. "He has more credits in his account than when he left the island. His Institute pay is automatically credited each pay cycle."

"That's odd. Why would they continue to pay him? The Institute pulls people's funding if they don't toe the line. Why would they bend over backward for Uncle John?"

"Good question. I have no answer for you. I've checked security cam feeds across the country, and there's no sighting of him since he left the island. It's as if aliens spirited him to another world."

"Aliens? Funny how aliens keep cropping up in conversations. Between the news feeds and the doomsayers, aliens are getting a bad rap."

The A.I. turned from the screen, his head cocked to the side. "You're pro-alien?"

"I'm pro-solution. People took Uncle John. We have to out-think them."

"We got nothing. They're very good at covering their tracks. If only we knew what they wanted, we could predict their next move."

Information clicked. "My family. Me. Somehow this is about us. That's the only thing that makes sense. Before he was abducted, Uncle John said my parents' deaths weren't accidents. Now, the bad guys are after you because you associate with me."

"You're right. I need a new boss. Wonder if the aliens are hiring?"

"Very funny. Knock it off; I'm serious."

"Me, too. Sorry, boss. Trouble is we have two things going on at once. World events. Landry events."

"Good thinking. We don't know why they want to exterminate Landrys, but I understand the other part."

"You do? Enlighten me."

"Someone's gone to a lot of trouble to show this world is in dire straits. Water's in short supply. So's food. Disease is a big threat, and thanks to nationwide tremors, the transportation system is mostly disabled. If the com system shut down, we'd have anarchy."

"How diabolical. God, you're smart, Dr. Geek."

Zeke ignored the backhanded compliment, intent on following his train of thought. "Who comes out on top in that situation? Who controls the power?

"The World Health Collective, for one," he mused as he answered his own question. "They're in charge of infectious diseases and coordination of planetary resources in the event of a large-scale disaster. From what I've gleaned online, food and water are being rationed by country, but leaders are conferring with the World Health Collective and following their safety recommendations before they make any moves."

He rounded on the robot. "Who is in the World Health Collective? Do we even know?"

Forman scoured the net, and forty faces popped up on the wide screen. "That's their executive board."

Zeke studied the international collective with interest. Two names he recognized from the water summit, the rest were strangers to him. "Search their backgrounds for commonalities. There has to be a connection here that we're not seeing."

"Roger that."

Zeke paced the room. "World Health Collective. Didn't see that coming." Why would health officials take over the world? Weren't they busy worrying about new disease outbreaks and delivering the same standard of drinking water to the world?

"Got anything yet?" he asked.

"Coming right up. About twenty years ago, the World Health Collective made a conscious effort to include lesser-known health professionals after they received flack for being too politically oriented. Of the present board, thirty attended college on scholarships and loans."

"Hell. I had a full ride. Only the wealthy can afford to pay full fare out of their pockets. If loans and scholarships are criteria for being a bad guy, then I fit that bill." Irritated, Zeke nodded to the screen. "Got anything else?"

"Nothing obvious. No familial connection. No alumni connection. No confluent career paths. They all studied health, or they wouldn't be on the board. In past organizational votes, conservatives have voted as a block and liberals as another."

"Go back to the money-for-school info cube. Where'd the funding come from?"

"Give me a sec."

Screens of data flashed past faster than Zeke could read them. After a few minutes, Forman sat back and nodded. "I had to dig to find this private think tank. The Foundation for Strategic International Relations has satellite campuses in fifteen world cities. FSIR has been around for a hundred years. They fund various research agencies, including your own employer, the Institute. Their U.S. mailing address is a St. Louis Post Office box."

"St. Louis? And we were routed to St. Louis. Hmm. I don't believe in coincidences. We're onto something here. How is FSIR connected to the World Health Collective?"

"They paid for the education of most of the appointees on the board."

Jessie wandered into the room, her wet hair shower fresh. "What's going on in here?"

"We're solving the world's troubles," Forman crowed. "Wanna help?"

"Sure," she said, moving to Forman's side. "Bring me up to speed."

"There might be a link between the people we've tentatively identified as key players to behind-the-scenes people. It's a long shot, but it's a start."

"And?" Jessie asked.

"We came up with the Foundation for Strategic International Relations."

"FSIR?" Her voice rose excitedly. "I've heard of them."

"You have? How? When?"

Jessie brightened. "They've got a place near here. Bea played for them last year. A private bash with champagne and scantily clad women. Some nearly naked guy dancers, too."

"We should go there," Forman said. "Scope it out."

"Good idea," Jessie said. "I know the way."

"We don't have proof of anything, only a few weak conspiracy theories," said Zeke. Their enemies played hardball. He didn't want Jessie or Bea in harm's way. "We can't walk in the front door and accuse them of world domination."

"What are we doing?" Tank asked from the doorway.

"We're hot on the trail of bad guys," Jessie said. "Wanna come?"

Zeke frowned. He didn't need more responsibility. "Forman and

I will check out this lead."

"No way. I know where the place is, and I'm not gonna wait here while you guys have all the fun spying on them." Jessie tipped her chin up and folded her arms across her chest.

Fun? Didn't she realize what they were up against? "If these people are responsible for the recent global troubles, they'll think nothing of killing us. They'll crush us like tiny ants."

Forman's fingers clicked across the keyboard. "The physical address isn't online."

Didn't anyone hear him? Zeke sharpened his voice. "I'm not taking a party of five on a stealth mission. Too dangerous and unwieldy."

"Bea's ankle isn't strong. Forman could stay here with her," Jessie offered.

"Mag idea." Forman clutched his battered hands to his heart. "I vow to protect Bea with every fiber of my being."

All eyes turned to Zeke. He swallowed thickly. His cautious approach had been rejected. A strong leader knew the merit of compromise. With a sinking heart, he examined the options and settled on the best plan.

"Okay," he began slowly. "Jessie can come along, but I'm in charge. We move out when I say. The recon team is Forman, Jessie, and me. Tank stays here with Bea. If we get held up, Tank is to accompany Bea to her home in Richmond. We'll follow as soon as we can."

Tank hooted with glee. "You guys will risk life and limb, and I get to hang out in this mansion with the hottest chick in the world? Cool."

Fifty-Two

While Forman wedged the transpo into a tight spot between two scruffy trees awash in moonlight, Jessie glowed with excitement. She'd transitioned from observer to activist, and it felt great. She would extend her wings and fly. About time.

Zeke helped her out of the unit. "You say the location is a playground of sorts?"

She nodded. "It's rustic, with rough-hewn structures, pavilions, and bathrooms scattered around the acreage. There are Frisbee courts, baseball fields, pony rides, and everything a kid could want. They had a barbeque pit going all day and the best corn on the cob you ever ate. You could eat all you wanted. Tank would have loved it."

"Tank thinks with his stomach." Zeke padded silently beside her. "The layout of the location puzzles me. You're describing a recreation park. Where are their offices? Where is the Foundation for Strategic International Relations headquartered?"

"FSIR is here, I tell you," Jessie insisted in a low voice. "While Bea sang, I walked around a bit. Little transpo trolleys ferried people to the pavilion. I tried to ride the trolley between sets but I couldn't because of the color of my pass. That made me curious, so I discreetly followed the transpo. It only made one stop, at a place I assumed was another bathroom shack. All the passengers got off, went into the shack, and another batch came out. It was more people than could fit in a bathroom facility. The trolleys ran every half hour, with different people on every train."

"The FSIR offices must be underground," Zeke said. "That explains a few things. Given the international scope of their business and the longevity of their venture, the concealed offices must be a security measure. Quite possibly it's a classified location. Which would explain why their physical address isn't in the locator database."

Forman patted her on the back. "Nice work, secret agent."

Jessie basked in the praise. It had been a long time since

someone besides Bea appreciated her, and it felt good. Really good. "Thanks."

Zeke glanced over his shoulder at Forman. "Did you download the real estate records for this sector? Who owns the property?"

Forman nodded. "Records before 1990 were scanned in and aren't indexed. One moment while I flip through the virtual deed books, which I also accessed."

"If we can track who owns the parcel, we'll have another avenue to pursue," Zeke said to Jessie. "Money leaves a trail, no matter how good you are."

"Get down!" Forman ordered. "Lie perfectly still. Don't talk. Don't breathe."

Heart in her throat, Jessie flattened herself into the dusty trail. Chasing bad guys was dirtier than she thought it would be. They were still a distance away from FSIR property. Why had Forman ordered them to the ground? She heard a high-pitched whining sound, akin to a large mosquito, and then the sound waned.

"It's all right to move," Forman said. "The danger is past."

"What was that?" Zeke asked.

Jessie brushed the dirt from her clothes, hands, and face. "Do they have attack mosquitoes?"

"Drone recon bug. Military grade. Not a good sign, folks. FSIR is guarded to the teeth."

Jessie shivered at his ominous tone. "Will there be more of them?"

"Undoubtedly. They must have something pretty sensitive going on in there to monitor this far out from their perimeter."

"How do you know it's theirs?" she asked.

"This land is owned by an agricultural cooperative," Forman said as they hit full stride again. "The co-op angled for an agridome to be located here in 2025, but that didn't happen. Since then the land has been idle."

"Any progress on the ownership of the FSIR tract?" Zeke asked.

"I traced it up until 1960. That's the last time the property changed hands. Jordan Blue, a professor of economics at Missouri University of Science and Technology, bought it."

"Dr. Jordan Blue?" Zeke's voice sounded strained.

"You've heard of him?" Jessie asked.

"You could say that. He's my mother's grandfather, a total SOB. My great-grandmother left him six months after they were married. He didn't want anything to do with her or the kid in her womb. Family lore has it that he obsessed about the fate of the free world."

"That fits," Forman said. He laughed, a melodic sound for a machine. "Dr. Z, you've got blue blood running through your veins."

Zeke's rubber-soled shoes scuffed the dusty ground. "Not funny. People think I'm odd enough already."

Jessie knew what different felt like. "You're not odd. You're thoughtful, caring, and compassionate."

Zeke shot her a strange look in the faint moonlight. Trust her to embarrass him. Time to redirect this conversation. Only, what could he say without sounding waspish?

"You're also stubborn and wrong-headed about John Demery," she amended. "I'm going to prove he's the man behind the global madness."

"This is gonna be good," Forman cackled. "Man versus woman in a showdown of galactic proportions."

"A bit over the top, but at this point, anything is possible," Zeke said. "I'm keeping an open mind about everything, and I suggest you two do the same."

They walked the rest of the way in silence, the silvery twilight giving the arid landscape an otherworldly feel. An open mind. How invigorating. Jessie felt truly alive. Her actions would make a difference.

With all that was going on, her mind had darned well better be open.

Fifty-Three

Zeke's trepidation increased with every step he took. Shadows dominated the landscape beyond the open gates of the recreational facility. Jessie's intel suggested that the wide-open upper level was a sham, that underneath this placid playtime scene thrived a large complex. That possibility, plus the appearance of the recon drone, worried Zeke.

If he'd guessed right, FSIR played for life-and-death stakes. This could get ugly. He turned to Forman and whispered, "Ideas?"

"Recon drones maintain a patrol loop. Following the next one would lead me back to the hive, where I can disable the drone system."

"Makes sense. Let's do that."

"Will do. Wait here until I return." Forman cocked his head to the side. "Get down. Another drone is coming. I'll follow it."

Zeke prostrated himself on the ground. So did Jessie with a little groan. Moments later, a metallic whine resonated in his ears. Knowing that the unit hovered about ten feet off the ground, Zeke carefully lifted his head to track its departure. Out of the corner of his eye, he saw Forman loping after it.

He sat up. Beside him, Jessie did the same.

A check of his wrist com affirmed the time sequence, about ten minutes between drone fly-overs. "Now we wait."

"Do you trust Forman?" she asked.

His eyebrow rose. "I trust him with my life. Why?"

"Because he's a machine chasing another machine God knows where, and we're sitting ducks." Jessie's tone reminded him of his mother making a point with his father. "We should find a new vantage point to wait. One where we could see if he comes back alone."

"Sneaky. And smart." Zeke grinned, helped her to her feet, and retreated back the way they'd come. "How long have you been doing spy stuff?"

"Those packets of information have been coming for a couple of years, but I couldn't afford to take action before. Bea's too emotionally fragile. I'm glad our paths crossed. Tonight, I feel like I'm finally doing my part."

"Tell me about the packets. What did they say?"

"Things like bumper crops of wheat eliminated by arson in the storage pods, governments that want to rule the planet, aliens that have infiltrated our society, parents relieved of their children for the greater good, and an ever-flowing source of water guarded by a secret society."

Aliens again. Zeke shook his head. "The first ones are rumor and wishful thinking. The last is a fairy tale. No one's ever found the Font of Gaia. If they had, the water shortage wouldn't be a global issue. We'd have an unlimited supply of water available, and quite possibly, everlasting life, if the myths about the font are true. Clean drinking water is our most limited resource, and the one we need the most."

"You don't believe aliens walk among us?"

"There's no proof. Conjecture doesn't pass as evidence. Besides, it doesn't make any sense. Wouldn't they want to control the planet and the human race?"

"What about the secret society?" Jessie asked.

"Secret societies exist, but a global secret society that controlled the Font of Gaia or a room full of aliens would already control the world."

"Guess we should be glad for small favors."

"Not necessarily. The font itself, if it exists, isn't good or evil. People, however, can be very cruel. The font is a myth, but the water crisis is fact. I'm trying to find where the bad guys hid the water."

Jessie's face lit with interest. "You think the bad guys hoarded our drinking water?"

"I'm sure of it, but I can't prove it yet."

"How'd they do it?"

"I'll get the how when I figure out the where. Could be a cave or a defunct volcano. Maybe an abandoned mine shaft, though that would acidify the water. I have access to real-time worldwide surface- and groundwater stats. Since the water cycle is steady-state, which means it exists in a closed box of our planet and its atmosphere, I concluded the deficit was hidden."

Jessie frowned. "Hidden water wasn't mentioned in my papers. You sure we didn't lose it to outer space?"

"Positively sure. I wonder if something unforeseen will happen at the International Water Summit next week."

"I've heard of IWS. Are you presenting?"

"No. I keep a low profile."

"Hmm."

They crouched behind thorny vegetation. Zeke listened intently for the whine of another spy drone, but the silvery night clung to its mysteries. He slanted a curious look at Jessie. When he'd last shared the moonlight with a beautiful woman, his mind hadn't been on world domination. Times had certainly changed for the worse.

"Zeke?" Jessie scooped up handfuls of sand and let the grains run through her fingers. "How'd you get involved with this?"

"My uncle. He's all the family I have left. Regardless of what you think about him, he's a good man."

"If your uncle never went missing, you'd still be back in your old life, doing your old thing?"

"I wouldn't have traveled across the country, that's for sure. With my altitude sickness, I'm best at sea level. Forman arranged for me to get a medical patch a few days ago, which helps with the spatial disorientation, but I feel off. I want to go home to Tama Island."

"Your home and your lab are gone. The fire made national headlines. Your uncle's disappearance merely added leverage. Multiple factors pried you out of your comfort zone. Why is that? What do you know that somebody else wants hushed up?"

Zeke shook his head. "Dunno."

He suddenly remembered Browning Charles, the Institute scientist who had wanted Zeke's lab space. He remembered his cousin Angie, who'd helped him row away from the inferno. Funny, he'd never looked at those events as leverage before. There had been a concerted effort to get him off the island.

Was it possible he knew critical secret information? His persecution didn't make sense otherwise.

After a long moment, Jessie sprang to her feet. "You know what? We're still reacting to whatever they are doing. Offense is how you win a game. If we stay in defensive mode, we'll never gain momentum."

He reached for her arm to tug her back down, but she danced out of his reach. "Get down, it isn't safe," he said in a curt tone.

"Doesn't matter. Whoever we're after is in there." She nodded toward the park before them. "They have all the answers. We can't get them by skulking in the dark. By waiting here, we're allowing them to control the flow of information. I'm tired of getting pieces of the big picture. I want—no, I *demand* to know more."

Zeke scrambled to his feet, his stomach knotted at the potential danger. "Don't be stupid. These people kill on a whim. We can't trust them."

"I agree with you on an intellectual level, but I'm frustrated. I want to clean this mess up now that I can finally take action."

"Have patience. Acting rash won't help. These people changed my name and threw me in prison. I could have died there, and no one would have ever known. I altered my destiny by staying cool and using my head, not by going off half-cocked. Rash actions are ill-advised."

"I agree with you, but I need to do something." Jessie shivered. "Forman's been gone a long time. Do you think he's in trouble?"

She shivered. He peeled out of his jacket and handed it to her. "This will warm you up."

"I'm worried about Forman," she said as she slipped it on.

"Forman can take care of himself. If he doesn't come back soon, I need to get you out of here."

She stiffened. "You'd abandon him?"

Fifty-Four

"He's an A.I. unit, Jessie," Zeke said dryly. "He'll survive until I get him back."

"He's not any old A.I. unit. Forman's special," Jessie insisted. "He has feelings."

"He'll survive captivity. Robo units are valuable assets. I don't want to lose him, but I have to think of your safety. If we don't have Forman, we have to regroup."

"He saved my life. I won't abandon him."

"He rescued me from prison," Zeke said. "Do you think this is easy for me to say? I have to prioritize. He's a machine. You're a person. In the eyes of the world, people count more."

Without warning, he crouched, tugging her down as well. Tension radiated from him in palpable waves.

She heard the high-pitched whine of a flying drone. Then another and another. She glanced up and saw a ring of them before her. Their red pinpoint lights glowed like demon eyes in the darkness. Her knees trembled.

This was bad. They hadn't stepped foot on the FSIR compound, but they'd been discovered anyway. Her mouth went dry. Forman hadn't neutralized the drones. She shuddered to think what had happened to him.

More drones arrived, their mechanical buzz an unwanted distraction in her ears. Overhead ballpark lighting flickered on, illuminating them starkly.

She blinked furiously at the sudden glare, wanting to run and hide. She backed into Zeke as a circle of strong-looking men in dark uniforms approached with large guns pointed at them. Zeke steadied her with a hand to her hip, pulling her to his side.

"State your business here," a brawny man with a shaved head said. His clipped tone demanded an immediate response.

"Is there a problem, officer?" Jessie turned to face them. She emulated the wide-eyed doe look Bea often used for effect on hapless males. Unlike Bea's admirers, these muscle-bound goons continued to glare at her. "We were having a little fun."

"This is private property," Brawny insisted.

A drone buzzed by her face. She swatted it away like an annoying house fly. "Sorry. We didn't see any signs."

Shaved Head stepped closer, and his gun dropped slightly. "Where's your transpo?"

"Down the road. We stopped for a romantic stroll in the moonlight. I'm sorry if we've intruded. We'll leave right away."

"Stand fast," the man commanded. He turned to Zeke. "Explain yourself."

Zeke's lazy grin surprised Jessie as much as the squeeze he gave her. "It's like she said. Moonlight. A beautiful woman. We lost track of where we were."

"You can't be here."

"We didn't mean any harm," Zeke said. "We'll leave right away."

Zeke tugged her forward, and they tried to step outside the circle of men. The circle narrowed. Jessie gulped and choked on her breath. Would it be her last breath?

"Not so fast," Shaved Head said. "The boss said to bring you in."

"Bring us in? Why? Are you guys the romance police?" Zeke asked.

"You picked the wrong place for a tryst, buddy. Hands up."

"Look, we're sorry," Zeke said evenly. "We made a mistake. Please, let us go."

Jessie nodded. "We're very sorry," she repeated. "We didn't mean to do anything wrong."

The leader ignored Jessie altogether, fixing his gaze on Zeke. Jessie wanted to crawl underneath a rock and hide. Why had she insisted on coming? She should have listened to Zeke and stayed away.

"No one is leaving. Butler wants to see you."

"We apologized." Zeke sounded like a weary parent. "We didn't know we were trespassing. We won't tell anyone about our mistake, I promise."

"Too late for apologies." The man raised his odd-looking handgun and shot Zeke.

"No!" Jessie screamed as Zeke crumpled. "This is wrong!"

"Sorry, chickie. Nothing personal." Shaved Head turned and

fired the weapon at her.

The impact knocked her to the ground. Jessie glanced at her chest, sure that a bright crimson stain must be blossoming there. Nothing. "What?"

The lights blurred, and her world narrowed to a pinpoint before it vanished altogether.

Fifty-Five

"Well, well, well." Number One stretched back in his chair, enjoying the luxurious slide of leather beneath his suit. He purred like a tuna-sated house cat at his overeager subordinate standing in the military at-ease position. "This is our lucky day. Landry fell into our lap?"

Dex Butler, head of security, nodded. "He was with a woman when my squad arrived. They were south of the east gate."

Butler had risen rapidly through the ranks, an earnest ex-soldier intent on righting the wrongs of the world. His performance today hinted of enough dedication for a promotion to a number slot.

One tapped his fingertips together. "Curious. How'd he locate our base?"

"Unknown. He didn't reveal any information before my team hit him with a tranq dart, and he's still out."

"The woman?"

"According to her ID, she's Jessie Stemford."

"What do you know about her?"

"Her singer-songwriter sister is an activist, but Jessie's not a public figure. According to public records, she's a college graduate, and she manages her sister's singing career."

Interesting. Why did Landry join forces with a nobody? One wanted to dismiss the woman as chaff, but he couldn't. Landry meant too much. "Landry doesn't have a girlfriend. Where'd she come from?"

"Unknown, sir."

Had he misjudged Butler's potential? He glared at the man. "Find out or be replaced, your choice."

"Yes, sir."

"Surveillance in place?"

"Yes, sir."

One considered the new information. He'd lost track of Landry after his Houdini-like release from prison. For him to turn up in St. Louis at the Chameleon Society home base was more than a coincidence. He didn't believe in coincidences.

"Any sign of his cell mate or other humans?" One asked.

Butler hadn't moved a muscle. "The only thing moving around up there was that A.I. unit that we neutralized, sir. To be sure, though, I ordered extra drones and foot patrols."

'Butler's smug tone irritated One. "What about trackers? You try them?"

"No need to pull the vermin out of their cages. I tell you, there's nothing else up there."

"You staking your life on it?"

"Yes, sir."

Why would a man of Landry's status bring a woman out here? The capture of Landry's A.I. unit proved he had a hidden purpose. Time to tease it out.

"Patch the vid feed from Landry's containment unit into my office. I want to know what they say and how they say it."

Butler clicked his heels together. "Will do."

"Fast-track that robot's reprogramming. Keep security on red alert. I don't want any more surprises. Dismissed."

One watched his underling scuttle out of the office. The door snicked shut, isolating One with his racing thoughts.

He had Demery.

He had Landry.

Soon he'd have the Master's chair, the keystone, and the Font of Gaia. He who controlled the water truly controlled the world, and with the Chameleons' hidden water reserves, he'd have it all. He'd own presidents and dictators, kings and queens. He'd have untold riches.

First, he had to get his son back. With that thought in mind, he picked up the com link and entered a series of numbers. Before him, the vid screen flashed on the image of Dr. Ira Cranfield-Meyers. According to the heat sensors his operatives had installed, Two was at home, with his wife, three children, and two dogs. *Pity about the dogs*, One thought.

A status light on his console changed from red to green. He savored a deep breath. His newest agent-prospect had come through for him. It had been a gamble to select a new operative for this sensitive mission, but this prospect had former military training and a keen desire to serve and please. Exactly the qualifications he sought in new recruits.

Green for go. His son was safe. A few taps on his keyboard, and the launch sequence activated. Minutes later, a rogue missile from a nearby Air Force base struck Two's house. One studied the crater of the house long and hard. Not one person staggered from the blast zone.

Two had crossed him, with full knowledge of the penalty for failure in the Society. Though Two had unique qualifications, he had been merely a foot soldier carrying out the orders of his superior. Once he'd failed to perform, his service had been terminated. Permanently.

Like hungry carrion, news choppers buzzed over the bombed house. Medical and police vehicles arrived next. The vid feed from the site showed the remnants of the Cranfield-Meyers house. His Chameleon associates at the nearby military base were already promoting the story of an unfortunate training accident.

One's com buzzed. He flicked on both audio and video feed, restricting his response to audio only. "Yes?"

"Package retrieved," the muscular brunette said in a crisp, feminine tone.

Ignoring the adrenaline rush in her eyes and flushed skin, One pushed ahead to the point of her call. "Damage report?"

The brunette stared resolutely into the vid cam. "Dislocated shoulder. A missing toe. Substantial bruises on face and torso. Facial swelling. Potential for internal injuries."

"See that he gets the best possible med care. Oh, and one more thing . . ."

"Sir?"

"Excellent work, Four. Welcome to the team. Report back to base for a new assignment. Terrorists tried to infiltrate our base and threatened national security. Question them."

The brunette beamed. "Sir, yes, sir."

One switched the com off and activated the vid feed from the containment unit. He fast-forwarded through the data stream until the point where Landry and the woman awakened. Rubbing his fingers together, he grinned and leaned forward.

Fifty-Six

I'm freezing was Jessie's first thought. She tried to huddle into a ball for warmth, but her arms and legs wouldn't comply. Frightened, she clawed her way up from sleep and gazed at unfamiliar surroundings.

The small room had thick, institutional walls and a solid ceiling. A musty scent reached her nose, reminding her of dark, damp places. One wall appeared to be glass, with another dark area beyond it. *Think, Jessie. What happened?* Reaching into the mental fog, she plucked a few salient facts. She'd taken action tonight. She'd overcome the numbing inertia in her life and now there was a price to pay.

Was she dead? It felt too darned cold for hell, and surely heaven was nicer than this. Alive. She must be alive.

She blinked a few times and noticed the room had a twilight illumination. After a few breaths, she tried to close her dry mouth. Nothing. Panicked, she renewed her effort to wiggle her fingers. No luck. Same with her toes.

She was in a strange place.

She couldn't move.

More of the evening flashed into focus. Zeke had been shot. Her lungs stilled. She'd been shot, too. *There should be pain,* she rationalized. *If I'm alive and bleeding, there should be pain.*

Instead, she had grits for brains and body numbness. She willed her fingers to move. Nothing. Tears blurred her vision.

She tried to raise her head. Nothing doing. She tried to roll her neck. Nothing there either. Wide-eyed, she scanned the edges of her field of vision. There. At eight o'clock. A movement.

Something else hovered in here with her.

Something else lurked, and she couldn't move.

Terror ripped through her, curdling her blood. Her head pounded with lurid imaginings. A monster the size of the Astrodome reared its ugly head and roared. Saliva dripped from its pointed teeth, light glistened on its scales. Oh God. She was about to be dinner.

"Jessie?"

At the sound of her name, Jessie fought for another breath, and the murk in her head thinned. She knew that voice. Zeke. Merciful heavens. She tried to tell him how very glad she was to hear him, but all that came out was "ZZZ."

"Don't fight it," Zeke said. "The drug will be out of your system soon. They must have hit us with the same dose of tranquilizer. It took longer for the dose to metabolize in your system. You'll be okay. I came out of the fog about half an hour ago, disoriented, like you."

Jessie clung onto each word, grateful he'd spoken slowly. With each breath, her mental fuzziness eased.

"Where?" she attempted.

Zeke took his time replying. "I don't know who has us or where we are. My com's gone, so's yours. We can't contact Forman. Unless they capture him, he will continue to work for our release. If they've got him, we're on our own."

His response crushed her hopes, the burden of them pressing her into the cold, hard floor.

If she hadn't been so sure she would put her mark on history, they wouldn't be in this fix. Remorse lapped at her in stronger waves, threatening what little equilibrium she had.

She struggled for speech. "Sorry." To her surprise, this word came out understandable.

"Not your fault. Capture was a strong possibility from the outset. I shouldn't have allowed you to come along. If there's any blame to be assigned, it's mine."

She sensed movement and saw Zeke's worried face hovering over hers, felt his strong hand cradling hers. "You're almost there."

His heat spread through her body. Moments later, she wiggled her fingers and toes. "Better," she said.

Zeke grinned. "You've been reborn as a woman of few words. I like that in a person."

"You would. What did they use on us? I feel like I've been run over by a tunnel crawler."

"Wish I knew. If I had access to a lab, I'd analyze a sample of our blood. Barring that, I'd say we got hit with a short-term paralytic. The headache fades with time. Other than that, I don't seem to be any worse for wear."

With sensation in her numb limbs returning, she lifted her head and scoped out the small space. About ten by ten, no furniture, no outside illumination. One wall seemed to be made of glass with more darkness beyond it.

They were underground, she surmised. Way off the grid of life. Outside of Forman, not one living, breathing person knew her location, not even her sister. That scared the snot out of her.

"Are we . . . " Her voice trailed off as she sat up gingerly and tried to make another location judgment. "Are we inside? Does FSIR have us?"

"That'd be my guess," Zeke said.

Jessie's heart wobbled. "What a disaster. Again, I apologize for exercising terrible judgment. Why did I pick tonight to start being spontaneous? I could've waited another forty to fifty years to be detained by a secretive group at an undisclosed location. We'll never find your uncle at this rate."

"Funny you should mention my uncle."

She glanced up at his wry tone. "Yeah?"

The pile of rags heaped on the floor of the adjacent room moved. At the spastic motion, Jessie let out a shriek.

"That's my Uncle John next door. Says he's been here awhile, and the concierge stinks. The food's nonexistent. So is the service."

With growing horror, Jessie focused on the broken, white-haired man next door. Despite her certainty that John Demery had done heinous things, she hated what had been done to him. No one deserved to be treated like an animal. No one.

"The food? The service? You're making a joke, right?"

"He says there's no meal service in this hotel."

"No wonder he looks emaciated. No food. Isn't that against the Geneva Convention or some other long-standing prisoner rule?"

"That assumes anyone would know about these containment units and inspect them for rule compliance. Trust me. We're flying way under the radar right now."

Jessie's hand came up to her mouth covered in grit. Sand, she corrected herself. They'd been sitting in sand before they'd been captured. She took stock of their situation. No com. No food. No sanitation. No real light to speak of. Very terrible.

Zeke nodded toward the next cell. "Tell her what this is all about, Uncle John. Tell her your daily routine."

"FSIR is a front for the Chameleon Society, a group on our terrorist watch list. They come for me each day." John Demery's thin voice wafted through the ventilation holes in the glass wall. "They used to take me to another room and beat me, but I can't walk there anymore. I'm too weak."

"What do they want?" Images of grotesque implements of torture flitted through Jessie's brain like an old-time horror flick. "Whatever it is, give it to them."

"If they had what they want, I'd already be dead."

"I don't understand," Jessie said. "What do they want?"

"The keystone. They kidnapped and murdered Zeke's parents for the keystone."

Zeke reeled. "My parents? Here? How?"

Jessie's heart lurched. How awful. She inched closer to Zeke, hoping to offer comfort.

"They were taken from their fishing boat,'" Uncle John rasped. "Rissa bragged about it in the helicopter."

"I should've kept looking for them."

"You couldn't, son. I didn't know about this place until I was brought here. This group, this secret place, it's a big operation."

"I feel terrible."

Jessie rested a hand on Zeke's shoulder. "I'm sorry this happened to you."

"Don't blame yourself," Uncle John said. "The best minds in the country brainstormed possibilities for foul play, and no one came up with this outcome."

"God. I can't think." Zeke hung his head, rubbed his face. "I want to scream. I want to hurt them back."

"Good. Get mad. It will empower you. Use the emotion to help us figure out why they want the keystone."

Zeke swore. His body jerked, dislodging Jessie's hand. "The keystone? Someone in prison asked me about a keystone. What is it?"

"I don't know," his uncle stated quietly. "The keystone must be important if they tortured Winston and Ruth for information."

Torture. Is that what they faced? Jessie felt as if the ground was trembling again. What the heck had she fallen into? Worse, how could she escape?

"My poor parents. Did you know the Chameleons had them?"

"I suspected they were involved, but I didn't know why. I was blindsided by this too."

Zeke held his silence for a long moment. Then his chin came up.

His eyes narrowed. "What about Rissa? Did you know she was a double agent?"

His uncle made a noise that sounded like a snort. "Rissa turned me over to these goons. I knew I was in trouble as soon as that chopper lifted off the island. They drugged me to get the keystone's location. Didn't work." Pride rang in his voice.

"Forman will figure this out and rescue us. He pulled me out of prison a few days ago."

"Prison?" Uncle John asked.

"I spent five days behind bars," Zeke said. "Through no fault of my own. Forman came through in spades. He'll do the same thing here."

"You realize he's a machine? That his programming can be overridden by any competent techie with a controller module?"

"Sure." Zeke beamed. "But I'm an optimist."

Jessie's courage faltered. What chance did the three of them have against a powerful terrorist group? She didn't want to like Zeke's Uncle John, but he'd been through so much, she couldn't help but feel sympathetic toward him. She had plenty of questions for him, but they had to take a back seat to escaping.

It's going to be all right.

She believed those words.

Until Uncle John's cell brightened, and the door opened.

Fifty-Seven

Through the glass, Zeke watched in impotent fury as two hulking men entered his uncle's cell. They were accompanied by an A.I. unit with ripped skin on his hands—Forman, to be precise. He'd hoped Forman had eluded capture. If they had the robot, help would not arrive anytime soon, if it came at all.

"Forman!" Zeke yelled, just in case. "Over here. Get us out of here."

The robot didn't acknowledge Zeke. He picked Uncle John up by the shirt collar while a beefy man used him as a punching bag. Flesh smacked against flesh. A bone broke. His uncle cried out in pain.

"Stop!" Zeke rose to his feet and smacked his fist against the clear wall. Even though he'd prepared himself for Forman being reprogrammed, he never expected them to use Forman to gather information from them. "He doesn't know anything."

His impassioned plea had no effect. Several more thuds followed. Then Forman released Uncle John. Both goons and the A.I. appeared distracted.

Ear coms, Zeke thought. They're soft-wired to someone else. Someone who can see what's going on. He scanned his cell for a camera and found two. He gulped. So much for privacy. So much for planning an escape.

Chances were their plight would get worse before it got better.

Forman and the two men left the adjoining cell and entered Zeke's.

"You're coming with us," Forman said, pointing at Jessie.

"I'm not going anywhere with you," Jessie said.

Zeke moved to protect her, keeping his body between the intruders and Jessie. Sure, he knew a few self-defense moves from prison, but Forman had every discipline of martial arts in his programming. He could anticipate any fight move Zeke made. He was a helluva lot faster, too.

Top that off with the intruders' well-muscled bodies, and Zeke's chances of fighting his way out of this underground hell diminished to zero.

But he had to try. He got in one minor lick on the shorter guy, but the larger one flattened him with a solid punch. By the time Zeke had lunged to his feet, Forman had Jessie in his grip. Out of ideas, Zeke padded along with the entourage.

They traveled down two empty corridors, turning first right and then left before they entered a larger room, one with day-bright lighting, carpeting, a utilitarian desk, and several chairs.

A stocky brunette in a black shirt and trousers rose when they entered. "Excellent work, team. Release the girl. Robot, secure the male. Guards, step outside."

When the men left, Zeke felt better about the odds. Two of them, two of us. Jessie shied away from Forman and the brunette. Smart woman.

"You have the keystone," the brunette said to Zeke. "Surrender it now, or suffer the consequences."

"I don't have what you want." Zeke winced as Forman yanked his wrists together behind his back. "I never had it. I don't know where it is. I'd never heard of a keystone before today."

The woman's unusual amber eyes blazed. "Now I know you're lying. You have, what—three, four college degrees, and you expect me to believe you don't understand the term?"

"I understand what a keystone is. It's a specially shaped piece that unites the others around it, such as the wedge in the crown of an arch. It isn't the terminology that has me baffled, but the application. I don't know of any keystones in my work, my family, or my home."

"You lie."

"I speak the truth," Zeke said. "I have nothing to hide."

Her eyes narrowed. "You want the keystone for yourself? There's a stiff penalty for each day of noncompliance." The woman turned her attention to Jessie. "Come here, girl."

Jessie backed toward the door, hands raised palms out. "I don't want any trouble. I don't have what you want." Her proximity triggered the automatic door to open, but the armed guards prevented her from leaving.

The brunette motioned for a man to hold Jessie. Zeke died a little inside. "Don't hurt her. She has nothing to do with this. Jessie is an innocent."

"No one is an innocent, Dr. Landry." The brunette marched

toward Jessie and slapped her hard in the face. "Where is the keystone?"

Jessie's face turned bright red. Her lower lip quivered, and an anguished cry passed her lips. Zeke struggled against Forman. "Let me go, you bucket of bolts. Leave Jessie alone. She's innocent, I tell you."

Forman's grip strengthened. No matter how much Zeke lunged toward Jessie, he couldn't help her. "I'm sorry, Jessie. I'm really sorry."

The brunette started walking toward Zeke, and then pivoted and planted a stiff jab in the center of Jessie's stomach. Jessie screamed and writhed on the floor.

"What's wrong with you people?" Zeke yelled, hoping to draw attention away from Jessie.

The brunette stalked over and gut-socked him. Pain radiated like a mighty furnace from his abdomen. He blinked the moisture from his eyes. "That all you've got?"

She came in again, her fists raised high, and landed a series of blows on his face. He watched her through narrowed eyes, waiting for his chance. The next time she bounced in close, he twisted to the side, as if cringing from the blow.

With rattlesnake quickness he kicked her solidly in the kneecap. Her face drained of color as she went down, screaming like a banshee. "You'll pay for that, mister. You'll pay with your life. No one touches me and lives. No one. Guards!"

Two burly men entered. "Shoot them," the woman shrieked through her moans of pain.

The shorter guy shot a dart into Jessie and another one into Zeke.

Not again.

Fifty-Eight

Zeke ran a systems check on his body once he revived in the cell. His jaw ached like a son of a bitch. One molar felt loose. He tenderly fingered his ribs, grimacing at the pain. Bruised, not broken.

Not yet, anyway.

He couldn't withstand many more beatings like the one today, not if he hoped to get them out of there alive. God, his head hurt. His stomach was tender, way too tender. At least he'd had an idea of what was coming, thanks to his prison fight experience.

This keystone they wanted—he couldn't imagine something so important. Or why his parents died to protect it. He needed more data to draw a conclusion. One thing was apparent. These people would stop at nothing to get the keystone.

The Chameleons had committed murder for their cause. They'd kidnapped Uncle John, and now they held Zeke and Jessie captive. Chances of rescue were slim to none, and escape seemed highly unlikely.

Gauging by the last time they got tranqed, he had about half an hour before Jessie awoke. How had his uncle survived a week of this? He crawled on hands and knees to the glass wall and the ventilation holes cut near the floor. He had to make this right. He had to pull it together. He had to save them.

He sat down with a groan. "Uncle John?"

"I'm alive."

Zeke talked softly because he knew the cameras overhead were recording him. His uncle sounded much weaker. "How long was I out?"

"All time is relative."

It had been bad enough as a kid when his father went into Zen mode. Zeke tried another avenue to reach his uncle. "Is there a way out of here?"

"Water seeks its lowest level."

The thought of something wet in his parched throat grabbed hold of his brain and wouldn't let go. "Do you have water over there? I'm so thirsty."

Uncle John shivered out a reply. "The water isn't safe."

"I don't see any water," Zeke replied. They must have broken Uncle John's mind with this last set of blows. "We have to get out of here."

"No way out."

"There's always a way." Cold seeped up from the floor, numbing his lower extremities. If only he could numb the pain in his face and gut. He needed a distraction. "Tell me about my parents."

"Your brilliant mother warned me."

He blinked away tears, needing to focus. "About what?"

"Trouble. She saw it coming. That's when I started planning Forman's strengths."

"Lots of good that did. The bad guys reprogrammed Forman. He doesn't know me from Adam."

"Adam who?"

"Figure of speech."

Jessie moaned on the slab floor beside him. She'd awaken soon. He turned his thoughts back to his uncle. "How bad are you hurt?"

"Bad enough. Right arm is broken. Ankle's busted. Several ribs are cracked. My gut's on fire."

Zeke swore.

His uncle didn't respond. "Uncle John?"

Silence met Zeke's ears. He prayed his uncle had merely passed out.

If only he could think clearly. His parents died protecting the keystone from FSIR and the Chameleons. Now his enemies thought he had the keystone. Worse, unless a miracle occurred, his entire family would be wiped out.

He wanted to live, and he'd do whatever it took to survive. Then once he got out of here, he'd make sure these terrible people paid for their crimes. He'd find that missing water and return it to the people of the world. He'd figure out the keystone's location and make sure they never found it.

The keystone had been hidden for a reason, and it needed to stay that way.

Fifty-Nine

Impossible.

Number One hurled an exotic vase at the stone fireplace. Pottery shattered, shards flew across the well-appointed office. No one knew a thing about the keystone. Not what it was. Not where it was located. Not even how it worked.

Chameleons had sought it for generations. Centuries, even. According to their intelligence, the keystone holder wielded great power. The Chameleons wanted it; One needed it. With the keystone and the Font of Gaia, he'd be invincible. But both of them were elusive.

At first the search for the font had been a fool's quest, much as searching for the Holy Grail or the Ark of the Covenant. But when Lovelock put forth the Gaia hypothesis in 1960, the Chameleons took note. The person who controlled the Font of Gaia could rule the world.

He'd been so sure that Ruth and Winston Landry owned the keystone, but nothing in their possessions resembled a key. Nothing on their bug-infested island resembled a keystone either. He'd killed them and moved on to softer targets, but the answer remained the same. The uncle didn't have it, and neither did the boy-wonder scientist. When was he going to catch a break?

With trembling hands, One pulled out a bottle of scotch and knocked back two stiff shots. Screw the Landrys. Screw them to hell and back.

He'd been so close. Poised on the brink of attaining his lifetime goal. He'd nearly had the Master's chair. His fingers tightened around the crystal glass, the myriad patterns cut in the design pressing against his skin. He appreciated the beautiful glass, but it was an empty vessel.

Like him.

In a rage, he hurled the glass at the fireplace. It shattered with a satisfying pop. Damn the Landrys. Damn the keystone. Damn the elusive Font of Gaia. He hurled the three remaining glasses of the set until all were reduced to glistening shards on his crimson carpet.

He wiped his brow, found it to be damper than expected, and wiped again. That felt good, letting go, venting his emotions in this private setting. Because it wouldn't do any good for word to get back to the Master about his out-of-control behavior or his failed power play.

The Master.

Did the old fart know that One wanted his seat so badly he could taste it? The current Master never got his hands dirty. When One became Master, policies would change. Everyone would be required to bust heads or leave the ranks.

What he wouldn't give to start this venture over, to follow different avenues of pursuit. If he hadn't focused so tightly on the Landrys, he might have discovered the keystone. With the botched earthquakes and the missing keystone, his days were numbered. He needed the keystone. He'd beat the truth out of Zeke Landry himself. His lips curled in anticipation.

His wrist com beeped. "Yes?"

A medical staffer in severe white appeared on his screen. "You asked to be notified when your lieutenant came out of anesthesia," the nurse said.

"His medical outlook?"

The nurse's lips quirked. "He will recover from his injuries. He's been asking for his father."

One nodded, flipped the com off. His staff believed him to be a strong leader, and that's what he showed them. He took another belt of scotch for courage and began the long walk down to the medical corridor.

When he entered the recovery suite ten minutes later, he saw his injured son sitting upright, his arm in a sling. Tough guy, like his dad, but with the pale, witchy eyes of his mother. He had big plans for his boy. "Looking good! How do you feel?"

"Never better," Three said.

One scanned the young man's battered face, noted the arm sling and bandaged foot. The thin nose, a mirror image of his own, now boasted a bulge where it had been broken. "No internal injuries?"

"That bastard Two did his best to kill me, but he didn't break me."

"He discovered your attempt to poison him. He thought if he gained control of you, he'd have me."

"He's a fool," Three said. "Two knew things about us, about the top tier of Chameleons. He spit in my face. You've got a leak in your power circle."

One grimaced. "I came to that realization after your abduction. I rescued you and terminated Two. He won't bother anyone again."

"What about the traitors—the men who leaked my information to Two?"

"I dealt with the problem."

"All of them? Jennings? Fernandez? Roswell?"

"Gone." Learning his longtime henchmen had betrayed him had been a body blow, but One had sanctioned their deaths without a qualm. Couldn't have subversion in the ranks. He wiped his brow again, found it beaded with moisture. Getting old wasn't for sissies.

Three nodded solemnly. "I expected as much given our policy on loyalty."

Full of paternal concern, One rested a hand on his son's good shoulder. "I'm sorry Two got to you. That won't happen again."

"No, it won't." Three shot him a pointed glance. "Are you all right?"

Conscious of the two clinicians with Three, he downplayed his fatigue. "It's nothing."

"Operatives are expendable—that's what you taught me," Three said. "Two paid the price for turning against us. Let me question Landry. I'll get the information we need."

"Next time," One said, a burst of pride swelling in him.

"As you wish." Three nodded solemnly. "Glory will soon be ours."

Sixty

Forman's gaze focused on an unfamiliar scene, a mechanical bay populated with robots. *Where am I?* Disoriented, he scoured his internal log for an answer. He'd awakened from his one-hour daily rest cycle three minutes ahead of schedule. Odder and odder. Data streamed full force through his processors, a river of chilling information.

Zeke and Jessie were prisoners here. They'd been beaten. He'd helped.

Information looped in and around and under a knot of remorse. He'd betrayed his friends. He'd hurt Zeke and Jessie. He should throw himself into the crusher.

He'd failed to protect Zeke, his prime directive.

But his thoughts were his own now. He had a shot at redemption.

He detected new programming, an implanted virus in his processors, and quarantined it. Unbeknownst to the techies here, his programming reset to his prime directive after each rest cycle. Thanks to Zeke, the default startup routine cloaked his original security mission, and when he'd been captured they had changed only his operational status, not his true mission.

The implanted directives tried to come online as core power initiated. As a security unit for the Chameleon Society, he would supplement the foot patrols for perimeter security, far from the prisoners in sector five.

They'd installed a direct link into his controller necklace. He suppressed the priority commands inserted there. Quickly, he accessed the structure's floor plan and devised an escape route. Names, ranks, and status of the humans and A.I.s were scanned. Zeke's Uncle John appeared in a file: prisoner Demery, health status poor.

The numbers of assets staggered him. Humans: five hundred people cycling in and out every eight hours. Flying droids: one hundred. Maintenance droids: twenty-two. Research bipeds: thirty-five. Security bipeds (including him): forty-six. Security quadrupeds: six. System defenses were layered but could be defeated.

He would fix this. He'd get Zeke out of this mess. The plan came together with grim certainty. He played out various scenarios, and the one with the highest probability of success wasn't good for his long-term outlook.

In the best case, Zeke, Jessie, and Uncle John escaped with their lives. Worst case, no one made it out alive. Either way, Forman accepted the risk.

He didn't want to be destroyed. There were more places to experience, more people to meet. And Bea. Beautiful, sexy Bea. He could spend a lifetime or two with her. Not that anyone gave a flying flip what happened to an A.I. unit.

His life didn't matter. It couldn't. If termination occurred, so be it. He'd go out protecting the people he cared about. His existence would have meaning.

A maintenance droid with a scanner tablet stopped in front of Forman's storage pod. He cloaked his true purpose and passed the routine diagnostic scans with ease.

As the droid uploaded information into him, Forman returned the favor, adding new routines for all the A.I. units. The exchange took less than three seconds.

Forman stepped from his resting pod. Around the room, other machines slumbered. A bench to the rear contained pieces of defective equipment. A maintenance drone fed the busted machinery into a crusher. Forman looked away as a droid headpiece went into the masher.

He exited security and began his appointed rounds, checking in as directed, staying on task. It would take three hours before enough droids had received the bogus tasking that would allow his rescue plan to take effect.

Meanwhile, he had more pieces of the puzzle. The Chameleons sought the keystone, which they thought was linked to the Font of Gaia. Folklore and legends concerning the font abounded. The Chameleons believed it to be the headwaters of planetary water. They believed the keystone could access the font, which would ensure their rise to world domination.

The Chameleons had targeted Zeke's family as being linked to the keystone, but Forman knew Zeke didn't have a keystone. As he patrolled the research facility's empty halls, he wondered why the

Chameleons hated the Landrys.

Zeke's parents had disappeared under mysterious circumstances, an alleged diving accident. Zeke, with his altitude sickness, thrived at sea level. Zeke studied global water resources. Two items linked all three facts: Zeke and water.

Scholars had argued for generations about the existence of the Font of Gaia. Was it wishful thinking or a secret resource? Most assumed the font referred to an idyllic place like Shangri-La. In such a place, there would be no sickness, no lack of food or drink. There would be long and happy lives. Seekers had studied deep sea trenches, mountaintops, volcanoes, rain forests, arctic circles, and more trying to find this heart of the earth with no luck.

Detractors negated each investigation, each wealth of species in places that seemingly couldn't support life, and poked holes in scientific theories, rendering the font to the realm of fanciful story, one that included a planetwide energy budget.

Chameleons viewed the font as an essential tool in their arsenal and devoted their lives to finding it. They'd looked everywhere for it. Empty-handed, they'd investigated water reserves around the world, thinking the font might literally be a physical column of water.

They reasoned a water expert like Zeke had a high probability of knowing where such a font might be. His parents, his uncle, his academic mentors, and even the Institute, his employer, had recognized Zeke's brilliance. Growing up on Tama Island, he'd been sheltered from outside influences, mentored initially by a father whose ancestors traced back to the earliest recorded history of the island, and by his double PhD mother, a gifted strategist.

Zeke Landry and a few similarly qualified individuals topped the Chameleon's candidate list. Their cold-hearted logic made sense. After reviewing the other possibilities, Forman agreed that Zeke's knowledge base made him an ideal candidate.

Which totally sucked for Zeke.

As the time approached for the breakout, Forman checked locks and sent dummy data streams back to the centralized processor. He disabled another A.I. and assigned himself to sector five security, where he looped the escape route cameras on a previous feed. Additionally, he requisitioned a maintenance cart one corridor over from the containment cells.

Plans in place, he opened the door to Zeke and Jessie's cell and froze. Jessie huddled in the corner. Zeke lay on the floor, an older man straddling him, punching his face.

Forman flicked the stun switch on his stolen weapon and fired. The assailant twitched, stiffened, and dropped to Zeke's left. He stepped forward, not believing what he saw. "Senator Holcomb?"

When the unconscious man didn't respond, Forman extended a hand to Zeke. "We must hurry. Come with me."

"We're not going anywhere with you." Jessie's voice quivered. "Traitor."

"I sincerely regret my actions of yesterday. I was not myself."

"When was your rest cycle?" Zeke asked, not taking his hand.

"Four hours ago. All is in readiness. We must go now," Forman insisted.

Zeke grinned and grabbed the hand. "About time." With a groan, he clambered to his feet and turned to Jessie. "He's with us now."

Jessie stood fast. "I don't understand."

"I'll explain later. Trust me. Forman is one of us."

"What about him?" she asked, pointing to the senator.

"Did you kill him?" Zeke asked.

"By law, I'm forbidden to kill a human," Forman replied. "I stunned him."

Zeke grabbed the gun, revved the blaster to max, and kicked the prone man. "The only way to deal with a rabid dog is to put him down. He murdered my parents. Wake up, you SOB."

The senator moaned.

"Don't do it," Jessie cried. "Don't be like them."

The burning look in Zeke's eyes worried Forman. "We have to go."

"Your mother cried when I raped her," the senator hissed, sitting up slowly. "She begged me to stop, but I didn't. Twenty men took her before she bled out. You walk out that door and I promise I'll do the same to your girl here. Give me the keystone, boy."

"I'm not your boy, and I don't have a keystone. You're crazy."

The senator lunged for Jessie, who screamed. Zeke fired point blank and killed the man. Though his action stunned Forman, he had to remain focused. With a nod toward the door, he said, "Jessie, help John Demery next door. We have to get him in the cart."

The weapon fell from Zeke's hand and clattered on the floor. Forman leaned over to check the man's pulse. "He's dead." He pocketed the weapon and herded his boss toward the door. "Are you okay?"

"My physical wounds will heal quickly." Zeke glanced over his shoulder at the door. "I've never killed a man before, but if I could revive him, I'd kill him over and over again. At least twenty times and still that wouldn't be enough."

Forman had no reference for an appropriate response. With each second of delay, their window of escape narrowed.

"We must hurry." He clamped a firm hand on Zeke's trembling shoulders and stopped him by the cart. Was his boss heading into shock?

"I will carry John Demery to the cart," Forman said. "Time is of the essence."

Moments later, he loaded the three humans in the maintenance cart and closed the lid. As they gulped down bottles of Global Now water and protein bars he'd stolen, he navigated upward through corridors with looped camera circuitry, using his security credentials to pass static checkpoints.

After they exited the elevator at ground level, he opened the cart. "There's a red service transpo five hundred yards that way. If we get separated, head there, and make your escape. I'll follow when I can."

Zeke rose cautiously, gripping the metal frame. "We made it?"

"I got us out of the underground facility. We still have to nav the grounds. Security up here is on a different system."

Zeke crouched again, studying the sky. "Understood."

In the distance, Forman heard the whine of the insect-like recon drones. "They found us. Can you walk?"

"Yes."

"Keep pushing the cart. I'll lay down cover fire."

"Shoot to kill," Zeke said.

"Can't do that unless they're robots. Push this cart as fast as you can. Your life depends on it."

Zeke hopped out and pushed.

A surface team of rabid drones and tracker dogs attacked them. Forman pulsed out a neural subsonic wave, stopping the attack. More units appeared, and they'd adapted to the beam's frequency. Forman lay down fire. As the enemy amassed behind them, he accepted his fate.

"Run, Zeke!" The drones attacked first with stun waves and

electronic stingers. Shock blasts jolted his neural net. With flickering vision, he took out eight drones with his fists. The robo dogs attacked next. He dodged the first charge, but the second wave knocked him down.

Before he could move, powerful jaws closed over his face plate and neck. His visual field blacked out. "I love you, Bea!" he called with his last pulse of energy.

Sixty-One

Thin clouds floated beneath Zeke's air transpo window as they winged east toward coastal Georgia. Every now and then, through a gap in the clouds he saw endless stretches of barren land. Anyone who doubted that the weather patterns had shifted the rainfall from the U.S. to Canada only had to look at the arid landscape and see the difference between now and historical images of forty years ago.

Zeke knew his world history, especially where it pertained to water. Global warming had been blamed for the first shortfalls in the water budget, and then for the shifting weather patterns. With the atmosphere a mess, people believed water had been lost to the depths of space.

The water hadn't left the planet. Thanks to his research that Forman had leaked, the world knew it, too. How did the Chameleons engineer such a massive deception? How did they control so many water reservoirs?

The Chameleons.

They'd tried to destroy him.

They murdered his parents, nearly killed his uncle, and hit Jessie. Though he'd struck down the man responsible, he'd become hardened. Worse, they'd taken something from him, something he had undervalued. Forman.

Thanks to the robot's heroism, Zeke, Jessie, and Uncle John had escaped the Chameleon stronghold in St. Louis. Forman's sacrifice assured their freedom. Such nobility in an A.I. The unit had been more than a programmed machine. Way more.

Zeke rubbed his eyes. He'd lost more than a research assistant. He'd lost a trusted associate. The Chameleons killed his parents and destroyed Forman. His heart lurched. He'd never held a grudge in the past, but now he wanted to strike back at the Chameleons, hard.

At the light tap on his arm, Zeke looked over at Jessie.

"I meant to give you this." With that, she leaned toward him and dropped a lightweight object into his hand. He glanced down to see his father's necklace. His fingers curled protectively around it.

"Thanks." Zeke knotted the rawhide cord around his neck, slipping the sliver of lightweight rock underneath his shirt. "Didn't know I'd lost it."

"It was on the floor of our cell," she said. "I noticed it as we were leaving."

"I appreciate your thoughtfulness. It belonged to my father. It was the only thing found in their boat after they went missing."

"Then I'm glad I found it. You're lucky to have a keepsake like that. Bea and I never knew our dad."

"If Forman were here, I'd ask him to find your dad." A wave of fresh grief tightened his throat at the thought of his parents' brutal murder. He waited until it passed. "I'm sorry I dragged you into this mess."

"Don't beat yourself up over it. I take full responsibility for my actions. Besides, we survived the experience."

"By the skin of our toenails. I wish I could do something to erase that terrible memory for you. I don't want you to have nightmares."

She shrugged. "What's a little nightmare among friends?"

"I'm serious. You could have gone your whole life without being beaten."

"We made it through, that's what counts. We're safe now."

"Only until they come after me again." He caught her eye. "After the transpo drops me and Uncle John at Tama Island, I want you to head home to Richmond to be with your sister. Tank and Bea are already there, just like we planned. He will keep you safe."

"Nope. Not doing it. I'm a part of this. Someone sent me those technical information packets. I want to see this through. I want to know why they chose me."

"These aren't reasonable people. Next time we might not get away. I want you out of the picture. You heard what they did to my mom. I won't let them hurt you that way."

"I'm aware of the risk, but it's a risk I accept. They know where I live. I believe there's safety in numbers."

"I don't have any answers. I'm headed home because I think clearest on Tama Island. I'm hoping to put all the pieces together."

"Yeah? What do you have so far?"

"They think I have the keystone, but I don't."

"What is the keystone?"

Zeke turned from her and stared at the horizon. "I wish I knew."

Sixty-Two

Jessie hugged her stomach as the air transpo hit a patch of turbulence. For all her brave words to Zeke, the Chameleons terrified her. Especially the bitch who'd punched her in the stomach. If justice existed, that woman would fry in her own hot oil.

Jessie Stemford didn't run from trouble. She wasn't made of spun glass. Challenges didn't stop her. She'd dealt with the international press corps. She'd handled legions of rabid fans. Her preventative efforts had kept the plague from signing her death warrant.

She knew what it was like to have nothing. Those days when she and Bea lived on the street had been rough. She'd vowed never to be that destitute or helpless again.

In the next compartment, machines beeped and whirred as medics worked on Zeke's Uncle John. Once they set his bones and checked for internal injuries, they'd induce two days of twilight sleep to accelerate his healing.

Was John Demery the bad guy from the technical documents she'd received? Or had he been framed by someone else? She didn't know what to think.

She trusted Zeke, trusted him with her life. He believed in his uncle, and she wanted to, but she didn't know enough about the man. Once they'd cleared the Chameleon compound, all it had taken was a few words on a com link from John Demery, and their rescue occurred. Troops appeared by air and land, transpo and medics, too. For that, she was grateful.

"Jessie?"

She drifted out of her fugue to see the com Zeke held out to her. "Is that for me?"

"Yes. It's a secure line to use, if you want to contact your sister."

Her spirits lifted. "May I call her now?"

He nodded and retreated. "I'll give you some privacy."

Heart thumping in her throat, she punched in the code for their home unit. Bea answered, her worried face filling the small com screen.

"You look good, Bea," Jessie said. "Are you feeling better?"

Bea's face hovered near the camera, her voice a terse whisper. "Where have you been? I leave you alone with a science nerd, and you fall off the grid. What's going on? Is that a bruise on your face? Did he hit you?"

"No. We had some trouble, but we're safe now. We found his uncle, which is good news. The bad news is that his uncle was being held prisoner and so were we. Thanks to Zeke and Forman, we escaped. Most of us escaped."

"Prisoner? Are you kidding?"

"It's all true. A nasty woman slugged me, and I crumpled like a baby. Zeke took a bunch of blows from the bad guys, but his uncle is in terrible shape. They'd had him for over a week. Medics are stabilizing him now."

"Where are you?"

"In transit," Jessie said. "Zeke needs to go back to Tama Island, so that's where we're headed, though you can't tell anyone. I'm not even sure if it's okay for me to tell you, but I don't want you to worry. I'm okay, maybe a little tender in the tummy."

"Holy cow." Bea exhaled in a whistle. "I'm struggling to take this all in. You guys found the uncle? Is he on our side or theirs?"

"I don't know. If he's one of them, he royally pissed somebody off. He wouldn't have made it out of there in another day or so."

Her sister's face blanched. "Come home. Let somebody else save the world. You're the only sister I've got."

"Zeke said the same thing, but I'm staying. I've got to see this through, to find out why I'm part of this issue."

"No one doubts you're strong, Jessie." Bea's lower lip trembled. "But I'm not strong. I need you."

"No fair playing the guilt card. You survived the plague and a great deal more. You're stronger than you think. Don't worry about me. I'm in good hands here."

Bea sighed. "What about that cute little robot? When can I see Forman again?"

"That's the bad news." Jessie forced in a shallow breath, not wanting to do this but knowing it had to be done. "Forman rescued us. He made the ultimate sacrifice, putting himself in harm's way for us." She gulped another breath. "Robo dogs tore him apart. I witnessed his destruction."

Bea's lower lip quivered. Her shoulders sagged. "I liked him."

Jessie wished she could have broken the news to her sister in person. She leaned in close to the cam. "I know you did, sweetie."

"He didn't act like an A.I. He's the best man I've ever known."

"I'm sorry, Bea. He was a genuine hero."

Tears spilled onto Bea's pale cheeks. "I had plans for him. What good's a dead hero?"

"He'll be missed, that's for sure, but he saved my life and two more. We can't forget that."

"Can't they fix him?"

At the hitch in her sister's watery voice, Jessie's heart ached. "I don't see how. I wish I could reach through this com and hug you. Both of us need to be strong right now. You're resilient, deep inside where it counts. Stemford women know how to keep going. We do what has to be done. We use our God-given talents to survive."

Bea sniffed in a few breaths. "You want me to write a s-s-song about this?"

"I don't want you to write any old song. I want you to write the best song you've ever written, one that people will take into their hearts and embrace because it gives them a glimmer of hope in these uncertain times."

"A song about hope? About miracles?"

Jessie nodded. "Yeah. This broken world needs a miracle."

Sixty-Three

Heartsick, Zeke huddled in the cockpit beside the air transpo pilot. He'd been certain that coming home would bring solace. Now that he'd arrived, he faced a stark truth. His island would never be the same. He inwardly cringed as they circled his intended destination.

Not one person stood on the once-bustling ferry platform on the mainland. The tattered flags hung limply. The open fields of marsh and dockside palm trees looked the same as ever. The gleaming mud banks and narrow blue-green ribbon of creek water proclaimed it was low tide.

But there were no boats at the dock.

Not even the island ferry.

Across the sound, a veil of thick fog cloaked the blackened island. A lump formed in Zeke's throat. His home. His work. Gone up in flames.

A wave of dizziness hit him, tilting his field of vision, knifing his gut. He wanted to live on Tama Island, nestled in the heart of his family. He hadn't realized before how ideal his life had been. He'd lost everything. Worse, his uncle hovered between life and death in the aft compartment.

He could have the pilot land them on the island, but Uncle John required constant medical attention and shelter. No telling who or what remained on Tama Island. Without the ferry to bring fresh supplies on a daily basis, native resources would already be strained. He needed another solution.

"Change of flight plan." Zeke leaned back in the narrow seat and rubbed his eyes, as if that would ease the gnawing tension he felt. "Your new heading is 31°27'16.0812" N 81°21'58.428" W."

The transpo whirled and covered the distance in minutes. Asia Minor's fortress of a house looked as secure as ever. No soot-blackened trees or picketing protestors here.

Asia's right-hand A.I. unit, Nola, met the transpo on the landing pad. At her welcome, Zeke breathed easier. If Asia had refused them, their options would have been sorely limited.

Jessie joined him in watching Uncle John get wheeled off the transport. They followed the medical team into the stronghold at a discreet distance. He tried once again to get Jessie to see reason.

"I can have you in Richmond in a few short hours," he said.

She shook her head. "I'm part of this, and I need answers. Two heads are better than one."

"You're being reckless."

"I'm being responsible, and I understand the danger. Where are we? Who lives here?"

"A family friend."

She studied the thick tabby walls ringing the fortress and numerous security cams as they hurried toward the house. "Looks like it would take an army to get in here."

"That's the idea. We'll be safe with Asia. Uncle John can recuperate here without fear of reprisal."

She shot him a sharp look. "Sounds like you're not staying."

"I need to go home, to see the damage for myself, to feel the pulse of the island."

"I saw the burned-out place we circled. Tama Island, right?"

He nodded.

"I didn't see any sign of human activity. It looked deserted. How will you get to your island?"

"I'll paddle out with the tide."

"Is that safe? Won't you be swept out to sea?"

"I'll be fine. I grew up here, remember?"

To Zeke's relief, Asia Minor stepped out of his home to greet them. After Zeke made the introductions, Asia took Jessie's hand in the crook of his arm and escorted her inside. Zeke followed.

"Sit," Asia implored. "Please make yourselves comfortable."

"Thanks for sheltering us," Zeke said. "The world's gone crazy. We nearly lost Uncle John."

"But you found him, and he's stable now. You did what you set out to do. Where's your A.I. sidekick?"

"Forman didn't make it out with us. He held off the Chameleons while we escaped. Without him, we'd all be dead."

"Here now. Let's not talk like that. The A.I. did his job. He extricated you from the throat of danger. That's the important thing to remember. Tell me about the underground facility."

"Not much to tell. I can describe the cell where they held us, and the woman who ordered the beatings. I saw elevators and empty corridors." Zeke shuddered. "If I ever step foot in St. Louis again, it will be too soon."

Asia Minor studied Zeke and Jessie. "The Chameleon Society has been around for over two thousand years, but outright violence is new to them. Our intel suggested they were a group much like the Institute—an assortment of thinkers and researchers."

"In reality they are more like a militia of armed guards and machines. Whatever they're up to, they don't want anyone to know about it."

"John transmitted the coordinates for the Chameleon compound when he made the distress call from the com. I dispatched a squad there to recon the area. When law enforcement arrived, they found dozens of bodies. No survivors. No artificial life forms remained on site."

Jessie's jaw trembled, and Zeke hated himself for bringing this darkness into her life. Forman's last cry for Bea still echoed in his mind.

"As you indicated, a US senator numbered among the dead. He'd been shot, but the poison in his system would've killed him within hours," Asia continued. "IDs from the sixty or so other humans dead there by gunshot wounds include scientists, clerics, academics, and militia members."

"What was that place?" Zeke asked, careful to keep his voice level. The fewer people who knew he shot Senator Holcomb, the better.

"That, my friend, is the million-dollar question."

"They kept asking me about a keystone. You know anything about that?"

Asia took his time answering. "Keystones are important."

"Uncle John said the Chameleons probably killed my parents over a keystone. If it's so important, why haven't I heard about it before now? Where is it?"

"The best hiding places are in plain sight."

Did Asia know the keystone's location? Zeke's pulse quickened. "My thought exactly. I'm paddling over to the island tomorrow to look around."

"Sounds like a plan."

Sixty-Four

Zeke's biceps throbbed by the time he made shore on Tama Island. Thanks to his quick-mending physiology and the still-active bloodstream nanites from his prison stint, his Chameleon-inflicted injuries were much better today. The ebbing tide had helped him travel toward the offshore island, but the cross breeze made him fight his way across the choppy waters of the sound.

Good thing he had Jessie's help. He'd wanted her to stay put at Asia's place, but she'd insisted on coming. She could give a lawyer debate lessons.

He glanced over his shoulder to see her paddle drizzling water on her clothes as she shifted to stroke on the other side of the small craft. "You doing all right?" he asked.

"Peachy."

"Take a rest from paddling. We're almost there."

"I can do it."

"No need to martyr yourself. Save your energy for the trip back this afternoon."

She rested her paddle on the sides of the boat and sighed loudly. "I'm not a wuss."

"Never said you were."

Zeke angled off into a narrow side creek that led to the settlement. The acrid stench of soot mixed with the cloying odor of river mud and tainted the salt air. Ahead, blackened stubs of trees reached in vain toward the blue sky. The absolute quiet unnerved him. Even with the near extinction of wildlife in this freshwater-deprived world, birds, insects, and small mammals flourished on the island.

Or they had before the fire.

With a heavy heart, he pulled the boat up on the marsh side of the island, hiding the lightweight craft above the low bank where he and his second cousin Angie had found it last week. Their escape seemed a lifetime ago.

He shouldered the backpack with food and water after he helped

Jessie out of the small vessel. "You can wait by the boat if you like. It'll take a couple of hours for me to hike through the settlement and down to the Institute on the south end and back. I'll return in four hours to catch the peak tide through the sound. With the clock ticking, I have to move fast."

"I won't wilt at the first sign of trouble. Besides, I want to look for the keystone that's turned our lives upside down. Chances are my fresh eyes will see something that you missed."

Her logic made sense. She didn't want to stay behind. Who could blame her? "We have to keep a quick pace."

"Don't worry. I can keep up."

"All right. Let's go."

Though the fire had long since run its course, charred husks of trees dotted the landscape. An isolated stand of pines stood tall with blackened bark but green pine needles left on their crowns. The palmettos and other understory trees hadn't fared as well.

Zeke headed for the residential settlement first. He'd grown up here, running down the many shaded paths. Now the shade and houses were gone. Concrete steps, toilets, and a few leaning chimneys littered the charred ground. A brick structure, the summer home of an off-island resident, remained, the wooden door gone, the windows busted out, part of the roof incinerated.

Even so, it might be inhabited. Zeke walked over and hopefully peered inside. "Anybody home?"

A thin, dark-skinned man clambered up from the tiled floor in the front room, hitched up his loose pants. "That you, Zeke?"

"It's me, all right. And a friend. How are you, Baggy?"

"I'm here."

Zeke introduced Jessie, and then glanced inside the house again. "Where are the others? Did anyone die in the fire?"

"We lost a few. Skipper. Granny. Jeremythia. That crazy protestor guy, Gabe something or another."

Skipper and Granny had been in their nineties. Jeremythia struggled with breathing difficulties her entire life. Curious about Gabe Servalis, though. He'd been young and strong and angry. Had Gabe been framed, as his associates claimed?

"Angie?" Zeke asked. "Did she come home yet?"

"She's still up in Savannah with her friend that had a baby. Everybody else is staying on the mainland until we get another ferry and federal disaster money for rebuilding. I got no people over there, so I just stayed put. Figured someone should keep an eye on the island."

"You could come back to the mainland with me. There's plenty of room at Asia Minor's place where I'm staying."

"Nah. Tama Island is my home. It wouldn't know what to do without a Whaley on the ground." His mouth stretched into a toothless grin. "Or a Landry. Good to have you back. You're here for good, right?"

"I wish. I want to come home, even if home isn't what it used to be."

Baggy nodded sagely.

Zeke checked the time on his wrist com. He had a three-mile walk from the settlement to the Institute grounds. "We'd better get going. I want to look around the Institute grounds, see what's left of my office, but we have to catch the tide on the way back to the mainland. Time is short."

"You'll only find ashes over there, but I understand your needing to see it. Hey, wanna take my mudpuppy?"

"You saved your four-wheeler?"

"Drove it right in here during the fire. It's good as new."

A vehicle would make short work of the distance. Some of Zeke's tension abated. "Yeah. We'd like to use the mudpuppy."

"Come on, then."

Moments later, Zeke and Jessie roared down the sandy track from the settlement to the Institute. The sun shone brightly on his bare head. During his entire lifetime, this single-lane road had been a shaded wonderland. Now, soot and ash littered the hot passageway. The entire island reeked of smoke and soot.

As he rounded the final bend, the shocking panorama caused his hand to release the throttle. The proud cluster of Institute buildings was gone. Here and there, a charred metal chair or table rose above the debris. Zeke's breath caught in his throat. He'd prepared mentally for the vegetation losses, but the twisted bits of rubble hit him hard.

"What's wrong?" Jessie asked.

"Fifty people used to work and live here at the Institute."

"Baggy said only three people died. Your colleagues must be on the mainland with the islanders." She glanced around him. "Explain the layout."

He laid down on the throttle, driving them past the meeting area, the canteen, the dorms, and the various labs, including his own, with increasing dread. When he stopped next to his former office, he walked over and squatted amid the ashes. Several items caught his eye. A metal bracket. A blackened doorknob. A steel bed frame. The charred husk of a refrigerator.

What a colossal waste. The protestors had set this fire on purpose. They'd wanted to destroy the Institute. Given the primitive fire-quenching measures on the island, it was lucky that more people hadn't died.

The protestors. His thoughts spun rapidly. Gabe died in the fire. Had he been eliminated once he'd served his purpose?

"What?" Jessie asked. When he didn't answer, she stood beside him in the charcoal-littered sand and tapped his shoulder. "You stiffened. Something occurred to you. We're on the same team. Tell me."

Zeke startled, half expecting to see Gabe and the protestors instead of Jessie. He rose to stand next to her. "There'd been a long-running dispute between the islanders and the Institute. Many islanders wanted the Institute to abandon its research facility. They wanted the island to be the way it was two hundred years ago."

She snorted. "Like that would happen. The island is no longer a cotton plantation."

"Right. The Institute owns this land, free and clear. Of all the Institute's campuses, everyone angles for a spot here. Why live in the snowy north when you could live on a balmy island?"

"Did you ever work at their other sites?"

"No. I said I'd only work here."

"Was that standard?"

"Can't say. I had an 'in' with my mom working for them, and my family living here."

"As an islander and an Institute man, didn't that strain your loyalties?"

Jessie had cut straight to the heart of his dilemma. "Though I didn't participate in the protests, the islanders treated me with respect. Then Gabe Servalis came in and got everyone riled up. Very militant. Very inflexible in his attitudes. He had it in for me."

"Gabe? Didn't he die in the blaze?"

He nodded. "My cousin Angie told me Gabe set the fires."

"So a militant outsider stirred things up, set the island on fire, and died. Tidy little package, isn't it?"

"Someone covered their tracks. Someone who sent Gabe down here to stir things up."

"The Chameleons?"

"We know the Chameleons we encountered are violent, they believe the keystone is here on Tama Island, and they don't leave any loose ends behind. At this point, I'd be more concerned if it wasn't them."

"Loose ends being people who will talk." Jessie shivered. "If that's so, we were darn lucky to have escaped their stronghold."

"We made our luck." Zeke scanned the charred landscape. "Since they captured us after the fire, they don't have the keystone yet. Where is it? The buildings are gone. There are no stone walls or arches. The fire leveled this complex."

"I don't see anything that looks like a keystone. Ever since Asia mentioned that the best hiding places were in plain sight, I hoped to see an arched tree or the like, but there's nothing to see."

Walking back to the four-wheeler, Zeke sunk into his thoughts. If Jessie weren't there, he'd sift through the debris at his feet and find a souvenir, something that survived the fire. Like a metal key. But he didn't want her to see him as weak or needy. Plenty of time to come back again later to rake through the ashes.

Wait a minute. A key. External electronic locks didn't work on the island because the high salt content in air corroded the delicate circuitry. He remembered his dad unlocking his lab door once he'd been hired by the Institute. They'd secured the buildings with metal keys and locks. "You've come full circle, son," his father had said. "I'm proud of you."

Since his parents' disappearance, he'd been increasingly drawn onto the international water stage. The Institute and Uncle John had pressured him to make an Institute-favorable report before the fire, which he'd done, a wasted effort for sure.

Afterward, Forman had released Zeke's extra water findings to scientists near the reservoirs in question. He'd been on the verge of resuming his search for the missing water when the fire occurred. That fire had nearly taken his life.

God. How long would it take the island to recover? He'd seen palmettos come back from a controlled burn—that usually took a year or two—but the live oaks, those had been hundreds of years old. What a senseless loss. He wouldn't see large oaks like that on Tama Island again during his lifetime even if they somehow survived in today's harsh climate.

No sense skirting the facts. The island had changed. He'd been targeted by a militant group. He wasn't a secret agent, but he'd better start thinking like one. He straddled the four-wheeler deep in thought.

The keystone.

The Chameleons wanted it.

He didn't have it.

But they thought he did.

"We're not getting anywhere," Jessie said. "Let's find some shade, eat, and rest for a bit before we row back to the mainland."

Zeke snapped out of his fugue. They should rest and refuel before making that journey. "Good idea. How about a picnic at my favorite spot on the island?"

"Lead on, McGenius."

Sixty-Five

Jessie thrilled to the wild ride behind Zeke. If they'd only found the keystone, the day would have been perfect. The brutal sun beat down on her head. She made a mental note to wear a hat the next time she visited a burned-up island.

They bounced down a narrow, sandy track, the rumble of the engine drowning out all other sounds. The charred husks of trees gave way to a row of tall sand dunes on her right. Nubs of grasses remained to hold the dunes in place.

At a dip in the dunes, she saw the Atlantic Ocean glistening mirror-bright all the way to the horizon. Ahead, a two-story lighthouse dominated her field of vision. Thick stripes of red and white paint alternated to the top glass cap.

Zeke slowed the four-wheeler to a crawl and stopped near the lighthouse. Up close, she saw that the fire had left its mark here as well. The chipped and charred paint on the structure looked like someone had torched it.

With the noisy machine turned off, Jessie heard the modest waves lapping at the beach beyond the lighthouse. Offshore, a solitary yacht rode the ocean swells. "Nice view," she said.

Zeke took the backpack from her and opened it up, handing her a water container and taking one for himself. "How old is the lighthouse?" she asked before taking a sip of water.

"This is the third light in the history of the island, but they were all built on the same site. They have to replace the stairs about every thirty years."

The lighthouse. An old stone structure. Generations old. Ideas whirled in her head as she ran her hand over the exterior. "Any chance it's hiding the keystone?"

Zeke glanced at the structure in a considering manner. "Me and every other island kid have climbed all over this thing, inside and out. If the keystone is here, it's well hidden." He took a deep breath. "I've always enjoyed coming here. I like to sit in the shade of the lighthouse and listen to the waves breaking on the beach. This place soothes me."

The riddle of the missing keystone seemed obvious to her. "Zeke, the keystone has to be here. Think about it. The lighthouse didn't burn. It's been on Tama Island for ages. Can we get inside?"

"There's no lock on the door. Knock yourself out."

"Aren't you coming?"

He shook his head. "I've been over this light, time and again. I skinned my knee on the twelfth step. I busted my lip when I fell against the upper window. I roasted marshmallows on its floor during a summer shower."

His dismissive attitude irritated her. Jessie reached for the metal door and opened it. Hinges creaked. A narrow, one-person-wide metal staircase spiraled upward. "I'm going to look. Stay here and count the grains of sand. Wouldn't want you to overtax yourself."

"I'm not tired." Zeke's eyes narrowed in speculation. Male irritation radiated from him in waves. He dropped the pack of food and followed her into the lighthouse. "I'll remember you goaded me into unnecessary exertion when I'm paddling back across the sound."

Jessie's steps rang out on the stairs. Energy snapped through her. "Pooh. You expected to hike the length of the island twice today. What's a few stairs for a strapping island boy?"

He didn't answer, but she heard him right behind her. As she climbed, Jessie kept her eyes peeled for arches, crowns, or anything that resembled a keystone. Nothing popped out at her, but the smooth interior of the lighthouse reminded her of something. She'd seen this color of stone recently, but she couldn't place it.

Gaining the top step, her breath came in labored gulps. So much for impressing him with her fitness. The white yacht she'd seen earlier rode the swells offshore, holding its position. She walked around the circular top deck, gazing in every direction. Sadly, the elevated view of the island confirmed what she already knew. There were no visible stone arches on Tama Island.

"Well?" Zeke asked. "Satisfied?"

"Not hardly. Frustrated is more like it."

"How about hungry?"

Trust a man to think of his stomach at a time like this. On cue, her stomach rumbled, and she laughed. "Yeah, I could eat."

"Smart girl."

She shot him a fulminating look as she clomped down the stairs.

"Don't patronize me. These people play for keeps. We have to stay ahead of them or we've got nothing."

"They don't know that."

"They'll follow us here, won't they?"

"They will."

"We need an army."

"We've got Asia. He'll have to do."

Sixty-Six

The wind at his back, Zeke's sure paddle strokes propelled the canoe toward the mainland. Disappointment tasted bitter on his tongue. He'd hoped for answers on the island today, but all he'd found was a sense of homecoming.

Nothing earth-shattering about that. He felt at ease here. That hadn't changed.

He paddled some more. How odd that his father had possessed an object that he'd died to protect, especially since Winston Landry had been known to literally give strangers the shirt off his back. He would voice an opinion about politics or worldly matters only if prodded. Tama Island had been his world.

If his father had owned the keystone, where'd he put it?

Had the information gone up in flames?

Surely his father would have made a contingency plan for something so important.

But who knew the island would be torched? Nothing like that had ever happened during Zeke's lifetime.

"Penny for your thoughts," Jessie said.

"The keystone. I keep coming back to it. Everyone wants it. Nobody knows anything about it, except they believe my father had it."

"He must have put it in a safe place."

"I hope so, but it would've helped if he'd left me a hint or two. As it is, I've got nothing."

Jessie took her time answering. "When we were kids, I thought Bea and I had nothing. It turned out we had a lot more than nothing. We had each other. You have your memories of your father."

"My memories are of him doing everyday things. I never saw him doing anything extra-ordinary. He went fishing and swimming. He cooked for our family. He read books. He did chores. How could anyone mistake him for a secret agent?"

"Your dad must have kept the keystone hidden. Out of all the people in the world, you're the most likely to know where he might have hidden it."

"One might assume that, but I feel like the village idiot due to the utter lack of information. My dad walked around the island every day. Something as small as a key could have been tucked in a centuries-old oak tree branch, buried on the beach with new turtle eggs, or submerged in a bottle at his favorite fishing spot for safekeeping. I don't even know where to start looking."

"Maybe he wove a clue into something he told you. Did he wax eloquently about any certain topic? Any words of wisdom he repeated?"

Zeke snorted. "He had plenty to say, but he often spoke in generalizations, as if he were Benjamin Franklin handing out worldly advice. He'd say things like 'Dream with open eyes' or 'Wisdom changes with the times.' He had hundreds of dad-isms like that."

"He sounds like a great guy, but you're right. It may take a while to visit all his favorite places and interpret his sayings." She sighed and started paddling again. "I had hoped to find the keystone for you, but I failed. I wish I could've done more."

"I'm not giving up on the search, but I need to regroup. A more focused effort will likely prove more fruitful than our broad sweep today." Waves lapped at the boat. Despite his frustration, Zeke felt better than he had in days. "It isn't a total loss. I enjoyed your company, and it felt great to be on my home turf again."

"Your island must have been a beautiful place before the fire."

It had been the most beautiful place in the world to him. His best memories were tied to the island and his parents. Unable to speak, he nodded.

I'll figure this out, Dad. I'll make you proud of me.

* * *

The sun hung low in the sky when they arrived at Asia Minor's private dock. Their host met them at the landing, a wide grin on his face. "Good news!"

"Is Uncle John better?" Zeke asked.

"He's much improved today, but my news is even better. The clean-up crew in St. Louis found your A.I. unit, and I flew him here. He's a mess, but Nola salvaged his processor modules, and she's down in the engineering lab with him as we speak. I've a spare unit if you want to reassemble him. I thought you'd want to know right away."

"Definitely. I want to rebuild Forman." Zeke paused to clear his throat. "We didn't locate a keystone on Tama Island. I had hoped we'd find it."

Asia nodded, his eyes twinkling enigmatically. "That is a disappointment, but we'll figure it out. Your A.I. unit can help—that is, once he's reassembled."

Zeke's spirits lightened at that thought. He'd have Forman again. "Roger that."

Sixty-Seven

Data surged through Forman's circuits. He rejoiced in the pleasurable sensation until his final memories surfaced. "Ow. That hurts."

Zeke looked up from the mound of spare parts on the workbench. "Give me a break. You don't have neurons or pain receptors, and you're in a serviceable body shell. Attaching a finger is at most a distraction."

"Just checking on your sense of humor, boss," Forman quipped. The outdated A.I. housekeeping unit junked in Asia Minor's storage area was a far cry from his original state-of-the-art body. The tuxedo-clad robot had been taken offline years ago after the finger had been damaged.

Information streamed through Forman's circuits at an extraordinary rate. Asia Minor's hypercharged com system delivered like nothing else. It felt great to be back on the grid. "Thought you might have one now that you're back on the Georgia coast."

Zeke scowled. "Do you want this finger or not?"

"Yeah, I want the finger, but I'd rather have my old shell. No one will give me a second glance while I'm stuck in this old thing."

"You're lucky to have your memory core intact. Even luckier that your electronics are compatible with this older butler unit."

"Those ferocious robo dogs. They really did a number on me."

"You're a hero, Forman. Never forget that. Uncle John, Jessie, and I owe our lives to you."

Forman played the sound of a human yawn. "Being a hero isn't all it's cracked up to be."

"Trust me, you'll have plenty of chances to screw up in the future, but at least you're getting a future. Asia went to a lot of trouble and expense to fly you here."

He hung his head. "I don't mean to sound ungrateful, but I'm so ordinary-looking Queen Bea won't recognize me. The love of my life will turn from me in disgust. My Gary good looks are but a faded dream."

"A.I.s don't fall in love."

"That's what you think. Bea's the one for me. I don't want to be with anyone else on the planet but her. When it comes to emotion, I'm more human than you."

"Come again?"

"You're very focused on the big picture of the world. You neglect personal interaction in your daily life, and you don't exercise any wish fulfillment. Sex makes the world go around. You should try it sometime. With Jessie."

"We're friends, not lovers."

"You could be more, if you'd make the effort."

Zeke's face flushed. "Let's talk about something else. Like the Chameleons. What do you know about them? You've been in their digital system, and you have unrestricted access to Asia's files. Cross-reference them and fill me in."

"The Chameleons are a secretive group with ascending cells of power," Forman began as he followed Zeke's command. "Senator Holcomb's cell is now defunct. Whether they were exterminated for failure or by a rival faction within the society is unknown."

"Why did they focus on me? Why do they want the keystone?"

"You're the last Landry."

"So?"

"Your family lineage is island-bound for generation upon generation."

"Other families live in the same place for generations. It's called putting down roots."

"Your argument is valid, yet they looked deeper than that."

"Forman, you're not making any sense. I think your processors are damaged."

"My processors are the only part of me that didn't get mangled by killer mutts. I never knew your parents, but I gather they weren't religious?"

Zeke didn't look up from his work on the finger socket. "They didn't attend church services."

"But?"

"But my father enjoyed nature, and my mother adopted his laid-back beliefs."

"Are these beliefs you now practice?"

Zeke pushed Forman's hand away and rose. "You don't understand. There's no practicing them. It's a way of living. And, yes, I live my life by my father's teachings."

"What does that entail?"

"Nothing earth-shattering. Respect others, respect nature, put forth your best effort in all that you do, and more universal axioms like that."

"It is my observation that you malfunction away from the island and that you are more at ease in natural surroundings than in man-made ones. Unlike most humans, you don't seek companionship; instead, you tend to repel others."

"My turn to say *ouch*."

"The truth sucks. Get over it."

Zeke jammed his hands into his pockets and leaned against the wall. "Are you suggesting I'm incapable of sustaining a relationship? That I'm not human?"

"Didn't say that. Your brush with danger shifted your focus to the frailty of human life. As the last of your line, it's your duty to father a son."

"A son?"

Forman nodded. "Ever since the island's earliest recorded history, resident Landrys have married and had exactly one son. The father-son line of your ancestry is statistically significant."

Zeke straightened. "It's true my father had no siblings. Neither did his father. How did you know about the rest?"

"Historical records in the Chameleon database. You and at least a dozen other individuals worldwide with similar male-dominated lineage were red-flagged."

"There are others like me?"

Forman activated a laugh soundtrack, wishing it sounded richer and less tinny. The retro shell needed major upgrades to suit him. "No one is like you, my friend. You've proven to be extremely resourceful and a royal pain in the ass to the Chameleons."

"Lucky me."

"They don't know if you have hidden the keystone, but the fact that they can't hold onto you has them seriously pissed."

"I have no idea what the keystone is. I looked around the island for it today, but I came up empty-handed. To my recollection, neither my father nor my grandfather ever mentioned that word to me. Why can't the Chameleons leave me to my water research?"

Forman paused. Zeke had turned the question around and presented a new avenue to pursue. Brilliant. "That is an excellent question."

"Which begs an excellent answer."

"Your water research halted once we left to look for your Uncle John. Those few water overages in plain sight were recently leaked to the press, and people are asking the right questions about the so-called water shortage now."

"All this chasing about the country didn't dull my brain. I remember the sequence of events."

"What if the keystone is a ruse? A means of applying pressure to keep you moving in a different direction?"

Zeke's head bobbed as if he'd been sucker punched. "Some ruse. It nearly killed all of us."

"If they can't stop your water research, they will expedite your death."

"Never thought of it that way."

Forman jerked a thumb toward himself. "I'm the brains of this outfit."

Zeke ignored him and rubbed his stubbled chin. "The fire destroyed my lab. We salvaged the data, but my customized analysis software, it's all gone."

"That's what they think, but I have your back, boss man."

"Yeah?"

"I downloaded your data and programs in Asia's computer palace and also buried it deep in the Bob mode of my tertiary processor. Redundancy is my religion of choice," Forman said.

"I think I love you." Zeke grinned. "Once I have you fully operational, I'm jumping back into research mode. I've been thinking more about them hiding the water in full sight. What if someone transported the missing water to the arctic and froze it? If they were sneaky about where they laid the ice, it would be virtually undetectable to the naked eye."

"How would they get it there?"

"Good question. They've had decades to do this. Maybe they used supertankers. Maybe they somehow used a land transport system. Or maybe they somehow tapped into the Alaskan pipeline. It would be interesting to know who rebuilt that thing forty years ago."

"I'll run those queries."

"What about under-the-sea storage possibilities? With a century of pumping oil out of the ocean floor, there are man-made voids down there, as well as natural ones. Let's check oil rigs and undersea maps for potential Chameleon activity. That missing water is here somewhere."

The motion detectors to the south of the estate alarmed. Cams activated, and a video feed streamed into Forman's head. "Trouble," he said, sending the feed to a nearby screen for Zeke to view. Zeke leaned in. "What's that?"

"We've got trouble outside. And I'm going to fight it with only nine fingers."

Sixty-Eight

Sunlight glinted off the security cam on the southeastern barrier of the coastal mansion. Three lowered his binoculars. The fortified summer home of philanthropist Asia Minor surprised him. He'd expected minimal security. Instead, he'd found a secure compound. His recon drone, a small insect the size of a horsefly, confirmed his gut-level analysis. With those thick concentric walls ringing the place, this would get ugly.

Using his wrist com, he reiterated the prime directive to his elite foot soldiers. He'd been anchored offshore in his late father's yacht while they marched north from the port of Brunswick. "Capture Zeke Landry alive. No tranq darts. I want him fully conscious for immediate questioning. Time is of the essence."

The brunette squad leader's image flashed on the small screen. "Understood."

Four's ambition spoke volumes. Her aggressive style and her fierce determination assured Three that no one would best her. She'd extricated him from Two's clutches, and she'd fallen hard for him. He hadn't hesitated to take advantage of her loyalty reversal.

The old man really knew how to identify people who needed a cause and a sense of belonging. Luckily, he'd learned a thing or two from his dad. He recruited Four immediately. Turned out she wanted sex from him and lots of it. Not a problem.

"And the others, sir?" Four asked.

"Eliminate anyone who impedes our mission."

"Yes, sir."

His father had promised Three the world if he played the game, but he'd wanted to share this moment with his father. Landry had taken that from him. Once he extracted the needed information, he'd kill the man with his bare hands.

The Master had contacted him after the St. Louis incident. If Three delivered the keystone in a week, he could assume his father's second-in-command position within the Chameleon organization and the coveted code name of One. After the new world order became law, he could set up an empire on any continent.

Sweeter words had never been spoken.

With his war spoils, his father's wealth, and his keen intellect, people would fall all over themselves doing his bidding. He'd control his destiny.

His father had been convinced Landry had the keystone. With time in short supply, Three had no option but to continue the same avenue of pursuit. His field promotion in the Chameleons depended on delivering the keystone to the Master.

Failure was not an option.

"The Bobs are in place, sir," Four stated. "Awaiting your order."

"You have my go."

Three picked up a blaster in his good hand, cursing the foul luck that had knocked his left arm temporarily out of commission. Two had paid for his audacity. Paid dearly. The power circle consisted of Three and Four now. They would succeed where Senator Holcomb and Dr. Ira Cranfield-Meyers had failed.

He followed a heavily armed squad of Killer Bobs. It had been his idea months ago to plant a virus deep in the Bobs' subroutine programming, his idea to raid the warehouse where they were sent for repairs. Supply Central had been embarrassed to the point of silence when a hundred defective robots vanished.

Three had shipped twenty to the Georgia coast to grab Landry. He had ten with him, and Four controlled the other ten about one hundred yards due east. *Should have brought them all*, he mused wryly, but a shipment of that size would've attracted undue attention.

Three hunched forward behind the Bobs, mirroring their silent approach, ignoring the wild slamming of his heart in his chest cavity. Adrenaline roared through his bloodstream, filling him with euphoria and optimism. This totally beat being a medical doctor.

Ammo whizzed over his head. The Bobs returned fire, knocking out an unmanned gun turret. A Bob went down.

Three scaled the first wall, sweating buckets inside his body armor. How could anyone stand to live in the godforsaken South? Too steamy for him.

The Bob to his far left exploded into the air, shattering into sharp projectiles. Three cursed a blue streak. They'd mined the approach. Not wanting to lose so much as a toenail, he adjusted his stride to follow in the footsteps of a Bob.

Robo dogs charged out of a concealed opening in the wall, snarling and snapping. The first four-legged unit lunged high, drew fire from every Bob, and fell silently to the ground. The second canine, a gangly, dark beast, surged toward him. Three emptied his entire clip into the pit bull, sighing with relief when the black monster dropped at his feet.

What did Asia Minor have in this place? Compounds in the Middle East had less security than Asia's "beach cottage," as it was listed in the property tax archives.

A barrage of fire from the next turret shot off the right hand of an adjacent Bob. Undeterred, the A.I. unit transferred the weapon to its other hand and disabled the turret.

Three inched forward in the sandy valley between barrier walls. That keystone had better be worth its weight in plutonium. His squad neutralized three more stationary turrets, four flying drones, and two more robo dogs with no losses.

Eight and a half Bobs and him. Four should've had similar success on the eastern attack front. The odds were still very much in their favor.

A squad of ancient robots advanced, pushing his group to the east, closer to Four's location. Sunlight glinted on their shiny chrome. "What are those things?" He squinted to read the names on the thick gold collars. "Nolas? I thought those clunkers had been retired years ago."

In the early days of robotics, those collars had been composed of pure gold. He made a mental note to harvest the golden collars on the robots here after he gained control of the compound. This firefight would be over in five minutes, and he'd have his hands on the prize. Landry.

Three stepped into a protective sandwich of Bobs. To his right, he heard the staccato sound of gunfire. Four had attacked from her landward position.

An athletic-looking man with naturally bronzed skin trailed the Nolas, a mini-blaster in each hand. To his right, a tuxedo-clad A.I.— a butler droid—tiptoed as if he walked on exploding eggshells. Three laughed at the absurd image.

What would they send out next? The robo vacuums?

"Target is outside and wearing light blue body armor," Three muttered into his wrist com. "Game on."

Sixty-Nine

Sweat plastered Zeke's shirt to his back under his body armor. He advanced behind the barrier of Nolas, firing when he had a clear shot. The mini-blasters hummed in his hands, raring to go. As gunfire pelted in his direction, he ducked instinctively.

"Shooter, ten o'clock," Forman said from Zeke's side.

Zeke whipped left and fired at the A.I. on the barrier wall. The machine spun off balance when the shot hit its upper left chest, but it didn't go down. "Perfect kill shot for a human. Not so good for an A.I."

"You want to take them out, it has to be a clean shot in the right eye."

"It would be easier if they didn't look so geeky. How did the Chameleons get so many Killer Bobs?"

Forman's arms moved like a mime on uppers, and his head swiveled from side to side. *Still need to do some fine-tuning on his movement controller*, Zeke thought. *If we get out of this alive.*

"When the Chameleons plugged me into their system, they had one hundred Bobs in their inventory," Forman said. "Coincidentally, one hundred Bobs went missing from Supply Central's rehab warehouse."

"All those Killer Bobs on the loose and not a hint of it in the media? Unbelievable."

"Can you hear me, Zeke?" Jessie's voice blared through Zeke's ear com.

Live rounds whizzed over his head. "Loud and clear. You and Asia find his secret weapon?"

"We accessed the hidden security console," she said. "The controller pad is a three-by-three grid of colored buttons. We don't know how to make it work."

"We're outnumbered three to one. They've neutralized the gun turrets and the robo dogs. Their Bobs are more maneuverable than our squad of Nolas. We need a miracle."

"Working on it."

Zeke hunkered down behind a thick Ionic column and waited. He glanced over at his companion. "Got any bright ideas?"

"My Brutus programming for hand-to-hand combat is no match for an assassination squad."

Zeke fired off another shot, this time in the money slot. The A.I. exploded with a loud bang, mechanical parts flying everywhere. He grinned at Forman. "Got one."

"Yeah, but they nailed two of ours in the same time frame. I could move into the open and draw their fire. That would allow you time to escape."

"We did that last time and look what happened. Besides, I'm not abandoning my friends or family. We're in this together."

"The odds of our success are poor. I calculate they are—"

"Hold up," Zeke interrupted. "Games of war aren't won on odds, they're won on heart. I believe we'll win this, as illogical as that seems right now."

"Fall back," the head Nola shouted as she zigged past Zeke's column. "We're outnumbered and outgunned."

Zeke and Forman complied, edging toward the house. Killer Bobs pushed forward en masse. Zeke's mouth went dry. Despite his best intentions, fear crept in. Sucking in a ragged breath, he tapped his ear com. "Jessie, we're out of options."

"I'm still at square zero. I've engaged each colored button individually, but the com screen stays locked. Asia tried a combo or two, but we've got nothing. Unless you brainiacs figure this out, we're doomed."

Zeke turned to Forman. "They can't unlock the console. There must be an activation sequence."

Forman looked solemn in his butler suit. "How many colored buttons?"

Zeke relayed the question over the com. Ammo sprayed the side of the column he hid behind.

"There are nine buttons," Jessie said. "They're the same primary colors as a child's box of eight crayons plus a white button. They're arrayed like a numeric keypad."

"Any identifying letters, numbers, or symbols?" Zeke asked.

"No," Jessie said. "All I've got are colors."

Forman leaned closer to Zeke. "The highest probability color sequence is a rainbow. Red, orange, yellow, green, and blue."

"But that doesn't use up all the colors," Jessie warned.

"What have you got to lose? Key in a sequence of ROYGB and see what happens."

"Okay. Here goes."

Zeke turtled his head into his shoulders, making himself a smaller target. If he ever built a fortress, he'd make sure it couldn't be invaded. Asia's mounted turrets, the Nola, and the robo dogs were a good start, but they couldn't withstand this level of assault. Asia needed an army of his own.

A moment later, Forman doubled over, his hands clamped over his fake ears. "My head. My head."

Zeke didn't hear or feel anything. "What?"

Forman clunked to his knees. "If I was a human, I'd be puking my guts out."

Zeke glanced at the battlefield, which had gone oddly silent. The other A.I. units, the Nolas and the Bobs, clutched their heads. One by one, they clattered to the ground.

Behind the Killer Bobs, a man with his arm in a sling shrieked in rage. "No!"

Zeke watched Forman twitch. "You okay, buddy?"

"I'll make it. My Holmes processor has an override that minimizes the sonic neutralizer."

"Is that what happened? A sonic blast disabled the machines?"

"Yeah. They're done. Fried permanently. We've evened the playing field: two of them, two of us."

"Can you shoot a human?"

"I can if it's trying to kill you."

"Let's take the fight to them. Come on. I'm going after one-arm. You take the woman with the knee brace. She pummeled me in St. Louis and would've killed me if not for you." Zeke fired at the male, who'd taken up a position behind a bullet-ridden statue of Venus. His opponent hunkered down, and Zeke waited for him to raise his head.

To his left, Forman zigzagged closer to the female's position near the eastern wall. The brunette had a good spot behind a massive oak ringed with large clay pots of flowers. Clumps of Spanish moss dotted the ground, cut from the tree by stray shots.

The brunette returned fire, pinning Forman to a column accessible to Zeke's shooter. Zeke kept up a barrage of fire so that his guy couldn't shoot Forman.

Without warning, Jessie slunk out of the robo dog access panel, wielding a shovel. Zeke's heart rose in his throat. If the female heard Jessie's approach, Jessie would be toast. Zeke fired off a steady volley into the tree above the woman until his blaster ran dry, raining down a flurry of leaves, moss, and tiny branches upon her head.

Behind Jessie, Asia Minor eased out of the dog panel, an old-fashioned .22 pump rifle in his hand. He sidled over to cover Jessie.

Jessie smacked the woman hard in the head with the shovel, and the brunette went down. "Don't mess with us, bitch," Jessie said. "That's for punching me in the gut the other day. I hope your head hurts worse than my gut."

The brunette groaned and reached for her blaster.

"Step aside, young lady," Asia ordered, his voice full of authority.

A crisp retort smacked through the air, and the brunette stilled.

Zeke cheered. One down, one invader to go. Forman, Jessie, and Asia fanned out, advancing toward the remaining shooter.

"Surrender," Zeke shouted during a lull. "You can't shoot us all. We've got you outnumbered."

"Never," the man shouted back. "And you're wrong. I don't have to shoot every one of you. Only the woman."

With that, the man aimed his blaster at Jessie. Zeke exploded from cover, hurtling forward, leaping over shredded greenery. In slow motion, he heard the man's blaster rev and pulse. Was he in time? *God, please, let me be in time. Please let me save my friend. Please let my effort, my life, matter.*

Red hot pain slammed through his body. He spun to the ground in a breathless void. Time hung and folded and wrinkled. Throughout it all, he clung to the searing pain. Scenes flashed before his eyes, a personal highlight reel. His family. His island. His home.

He heard more shots.

His friends might be in danger.

He clung to that thought and fought his way back through the jungle of pain. Clamping his right hand over his wounded shoulder, he attempted to sit up but only succeeded in turning on his right side.

Jessie and Forman appeared in his field of vision. Jessie's face had gone chalky white. Forman looked dapper and poised in his butler robot guise.

"Is your shoulder the only injury?" Forman asked.

No sound came out when Zeke tried to respond.

Jessie's hands ran over his front and back. "One entry wound," she said.

Another shot rang out, and Jessie dove for the ground next to him. She raised up to see. "Oh no!" she wailed. "That guy shot Asia. Asia's not moving. I think he's dead!"

Darkness edged Zeke's vision but he fought it. Asia. Dead. It didn't seem possible. Not fair. Not his fight. He stared at Forman, willing him to do what he couldn't do.

Forman picked up blasters in both hands and fired four charges at the invader. "This time you'll stay dead if you know what's good for you."

"It's over," Forman said, squatting next to Zeke. "We got 'em. Never bet on a Chameleon, not when you're around."

Jessie's drawn face orbited over Zeke, blood streaked down her cheek. Forman hovered over her shoulder, a worried expression on his butler face. Zeke tried to thank them for helping him, but the words wouldn't come.

Darkness rode in on the barbed wings of pain.

Seventy

Like a distance swimmer desperate for air, Zeke shot out of an uneasy sleep into a bedroom of dark antiques and thick drapes. His room at Asia Minor's house. The muted illumination and drawn curtains created a timeless sensation. Was it day or night?

He glanced down at his wrist com. Nothing there but wrist. He scanned the room. No timepieces. No electronics. Just the bed, two chairs, a bedside table, and a dresser.

When he tried to rise, sharp pain lanced through his shoulder. Wearily, he laid his head back on the pillow as bits and pieces of memory surfaced. He'd rescued Uncle John and brought him to Asia's place. The Chameleons had followed and attacked. He'd been wounded.

Beyond that, he had no clear memories. Blurry snips dogged his thoughts. There'd been cops. White-coated medics. The pungent smell of antiseptic.

He glanced down at the snowy bandage on his bare chest. A serious bandage. He wiggled the fingers on his left hand. They worked. The damage wasn't crippling. Just painful.

"You're awake!" Jessie padded into the room, her shoulder-length blonde locks darkened by moisture. "I stepped out for a shower. How are you?"

His shoulder hurt like a son of a bitch. "I'm okay."

She burst out laughing and touched his good arm. "For a genius, you're not too smart. You jumped in front of a crazy person with a blaster. It shredded your body armor."

"He would've killed you."

"I appreciate the heroics, I really do, but I'm putting my foot down. No more blaster dodging. A dead hero is no good to anyone."

He didn't have a comeback for that. He'd acted on instinct, nothing more. "What happened? Is Asia dead?"

"Yes. The man with the scary eyes killed him."

Zeke shuddered, causing a fresh wave of pain to radiate from his shoulder. "I feel terrible. Asia didn't deserve to die this way."

Jessie's eyes misted. "Asia was sweet to me, and I wanted to spend more time with him. I wish he'd stayed inside during the firefight, but he wouldn't hear of it. He wanted to defend his property."

"If he'd stayed inside, he'd be alive."

"Don't punish yourself. God knows, I've replayed that scene over and over in my head, wishing for another outcome. Asia knew the risk of entering the battle. He died a hero."

Though Jessie spoke the truth, it didn't lessen his grief. "What about the woman with the knee brace, the one that socked us in St. Louis? What happened to her?"

"She's dead. I smacked her with a shovel, and Asia shot her. After you took a blaster ray for me, Asia wounded Mr. Scary Eyes. Forman and I rushed over to check on you, but the bad guy tricked us. He shot Asia, and then Forman blasted the bad guy's face off. This time he stayed dead."

Zeke nodded, piecing the snips from his fractured memory into that framework. It fit, not that he wanted Asia dead. Not that he wanted a throbbing shoulder injury, either.

"What did you tell the cops?" he asked.

"Your Uncle John rallied to take charge of the situation. His medical team stabilized you. Forman temporarily loaned his Brutus processor to the head Nola. Together they removed and destroyed all the Killer Bobs and hid the deactivated Nolas in storage. The two dead people were then dressed in what Forman called island protestor robes. That's when we called the local cops."

Zeke appreciated the logical approach to the situation. "And?"

"We told the cops that renegade island protestors stormed the compound with blasters. With Asia dead and you wounded, they accepted our story. Once they left, Uncle John's medical team removed your bullet and stitched you up."

"No one mentioned Chameleons or keystones to them?"

"Nope. Everything is all tied up, nice and tidy."

"Not so tidy from my perspective. Asia is dead. I've got a hole in my shoulder. And we still have no idea where this keystone is. Or if there are more Chameleons poised to descend upon us. Did the cops ID the invaders?"

"Don't know what they have. Forman ran their prints, and we had an ID in minutes. The leader was Senator Holcomb's son, an orthopedic surgeon named Travis Holcomb." Jessie shuddered. "The woman was an anesthesiologist named Nancy Abner."

"They were more than that. The way they commanded those killer robots and handled themselves under fire, they were combat trained, most likely Chameleons. Any chance we got them all?"

"Ask your Uncle John or Forman about that. I'm done with conspiracy theories. One firefight will last me a lifetime. I'm not cut out for a life of nonstop action and adventure."

"You're right. It isn't safe here." He pushed up to a seated position. "We'll arrange private transport for you to go to Richmond. The Chameleons won't stop until they have the keystone. They have to be neutralized."

"Take your own advice, and let some hotshot special forces guys hunt them down. You've done your part and then some. Why don't you recuperate in Richmond?"

Going to Richmond would put Jessie and Bea in danger. "Thanks for the offer, but I won't bring my troubles to your door. What of your connection to this? Have you changed your mind about Uncle John?"

"Oh, that." She brushed aside his query with a flip of her wrist. "We worked through that days ago, while you were in twilight sleep recovering. Your Uncle John is a great guy, just like you said. He's been pouring through Asia's records, and we learned a few things."

"Such as?"

"Turns out Asia knew about the documents I've been receiving from the Chameleons. Remember that albino, Rissa? Asia had her followed from the start, and he knew she'd been dropping off those packets for me. Once Rissa vanished, he sent me another packet, sure that I'd jump at the chance to meet the man he fingered. He selected your uncle because he knew I'd come to no harm through John Demery and that I'd meet you. It's all in his notes. Your uncle is an innocent. Asia—well, I don't understand the things he did. He made many unusual choices."

Some of his grief for Asia abated. The man had played roulette with their safety. "I don't understand. Who did Asia work for?"

"Not sure, but your Uncle John inherits Asia's wealth and his home."

Zeke whistled under his breath. So much had happened during his recuperation. "Didn't see that coming."

"Neither did I." Her eyes twinkled. "It gets better."

"How?"

"As your uncle's heir, you're going to be mega-rich."

Rich?

What did he want with money?

Wealth wouldn't bring his parents back. His dad used to say money caused more problems than it solved. Would it change him?

Would it change how people reacted to him?

Zeke's suspicions intensified.

Had Jessie invited him to Richmond because of the money?

Seventy-One

The cold, hard lines of Asia's private office suited Zeke. The deluxe com hardware, the quad servers and processors, the state-of-the-art software, the bank of monitors—the entire room buzzed with power and possibilities.

"Computer," Zeke said, resting comfortably in the body-conforming chair, "Call up the current global water data and run it through my water analysis software."

"Processing," the sultry female voice replied.

"Found something water related." Forman turned in his seat to face Zeke's chair. Data streamed through an air bridge from console to robot. A shimmering blue cloud linked him to the com module. "Computer, run the vid footage on screen five."

Zeke leaned forward to study the people in conflict on the monitor. "What's all this?"

"Remember the International Water Summit? The meeting the Institute needed your water report for?"

Zeke nodded.

"This is it. Doomsayers armed with blasters disrupted the proceedings yesterday. Organizers canceled the summit."

"Why didn't security handle the intruders?"

"They did, but the water authorities were terrified by the violence. They packed up and went home."

The news struck Zeke like a sledgehammer. "Why didn't they meet elsewhere to rework the water rationing system?"

"Without a quorum, they couldn't vote. The Institute's position paper wasn't scheduled to be released until noon the second day. All that pressure they put on you to write that report in a short time frame was for naught."

"Maybe not. Uncle John's friend Rissa Porter knew about my findings and my report. As a double agent, she surely passed along my information to FSIR and the Chameleons."

"The probability of her leaking your results approaches one hundred percent. They've been trying to silence you from the start.

Your water research threatens their plan for world domination."

"My research involves tracking the water cycle. Nothing subversive or world-rocking about that, unless they control the remaining supply. From our earlier search it looks like they control most of the water and mineral rights in highly populated areas. They're making money hand over fist through the Global Now water products. Whatever happened to the query we were going to run about the arctic and deep sea as hiding places?"

Forman's mouth gaped. "I forgot."

Zeke mirrored his expression. "A.I.s have perfect recall. What do you mean you forgot?"

"I forgot. Sue me. We had a huge battle. You got shot. We had the cops to deal with. Then your Uncle John needed me. I haven't had time to do one more thing in days."

"Some fancy research assistant you are. I'm out cold, and you're working on other things."

"I apologize. I haven't been myself since … the accident."

Since his rebirth in a butler suit. Zeke relented. "All right. I give. Your level of trauma trumps mine. We both need time to heal. But we can continue our water research as we convalesce."

"I am checking out the Alaskan pipeline as we speak. Elite Eagle Engineering had the contract for the refurbishment of the line in 2020. It took them three years to complete the upgrade. EEE built the new line next to the old one, and decommissioned the old one in place. Historical footage coming up on screen three."

Zeke studied the image of the construction crew in the frozen terrain. "Could they have used the old pipe to carry water up to Alaska?"

"It leaked like a sieve in places. The water would've been noticeable. My bet is there's a hidden supply line under or attached to the new pipeline."

"Can you rotate the cam angle to check?"

The onscreen image changed from a historical vid to a current day image. With the white snow underneath and the white pipeline, Zeke couldn't discern a noticeable addition. "See anything?"

"Not with this lousy equipment. I'll help myself to a Chinese government sat. We'll only have a few minutes before they notice us and kick us off. Wait for it." Another image flickered onscreen, with different color signatures. The cam panned the pipeline. Along the bottom, a different color scheme fluoresced. "Got it. You were right.

There's an auxiliary line underneath the oil trunkline. From the colors detected, water is inside."

"Heads of state will want to know about that. Release that image to the press before anything else happens. We want to stay proactive on this."

"Got it. What about the ocean floor?"

"Do you have charts we can review?"

"Better than that. I have a complete listing of Chameleon properties around the world."

"Good deal." Zeke scanned a portion of the list. Many properties fronted the Gulf of Mexico. "Can't be coincidence they own this shoreline. I bet if you go back far enough, there are air pockets in there, pockets where water could hide without a trace."

"How will we prove it?"

"We won't do anything, but the Institute can use images from their dolphin research program to investigate. Make sure Uncle John has this information."

"Done. Anything else?"

"Something else occurred to me. We checked drinking water reservoirs. What about the contaminated impoundments? Some of those contain a lot of water, even if it isn't potable. Let's look at five of them."

"Can do," Forman said. The stream of data around him dimmed to a pale blue momentarily until it darkened with new data input. "Every site checks out to the milliliter."

Zeke's pulse jumped at the coincidence. "That's odd, given natural evaporative processes, rainfall, and lack of groundwater recharge due to the impenetrable basin liners. There should be some variance in the readings."

"Nope, the number is rock solid out to four decimal places, and has been that way for two years. Did the monitoring gauges malfunction?"

"Perhaps. I'd like to see the impoundments for myself. Which site can we visually monitor by satellite right now?"

The number stream fluctuated again. "The Central American one. I'm redirecting the sat cam now. Volume measurement coming to you in five." After a pause, Forman turned to Zeke. "It checked out. Same volume as in the data feed."

Zeke shook his head. "Impossible. Nothing in nature is that precise."

"Good point, Dr. Z. Nature is fraught with variance. Machines, on the other hand, are extremely precise."

He couldn't think straight with the therapeutic chair wrapped around him like a sweater and massaging his lower back. Zeke rose and paced the office. "A machine. That makes sense. A machine could monitor water levels and adjust to a constant value. Only who would be foolish enough to add fresh water to a contaminated basin?"

Forman tightened the shot of the lake. A dark amorphous shape showed beneath the crystal-clear water.

"What is that?" Zeke asked. "Can we get compositional readings?"

"Not with the satellite cam. What I can do is compare the image to a historical photo in Asia's extensive natural resource photo inventory. Here's a contrasting shot on screen three from five years ago. No dark areas at that time."

"That water is biotoxic, so the underwater shape isn't the creature from the dark lagoon."

Forman cracked a smile. "Uh-oh. Your sense of humor's showing. How'd that happen?"

"Life is short. No sense in always bottling yourself up."

"Now you're talking my language. Love. It."

Zeke blushed and cleared his throat. "Getting back to the problem at hand, the contaminated basin maintains a steady state volume. Since that didn't occur naturally, it's an artificial construct, leading me to believe contaminated water has been removed. Why would someone want toxic water?"

"To poison people?"

"You may be onto something there. Let's see if this is an anomaly or a pattern. Can you obtain recent aerial shots of other contaminated impoundments?"

Within a few minutes, Zeke made a chilling discovery. "Another disaster is in the works. This contaminated water can be used as a bioweapon. Depending on concentration, these toxins can kill or sicken those who drink it or shower with it. We need to alert the authorities, but first we have to discover their target."

"The toxic water has to be transported in an innocuous way. Want me to search for water bottling companies operating under the umbrella of FSIR and the Chameleons?"

"Yes. Forward your findings to Uncle John's com station. I'm headed there now."

"You got it, boss."

Zeke hurried down the corridor and knocked on his uncle's door. A medic answered. "Yes?"

"I need to see my uncle."

"He's resting. Can't this wait?"

"No. It's a matter of national security, maybe even global security." Zeke pushed his way in, ignoring the medic's sputtering protests. At his uncle's bedside, he noted a healthy skin tone, fading bruises, and rounder cheeks. Much better. His eyes were still razor-sharp, as ever.

"Sorry to barge in on you like this, Uncle John," Zeke said.

"Zeke. Good to see you up and about. I heard the sanitized version of the Chameleon attack. You handled yourself well, acting with courage and integrity. Your parents would be proud of you."

"It isn't over yet. Forman and I were searching for the missing water and stumbled into something with the potential to overshadow the locusts, the plague, and the earthquakes. May I speak in front of your staff?"

Uncle John nodded his medic toward the door. "Out." When they were alone, the elderly man nodded. "Continue."

Zeke briefed him on the findings. "I discovered several more hiding places, and I will continue to work on the problem. However, today's findings horrified me, especially the toxic water."

"As well it should. How do you think it will be used?"

"If we're dealing with Chameleons, they tend to be aggressive in their strikes—no lingering poisoning for them. Concentration matters when dealing with a waterborne toxin, so my guess is that they'd target groups of powerful people, such as world leaders. Or they might target one side of a long-running feud—say, pitting the Arabs against the Israelis. Any such implementation would incite violence, chaos, and worldwide panic."

"Sounds like the Chameleons. Determined rat bastards, aren't they?"

The room chimed before Zeke could reply. Forman's butler mug appeared on the far wall. "I have more information. These four companies have bottling operations near the contamination sources."

Zeke paled at the sight of one of the names. Green Earth provided bottled water for the Institute and to many government agencies. "That gives us a means and a motive. Compile a list of known meetings in the next three months of heads of state or other world leaders."

Forman nodded. "One moment."

A new list flashed on the com wall. Zeke scanned the list, tripping over one meeting in particular. "The One World Water Association annual meeting is in two weeks. Forman and I previously determined that many World Health Collective delegates attending this meeting owe FSIR and the Chameleons. They could strategically target their enemies at this gathering, inserting more FSIR-friendly delegates to fill in the vacancies, and they would control water across the planet."

"I'll pass this to my superiors, and we'll neutralize the threat," Uncle John said. "Well done."

"Thirty percent of the world's drinking water is still missing. My working hypothesis is it may be hidden in the arctic and under the sea. I'll find it."

"I'm sure you will. You've proved your worth many times over during this crisis. I salute you, and your country salutes you."

His uncle's praise made Zeke nervous. He backed toward the door. "Well, okay then. I don't want to overtire you. And, sir?"

"Yes?"

"I'm sorry about Asia."

"My friend was a fine man, and I miss him. Having his ear meant a lot through the years."

"I feel the same way about you, Uncle John."

"Feeling's mutual, kid."

Seventy-Two

Forman let the shredded flowers slip through his white gloved fingers, their sweet fragrance adding to his growing distress. He ignored the rabid voices of Pauline and Connor on the kitchen vid screen as they vented about the surprising water supply line that had been found beneath the Alaskan pipeline. The Chameleons would have to find another way to dominate the world. With their external reserves of water confiscated, the Chameleons, especially their affiliates, would be busy trying to stay out of prison.

But world affairs didn't hold the robot's interest today. "I'm doomed," he moaned.

Zeke sipped coffee at the nearby table. "How so?"

Forman lifted his head and looked at Zeke. "I've disassembled fourteen varieties of flowers with 'she loves me, she loves me not,' and the overwhelming result is she loves me not. I don't want to live in a world where Bea doesn't love me. And how will she know it's me in this tin-can butler suit? I don't even look like myself."

"Looks aren't what counts. What's inside matters most."

"Easy for you to say, your heart isn't on the line."

Zeke nodded soberly. "I wish you luck. My father always said to be yourself."

Another wave of despair cascaded through Forman's neural net. What good was it to have emotions if they weren't reliable? "I have even less to offer Bea than before. In this retro butler shell, I'm not even anatomically correct. I resemble a plastic fashion doll of a hundred years ago. I can't pleasure her fully."

"I didn't consider your love life when I reactivated you, but this setup is temporary. That Gary robo shell Uncle John ordered for you will arrive any day now."

Forman momentarily covered his ocular sensors with his hand, as if blocking his sight would improve his physical attributes. "But Bea will arrive first. I should keep away from her until I'm restored to my physical stature."

"Suit yourself, but that's not necessary. From what I gather, the

Stemfords aren't superficial."

"Bea is the hottest chick on the planet. She can have any man she wants."

"Maybe she doesn't want a man. Maybe she wants you. Did you ever think of that?"

"Don't tease me. This is too important."

"I see that."

"What if she's sleeping with Tank now? They've been living under the same roof for nearly a week. He's had the inside track."

"Take a deep breath, Forman. Women are the eighth wonder of the world. You can't change what's in Bea's heart. What will be will be."

Zeke's advice resonated with truth, but the humor of the situation brightened Forman's dour mood so much that he chuckled aloud. "Hold the com! Is Zeke Landry giving me relationship advice?"

"I don't have a data set to analyze for this, but it seems straightforward. Bea likes you. You can work with that."

An electronic signal pulsed. Forman sighed deeply, his worries rebounding in full force. "She's here."

Zeke rose and waved Forman forward. "She knows about the butler guise. It will be all right."

Jessie joined Zeke and Forman at the front door. They watched as Tank parked the armored transpo in the circular drive. Bea popped out of the stopped vehicle with a happy shriek and dashed right into her sister's arms.

The women talked a mile a minute, and the rest of them might as well not even have been there. The delay wreaked havoc on Forman's operating system. To steady himself, he reached over and shook Tank's hand. "You okay?"

Tank grinned. "Yeah. I spent the week chillin' with Queen Bea. Hanging with the hottest female on the planet. Eating to my heart's content. Groovin' to cool tunes all day and all night. Can't beat that."

Forman's system flooded with jealousy. He flexed his nine fingers. "Lucky dog."

"She talked about you, dude," Tank said. "Said you were a big hero for saving her sister's life. She's got a thing for you, even though you look ridiculous in that butler suit."

He stilled the data streaming through his processors. She

approved of his actions. She cared about him. Would it be enough?

Finally she turned to him.

He couldn't move a millimeter if he tried.

He registered that Jessie and Zeke had stepped back into the house to give them privacy. Tank, darn his sorry hide, didn't budge an inch.

"That you, Forman?" Bea said.

Frozen, he could only stare at her. Tank thumped the back of his head, and his circuits unscrambled. "It's me. I apologize for my temporary appearance. I'll look like my old self in a few days."

"Don't ever apologize for your appearance. Jessie told me how you saved the day, twice. You gave your life for her. You are so brave, so courageous. You're my Mr. Wonderful." Bea rushed him, hugging him tight, raining kisses on his unfeeling face.

He cursed his wretched, sensory-deprived state even as his arms tightened around her. He loved this woman. "I've missed you."

"Miss no more. I'm moving in."

"You are?" Data streamed at light speed through his processors, whirling in three dimensions at once. The universe of possibilities expanded in hopeful shades of light.

"Yep. Jessie and I are relocating. Didn't she tell you?"

"No."

She patted his back. The sound echoed through his mostly hollow core. "Poor guy."

"I'm moving in, too," Tank said.

Forman glared at the ex-con over Bea's head. "You heard Zeke's in line to inherit millions, right?"

"What? That's awesome, but that's not why I'm staying. Back in prison Zeke offered me a place to stay on the island. After all this stress, I'm ready for some island time before I start my new job."

"I've invited Tank to tour with me," Bea said. "With him watching my back, I don't have to worry about crazy fans."

Her remark sliced through Forman. She thought of him as a crazy fan? But what could he offer her, realistically? He was a machine, not a man. He existed to protect Zeke. He couldn't follow Bea all over the globe because Zeke would move back to Tama Island.

His hopes for a rosy future with Bea faded.

"That's great," he managed.

"Don't pout," Bea said, pushing herself at arm's length from his abdominal cavity. "You're invited, too."

"Thank you, but I can't accept a bodyguard position no matter how much I want to be with you. My primary function is to assist Zeke."

"That slave driver can't give you a weekend off, here and there? That's unreasonable. I'll set him straight."

Forman laughed, and his mood brightened. "You do that, sweetheart."

Someone cleared his throat behind Forman. He automatically checked the pitch and timbre against those of the household occupants. Zeke.

"If you lovebirds are finished with your reunion, Uncle John requested a private meeting with Forman and me," Zeke said.

Bea kissed him again, this time full on his mouth. "Go do your guy stuff while I get unloaded," she said. "See you in a few."

Forman followed Zeke down the hall and into the elevator, his heart as light as a helium balloon.

Zeke shot him a penetrating look. "Gonna make it?"

Forman grinned as big as his rigid butler face would allow. "Yeah. She doesn't hate me."

"You're right about that. You got a clinging violet hug. She never even acknowledged me."

"She didn't mean to be rude. This is the longest she and Jessie have been apart in years."

Zeke's palms went up. "I wasn't judging her. I have no problem with Bea."

"Good. Bea and Jessie are moving to Tama Island. But Tank's in the picture."

"Tank is her friend. He didn't pop a cork when she hugged you. I know for a fact that he likes women with large butts. He said they were his dream women while we were in prison. Bea, if you notice, has a petite butt to go with her petite frame."

"Don't you be looking at Bea's butt."

"I promise to never mention it again. Just know that Tank's not a romantic rival."

"You've made my day."

Seventy-Three

Word came down the wire the next day that a strike force had successfully raided three of the water-storage sites Zeke had identified. The secure feed for those raids was now temporarily available for Zeke to review, but first, he and Forman were invited to watch a real time takedown on their vid screen at 0900 their time.

Forman dialed in the contaminated Central American impoundment on the sat cam. Dawn had brightened the sky, but the light intensity was weak.

"Keep the field of vision wide-angle for now. I don't want to miss anything," Zeke said.

The lake came into view, along with the darker central splotch of the hidden water. The image filled with static, then reset. "Having trouble with interference in the signal," Forman said. He'd let Zeke down at the Chameleon compound. He couldn't let him down again. "It keeps fading in and out."

"Wonder if the Chameleons are trying to jam the sat feed. Can you do anything to focus the image?"

Forman's fingers flew over the keyboard. "This is as good as it gets."

Four black SUVs caravanned onto the property, one of them towing a small boat. "Here they come," Zeke said. "Will the Chameleons rush out of that building with their blasters blazing?"

"I'd like to see them try," Forman said. "According to the security badge scanner on the sat cam, these vehicles are full of elite commandos. It won't be like the Chameleon's twenty-two-man attack on Asia's place. This time the good guys have the advantage of surprise."

The building door opened, and four guys walked out, hands raised high in the air. "Who are they?" Zeke asked, leaning closer. "Zoom in and get their faces for us."

The image changed, showing the men's faces. Forman captured the image and saved it to the local system. "Given their grungy navy blue uniforms, they work in mechanical systems. I'm running their faces through my facial recognition program." Forman tapped a few more buttons. "Got three out of four identities so far. All of them are blue-collar workers. No big bosses here."

"Hmm. Zoom back out to the immediate vicinity, keeping the building and the edge of the lake in view. We need the top guy. Who is he?"

"Don't know and don't care as long as he leaves us the hell alone."

The four men were cuffed and escorted to two of the vehicles. Two commandos stayed with the prisoners while the rest stormed the building.

"I wish we could see what's happening inside," Zeke muttered. "I have a bad feeling about this. The Chameleons had to know this raid was coming since three of their other locations were hit yesterday."

The wistful note in Zeke's voice made Forman wince. "Let me try something else. Those commandos are wired for vid and sound. Perhaps I can isolate their feed uplink."

"I don't trust the Chameleons to play fair."

"Got it," Forman gloated. The black-and-white image flickered and pulsed in a nauseating manner. Uh-oh. He had to work fast, or he'd lose the feed.

Zeke shut his eyes. "What's up with that?"

"Jammer. Wait. I've got a clear signal now."

A control room hove into view. Gauges and dials had been busted. Smoke rose from a sink in the room. A man in a suit slumped in a chair, a bullet hole in his temple. A handgun lay near his feet.

"What are they saying?" Zeke said. "Where's the sound?"

"The sound is off. They must have anticipated others would listen in."

"Damn. This is so frustrating."

One more scan of the instrument room, and to Forman's dismay, the feed died. He tried six different ways to locate the signal, but it was gone.

"Did you get the dead man's face?"

"I did." Forman clicked a few keys, then the images of all five men from the raid came into view. He felt a wave of satisfaction. He'd accomplished a Herculean task and made it seem easy. All in a day's work. "While we were watching the live feed, I tracked down the fourth man who surrendered. Like the others, he is a worker bee. The dead guy isn't in the Chameleon database. It may take longer to

ID him."

Zeke nodded. "Show me the other raids before those feeds disappear. I want to see all the people involved. We need to know at what level these people are embedded in the decision-making process. For this plan to advance so far, they must have had help from local, state, and federal officials."

In the first raid, site personnel were armed. Heavy fire netted the loss of one soldier, with two others sustaining injuries. All site personnel went down in a blaze of blaster fire.

"Looks like suicide by cop," Zeke said. "Capture their faces and show me the next site."

Similar scenarios played out at the next two sites. Five minutes later, they had the faces of twenty men. Forman matched images with locals for sixteen of the men. He clicked on each man's bio in turn for Zeke.

"Worker bees, as you predicted," Zeke muttered. "We're missing something. Any luck on the top guy at each site?"

"They are not in the system."

Zeke's jaw dropped. "How is that possible? IDs are required everywhere."

"They might have been in the system previously, but they aren't there now. Someone has erased them."

"And the top guys are all dead. That's tidy. Someone is very good at tying up loose ends." Zeke rose and paced the room. He let out a low moan sound.

"Boss. You okay?"

"What? Oh, sorry. I was thinking about something else. So much has happened so quickly, I can't get any distance from the data to analyze it. I'm missing something important."

"I got this. I've analyzed the data and I'm 99.999 percent sure I have arrived at your elusive conclusion. We believed we saw all there was to see of the Chameleons. It's true we've wiped out a large number of their foot soldiers and middle managers."

"The boss!" Zeke clapped Forman on the shoulder. "You're right. The head of this Chameleon organization is still out there, anticipating our moves."

"Exactly. But this guy is uber smart. Worker bees can't ID him. That's why no middle people survived. They had orders to do or die."

Zeke slumped into the wraparound chair. "I wanted to get rid of the Chameleons for good, but the threat is still out there."

"You took down a plan that had to be years in the making, don't you forget that. Finding that stolen water, exposing their lair in St. Louis, and taking down their army hurt them. World domination isn't the cakewalk they expected it to be."

"Thanks for the pep talk, but it seems anticlimactic. We'll need to tell Uncle John."

"I'll be a few more minutes here. I need to erase our tracks in the system."

"All right."

After Zeke left, Forman punched up the four mystery men. Three of the men held no interest for him. But the last man—he recognized the face. How, he did not know.

According to his memory, he'd been created four months before he was assigned to Zeke. There was nothing in his system that held any trace of data about the man, but he knew the man's face. And feared it.

Should he tell Zeke?

According to the directive, it was his duty.

But Zeke thought he'd failed, and the bad guy was already dead.

Passing along the information wouldn't be helpful. Worse, Zeke might assume Forman couldn't be trusted if he had memory fragments from before Zeke. Thanks to the Killer Bobs, humanity's latent fear of robots had been reignited.

He couldn't lose everything over a stray wisp of data.

What Zeke didn't know wouldn't hurt him.

Seventy-Four

Zeke selected the chair closest to Uncle John's recliner; Forman sat rigidly in the chair near the door. Though a plastech sleeve covered Uncle John's arm, he would soon be back to one hundred percent. The twilight sleep healed his internal injuries; the bloodstream nanites would continue the revitalization process. Light streamed in the windows, heating the small room to the point of discomfort. Zeke tugged at his shirt collar to loosen it.

His once-peaceful existence had been ripped apart this last month. A powerful secret society had targeted him, endangering his health, his sanity, and his life. His uncle had paid a heavy price too, barely surviving his ordeal.

Zeke relayed his conclusions from watching the raids at four water-storage sites. "They knew we were coming. The four survivors have no knowledge of the Chameleons. It's a dead end."

"As often happens in our line of work. We'll live to fight another day." Uncle John's voice sounded full and deep again. "I expect you two have questions. Where would you like me to begin?"

"At the beginning. Were you and Asia members of the Chameleons?" Zeke asked, dreading the answer.

"No. The Chameleons are our enemies. From its inception, that society has had a take-over-the-world mentality. Consequently, the Institute plays a dual function with respect to the international scene. First, it supports the most brilliant thinkers in the world, keeping them on our payroll and accessible to us. Second, it protects the world from the Chameleons."

He should've been shocked by his employer's secret agenda, but not much shocked him these days. It would take an organization with the breadth and scope of the Institute to stand up to the Chameleons.

Looking back, he saw how the Institute's "thinkers" could have shaped world policies and more. Odd that he'd never noticed the direct link between Institute policy papers and current events before. For a smart guy, he suddenly felt very dense.

"You're an administrator and a warrior?" Zeke asked.

"I'm those things and more. I'm very sorry about your parents, Zeke. I looked for them after the Chameleons kidnapped them, but I had nothing to go on. After they disappeared, I commissioned Forman to be your bodyguard. He's more than earned his keep. Truthfully, I didn't expect to survive my captivity. I owe you both for that."

Uncomfortable with the praise, Zeke glanced over at his A.I. unit. "Thank you, sir. Forman saved my life, twice. He's worth his weight in gold."

"That he is. And so are you."

"What about the Chameleons and FSIR? Will they come after us again?"

"Historically, the Chameleons take years to regroup after a botched attempt like this. My sources indicate Senator Holcomb's cell orchestrated the water shortage, which you uncovered, thank you very much. They spread the plague, released the voracious locusts, and engineered the earthquakes. In addition, they tried to kill you and burn your work. Nasty bunch, aren't they?"

Uncle John paused to drink a glass of water. "We have a little breathing room before they try to take over the world again, but, to cover our bases, I must insist that Forman remain your permanent assistant."

"I'm okay with that, but Forman may have other ideas. He's got a girlfriend now."

Uncle John's snowy eyebrows shot up. A smile tugged at his lips. "Is that right?"

Forman nodded solemnly. "I'm in love with Bea, Jessie's sister."

Uncle John appeared to be biting his lip. Curious. "Did you engineer that, Uncle John? Program him to like Bea?"

"Asia and I had specs written into his programming to predispose him to environmental welfare, but we also engineered an emotion module for him. Asia wanted to push the bounds of artificial intelligence, and it appears Forman exceeded his expectations. We didn't plan the physical attraction, I promise. That's all Forman."

"I see." He fell silent to absorb all the information. "You called Senator Holcomb's group a cell. Are there more cells? Is there a head guy?"

"Our intelligence indicates there are more Chameleon cells, though none are currently active in the U.S. Asia believed there's a mastermind behind the Chameleons, but we've never taken any members of their group alive. Don't worry, though. Our people are looking for him. Sooner or later he'll make a mistake."

Asia and Uncle John had been powerful men determined to save the world. Zeke wanted to believe his uncle spoke the truth, but he believed their meddling hadn't ended with the robot's processors.

Zeke leaned forward, his gaze intent on his uncle's expression. "What was the deal with Asia sending Jessie those classified documents? Jessie said Rissa told Asia about it."

"Rissa, poor woman, both betrayer and betrayed. Her early information about the Chameleons helped us. Once Asia learned Jessie had been targeted by the other side, he investigated her thoroughly. Since she appeared to be in no physical danger, Asia didn't interfere with the document transmission. After Rissa disappeared, he decided to bring Jessie into the fold using me as the bait to lure her to California."

"Why all the secrecy? Why not call Jessie up and explain?"

"Asia expected to explain everything, but he ran out of time."

"You two played God with our lives. What gave you the right to do that?"

"It's our job, though that doesn't make it any easier to stomach." His uncle grimaced. "Asia had a talent for assessing situations. He'd even come up with Senator Holcomb's name as a potential Chameleon member, but Holcomb kept slipping through our surveillance. However, with Rissa's defection, my kidnapping, your incarceration, and other national security issues, Asia had no time to dig deeper into Holcomb's life. Thank goodness you and Forman rose to the challenge. You make an excellent team. Thank you both."

Zeke glanced out the sunny window, avoiding his uncle's gaze and blinking away the moisture in his eyes. Out of the corner of his eye, he saw Forman glancing down at his shiny butler shoes.

"What happens now?" Zeke asked.

"We rebuild the Institute stronghold on Tama Island. I've already ordered ready-made office buildings and homes to be airlifted to the island."

"Won't the protestors come back?"

"If anyone protests who doesn't live on the island, we'll have them discreetly removed. Angie will make sure of that. The Institute needs Tama Island to be a research sanctuary. We won't let things get out of hand again."

"Angie? Is she part of this?"

"She's one of my best undercover agents. That's another secret I'm trusting you to keep."

"Where is she? Is she okay?"

"Officially, she's visiting a friend in Savannah."

"But unofficially?"

"Unofficially, she's on another assignment."

Zeke shook his head. "How could I have missed all of this subterfuge? For a smart guy, I've missed a lot."

"You weren't meant to know. Knowledge can be a burden."

"Lack of it can get you killed."

Uncle John's expression soured. "I understand that truth very well. Like you, I'm being thrust into a new role. I'm no Asia Minor, but I promise to do my best to live up to his legacy."

Sounded like Uncle John had accepted his field promotion. Zeke felt uncertain about his changed status. The need to return to the island pulled at him like a riptide. He could row back out there every day, but that kind of individual effort would be noticed.

He needed ordinary, regular transport to stay low profile. "Will the Institute pay for a new ferry as well?"

"It's motoring down the Intracoastal Waterway as we speak."

Zeke took a full breath. Uncle John had everything under control. He replayed recent events in his head. Every way he looked at it, Asia's name came up. "Who was Asia Minor?"

"The big boss at the Institute."

"You're kidding. I thought your longtime friend was a recluse."

"He was that and more."

"Are you in charge at the Institute now?"

"Yes and no. Officially, I'm a midlevel manager at a think tank. Unofficially, I'm in charge of the warrior side of the firm."

Zeke had suspected as much. "What about your coworker? What's Rissa's story?"

"She changed sides and turned her back on us. On me. That hurt."

"You cared for her, Uncle John?"

"I do—I mean, I did."

That sucked. Zeke took a long breath, considering the larger picture. "We've talked all around it. Tell me about the keystone. Where is it? What is it?"

"We don't know. The guardian controls the keystone. Your

father was a guardian, but he died before he passed the knowledge to you."

He couldn't keep his irritation out of his voice. "I don't know anything about being a guardian, and the keystone might as well be water vapor. I don't want a top-secret role in the company. I want to live quietly on Tama Island and continue my research. I reject the role of guardian, whatever it entails."

Uncle John shrugged. "Time will tell. Meanwhile, you'll have the first choice of the housing options on the island. You can set up housekeeping there in two days, though you will always have a place here."

Sounded like he still had a job and a home on the island. With any luck, the Chameleons would leave him alone. "Cool."

Seventy-Five

Zeke lounged on the sandy blanket. Since he had moved back to Tama Island last week, he kept returning to this spot near the lighthouse. The mystery of the keystone continued to plague his thoughts. So did the idea of being a guardian. What had his father guarded? How did the keystone fit into any of this?

Jessie planned to meet him for a swim later this afternoon, but he had time now to focus on the keystone and guardian. He'd found the hidden Chameleon water in the arctic and under the sea, and he could solve this problem if he put his mind to it.

The facts were simple. His father knew about the keystone. His father guarded that secret. His father rarely left the island. Through the years, his father had taught him a code, a set of rules for living his life as they'd relaxed here in the shadow of the lighthouse.

Whenever he wanted to talk to his dad, he'd found him here.

Zeke touched his father's necklace. It was a bit of gray stone on a simple thong. He removed it, wrapped the leather around his hand as his father had often done. The stone fit naturally in the palm of his hand, almost like a key.

A key.

A stone key.

A keystone.

Was it possible?

Anything was possible if you dreamed with open eyes. Those familiar words of his father's took on deeper meaning. Could he have been such an idiot as to overlook the obvious? *Don't be too hard on yourself. You thought of the necklace as a memento, a cherished heirloom. You hung on to it because it reminded you of your father. Think like him. Dream with open eyes.*

Going further down that road, if the necklace was a keystone, what did it unlock? Thanks to the fire, the only structure within a mile of here was the lighthouse. He studied the tall, narrow building. During his lifetime, he'd been up and down those stairs hundreds of times.

But now that the fire had peeled away the exterior paint, the underlying structure matched his necklace stone in color.

Excitement pulsed through him at the speed of light. Something was hidden here. Something that people had killed for. Something that affected the fate of the free world.

He'd better find it.

Holding the tiny stone out like a door key, he circled the outside of the structure. Nothing caught his eye on the outside. Inside, then.

The thick walls offered no clues. He'd been in and out of this place his entire life and never once noticed a keyhole, but it had to be here. With quickening steps, he walked all the way to the top and back down again. Nothing.

He gazed at the shape of the key again. The keystone was narrow but thicker on one side. Egg shaped. Wait. He remembered an oval hole. As a kid he'd tried to fill it with sand, but no matter how much sand he'd poked in the hole, it never filled up.

The hole had been directly across from the door, about two feet off the ground. He turned and studied the wall. There. The hole. Just as he remembered.

Taking a deep breath, he inserted the key. Slowly a well-oiled false wall slid out of sight, revealing a narrow descending ladder.

He stared at it in stunned surprise.

Where did it go?

How had he not known about this passageway before now?

Curious, he entered the shaft, climbing down the narrow metallic rungs. Behind him, the panel slid closed. Recessed lighting allowed him to descend safely. Twelve steps later, he stood in a stone cavern of sorts.

Machinery whirled. Sand crunched underfoot. A golden chair sat across the room. Thick books lay scattered on a nearby table. Zeke approached an open book and recognized his father's handwriting. A sealed envelope with his name on it rested beside a book.

He tore it open and read the brief note.

Son,

If you're reading this, I'm gone. Hopefully, I found the right time to fill you in on your role as a guardian. Our Tama Island lighthouse dates back nearly seven hundred years. There used to be an artesian well here, though it dried up during my lifetime. As you can see from the stains on the wall, water occasionally gets in here. It's your job to keep this place dry and protect the records and the transmission chair.

We're Guardians, son. Sentinels from another place and time sent here to observe and report back on the state of Earth. The pull of this sanctuary is strong; that's why you feel so comfortable here. The slight pulse from the metallic stone is essential to our cellular processes.

When you're ready, sit in the chair, and the transmission will begin. There's no set schedule for your broadcast, but I maintained a monthly schedule of reports.

You've grown into such a fine young man. Your mother and I are so proud of you.

By the way, every grain of sand in this place is your doing. Figured I'd leave the mess for you to clean up.

Keep the secret, Son. It is not to be shared with anyone, not your cousin Angie, not Uncle John, not even a future mate.

You will be blessed with a son, just as I was. It's our way. Raise him as I raised you to be a man of honor and integrity.

Love, Dad

Stunned, Zeke read the letter again.

He was a guardian by virtue of birth, whether he wanted the job or not.

He hailed from another planet, or at least his ancestors did.

What did that make him? Was he human? Seven hundred years with five generations born every hundred years—that would be thirty-five generations of mating with human women. Wait, human genetics might not factor in at all when it came to alien reproduction.

In shock, he gazed around for a place to sit, but the only seat in the room was the broadcasting chair.

Nope.

Not happening.

Instead, he sank to the floor, letter in hand. How was this possible? He glanced around the chamber again, heart thumping in his ears. This had been his father's secret place; now it was his. Unfrickin' believable.

Zeke set the letter on the floor to run his fingers through his hair. The action helped ground him. He gazed at his fingers. They seemed normal. He knew he looked human. No one had ever questioned his origin. But, according to the letter, he was alien, as in a foreign being, as in not from Earth.

It seemed beyond comprehension, except his father never lied.

He was an alien.

So what? He was still himself. That hadn't changed. He could sit here and bemoan the fact, or he could figure out what it meant. With that, he scrambled to his feet, depositing the letter on the table where he'd found it.

He wandered over to study the chair. The shape of it reminded him of an old-timey dental chair, but the leatherlike material covering the chair glowed in response to his tentative touch. Interesting.

There were no wires or straps, no auxiliary probes to bore into his head. Just the chair.

Now that he'd touched the chair, he really wanted to sit in it.

Dare he?

According to the letter, his father had done this once a month for years. It couldn't be life-threatening. His father had been the very picture of health. In fact, he couldn't remember his father ever being sick a day of his life.

His father had been dead for over six months. No one had reported in during that time. What did that mean? Were alien spaceships on their way here now to investigate—or worse, to exact a deadly reprisal?

He shuddered.

Given the state of global politics and the existence of power-hungry groups like the Chameleons, the world wouldn't survive a visit by alien spaceships. He had to do his part.

Looked like it was the chair for him.

With that thought, he eased into the transmission chair.

Seventy-Six

Zeke's head sank into the plush headrest, and his feet slid into the footholds. His fingers tightened on the armrests. He let out a slow breath. So far, so good.

When he glanced down, the fabric of the chair glowed. So did his skin. The radiance dispelled the shadows in the room and became brighter still. In moments, the details of the room faded into the light.

Strange.

And yet oddly thrilling.

Without warning, the light narrowed to a pinpoint in a dark field and vanished. Devoid of sensation, orientation, and landmarks, Zeke screamed silently. He had the vague sense of swift motion unlike anything he'd ever experienced before.

A star appeared, then another. They cast light in the darkness, permeating the dread and nausea that overtook Zeke. More light dawned.

What is this place?

The radiance intensified to a near-painful level. He blinked against the strong light, noticing that some areas blazed brighter than others. They seemed to be in motion. Were they coming toward him? Not good. He needed to be low profile.

Time to move out of harm's way. Except he couldn't move. He couldn't see his hands or his body. The bright light hurt his eyes.

Another stray thought caught him. Was he breathing? Was he alive? He couldn't tell. What was happening to him? How did he get out of this crazy chair?

Powerful waves of energy rolled through him. He fought the tide, but the relentless pull undermined his feeble barriers. He couldn't hold out. Couldn't fight what he couldn't see. He surrendered to the next wave.

Currents surged in, permeating eddies, voids, and channels Zeke never knew he had. He marveled at the difference. He'd been invaded, but he didn't feel conquered.

He felt . . . whole.

Lethargy overtook him, as if the transformation to this new state had exhausted him. He longed to let go and float on his thoughts, to completely shut down his external senses. Could he trust that urge? Wasn't he vulnerable in this strange place?

Relax. Close your eyes.

"Who said that?" He strained to see through slitted eyes, but the bright glow washed out everything else.

Did he say that out loud? Or did he think it? Was someone else in here with him? Was he in danger?

Take it easy.

His thoughts locked. He was in trouble. Thoughts appeared in his head, but from where? From who? Another being? An alien? He had to get out of here. He'd made a mistake in thinking he could be a guardian.

A giant mistake.

He tried to move but his body didn't respond. Did he still have a body? He seemed to flow and billow as if he were a cloud in a windy sky.

Discordant noise registered, sounds he didn't recognize. Was he still alive? He couldn't tell. He needed to get away from this place. He needed to go home to Tama Island.

Don't fight the link. You'll be fine if you relax.

That voice again. It sounded familiar. Could it be? "Dad?"

"It's me, Son."

His father's voice sounded stronger now.

"How? What? Where are we?" Zeke babbled.

"My father and his father before him called this place Tween," his father answered. "As for the how, the chair facilitates your presence in our dimension."

"Is Mom here?"

"No." His father sounded sad. "This is not her place."

"Why not?"

"She isn't one of us."

"This is confusing."

"You're trying to understand with your human perceptions."

"I am human."

"And something more. You're a Taman."

"How is that possible? Why didn't you tell me?"

"Men in our family have long life spans. I thought I had more

268

time. I planned to pass the title of Guardian to you in due time, but I waited too long. I'm sorry."

"I miss you, Dad. Everything is different now. The island is different. I don't feel like myself anymore."

"A house divided cannot stand. Once you embrace your duty, your dual nature will resonate harmonically."

"What are Tamans?"

"Beings that are compatible with many species. Our line monitors the sentients on Earth. You are to carry on our mission. Blend in and settle down. Those should be your top priorities."

These thoughts streamed through Zeke's head as if an actual conversation were taking place, but there were no people here. No real voices. No external sensations at all. It felt as if he'd gone someplace deep inside himself, though that was theoretically impossible. "I plan to live here. Is that what you mean?"

"You have to reproduce. It is critical to the success of our mission. Keep your son close and train him in our ways."

There was so much he wanted to ask his father. He barely knew where to start. "Was death painful, Dad?"

"I don't dwell on that aspect of my time on Earth."

"I killed a man, Dad. The man who tortured and killed you and Mom. I value life as you taught me, but I'm not sorry I did this."

"I understand your need for vengeance, but you must let those destructive feelings go. They will not bring you peace."

"If I'd known about the Chameleons, I would still be looking for you. I didn't know. I'm sorry I failed you."

"You failed no one. I protected your innocence for too long. The fault is mine."

"I'm no innocent."

"You're strong, Zeke. A true Taman. With your mother's brains and my superior physiology, you're our shining hope for the future. There's never been a Taman like you."

"I didn't ask for this. I don't know how to do this."

"Easy. Be yourself."

As Zeke pondered those words of wisdom, several hot spots of light neared. Instinctively, he shrank from the unknown. "Who or what are they?"

"Us."

Zeke mentally shook his head at the circular logic. "They can't be us if we're us."

"They are us, and we are them. In Tween, we're a single entity. We've been expecting you."

"I didn't know about this place before now. How was I expected to find it?"

"You're brilliant, Son, as we'd hoped. I knew you'd find a way to reach us and beyond."

Zeke wanted to stop and put these thoughts in a decision matrix and figure out how they connected. Unfortunately, he didn't have that luxury. "Tell me more about the beyond part. Who are we contacting and why?"

"Us. We're contacting us."

Zeke scoffed. "Being in this realm has changed you, Dad. You used to make sense."

"Let go of your human logic. Surrender your will. Relax."

If he had a voice, surely it would have risen two entire octaves. "The problem is my analytical thinking, not you?"

"There are no absolutes in life and death. Everything is changeable."

"I don't understand any of this. Spell it out more plainly, please. What am I expected to do?"

"Log into Tween on a regular basis. That's how you pass along the knowledge we need."

"You're inside my head?"

"Not in a literal sense. Our connected consciousness transcends the ordinary bounds of space and time. We link the future and the past. We link galaxies in space."

"I still don't understand. What exactly is it that I'm guarding?"

"The portal to our world. After all these generations, Earth is on the verge of having a planetary civilization. If they survive the transition, we'll bring them into our interplanetary alliance."

Talk of planetary civilizations and interplanetary alliances sounded like fantasy. The concepts were too massive to assimilate instantly. He needed time. But he could guard a single access point. "Do others know about the portal? Is that why the Chameleons want the keystone?"

"They crave the keystone's power, but they've got it wrong. The keystone doesn't bring power—it opens the Guardian's gateway. It brings clarity and enlightenment to the Guardian."

He held the keystone, and he was the Guardian. That made him pretty important for a messenger. Still, nobody liked a tattletale.

"I'm not betraying my fellow earthlings by accessing the portal?"

The other lights moved closer and then merged into his father's light. "You're one of us. You belong here. We require your information."

"I need to think about this. How do I return to Tama Island?"

The light dimmed. "Easy. You never left. You're both here and there."

With that, the light receded, and the sense of wholeness dissipated, as if a great magnet had passed through his consciousness, retrieving the similarly charged pieces.

* * *

Cold.

He was very cold.

He blinked against the pale light in the lower reaches of the lighthouse. Judging by his familiar surroundings, he'd returned to Tama Island, alive. Two things that made him very grateful.

With caution he moved his fingers and toes. The numbness slowly dissipated, and he rolled out of the chair onto the stone floor.

What had happened? Had the chair transported him to another galaxy? Was it a time machine or a spaceship?

It didn't seem possible that he traveled to another place and conversed with his dead father. But it had happened. He believed it. He gazed at his human skin. He didn't look anything like an orb of light. He was a man.

No, he wasn't.

He was an alien.

He frowned.

That wasn't right.

He was half human and half alien.

He wanted to reject the premise outright, but he couldn't. Too much of his personal history consisted of being out of step with everyone else. He rarely fit in. He didn't get as teary-eyed or as jubilant as others did.

With this new information, his life made sense.

He lived here in an observatory role. He should keep a low profile; he should stay off the grid of public notice. Except he'd been in the spotlight a lot lately.

Not much he could do about that now.

If he believed the experience, he needed to reproduce. He needed a mate. Jessie? He felt a physical attraction to her. They were compatible on an intellectual level. Was that a foundation for a relationship?

He needed more data.

He hurried up the ladder and out into the fresh air and sunshine. The sunbeams and gentle sea breeze bathed his face. He sank down on his sandy blanket again and watched the crash of waves on the shore. The rhythm of life here sustained him. Would it suit his future mate?

He surveyed the entire shoreline and the vast horizon. This island outpost functioned as a gateway to the Atlantic Ocean, but it had been named for his alien race, the Tamans. His kind had been here a long time.

"Looking for something?" Jessie smiled as she lowered a tote bag full of towels and food.

"Little green men, demons, angels, and an alien or two," he quipped with a silly grin, knowing he was flirting with danger. Who knew the doomsayers had it right all along? Aliens were embedded into human culture. He was living proof.

Her eyes narrowed. "I don't understand."

He waved off her comment and rose. "Bad joke. Forget I said it."

She searched his face. "Is something wrong?"

His head reeled from his discovery. Keeping his cool and blending in mattered to an alien like him. His father had been clear on that. No one could know his secret.

He marveled that he could hold the news in, especially since he'd just discovered his non-human heritage. After the transmission, he glowed with Taman energy. Was it visible to human eyes?

Time to run a small experiment. "Do I seem different to you?"

She studied him for a long moment. "You're more relaxed since you moved back to the island. Is that what you mean?"

"I mean different from other men."

"Sure, you're different. But I'm different. Bea is too. Different is good."

He didn't know much about being a guardian, but he could sit in that transmission chair once a month. Whether Jessie was the right woman for him, time would tell. Meanwhile, he'd dedicate himself to his work and reproducing.

He nodded in agreement. "Different is good."

ABOUT THE AUTHOR

Formerly a contract scientist for the U.S. Army and a freelance reporter, Southern author Rigel Carson, the pen name of Maggie Toussaint, is a multi-published, award-winning author in suspense and mystery fiction. Her background in environmental science and toxicology, as well as years spent doing water research, provided the impetus for this new dystopian thriller series set in a futuristic Earth. The digital version of this book is a Kindle Scout winner. Look for releases of G-2 and G-3 in the coming months.

Maggie lives in coastal Georgia, where secrets, heritage, and ancient oaks cast long shadows. Yoga, beachcombing, and music are a few of her favorite things.

Visit her online at:
http://www.maggietoussaint.com
http://www.RigelCarson.com
http://mudpiesandmagnolias.blogspot.com
http://www.facebook.com/MaggieToussaintAuthor
http://www.twitter.com/MaggieToussaint
http://www.twitter.com/RigelCarson
http://www.BookloversBench.com

Bonus excerpt from G-2

Zeke used the transmission chair a little before midnight. He wasn't due to make a report for another week, but he felt oddly compelled to connect with the Tamans tonight. In a few moments, the ocean-scented air of his island home faded as his thoughts hurled through space.

The disembodied sensation of this invisible means of communication no longer freaked him out. He'd gotten used to the darkness, the shifting shadows of Tween, and the occasional glimpses of orbs of light. He'd even made his peace with reporting conditions on Earth to his distant relatives.

In short, he'd accepted his role as Guardian of Earth.

Trouble is coming.

Like thunder across the ocean, his late father's message boomed through Zeke's mind. In the shuttered darkness of the Taman mindlink, his thoughts iced. Instinct demanded he leave the thought plane and take cover, but he couldn't disconnect without knowing more. The chilling tone of the transmission rattled his nerves.

He didn't doubt his Taman ancestors. He believed them. Trouble *was* coming to Earth. The emotion piggybacked on the message radiated danger loud and clear. His thoughts scrambled in fear, and he wrangled the paralyzing emotion to the corners of his mind.

He wasn't a superhero. Except for his intellect, most people thought him average. Dr. Zechariah Landry, hydrologist, and coastal Georgia beach bum. Just your average, every day alien, though that last part was a closely held secret.

Trouble? He shot back, as if he weren't quaking in his mental boots.

More voices joined in, drowning out his father's voice. *Trouble like you've never seen. Trouble like you don't want on Earth. The Maleem. If we could recall you, we would.*

Recall him? How? That possibility rocked through his expanded consciousness, shaking the tenets of all he held dear. With the retirement of the U.S. Space Shuttle program some fifty years ago, manned space exploration had been abandoned by the entire planet. But the Tamans had mastered space travel, or he wouldn't be embedded in Earth's population halfway across the universe.

He didn't want to be recalled. Earth was the only home he'd ever known.

One problem at a time. He needed to focus on this new threat. The Maleem.

What can I do? he asked.

Look and learn.

The Taman link shuddered, jarring Zeke. A flood of stark images arrived. Vegetation on fire. People dead, gaping holes in their abdomens. Like the worst vid of his life, the terrible scenes unfolded at breakneck pace. Structures leveled. Forests crackled with crown fires. Water fouled with bodies. People screamed in mortal terror, others wailed softly as they huddled in bolt holes.

He mentally gagged. The link strobed. The darkness whirled in a dizzying freefall as devastation images blanketed him. This was awful. Beyond terrible. He'd never seen anything like this. Never thought this level of genocide could occur in the modern world. Earth had to be protected. He had to pull it together.

He could analyze and review later. His time in the mindlink was short. He wrestled his emotions aside to focus on the problem. *What is this?*

The planet Drigil Eight during the Maleem attack. Forty survived out of three million.

Zeke sickened at the horrific images, a ghastly panorama of destruction in the obsidian darkness of the mindlink. The Taman collective intoned the names of the faraway places as the images scrolled across his mental blackboard. *Cantoon. Asphix. Thorian. Xantavian. Agathe. Naum Three. Shomari. Ruiz. Wailea-Molkini.*

Places he'd never heard of, places he'd never imagined.

Places no one would ever see again.

Stop! he begged. *You've convinced me. Maleem are destroyers. What are my options?*

They come. They take.

Zeke struggled to grasp the ramifications. These terrible beings were on the way to his planet. *How do they even know Earth exists?*

We know. Others know.

Though only thought energy was present in the mindlink, Zeke's whole body tensed. *Others? How many others are there?*

Too numerous to count.

The chilling news jarred his careening thoughts to a dead stop. He'd discovered his Taman heritage two months ago, the same time he'd learned there were sentient beings in the distant universe. He'd love to have his quiet life again, but he was the Guardian now. He needed to do his job. He needed to guard Earth.

Are the others destroyers like the Maleem? he asked.

The lightning-fast exchange faltered, worrying Zeke. What weren't the Tamans telling him? Were worse people than the Maleem out there?

The reply came in an eerie monotone laced with doom. *Tamans seek advanced civilizations to join the Alliance. Others have different goals.*

After the horrific images he'd seen, Zeke had no doubt of the Maleem's intentions. *We have to do something. Can we deflect the Maleem? Can we bargain with them or threaten them?*

His father's voice blasted through the group link. *They have no honor. You're forbidden to contact the Maleem.*

Forbidden? Was he a child to be scolded? So what if these Maleem were the bullies of the cosmos. Even bullies had weaknesses. They weren't invincible. He needed a plan of action.

You can't tell me Earth is doomed and leave it at that. There must be a strategy we could employ to make a difference. Can we taint our resources to make them unpalatable? Can we shield the planet? Can we give them engine trouble?

Once again, the exchange faltered. The edgy silence taunted him. Were they conferring about a solution? Were they debating about cutting him loose? Would they abandon him and Earth?

Shadows flickered in the darkness, black on black, his mental gaze keenly attuned to the dark nuances. Frissons of dread peppered his thoughts, rattling his senses. He floated in the timeless void of space. Cold. Alone. Afraid.

Without warning, a line drive of thought energy socked him. He struggled to hold the link. The vermillion-tinged darkness reminded him of primordial ooze from which there was no escape. Was his planet destined to go the way of the dinosaurs?

Several voices spoke in uneasy unison, adding to Zeke's disembodied sense. *We have not been successful in dealing with Maleem. They take. They do not negotiate. They do not compromise.*

His spirits plummeted. There had to be a way. He couldn't give up on his planet without a fight. Someone must have beaten them before. They needed to build on that success. He fired a query across the vacuum of space. *Wait! What about those few stragglers on Drigil Eight? How did they survive?*

The link hummed with energy. It buzzed bright in his head as if hundreds spoke at once. Zeke allowed himself to hope. All wasn't lost. It couldn't be. More than seven billion people lived on Earth. So many innocent lives at stake.

We have sent a query, young Zeke. We will advise you in due time.

The link started to fade. That was it? He needed more information. *How long do we have? When will the Maleem arrive?*

Soon.

BOOKS BY MAGGIE TOUSSAINT

Science Fiction
G-1 (as Rigel Carson, book 1 The Guardian of Earth series)
G-2 (coming soon, book 2 The Guardian of Earth series)
G-3 (coming soon, book 3 The Guardian of Earth series)

Mystery
In for a Penny (book 1 Cleopatra Jones series)
On the Nickel (book 2 Cleopatra Jones series)
Dime If I Know (book 3 Cleopatra Jones series)

Death, Island Style
Murder in the Buff
Gone and Done It (book 1 Dreamwalker series)
Bubba Done It (book 2 Dreamwalker series)
Doggone It (coming soon, book 3 Dreamwalker series)

Romantic Suspense
House of Lies
No Second Chance
Muddy Waters (book 1 Mossy Bog trilogy)
Hot Water (book 2 Mossy Bog trilogy)
Rough Waters (book 3 Mossy Bog trilogy)

Sweet Romance
Seeing Red

Reviews are welcomed and encouraged!

43919312R00161

Made in the USA
Charleston, SC
12 July 2015